PINO

D0681258

HUNGRY HEARTS...

"I'm not going to let you do it again," Nicky warned softly.

"Do what?"

"Chase me off like a child. I'm not, you know."

"I know," he said. "I also know that doesn't change the rules. You're still untouchable, Miss Thompson."

"I didn't think you were the kind of man to follow rules." It was a challenge.

"I'm not," Kane said flatly. "But on occasion, it seems a wise thing to do."

She seemed to think about that for a moment, then asked, "And if I wasn't ... untouchable?"

Kane saw she was holding her breath, that it had taken a measure of bravery to pose the question.

He stood and walked over to her. He touched her hair, feeling the softness of the curls.

She leaned into him, and his arm went around her.

Against every ounce of sense he'd ever had, he bent his head and touched his lips to hers.

Diablo

Patricia Potter

BANTAM BOOKS

New York   Toronto   London   Sydney   Auckland

DIABLO

A Bantam Book / April 1996

ISBN 0-553-56602-4

Published simultaneously in the United States and Canada

Bantam Books are published by Bantam Books, a division of Bantam Dou-
bleday Dell Publishing Group, Inc. Its trademark, consisting of the words
"Bantam Books" and the portrayal of a rooster, is Registered in U.S. Patent
and Trademark Office and in other countries. Marca Registrada. Bantam
Books, 1540 Broadway, New York, New York 10036.

PRINTED IN THE UNITED STATES OF AMERICA

RAD   0   9   8   7   6   5   4   3   2   1

Chapter One

TEXAS, 1867

It was not so much the prospect of dying as the way in which he would die in two days that kept Kane O'Brien awake.

The cell was small and stifling in the July heat. The sun baked the prison during the day with smothering intensity, permeating the rock and stone and iron so that its disappearance at night did little to cool the interior. Kane had taken off his sweat-soaked shirt. That gave insignificant relief, but at least it no longer clung to his body.

Maybe dying wouldn't be so bad, even at the end of a rope.

The walls closed in on him. He'd never wanted to see the inside of a prison again, not after the year he spent in a Union prison camp. His hand went to his cheek, to the scar running down the side of his face. A devil's face, one of his enemies had called it. Diablo.

And Diablo he had become.

He sat on the stone slab they called a bed, facing an iron door fixed into a wall of stone. Only a minimum of light crept inside. David Carson was somewhere within this cellblock. Davy, his best friend for the past twenty-five years, was to die with him. That's what Kane regretted the most—that his own anger and impulsiveness were leading not only to his own death, but to Davy's. It was damned unfair. Still, they'd given the bastards a good chase.

He paced the small cell, wishing for a breath of sweet air, but the cells for the condemned were underground.

Condemned! It was ironic that he'd survived four years of war to die this way. The trial had been short, the verdict a foregone conclusion. Even he couldn't deny his guilt, some of it, anyway.

Footsteps echoed in the corridor. It wasn't time yet for the slop they called food. Kane took the few steps to the cell door, peering out of the small grated opening. He couldn't see much, but the sound of boots and spurs against the rock floors grew louder.

Momentary hope surfaced as he made out a tall figure, a marshal's badge pinned on the leather vest he was wearing. He stepped back, unwilling to allow anyone, much less his enemies, to see his fear and anxiety.

A key grated harshly in the door, the sound of metal against metal echoing in the corridor. Then the door was pushed open, and the man entered, limping slightly. He was tall, rangy, and just a touch familiar. Kane studied him, insolently, as the law officer did the same to him. The visitor's gaze was sharp, his eyes missing little. For a moment he focused on the scar distinguishing Kane's face.

"Captain O'Brien," the man finally said.

Kane bowed mockingly. "I haven't been a captain for a long time. I am, though, at your service, but not particularly from choice."

The lawman smiled slightly. "You don't remember me. Well, there's no particular reason you should. I, on the other hand, have a very good reason to remember you."

Kane was intrigued despite himself. There was no anger in the man's voice or expression, only interest. The marshal turned around and with a gesture of his head dismissed the guard.

The key turned again. Kane was once more locked in, but this time he had a hostage. Too bad the marshal didn't have a gun in his holster.

"Don't even think about it, O'Brien," the visitor said.

"They have orders. They won't let you go, even if you threaten my life, and I think I'm probably in better shape right now than you."

Kane shrugged. "They can't kill me twice. I wouldn't mind taking another Yank with me."

"Even one whose life you saved three years ago?" The question came unexpectedly, and was uttered with little feeling.

Kane's eyes narrowed as he studied the officer more closely. "If I saved a Yank's life, it was a mistake."

"It probably was—for you. You were taken prisoner because of it," the marshal said, forcing Kane to remember.

It came back in flashes. The wounded man in blue calling for water—a captain, his face bearded, his light-colored hair dark with blood. As hardened to battle, to cries and screams, as Kane had been, something that day had stopped him, made him pause and look back. Some of his men lay in that killing field, too, but they were still.

As he watched the rest of his troop disappear into the woods ahead, he retraced his steps. He took his canteen from his belt, helped the Yank drink, and then tied a tourniquet around his leg. He turned to leave, and suddenly he'd been surrounded.

It had been the most damn fool thing he'd done during the war, and it had cost him a year of his life, a year of freezing cold and near starvation. He hadn't really hated until then, but he hated after that. He'd experienced cruelty for cruelty's sake. There had been no honor, no humanity, in the prison at Elmira.

"You shouldn't have reminded me," he told the marshal. "Unless, of course, you're here to return the favor."

"I wish I could," the lawman said. He held out his hand. "Ben Masters."

Kane refused it. "I suppose there's a reason for this visit?"

Masters looked at his outstretched hand, then dropped it. He seemed to take no particular offense, though.

"There is. I can't save you myself, but others can. I have a proposition for you."

A thread of hope stirred within Kane. He tried not to show it. "What kind of proposition?" Suspicion hardened his voice.

"Have you ever heard of the Sanctuary?"

"No," Kane said. "But it sounds like a good place at the moment."

"A lot of outlaws think so." Masters hesitated. "It's a hideout. Expensive. Well-protected. Lawmen in four territories have been trying to find it for years." He paused. "Your . . . reputation might get you inside."

"To spy for you?" Kane's mind was racing ahead. The law must be desperate to take a chance with him. He'd been wanted for two years. At one time, he thought the whole U.S. Army was after him. The fact that they were ready to use him explained real well how much they wanted Sanctuary.

Masters must have heard the derision in his voice. His mouth grew grim. "Yes."

"And what do I get in return?"

"You get us a location, and we find the hideout, you'll have a pardon."

Kane turned away from him. "Go to hell. I don't like spies. I don't like your government."

"You'd rather hang?"

"Than to spy for you against my own kind? Yes."

"What about your friend?"

Kane turned around slowly. He stared at Masters. He tried to keep his face from revealing anything. "Davy goes too? Have you talked to him?"

"No," Masters replied. "He stays here. But if you do the job, he won't hang."

"That's not good enough," Kane said. "A pardon. A full pardon for him?"

Masters shook his head. "I can't guarantee that. Just that he won't hang. It took all my persuasion to get the governor to agree to pardon you."

"Why me?"

"You have a reputation no one can question. We can't manufacture that kind of past."

Kane hadn't survived the war and two years as an outlaw without sensing danger. "How many men have you sent looking for this place?"

Masters considered his answer long enough for Kane's instincts to go on alert. "Two," the lawman finally said.

"How many came back?"

"Neither."

"Trying to save Texas the hangman's fee?"

"I would think a bullet would be preferable to a rope." For the first time, Masters's gaze left Kane's and seemed to focus on a particular rock in the wall.

"Where is this place? Texas?"

"That's the hell of it. It could be in any of four jurisdictions—Indian Territory, Colorado Territory, Texas, New Mexico. Outlaws just seem to disappear when lawmen start to close in. We keep hearing rumors about this place, but no one has any idea where it is. My territory is southern Colorado, but we're cooperating with Texas and the marshals in the Indian and New Mexico territories." Masters's gaze now bored into Kane. "When I heard about Diablo, that Kane O'Brien was Diablo and that you had been condemned, I suggested a deal. Texas authorities were reluctant, but—"

"I bet they were," Kane interrupted.

Masters ignored him. "I thought you might be willing to make a trade."

"You thought wrong. You're asking me to betray my own kind to save my skin."

"*Those* kind wouldn't have stopped to save an enemy soldier," Masters pointed out.

"A grand moment of idiocy," Kane said bitterly. "It cost me a year of life. It's a mistake I won't make again. You sure as hell weren't worth it." He allowed a second to go by, then muttered in disgust, "A lawman, by God."

"I read the report on your trial," Masters said quietly. "I know how Diablo was born. You haven't changed that much in three years. You're still tilting at windmills."

"You know nothing," Kane said.

"I know you have one chance to save yourself and your friend from dying in two days. Maybe you don't care about yourself, but David Carson is different, isn't he? Maybe he wants to live. Maybe his family wants him to live."

It was a shot in the gut. Kane felt it rip through him. That had been the worst of his trial, seeing Davy's wife and son sitting in the courtroom, watching their faces as the verdict was announced. He suddenly made a decision. "I'll agree on one condition," he said. "Davy gets a full pardon."

"I can't promise that," Masters said again. "I got a pardon promised for you because you would be risking your life. Carson's sentence is to be commuted to prison."

"Then the answer is no," Kane said. "Davy couldn't survive years in prison. I had a year of it, remember? We'd both be better off dead."

Masters hesitated. "I'll do what I can."

"I want him with me."

"No," Masters said firmly. "He's the only reason I got the governor to agree. The fact that he'll hang if you run is the only leash we have."

Kane's fingers clenched into a fist. "You have it all figured, don't you?"

Masters was silent, his eyes watchful as he waited.

"A pardon for David Carson," Kane said. "I don't care about myself. Take it or leave it."

"If I can convince the governor to give your pardon to Carson, you'll go?"

"Yes."

"And return to face your own sentence?"

Kane's lips moved into a slight, sardonic smile. "Don't ever go into the drummer business, Masters. You couldn't sell a dying man a sip of water."

"I just want to be sure we understand each other."

"We understand each other," Kane repeated. "But I want Davy's pardon in writing, and I want it in the hands of someone I trust."

"I'll see what I can do."

"You'd better hurry." Kane leaned against the stone

wall of his cell. "Oh, and I want that pardon for Davy even if I'm killed."

"I might be able to convince the governor ... if we find your body."

"I'll try to die where you can find me. Don't want to inconvenience you any."

Masters didn't answer. He went to the door and yelled for the guard, then said to Kane, "I'll be back."

"Even if the governor turns you down?"

"I'll be back," Masters said again. "Either way."

"Don't bother coming if he says no. I don't want to waste my last hours being reminded of an error in judgment."

Masters was spared making a reply. The door opened, and he started to leave. He paused a moment, looked back as if to say something, then shook his head. He disappeared out the door, and Kane was left with the sound of iron closing on iron and the echo of spurs on the stone floor.

Kane stood where he was, his mind running over every word of the conversation. Maybe he could save Davy. Maybe. He rubbed the scar on his face. It itched, as it always seemed to do when he was troubled. To save Davy, he would have to become a marionette, his strings pulled by a man he despised: a lawman who wanted to use him for his own purposes, who would hold the life of his friend hostage.

He hated the idea. He hated the prospect of being a spy, of betraying people who trusted him. But he would do anything for Davy.

Masters had a day and a half before he and Davy were scheduled to die. Kane wondered whether the marshal would succeed.

TWELVE *hours until the noose would drop around his neck.*

Kane had given up on Masters. He'd asked too much. He tried to tell himself the offer had been a hoax from the beginning, a final indignity. But part of him wanted to hang on to hope just a little bit longer. All of him wanted Davy to see his family again.

He refused the plate of beans that would be his last meal. He drank the coffee, though. Drinking it passed the time. He tried not to think of the next morning.

The guard had been taunting him all day, telling him how various men had died on the rope. All of them, according to the guard, ended up begging. Some, he'd smirked, had taken ten minutes or more to die. There were wagers on how fast Diablo would die. Kane had ignored him, and finally the guard left.

Kane lay down on his bed, leaned his head against the wall, and closed his eyes. He sorted through memories as if they were cards in a poker deck. He discarded the jokers: the war, his quixotic rescue of Masters, his fated plunge into outlawry.

Instead, he focused on the aces. Ah, the aces. The horse races with Davy across the fields. The swimming hole where he and Davy used to splash after a day of tending cattle. A table brimming with biscuits and chicken and fresh vegetables. But Davy was waiting to die, just as he was. And a tin plate of cold, mushy beans sat on the floor near the door, mocking him with their rancid smell.

Back to the jokers. They were easier to bear.

Then he heard the footsteps, just as he had yesterday. He didn't move, but he felt his muscles tense. The steps neared. He didn't turn his head, but he heard the sound of the key in the lock, and the heavy door groaning as it opened.

"Get up," the guard said as he entered the cell. He was followed by Marshal Ben Masters.

"What are you going to do if I don't?" Kane drawled.

The guard took a club from his belt and moved threateningly over to the slab. His arm was caught by Masters. "No," Masters ordered. "Leave us."

The guard reluctantly retreated.

Kane sat up lazily, leaning his back against the stone wall. And waited.

"I have what you wanted," Masters said. "You find Sanctuary for us, and Carson goes free."

"In writing?"

"In writing."

A glimmer of triumph snaked through Kane, but he was careful not to show it. "I want to see it sent to an attorney in Austin." He gave the name. And agreed, at Masters's insistence, that the envelope be labeled OPEN ONLY IN THE EVENT OF MY DEATH.

"There are some conditions," Masters said after a moment. "I'll need your word that you will return."

"The word of Diablo?" Kane asked sarcastically.

"The word of Kane O'Brien."

"Why do you need that? You have Davy. My leash, you called him."

For a moment, Masters looked discomfited, and Kane drew a small measure of satisfaction in that.

"All right," Kane said after a moment of silence. "You have it. For what it's worth. What else?"

"You have three months," Masters said. "It took one hell of an argument to get you that much."

"And if I can't do it in that time?"

"Carson dies."

Kane stood at that, his fingers fisted at his side. "You are a bastard, Masters."

"Remember that, O'Brien. I'm your other leash. Your contact. Your lifeline." The marshal's voice was hard, callous.

"What if I want someone else?"

"What you want doesn't matter. You're a condemned murderer."

"A condemned murderer you want to use," Kane replied bitterly.

"We *have* to use," Masters corrected. "I don't like it any better than you."

"Don't like getting your hands dirty, working with an outlaw? A reb?"

Masters sighed. "I don't have a choice, and neither do you. It's me, or you and Carson hang on schedule. Do we do business or not?"

"We do," Kane said. "But don't push me."

Masters shrugged. "Let's get one thing clear from the

beginning. You don't make the rules. I do. If you're not willing to accept that fact, the deal's off."

Kane wanted to throw the offer back in his face. If it were his life, he would. But Davy's life was important enough that he would swallow his pride. Even if it choked him. He nodded reluctantly.

"You'll escape tonight."

"How?" Kane said with a touch of humor. "I've been trying with little success."

"A priest will visit you in a few hours. You knock him out, take the cassock."

"Now why didn't I think of that?" Kane said sardonically. "He approves of all this?"

Masters ignored the sarcasm. "The priest will be a deputy marshal. There will be a gun in his cassock."

"Loaded?"

Masters looked at him steadily. "Could I trust you with one?"

"I don't know," Kane challenged. "Could you?"

"I don't think so, not yet."

"Trust is truly a beautiful thing. I can tell we're going to have a long, fruitful partnership. A little lacking in warmth perhaps, but that should be more than balanced by your astounding faith in me."

Understanding flickered in Masters's eyes, but Kane knew he wasn't going to change his mind. He itched to hit the man. "I want to see Davy."

"No."

"Are you going to tell him?"

"It would only endanger you if we did," Masters said. "Only five of us know and, of course, the governor. Even the warden here won't. Carson's execution will be delayed on the pretext of his being needed to help find you."

Kane took several steps toward him. "You're going to keep him believing he's going to hang?"

"He *will* hang," Masters said bluntly, "unless you do what's expected. Why give him false hope?"

"I should have left you to die."

A muscle worked in Masters's cheek. "Maybe so," he said, "but right now I'm all you have."

"I'd rather have smallpox."

Masters smiled wryly. "Let's get on with it. If you have those robes and a gun, do you think you can make it out the gates?"

"Oh, I'll make it all right," Kane said.

"The drainage ditch outside . . . I'll be about an eighth of a mile south with a horse."

Kane nodded.

"And don't try to find Carson on the way. He's being moved to another section of the prison."

"You think of everything, don't you?"

"I try," Masters said. He turned toward the door and yelled for the guard. He looked back for a moment. "Good luck." He didn't hold out his hand.

Kane didn't answer. He just watched as Masters left the cell and thought about the next few hours.

A priest for Diablo. A priest with a gun. It was somehow fitting.

Chapter Two

SANCTUARY

Nicky looked up at the ridge of mountains that represented the walls of her existence. She yearned to ride beyond them, to take her brother away from this place and never look back.

But she was like a butterfly pinned to a board, bound there by loyalties she couldn't ignore. She'd almost decided to leave—any way she could—when she'd chanced on her uncle this morning. He'd been doubled over in pain. It was not the first time she'd seen him that way, though he'd tried to dismiss it as something he'd eaten.

Her uncle or her brother—she would have to choose between them soon. Her brother, Robin, was already too eager to reach for a gun, too ready to admire the desperadoes that stayed at Sanctuary. Jesse and Frank James were his heroes. She didn't want him to travel down the same road as their father and wind up in an unmarked grave.

Sanctuary. It had been that for her and Robin years ago. Now it was more a prison.

Her mare, Molly, snorted and pranced impatiently under her. Nicky wanted to run, too. At twenty-two, she wanted to be a woman, an ordinary woman, who wore pretty dresses and attracted men she could admire. Instead, she wore trousers and a loose shirt. Her hair was cropped short, like a halo of curls, because her uncle feared—she feared—that if she looked like a woman some of the outlaws might well be inspired to want a lot more than what they were paying for.

She had skills, some womanly and some not so womanly. She could cook well enough, and she had a way with a needle and thread. She could shoot and fight dirty. She could ride like the wind and do some doctoring.

She could play the fiddle, but couldn't dance. She didn't know nice manners or how to dress properly. She didn't know how to flirt or tease or be courted. She was twenty-two, and she'd never had a beau, mainly because the only men around were thieves and murderers and worse—and her uncle would kill anyone who laid a hand on her.

Molly snorted again. Nicky gave the mare her head, and they raced across the barren valley, ignoring the lookouts stationed all along the hills surrounding Sanctuary. Not that they had much to worry about. The Commanches protected them—for a price. And the place was as well guarded as any medieval castle Nicky had read about in her small collection of books.

What worried her most was Robin. She was so afraid for him. She should have left years ago and taken Robin with her, but she owed her uncle so much. Besides, she hadn't had the faintest idea how to earn a living to support herself and Robin. She had thought of starting a ranch, or a boardinghouse, but both required a great deal of money. Money she didn't have. If she'd been alone, she might have risked striking out, but Robin was a different matter.

Now, she feared that Robin might be in greater danger here. That feeling had been growing stronger since she'd discovered Robin practicing quick draws with Cobb Yancy, a ruthless killer. But just as her resolve to leave hardened, she'd found her uncle doubled over, his face pale and sweaty. To be sick here, to show any sign of weakness, was death. The men in Sanctuary would turn on him as hyenas turned on their wounded and dying.

She had to convince him to leave, to find a good doctor, not the lawless quacks who sought refuge here.

She ran Molly until the horse slowed. Then she turned the mare's head and started back. Her uncle didn't like her being out here alone, even though she could take care of herself. He always wanted either himself, Robin, or Mitch Evers, the only man her uncle really trusted, to ride with her.

Nicky rode back into the settlement called Sanctuary, a string of mostly stone buildings huddled along the rocky side of a mountain. They fit perfectly into the terrain, almost invisible from a distance. She ignored the men swaggering from the saloon to Rosita's brothel. Not enough of them visited the washhouse and barber's. There always seemed to be a stench in the air. Still, Sanctuary had the look of any small cow town, although it was anything but.

John Reno lifted his hand in salute, and she acknowledged it, but barely. She knew them all, the current residents, both by reputation and sight. She knew how much money they had, for without money they were not welcome at Sanctuary. There were twenty "guests" now, all wanted men successful enough to afford her uncle's protection. The permanent residents were former guests with certain skills. Andy Lonetree was the blacksmith, Sam Dunn ran the general store, and Jeb Gibson the hotel and restaurant. Cray Roberts and Bob Berry managed the saloon and its games. Old Cracker was a piano player. All had been on the run, and their money had given out in Sanctuary. Her uncle, Nat Thompson, chose his permanent residents very carefully. Once they chose to stay, few ever left. It was exile forever, and each was made to understand that.

Her exile, too. Her prison. And yet she hadn't been unhappy. She'd had love from her uncle, from her brother. She'd had a certain freedom in dress. She loved riding, and as a child she'd been doted on by Nat's friends. But as she'd grown older and her body had changed, their looks had changed. They were no longer indulgent, but hungry. She could no longer sit on someone's knee and learn a bawdy song. She sure knew her share of those.

Nicky reached the house, low and sprawling and comfortable, and hitched her horse to a rail, then went inside. Her uncle was sitting at his desk. He was looking better, the color back in his face.

"We might have a new guest soon," he said, looking down at the papers in his hand.

Nicky sighed. She'd been hoping he would slow down, limit the number of guests, gradually eliminate them. She'd been trying to guide him in that direction.

Her uncle was looking at her expectantly, obviously waiting for her to ask the identity of their new guest. She might as well. She would learn it soon enough, anyway.

"Who?" she asked.

"Diablo," Nat said with satisfaction. It always pleased him to get a well-known desperado. It enhanced Sanctuary's reputation among potential guests.

Nicky searched her memory. They often got newspapers here, bought by guests or by the two guides who led guests into and out of Sanctuary. Her uncle saved articles on outlaws, holdups, stage and bank robberies. They were invaluable in weeding out potential spies. One robbery did not a fugitive make, in his cautious opinion, especially after a guest recognized a lawman who had infiltrated Sanctuary. Nicky wasn't sure what happened to the man; he'd simply disappeared, just as another had who was suspected of being a spy. She tried not to think about it.

"He's been wanted in Texas nearly two years," her uncle said. "Murder. Robbery. Broke out of prison three weeks ago, has nearly the whole state looking for him. He's been making inquiries about Sanctuary."

She asked the obvious question. "Does he have any money?"

"Apparently. My sources tell me he's been spending enough."

Nicky took a deep breath. "Uncle Nat, maybe you should close up. That last lawman got too close, and we have enough money to start a ranch, and—"

"Soon," Nat said. "Another year, and we can head toward California. Far enough away the law won't ever find Nat Thompson. But I want to make sure there's enough

money so Robin will never have to . . ." He trailed off, a
muscle throbbing in his cheek.

She could have finished the sentence for him. *So he'll
never have to rob like your father did.* She knew the guilt
he felt for that, for her mother's death, for leading her
father on that last bank robbery. John Thompson hadn't
survived the shoot-out that followed.

Nat had tried to make it up to Nicky and Robin. He
had taken them in, had hired housekeepers for them when
he was away. She hadn't known then he'd been robbing
banks. "But we've grown up, Uncle Nat. We can take
care of ourselves."

"What I want is for both of you to be taken care of,"
he said. "A few more guests, and you and Robin can go
anywhere." She didn't like the tone in his voice, the words
that didn't include him.

"Is anything wrong?" she said, trying to keep the worry
from her voice. He didn't like worry. He didn't like fuss-
ing.

He shook his head. "Now let's talk about Diablo."

"Why don't you go to Denver and see a doctor?"

His mouth thinned as it did when he didn't want to
discuss something. It was an expression he seldom used in
her presence. "I'm fine. Doc Cable said so."

"Doc Cable is a quack," Nicky countered. Doc Cable
had been one of their guests several months earlier.
"That's why he was here. He killed a few patients."

"When he was drunk," Nat said. "He wasn't bad when
he was sober. Now let's talk about Diablo."

Nicky decided to try once more. "Tell him no, Uncle
Nat. It's getting too dangerous."

"Nine more months," Nat bargained.

"And then we'll go to California?" Nicky countered.

"I swear."

Nicky didn't like it. She sensed they didn't have nine
months. But she knew her uncle, and this was the best
she was going to get. He would stick by his word. He
always did. She nodded reluctantly. "Tell me more about
Diablo."

• • •

KANE was hot, tired, and thirsty. It had been a hell of a long ride. His eyes had been blindfolded for two days, and his horse guided by a man he'd met for the very first time three days before.

Breaking out of prison had gone smoothly. Then three frustrating weeks had followed as he kept moving from town to town, saloon to saloon, seeking entrance to Sanctuary while avoiding posses and lawmen.

Masters was on his heels the entire time. When Kane had finally gotten a bite in a little Texas trading town, Masters had provided him with cash to pay the way into Sanctuary. One thousand for entry, another thousand as down payment on the hundred-dollar-a-day privilege of staying.

Kane remembered clearly how three days ago, his escort had shown up in Kane's hotel room, a knife at Kane's throat. Their conversation had been brief.

"You got the money?"

Kane had nodded. If it had been his own money, he would have been reluctant to give it to the man in a calico shirt, dirty buckskin trousers, and an even dirtier hat. But it was the federal government's money, and he surrendered it easily enough. He'd been given no time to alert Masters, who was in another hotel, no time to do anything but throw a change of clothes in his saddlebags, which contained several thousand dollars more. His horse, he was told, was already saddled and waiting in back of the hotel.

That was in Gooden, Texas, and now he didn't know where he was.

The pace slowed. The horse was climbing upward. They must have reached a mountain somewhere. Damn. Two months and four days left, and he couldn't even tell which was north or south.

Another hour passed, and the horse began to move downhill. Time crawled by, but finally his horse came to a stop. His escort said in a gravelly voice, "You can take off the blindfold."

He did and was instantly blinded by the sun. It was high overhead and glaring. Kane half closed his eyes until they gradually adjusted to the brightness, then opened them again. They were in a canyon, surrounded by rugged mountains he couldn't identify. He turned his head and saw the main street of a town.

"Welcome to Sanctuary," his guide said as Kane peered around. A blacksmith shop. A barber. A saloon. A general store. Even a mayor's office and what looked like homes. Some were neat, some ramshackle. All in all, he could have been in any of a dozen small towns.

Except there was a preponderance of men, and none of them were wearing gunbelts. His own had been taken at the beginning of this journey.

His guide followed the direction of his eyes. "No guns are worn in Sanctuary. Except by Mr. Thompson and his deputies, like me," the man added with a small smile. "He'll tell you all the rules."

The guide gestured to the mayor's office. "He'll be expecting you."

Kane dismounted. He looked around again, trying to identify something, anything. He thought he saw flashes of light and believed them to be from lookouts in the hills, gun barrels glinting in the rays of the sun.

"Who will be expecting me?" Kane asked.

The guide shrugged. "He'll tell you what he wants you to know."

Kane approached the office just as the door opened, and a boy ran into him. His hands went out automatically to steady the boy and found something soft instead. He heard a gasp, then the stranger stepped back with a short curse.

Startled, Kane stepped back also. The stranger, about half a foot shorter than his own six feet, was dressed in worn, ill-fitting denim trousers, a dark shirt, and vest. The light brown hair was cut short, shorter than commonly worn by men, and was carelessly brushed back from a face he couldn't quite see. Then the face tilted up toward him, and he realized it didn't belong to a boy.

Large brown eyes the color of dark chocolate, shaded

by long, black lashes, looked at him contemptuously. A small nose in an elfin face wriggled as if it were smelling something undesirable. Kane was instantly aware of his three days' growth of beard, and the trail dust and sweat that covered him. With the scar on his cheek, he must look like the devil himself.

He bowed. "My apologies, miss, both for my clumsiness and my appearance. I've been riding—"

"I know," she interrupted, her mouth grim. "You're Diablo."

He tried to hide his astonishment as he wondered who she was. Her exact age was impossible to judge, but clearly she wasn't a child. She obviously was unimpressed by Diablo's reputation, and he doubted she was an outlaw on the run. He tried again. "I prefer Kane. Kane O'Brien."

"Like the man who killed his brother." Her remark, said with disdain, hurt more than she could know, and inwardly he winced. She was angry with him and he didn't know why. He was usually successful with women, even with the scar on his cheek. Or perhaps because of it. He frightened even while he attracted. But this woman's gaze didn't focus on the scar. She just dismissed him, something that had never happened to him before. And he found that intriguing, challenging.

Nearly as much as he found her face fascinating. He'd seen far more beautiful ones, but few that piqued his interest as this one did.

Maybe he'd been too long without a woman's company. He'd spent the last three months in a cell, and two years prior to that on the run.

"Who do I have the pleasure of . . . almost running down?" he said in a voice that usually charmed the most reticent of women. But there was no answering smile. Only when her eyes met his did a flash of uncertainty streak across her face. Something passed between them, something so swift and strong that Kane felt jolted. She must have felt it, too, for she took a step backward, then another.

Kane suddenly feared she would fall from the porch, and he reached out a hand. His gloved fingers brushed hers, and a new kind of heat ran up those fingers and through his arms, settling deep in a most sensitive place. The woman jerked back her hand, as if she too had been burned. She stared at his outstretched hand, turned and walked away. Kane took some pleasure in noting that her gait was none too steady, but then neither was his as he took a step in her direction. A harsh voice behind him brought him to a quick halt.

"She's out of bounds."

Kane turned and stared at the man framed by the doorway. He was as tall as Kane, his build heavier. Time had carved canyons in his face, but his pale blue eyes were ageless—and as cold as any Kane had seen.

"Why?" Kane asked.

"Because I say so," the man said. "You're Diablo?"

Kane nodded. The man held out his hand. "I'm Nat Thompson. I run Sanctuary, and the first rule is to keep your hands off that girl." The tight grip was more than friendly. It was a warning. Thompson released his hand, then headed inside the office, obviously expecting Kane to follow. He did.

Thompson went to a desk and took the chair behind it. "Sit down," he said. "Welcome to Sanctuary."

"How safe is it?"

"As safe as you can get," Thompson said with obvious satisfaction. "There's several ways out, if a trail to Sanctuary is ever found. Even then, we're protected by several Indian tribes, and our lookouts can see miles away. You're safe enough here. If you follow the rules."

Kane felt the muscles in his stomach tighten. This wasn't going to be easy. "What rules?"

"No guns in Sanctuary except my own and my deputies'. No fighting unless it's for entertainment—in a ring and with rules. No questions of other guests unless they wish to volunteer information. You can't ride outside the ring of mountains without one of my guides."

"A lot of rules for a hundred dollars a day."

Thompson shrugged. "You can leave. A guide will lead you out same way you came. You can take your chances outside."

"What do you have except for rules?"

Thompson's lips cracked into a small smile for the first time. "Everything you want. Women. A saloon. Gambling. Good food. Feather beds. Hell of a lot better than a jail cot. Or a grave."

Kane nodded. "I don't have much choice. Every lawman west of the Mississippi is after me."

"So I hear." Thompson eyed him with interest. "No one ever escaped from that prison before."

Kane shrugged. "Wasn't that hard. They're not very smart." He paused. "Tell me more about the women."

"Mexican, mostly," he said. "Have some real little fireballs here."

"The girl . . ."

The smile disappeared. "I said no one touches her. My rules include certain punishment for breaking them. Lashing's one of them. Indians are another. They rather enjoy seeing how brave a man is."

"I get your point." An odd disappointment swept over Kane. So she was private property—of a man twice her age.

"No, you don't," Thompson said, his eyes narrowing. "That girl is my niece. She and her brother, Robin, are my only family."

Relief flooded Kane, quickly followed by something ominous. Thompson's niece. A part of Sanctuary, which Kane was sworn to destroy. If he didn't, his best friend would die.

"I don't think she liked me much."

Thompson shrugged. "The clerk at the hotel is expecting you. You might want a bath and shave. There's a barber and washhouse three doors down."

Kane was hesitant to leave. He wanted to know more. "It's a regular little town."

A glitter of pride flickered in the older man's eyes. "We tried to make it that way."

"We?"

"You ask a damn lot of questions."

"Just curious," Kane said. "I've never seen its like before."

"We try to please, make our guests as comfortable as possible."

Kane felt more like a prisoner than a guest. He turned to leave.

"Let me know if you need anything."

Kane nodded and walked outside. He scanned the streets for the girl, but he didn't see her. Thompson's niece. She must be used to renegades and outlaws. So why the particular distaste when she saw him? Why, when she was as guilty as her uncle of perpetuating Sanctuary?

Kane led his horse to the hotel. Maybe he could think better with a bath and shave. Maybe for a few moments he could stop thinking about Davy and his family.

And about a brown-haired, brown-eyed woman he sensed was pure trouble.

Chapter Three

Nicky wanted to run home, but she forced herself to walk slowly. It wouldn't do to let the man called Diablo know he had a disturbing effect on her.

But he *did*. Her legs had turned boneless the moment their eyes had met. His were silver-gray and fathomless with a hint of deviltry that was beguiling. She'd been caught like a rabbit by a hawk, and it had confused her. She'd never had that feeling of helplessness before.

He was certainly not among the most handsome of men who'd come to Sanctuary. He'd looked like the most desperate of desperadoes, which he was, by all accounts. And the dirt and dust were not the worst of it. A scar snaked down his left cheek, turning the corner of his mouth into a rakish smile that went with the glint in his eyes. Yet when he had bowed, he appeared every inch a gentleman, as if the exterior hid something fine.

He was a renegade, she reminded herself. He was wanted for murder and crimes too numerous to remember. And he was one of the reasons her uncle wouldn't leave Sanctuary. For that alone, she'd been prepared to hate him.

Why, then, had her heart raced? Why, then, had she fled when she'd never fled before, not from the most ruthless of men? She had learned to stand her ground, to glare

them down, to curse as soundly as they. It wasn't only her
uncle who had kept them away, it was her own frostiness.

Muttering a few of those curses, she decided to find
Robin. He wasn't at the house or the stable. His horse
was in its usual stall, though. She started for the blacksmith's. Andy Lonetree, who was part Cherokee, had been
here five years. He'd decided to stay when he'd fallen in
love with Juanita, a Mexican girl working at Rosita's.
They were married now, the only married couple in Sanctuary. Andy was wanted for murder, and Nicky knew he
would never leave.

Andy was at his forge, his big biceps bulging as he
hammered on a horseshoe. He glanced up and grinned in
welcome.

"I'm looking for Robin," Nicky said.

The smile disappeared. "He went with one of the
Yancy brothers," he said.

Nicky felt her heart plummet. Of all the current guests,
Cobb and John Yancy were among the worst. Nicky had
asked Robin to stay away from them, but these days he
considered that a challenge. He was fifteen, and he felt
trapped here, too. His only friends were outlaws, so he
wanted to be one, too, to learn everything about being the
best there was, to earn the admiration of the only men he
knew. The worse their reputations, the more he sought
them out. He would probably shadow Diablo, whose reputation was only a little less notorious than the Yancy
brothers'.

"Where did they go?" she asked.

"Toward the stream. I heard Robin ask Cobb to teach
him to draw fast."

"They don't have guns."

Andy fanned the bellows, and flames reached toward
the ceiling. "You know your brother. He probably cajoled
one of the guides to loan him one."

Nicky did know him. Robin could tempt birds from a
tree when he so pleased. He had a grin that spread halfway across his face, an eagerness to learn and please that
sometimes frightened her. It could be used—twisted—so
easily.

"Thank you," she said. "Say hello to Juanita for me."

"I will," Andy said, then beamed. "She's going to have a little one."

"Oh Andy, I'm so glad."

His obvious pleasure faded. "But I don't want him raised here. Too much—" He stopped as if he suddenly realized who he was talking to.

"I know," she said softly. *Too much evil.* The unsaid words hovered between them for a moment. "Where would you go?"

"Mexico, maybe. Juanita has family there."

"We would miss you."

"You should leave too, Miss Nicky, you and Robin, before he joins up with some bad 'uns."

"I can't leave my uncle now," she said.

Andy nodded, and she knew he'd noticed her uncle's ill health. He was loyal to her uncle, and he'd been content at Sanctuary until now. She understood, though, about the baby. She felt the same need to protect Robin, who sometimes seemed more like her child than a brother. She had been the one to hold him, to rock him, to feed him when he was a baby, even though she'd been little more than a child herself.

"When will you leave?" She suspected Andy would be one of those her uncle allowed safe passage out of Sanctuary. Others, though, had died when they proposed leaving, Nat Thompson forcing them into a gunfight. And no one had ever outdrawn Nat Thompson.

Andy hesitated. "A month or so."

Had Nat talked to Andy about his own plans to leave Sanctuary? She doubted it. Nat Thompson might like and trust Andy, but his trust didn't extend very far. He'd often told Robin that an outlaw didn't have friends. Loyalty between thieves was a myth. You always watched your back. Always.

Nicky wished Robin would listen to their uncle's warning.

She hurried to the stable and saddled Molly. She would find Robin. Perhaps her search would also take her mind from the new "guest," and those silver-gray eyes she couldn't forget.

WITH a sigh of pure physical contentment, Kane relaxed in the big tin bathtub in an alcove off the barber's shop. One hand rubbed his newly shaved cheek. The barber had been good, the water hot. The shave had been sheer luxury, costing five times what it would have in any other town, but that didn't bother him. In truth, it amused him. He was spending Masters's money.

He lit a long, thin cigar that he'd purchased, also at a rather high price. He supposed he was as close to heaven as he was apt to get. Sinking deeper into the water, he tried not to think beyond this immediate pleasure. But he couldn't forget Davy. The leash, as Masters so coldly called it, pulled tight around his neck.

Reluctantly, he rose from the tub and pulled on the new clothes he'd purchased from the general store. Blue denim trousers, a dark blue shirt. A clean bandanna around his neck. The old one had been beyond redemption. He ran a comb through his freshly washed hair, trying to tame it, and regarded himself briefly in the mirror. The scar stood out. It was one of the few he'd earned honorably, but it was like a brand, forever identifying him as Diablo.

Hell, what difference did it make? He wasn't here to court. He was here to betray. He couldn't forget that. Not for a single moment.

With a snort of self-disgust, he left the room for the stable. He would explore the boundaries of Sanctuary, do a reconnaissance. He had experience at that. Lots of experience.

NICKY rode for an hour before she heard gunshots.

She rode toward the sound, knowing full well that a stray bullet could do as much damage as a directed one. Robin was crouching, a gunbelt wrapped around his lean waist, his hand on the grip of a six-shooter. In a quick movement, he pulled it from the holster and aimed at a target affixed to a tree. Then he saw Nicky.

The pride on his face faltered, and then he set his jaw rebelliously and fired. He missed.

Nicky turned her attention to the man next to him. Arrogance radiated from him as he leered at her. Her skin crawled as she rode over to them and addressed Cobb Yancy. "If my uncle knew about this, you would be out of here faster than a bullet from that gun."

"That so, honey?" Yancy drawled. "Then he'd have to do something about your baby brother, wouldn't he?" He took the gun from Robin and stood there, letting it dangle from his fingers.

Nicky held out her hand. "Give me the gun."

"Why don't you take it from me?" Yancy's voice was low, inviting.

"You leave now, and I'll forget about this," she said.

"What if I don't want to forget about it?" he asked, moving toward her horse. "The boy can take your horse back. You can ride with me." His hand was suddenly on the horse's halter.

"Robin can walk back," she said, trying to back Molly. Yancy's grasp, though, was too strong.

Yancy turned to Robin. "You do that, boy. Start walking."

Robin looked from Yancy to Nicky and back again, apprehension beginning to show in his face. "I'd rather ride back with you, Mr. Yancy."

The gun was suddenly pointed at Robin. "Do as I say. Your sister and I will be along later."

Nicky was stiff with anger and not a little fear. "My uncle will kill you," Nicky pointed out.

"He may try," Yancy said. "I've been wondering if he's as fast as everyone says."

Nicky knew then that Cobb Yancy had just been looking for an excuse to try her uncle. Had he scented weakness? Was he after Sanctuary?

She felt for the small derringer she'd tucked inside a pocket in her trousers. "Go on, Robin," she said. "I'll catch up to you."

Robin didn't move.

"Go," she ordered in a voice that had gone hard. Softness didn't survive here, not in these mountains, not among these men.

Instead of obeying her, Robin lunged for the gun in Yancy's hand. It went off, and Robin went down. Nicky aimed her derringer directly at Yancy's heart and fired.

He looked stunned as the gun slipped from his fingers and he went down on his knees, then toppled over. Nicky dismounted and ran over to Robin. Blood was seeping from a wound in his shoulder.

She heard hoofbeats and grabbed the gun Yancy had been holding. It could be his brother coming.

But it wasn't. It was Diablo, looking very different than he had earlier. He reined in his horse at the sight of the gun aimed in his direction. His gaze moved from her to Robin to the body on the ground.

"Trouble?"

"Nothing I can't handle," Nicky said, keeping the gun pointed at him.

The side of his mouth turned up by the scar inched higher. "I see you can," he said, then studied Robin. "What about him?"

"My brother," she explained stiffly. "That polecat shot him."

"I think he needs some help."

"Not from you, mister," she said.

His brows knitted together, and he shifted in the saddle. Then ignoring the threat in her hand, he slid down from his horse and walked over to Robin, pulling the boy's shirt back to look at the wound.

Robin grimaced, then fixed his concentration on Diablo's scar. "You're that new one," he said. "Diablo."

Diablo nodded. "Some call me that. How in the hell did everyone around know I was coming?"

"There's not many secrets here," Robin said, but his voice was strained. He was obviously trying to be brave for the gunslinger. Nicky sighed. Hadn't he learned anything today?

Diablo studied the wound a moment, then took off his

bandanna and gave it to Robin. "It's clean. Hold it to the wound to stop the bleeding."

He then went over to Cobb Yancy, checked for signs of life and found none. He treated death very casually, Nicky noticed. "He's dead, all right," Diablo said.

Before she could protest, he returned to Robin. He helped Robin shed his shirt, which he tore in two and made into a sling. When he was through, he offered a steadying arm to Robin.

"Don't," Nicky said sharply. "I'll help him."

"He's losing blood," Diablo said. "He could lose consciousness. You prepared to take his whole weight?"

Nicky studied her brother's face. It was pale, growing paler by the moment. "We'll send someone back for Yancy. He has a brother. It would be best not to meet him."

Diablo didn't ask any questions, she'd give him that. She looked down at her hands, and noticed they were shaking. She'd never killed a man before.

Diablo's eyes seemed to stab through her, reading her thoughts. Then he was guiding Robin to Yancy's horse, practically lifting her brother on the gelding. There was an easy strength about him, a confidence, that surprised Nicky. He'd looked so much the renegade loner this morning, yet here he'd taken charge automatically, as if he were used to leadership. Resentment mixed with gratitude.

She tucked the gun into the waist of her trousers and mounted her mare. She kept seeing Yancy's surprised face as he went down. Her hands were shaking even more now. She'd killed a man. A man who had a very dangerous brother.

She had known this would happen one day. But nothing could have prepared her for the despair she felt at taking someone's life. She felt sick inside.

Diablo, who was riding ahead with Robin, looked back. He reined in his own horse until she was abreast of him, and she felt his watchful gaze settle on her. "Tell Yancy's brother I did it."

Nothing he could have said would have surprised her more.

"Why?"

"I can take care of myself."

He couldn't have insulted her more. "What do you think I just did?"

"I think you just killed your first man, and you don't need another on your conscience. You certainly don't need it on your stomach. You look like you're going to up-chuck."

She glared at him. "I'm fine."

"Good. Your brother isn't."

All of Nicky's attention went to Robin. He was swaying in his saddle. She moved her horse around to his side. "Just a few more minutes, Robin. Hold on."

"I'm sorry, Sis. I shouldn't have gone with . . . Cobb Yancy, but—"

"Hush," she said. "If you hadn't, Yancy would have found something else. He was after more than me."

But Robin wasn't listening. He was holding on to his saddle horn for dear life, and his face was a white mask now.

"Maybe I should ride ahead," she said. "Get some help."

"You got a doctor in this place?" Diablo asked.

"Not right now. But Andy—"

"Andy?"

"The blacksmith. He knows some medicine, and I can sew up a wound."

"Go on ahead, and get him ready," Diablo ordered. "I'll get your brother there." He stopped his horse, slipped off and then mounted behind Robin, holding him upright in the saddle.

Could she really trust Diablo that much? Dare she leave him alone with Robin?

"I'll take care of him," Diablo said, more gently this time.

Nicky finally nodded and spurred her mare into a gallop.

• • •

KANE handled young Thompson gingerly. The boy reminded him of himself years ago, particularly the bravado. The kid was obviously in severe pain, but he wasn't going to show it.

"Hang on," Kane said. The wound wasn't too bad. The boy would survive. But for what? To get caught in a shoot-out here? To see his uncle and perhaps his sister go to prison?

He thought about how the girl had looked so determined as she'd held a gun on him, and yet she had to have been scared. And the boy trying so hard to be a man . . .

What in the hell were they doing here?

Keep your distance, he told himself. *You can't afford pity, or sympathy or . . . anything else.*

The boy slumped farther in the saddle. "What's your name?" Kane asked.

"Robin," the boy replied in a weak voice.

"Well, Robin, you're going to be fine. Just try to keep awake."

The boy struggled to sit up straight.

"Don't," Kane said. "I'll hold you."

"I can do . . . it myself."

"I know," Kane said softly, fighting off the unwanted memories that were beginning to surface. Memories of Davy's family rescuing him from hunger and fear.

The strange little town came into view, and the street that wasn't anywhere on a map. "The first house," the boy said. Several people had gathered in front of the stone and adobe house, which was the finest in Sanctuary, Kane had noticed.

He guided the horse to the hitching post, and Nat Thompson, his face red and full of anger, reached for his nephew.

Kane helped lower the boy, and another man, a huge man with biceps like tree trunks, carried him inside. The girl, who had been watching from the porch, followed, leaving Kane alone in the street.

He was ready to turn his horse and return to the hotel when an older man he hadn't seen yet walked out the door.

"Come inside," the man said.

It wasn't an invitation, and Kane had to tamp down his resentment before he dismounted.

When he reached the door, the man stuck out his hand. "I'm Mitch Evers." Wondering exactly what Evers's role was, Kane took the man's hand, somehow understanding that he didn't extend it often.

"I hear you offered to take blame for the shooting," Evers said. "That won't be necessary. John Yancy is now being escorted from Sanctuary. He won't be back." There was a hardness to his voice that belied the slight smile on his lips.

Kane didn't ask any questions. He just nodded and turned to leave.

"Nat wants to see you. He'll be here as soon as he makes sure Robin is all right."

"The boy should be okay," Kane replied. "He lost a lot of blood, but I don't think the bullet hit anything serious."

"You sound like you know a lot about wounds."

"I was in the war four years."

Evers nodded, and the two men went inside to a large main room. Evers went to a cabinet and turned to Kane. "Want a drink?"

Kane nodded.

Evers poured one. He didn't look at Kane. "Not curious about Yancy?"

"It's none of my business."

"Then why did you interfere out there?"

"I figure a gunshot in my vicinity *is* my business."

Evers chuckled. "Mebbe so." He handed Kane a glass filled with amber-colored liquid. Kane took it, sipped appreciatively. It was good whiskey.

Evers waved a hand toward a chair, and Kane sat. Like everything else about this house, the chair was good quality and comfortable.

Kane sensed that being invited inside Nat Thompson's home was unusual. His first meeting with Thompson had suggested nothing but cold professionalism. Through no design on his part, Kane had apparently made a unique place for himself, and he didn't care for it. He had made his offer to the Thompson girl instinctively, and now he was in the home of Sanctuary's mayor, drinking his whiskey. Masters would be proud. Kane squirmed a little, feeling dirty inside.

The door to another room opened, and Nat Thompson appeared. Kane stood and was gestured back down again. He endured a very long searching study.

"What were you doing out there?" Thompson asked. The question came unexpectedly, like a lightning bolt from clear skies.

"I like to know something about the place I'm in," Kane replied.

"I'd think you'd rather be drinking after that long ride."

Kane shrugged. "I've been on the run too long to give up certain habits."

Thompson visibly relaxed as if he understood that line of thinking. "Not too many of my customers feel that way. They generally spend the first few days in the saloon or in bed."

"Maybe they haven't spent time in jail . . . or getting as close as I did to the noose."

"Most of them wouldn't have interceded in something that didn't concern them, either."

"I didn't have to intercede. Your niece had everything under control."

"You helped my nephew. You made an offer that could have got you killed. I owe you for that."

The last thing Kane wanted was this man's gratitude. Not when Kane's sole aim was to see Thompson hung or sent to prison.

Kane gulped the rest of his whiskey and stood. "How's the boy doing?"

"Andy says he'll be fine in a few days."

"He's got spunk."

"Too much for his own good."

Then why is he here? Kane wanted to ask. Thompson was crazy for allowing a kid and a girl to run loose among men like him.

Thompson seemed to read his mind. "They don't have

anyone else. I try to protect them, but . . ." He stopped, then sighed. "You have my thanks."

Kane shook his head. "It isn't necessary. I think I'll go get some of that rest you mentioned."

Thompson smiled for the first time. "When I said bed, I didn't particularly mean rest."

Kane smiled. "Maybe later. Your method of traveling was none too comfortable."

"Maybe not, but it's effective in keeping you and the others safe."

And you. Kane kept that thought to himself, inclining his head slightly in acknowledgment.

"You want a woman, it's on me," Thompson said. "For as long as you're here."

That the offer left him cold stunned Kane. It had been a long time since he'd last slept with a woman, and yet the thought of being with just *any* woman didn't appeal to him. He cared even less for the thought that maybe a toffee-hair girl in pants did.

He nodded again, put the glass down, and headed for the door before Thompson's all-too-perceptive eyes read his mind.

Chapter Four

Kane slept through the night and much of the next day, not waking until late afternoon.

He'd had only one nightmare—of being hit by his father.

Kane was incorrectly named for the biblical character who had killed his brother. For it was his mother he had killed—though not through evil intent. His birth had been fraught with complications, and his mother had died. His father had never forgiven him; and, being illiterate, had never known the name was misspelled.

Kane rose from the bed and, without bothering to cover his nude body, went to the window. Sanctuary could get monotonous, with its one street, one saloon, one house of joy. Safety had its price, and not only in money. The street looked as it did yesterday; men wandered it with no particular purpose in mind. He wondered how many knew what had happened yesterday. Or if they even cared.

Kane stretched as if he could remove the kinks in his thoughts as well as his body. He was still looking out the window when he saw Thompson's niece heading toward the hotel. She looked up and he realized she could see him. Her eyes widened, then she quickly headed toward the store across the street. How could her innocence have survived in a place like this?

Kane dressed, then walked down the stairs to the dining room. One man was sitting at a table; the other six tables were empty.

"Mr. Diablo," the man said as he rose from his seat.

"O'Brien," Kane corrected him.

"Mr. O'Brien it is," the man said cheerfully. "We've been waiting for you to wake up. This meal is on the house, Mr. Thompson said."

If this was a singular honor, it was one he could do without. "Steak, if you have it."

"Oh, we have nearly everything, particularly beef. Have our own herd here."

Kane grinned his most disarming grin, the one that usually got him what he wanted. "Seems you have everything a man could want."

"Mayor Thompson planned it that way," the man said. "I'm Jeb Gibson."

"You a permanent resident?"

Jeb nodded. "I run the hotel, do most of the cooking. Help's hard to get."

"How many live here?" Kane asked, true interest behind the question. He was fascinated by Sanctuary's resemblance to a real town ... and the violence that lay simmering beneath the peace.

"Oh, about twelve to fifteen, depending."

"Depending on what?"

Jeb Gibson's loquaciousness came to a sudden end, as if an invisible gag had been shoved in his mouth. He turned toward the door, muttering. "Better get that steak. Be just a few minutes."

Kane found himself a chair, one backed to the wall so he could see anyone who entered. He wondered where the other "guests" were, and who they were.

He was halfway through a steak when several started wandering in. They eyed him curiously, gazes quickly going to the scar on his face. He would have recognized them anywhere, not particularly who they were, but what they were, even without their gunbelts. There was a coldness in their eyes, a cautiousness as they surveyed the room—and himself. He felt a sudden chill. He was one of these men, so much so that the law sent him here: an outlaw to catch outlaws.

Only one came up to him. He was a tall, rangy man, and he walked like a panther. He thrust out his hand. "Sam Hildebrand," he said. "Heard you was a reb. I fought them Yanks in Missouri."

Kane knew the name. The man was rumored to run with Frank and Jesse James. He took the hand and acknowledged the introduction with a nod.

His reticence didn't seem to bother Hildebrand, who dropped down on a seat at his table. "We're having a poker game this evening. Thought you might like to join us."

"Why not?" Something about Hildebrand made Kane's skin crawl. Kane had turned outlaw to survive. Hildebrand was a man born to banditry and death. Kane had heard tales of the bushwhackers in Missouri; as far as he was concerned they had nothing to do with war, and everything to do with personal greed and blatant killing. But every bit of information he could gather would help him.

He finished his steak and rose from his seat. "When is the game?"

"A few hours. Over at the saloon," Hildebrand replied.

"Think I'll take a look around first."

"Heard you did some lookin' yesterday. Some men saw you come riding in with the kid. Strange about that. Some of Thompson's men came and fetched John Yancy about the same time. Escorted him out, they did, and without his brother. Which means Cobb is dead."

Kane should have guessed. Gossip seemed to be the chief activity here. Now he knew why he'd been asked for poker.

Kane shrugged. "Found the kid hurt, that's all."

"Just the same, John might wonder about your part in it."

"That's his problem." Kane brushed past him.

"Just a friendly warning. The Yancys have a reputation for getting even."

Kane didn't answer. This whole thing was turning into a mess. But John Yancy was the least of his worries.

He strode to the stable, found his horse and saddled it. The blacksmith came over to him.

"Going someplace?" the man asked.

"Feeling a bit restless. Any suggestions for a ride?"

"I would think after yesterday you might want to stay in town a while."

"It goes against my grain to stay still long," Kane replied. "I've been running nigh onto two years now. I like to study my exits."

The blacksmith stuck out his hand. "We didn't get introduced yesterday. I'm Andy, blacksmith and stabler. You need anything, you come to me. You did real good with the boy yesterday."

"Everybody call him 'the boy'?" Kane was curious about the relationships in Sanctuary.

Andy raised an eyebrow. "Someone else did?"

"Man named Hildebrand."

"He must have been asking you about yesterday then. Natural enough, I guess. One Yancy disappearing like that, the other being asked to leave."

"Asked to leave?"

Andy grinned suddenly. "Guess he didn't have too much choice."

"Does that happen often?"

The smile disappeared. "No. Not many challenge Mr. Thompson nor fool with his kin. Them that do don't live long."

"So I understand." Kane mounted his horse. "Any suggestions as to where to ride?"

"Just don't go too close to the canyon walls without escort," Andy said. "You saw the creek yesterday. There's some right pleasant places along it, even a pretty good fishing spot a few miles down."

Kane nodded. "How's the boy doing?"

"Well enough. Madder 'n hell at being shot. Even madder at being used by that coyote. One good thing—he'll sure as hell be more careful next time."

"It has to be hard on him, no other kids here."

"Better than an orphanage." Andy scowled as if he'd said too much. "Remember about not getting too close to the canyon walls."

Kane touched his spurs to the sides of his horse and cantered off down the street.

EXCEPT for a brief trip to the general store, Nicky spent most of the day with her brother, who slept, aided by laudanum. His wound looked ugly, but Nicky guessed his pride suffered the greater damage. Who wouldn't hurt at being used and being seen helpless and weak? Perhaps it was just as well; his embarrassment might keep him away from Diablo.

Funny, but Diablo hadn't seemed much like the devil yesterday. He'd been compassionate, and his offer to take the blame had completely blindsided her. There had to be a reason, she kept telling herself. No one did something for nothing, not in her world. Maybe there were knights in shining armor in books, but not in real life. Diablo wanted something. But what was it?

Right now, Nicky only wanted him to stay away from Robin—and from her. Although he didn't act like the devil, he looked like the devil, the devil of temptation. A vivid image of his nude form, only partially concealed by a curtain, flashed in her mind, bringing color to her cheeks. In that brief moment before she'd torn her gaze away from him, she'd been unable to breathe. He'd looked magnificent.

Suddenly unable to sit still, she stood and started prowling the house. Her uncle kept most of the Wanted posters and articles about outlaws at home, and she found the file on Diablo. She'd read it before, but she wanted to read it again. There were two Wanted posters, one dated a year ago, the other a more recent one. She knew the particulars: six foot one, one hundred and seventy pounds, dark hair, gray eyes. Wanted for murder and numerous robberies. He was an ex-cavalry man, a captain with the reb army, who had turned outlaw after the war.

Sanctuary had seen its share of others like him, men who hadn't been able to return to civilian life after the war. Despite that similar background he wasn't like the others, which made him dangerous to her. Instinct told her he was also dangerous to her uncle, but she didn't know how or why.

Later, toward dusk, she went outside on the porch for some fresh air and saw him riding toward the house. He was barely touching the reins, which were draped over the saddle horn, and his hands were holding something.

"Miss Thompson," he greeted her.

She nodded in acknowledgment.

"I found a baby hawk. It must have fallen from a nest in the canyon wall." He hesitated a moment, then continued. "I thought maybe your brother might like to take care of it."

Nicky was delighted. She loved animals, and so did Robin. Their dog, Caesar, had died last year, and Robin had been heartbroken. She held out her hands for the bird, cuddled the small thing for a few seconds, and looked up at O'Brien. "How did you know?"

Color rose in his face. If she hadn't known better she almost would have called it a blush.

"Kids and animals go together," he said curtly, almost rudely, then moved his horse back a few steps and continued his way to the hotel.

She could only stare at him in astonishment. None of the other guests would have cared about the bird or Robin's feelings.

He's an outlaw, she told herself. A deadly one. And yet his guarded gray eyes held little cruelty. She didn't get that icy feeling around him as she did with the others, as though they were rattlesnakes coiling to hit. Maybe he hid those snake bands better than most.

She'd also seen her share of charmers, whose laughter turned lethal in a matter of seconds. Her uncle was like that. His magnetism was the first secret of Sanctuary's success, his hardness, the second. When one didn't work, the other did. Could Diablo be setting her up for the kill?

"Hellfire," she muttered. Cradling the small bird in her hand, she took it in to Robin.

• • •

KANE stabled his horse, then went directly to the saloon. He needed a drink. He'd discovered that Nat Thompson protected his valley very well indeed. Guards seemed to be at every possible exit. The only way to discover Sanctuary's location was from within. None of the guests knew what that location was, but he'd lay money that Thompson's niece did.

Miss Thompson. The woman with tough talk and eyes that had warmed when he'd handed her the bird minutes ago. Her mouth had turned up into a delighted smile. Her hands had been gentle as they'd stroked the small hawk, and he'd felt a sudden, unexpected ache to have them touch him.

Had anyone ever touched him with such care and tenderness?

He'd had a hawk for a brief time as a boy. His father had wrung its neck, saying it would kill the chickens when it grew up. So when he'd found the baby hawk today, he couldn't have left it to starve to death. But nursing it didn't exactly go with his image as a hardened gunfighter. Then he'd thought of Robin.

Taking it to the house was a foolish thing to do. He'd realized it the moment he saw the woman.

He tried to shrug away the confusion she stirred in him. With Davy's life at stake, he shouldn't be concerned with the likes of Miss Thompson. Still, he wasn't able to keep himself from wondering about her first name. He went over possibilities in his mind, but none fit. Some were too soft, some too hard. She was neither, but a fascinating combination of grit and vulnerability.

He would never know her name, because he was going to stay away from her. Everything in him rebelled against using her, betraying her. But what if that was the only way to save Davy?

He entered the busy saloon, and everyone turned to look. Some automatically reached for guns that weren't there. He sauntered up to the crowded bar, saw Hildebrand motion for Kane to join him at the other end where he stood with several men.

"Meet the others," Hildebrand said, and ran off a series of names, some of which Kane recognized.

"How do you like our little town?" one asked him.

"Interesting," Kane replied noncommittally.

"You here for long?"

"Long enough for a posse to lose my trail."

One man sidled up to him. Like Kane, he wore a scar across his cheek. The man put a hand to his. "How did you get yours?"

"The war," Kane said curtly.

The other man looked disappointed and walked away. Kane wondered what kind of answer he had wanted. He turned back to his drink, discouraging conversation. He felt like a wolf among coyotes. They might have some ancestry in common, even some interests, but he didn't like the association.

The men he'd ridden with the last few years had all been ex-rebs. They hadn't been thieves by choice but by injustice. Their land had been taken, and in some cases their families killed. They'd come back from war to nothing, to carpetbaggers stealing land settled and worked by their fathers. Their families had fought the Mexicans and Indians and drought and flood for their small dreams, for the right to live and farm and ranch on their land. They'd been fighting for that these past two years, as they had fought four long years of official war. The stakes had been the same, but the odds had been stacked even more heavily against them.

That was *his* justification for outlawry, anyway. He wondered whether Nat Thompson had any.

"Come on, Diablo," Hildebrand said. "Join us in a poker game."

Kane nodded. He followed Hildebrand and three others to a table. Parker. Kayo. Curry. Curry, he remembered, was wanted for a bloody bank robbery where two kids were killed. Kane shuffled the cards and started dealing.

The game broke up three hours later. Kane was the

big winner, which did not endear him to the others. Curry, in particular, was a poor loser as well as a piss-poor poker player. He swore several times and kicked over a chair when he rose.

Hildebrand shrugged. He and Kane were the only two left at the table. "He'll get over it."

Kane poured his companion a glass of whiskey from the bottle he'd just purchased. "Does he always play that badly?"

"Only when he drinks too much."

Which was often, Kane thought, if one paid attention to the unhealthy color of his face.

"What about tomorrow night?" Hildebrand said. "I want a chance to get my money back."

"Don't know why not. Nothing else to do here," Kane said. "You been here long?"

Hildebrand sighed. "A month. I'm just about broke. I'm trying to recruit a couple of men for a bank job. You interested?"

"Might be," Kane said slowly. "Right now it's pretty hot out there. Whole state of Texas is looking for me."

"I'm not thinking about Texas."

Kane allowed his interest to show, though he said nothing, just waited for more information.

"Kansas," Hildebrand said. "Cattlemen are taking their herds up there, and buyers have lots of money in those banks. I could use a man like you."

"Who else is going along?"

Hildebrand's eyes grew cautious. "I'm not sure yet."

"I want to know the men I ride with," Kane said. "I don't take chances. I'll let you know when you recruit the others." He poured Hildebrand another drink. "You have any idea how far that bank is from here?"

"Depends on where you tell Thompson you want to go. I figure about ten, twelve days hard riding from the Texas border.

That was little help. Hell, he might as well ask. "You have any idea where we are?"

Hildebrand shook his head. "Don't really want to know. That's dangerous knowledge. Real dangerous."

"Thompson's got a good thing going here."

"Wish to hell I had some of it," Hildebrand said. "No risk. Just money pouring in."

"I think I would get bored real quick," Kane said. "Risks are what makes the game interesting."

"Speaking of interesting, I saw you talking to Nicky Thompson."

"Nicky?"

"Thompson's niece. She's real class, but she doesn't have anything to do with us. That's Thompson's first rule. First time I came here two years ago, a man tried to kiss her. Thompson had him whipped near to death. Never saw or heard of him again."

"I'll remember that." Kane took another glass of whiskey. He shouldn't. He needed his wits about him. But the mention of the woman had rattled him. Nicky. The name suited her.

He abruptly rose, shoving the bottle over to Hildebrand. "Take it. I'm going to Rosita's."

Hildebrand leered. "If you're going to Rosita's, ask for Cara."

Maybe he *would*, Kane thought. Maybe that's all he needed: physical release. He started for the brothel next to the saloon, but stopped when he saw a light on in the stone house at the end of the street.

Nicky.

Damn it all to hell. He had as much business thinking about her as he did about a future. Muttering a curse, he continued on to Rosita's.

So he was like the others, after all.

Jealousy whipped angrily inside Nicky as she watched through the window, though there was no reason for it. She had no claim on Diablo, wanted none. Still, it hurt so much to think of him with one of the women at Rosita's.

Men had needs, Nicky knew that. Andy's wife, Juanita, had whispered the intimate secrets to her, and she'd heard men talk about it when they thought she wasn't listening.

Would she ever find out those secrets for herself? Certainly not unless she left Sanctuary.

Feeling empty and lonely, she left her room to check on Robin. He was asleep. On the floor beside him lay the hawk in a makeshift bed. Robin had already named it Diablo.

She crawled into her own bed, suddenly feeling seven years old—and deserted again. It was the way she'd felt when her mother died, and then her father. It didn't make sense. Still, the ball of misery rolled around inside her. She wanted something. She wanted it so badly it hurt. But she didn't know what it was. It couldn't be Kane O'Brien. She would never fall in love with a man like her uncle or father. She'd loved them both dearly, but losing her father had hurt too much, and she didn't doubt that losing Uncle Nat would be as bad. She felt a dampness on her cheeks and touched them. Tears. She hadn't shed tears since her father died.

Nicky wiped them away angrily. No, she would never allow herself to care for a man like Diablo.

KANE slammed around his room, taking out his frustration on everything he touched. He cursed Masters repeatedly. He even wished a return to his prison cell. There had been fewer moral dilemmas there. Just waiting. Just emptiness.

He'd found Cara at Rosita's, had taken her to one of the rooms in back. He'd watched appreciatively as she'd stripped slowly and seductively. But as he had leaned down to kiss her, another face came between them, a pixielike face with big brown eyes, a wide mouth, and a too-serious expression.

He'd suddenly backed away, leaving Cara to look at him in puzzlement. "I do something wrong, senor?" she'd asked.

She was a pretty little thing, and her smile said she enjoyed her work. So did her hands that started to work on him, unbuttoning his shirt and caressing his chest. He felt his body react, but for some reason he couldn't make his mind do the same. Somehow, an act he'd always enjoyed seemed wrong. Hell, there was nothing wrong with paying for a bit of sex.

He'd tried. He'd really tried. He'd admired the roundness of Cara's body, even while part of his mind compared it with the slender grace of Nicky Thompson's. In the end, the act had been a clumsy, hurried affair that left him more frustrated than ever. He'd just wanted it over. He'd given Cara an extra large tip and left quickly. He knew he wouldn't be back.

He felt as if someone had drilled a hole into him, allowing the best part of him to drain away and leaving the worms. How in the hell had he ever gotten into such a mess?

He had to get one single thing right in this life. The problem was, he no longer knew what that one single thing should be. He'd been given a choice: Davy's life or death. But he should have known it wouldn't be that simple. It had whirled into something else completely, like a kaleidoscope he'd once seen: colors and shapes always changing. One choice was leading to another: betrayal of his best friend, or betrayal of a vulnerable woman who moved him more than he was willing to admit.

Chapter Five

Morning was Nicky's favorite time. She usually rose at dawn and took a ride. The inhabitants of Sanctuary were almost all asleep then; they thrived on darkness.

Nicky had a particular spot she loved, a rise on the west side of the valley where she could watch the sun ascend and the soft colors brighten the earth. She knew, when she rose after a sleepless night, feeling slow and drugged, that she needed to visit her special place, needed to be alone to think.

Not another soul was yet in sight when she arrived at the stable. Molly whinnied her usual welcome. Nicky didn't bother with a saddle and bridle this morning; using only a halter, she headed the mare out of town.

She gave Molly her head, and the mare danced a few steps with pleasure. Dark night had surrendered to the first rays of a sun still lurking behind the mountains, and a soft morning gray was promising a fine day. A breeze was pushing a few wispy clouds over an otherwise clear sky like bits of lace over fine cloth.

Nicky avoided the area where she'd shot Yancy and went farther upstream where the land started to slope upward into the hills. Cottonwoods and scraggly oaks struggled to exist among the rocks, and she'd always felt them very gallant indeed to keep trying. She guessed it had been nearby that O'Brien had found the baby hawk, for she'd seen several hawks soaring around the top of the canyon wall. She wondered which one had just lost its offspring and if it mourned the loss. The thought saddened her, strengthening the bittersweet longing that still lingered inside her.

Nothing seemed right this morning, right or natural, even on a morning as sweet as any she could remember.

Molly went straight to the top of the rise. Nicky slid off the horse, taking a seat on a rotting log as Molly found a patch of grass to nibble. Light was exploding now like a halo around the mountains. In moments, the top of the sun would tip the mountain in a glorious awakening.

She swallowed hard. There must be so much life beyond these majestic walls. She had never realized how lonely she was until now. Or maybe she simply hadn't admitted it.

The sun edged up, its rays hitting the jutting boulders of the crags like flecks of silver and copper. She glanced around and noticed a rider following the wall of the canyon. He was a long distance away, but she knew him instantly. She recognized the horse, for one thing; it was a gray, and there were few grays in Sanctuary. And then there was the way the rider held himself. She watched from a distance. He appeared to be looking for something. A way out? But why? He had paid a fortune to get inside.

The guards, stationed at strategic places, probably couldn't see the man now moving along the wall, stopping occasionally as if to study an outcropping. The brilliance of the morning dulled. She watched for another few moments, and then he turned, the metal trim on his saddle glinting in the sun. Then he stilled, and she wondered whether he had seen her. He apparently had, for he turned the horse in her direction and rode at a leisurely pace toward her.

Nicky wondered whether she should mount and ride like a demon for her uncle's. She was only too aware she hadn't brought a gun this morning—bringing even her derringer stole something from the peace of a sunrise—but her legs didn't move. She only watched as the figure grew larger.

Nicky ran her fingers through her hair, trying to comb it, recognizing the action for the vanity it was, despising herself for caring. He was an outlaw, an outlaw who'd visited a fancy lady last night. She wished, though, that her heart wouldn't thump so loudly.

She didn't move as he approached. He sat for a moment on his big gray, then slid easily down from the saddle. He took off the hat he wore and bowed slightly, just as he had that first day. The thump in her heart moved up to her throat.

"Miss Thompson," he said. "A pleasure. I thought I would only see birds this morning."

Nicky sought to find her voice. It came out unintentionally accusing. "I'm surprised you're up so early . . . after a late night."

He looked surprised. "Late?"

Nicky bit her lip. She didn't want him to think she was spying on him. And she hadn't been. She'd just been looking out the window. "Everyone goes to the saloon and Rosita's."

"Do they now?" he said, an edge of amusement in his voice.

She wanted to slap him. She went on the attack instead. "What are you doing, prowling around?"

"I always get up early. I'm just exploring. Thought I would try to find that hawk's nest."

"Why?"

He looked her straight in the eyes. "Something to do, Miss Thompson. I get bored easily."

"Why?"

He raised an eyebrow in question.

"There's always Rosita's."

"That's the second time you mentioned Rosita's."

"I saw you go inside last night," she said acidly. She knew she was being unreasonable. She hated allowing him to know she cared enough to mention it. But the words kept popping out, sputtering like steam from a teapot.

"I suppose you see a lot of men go in Rosita's," he said reasonably.

"Of course," she said airily. "I just wondered why you

were up this morning. My uncle doesn't like his guests sneaking around."

He chuckled. "I don't think I'm sneaking around. If I am, I'm doing a damned poor job of it."

"Are you laughing at me, Mr. O'Brien?"

"No, Miss Thompson, I'm not. I'm simply trying to explain something, and I rarely do that." His voice hardened. "Very rarely."

She bit her lip. He confused her. One minute, he was exuding charm, the next, menace. Yet she sensed that menace wasn't directed toward her. Nicky quickly changed the subject. "I come up here every morning."

He looked toward the east, at the sun now fully clearing the mountains. "I understand why. But isn't it dangerous?"

He was thinking about Yancy. She was thinking about Kane O'Brien. He was far more dangerous. She didn't know the rules of *this* game. She didn't know how to flirt and was muttering all kinds of silly things. Nicky cringed at what he must think.

"I can take care of myself," she said defensively.

"So I noticed. But it doesn't look like you have a gun today."

"I do," she bluffed.

His eyes roamed over her. She felt as if she were sizzling inside. When she could stand it no longer, she stepped back, stumbling, heat rising in her face.

He reached out to steady her, his slight perpetual smile turning into a frown. "I didn't mean . . ."

Nicky would have fled if she weren't afraid that she would stumble again. His hand touched her shoulder, his gloved fingers moving to her cheek, touching it lightly.

"I wouldn't hurt you," he said.

His fingers left her skin and she felt bereft. She looked down at his hands and watched him pull off a glove. Then his fingers were back and this time she felt his skin against hers in an agonizingly intimate way.

Intimate because she'd never felt a man's hands on her before. She didn't know they could feel this way, that a mere touch could warm her blood and make her toes curl, that a kind of fever could rip through her like a tornado, leaving ruins in its wake. She tilted her face upward to look at him. That perpetual half smile, drawn by the scar, appeared gentler.

She reached up and tentatively touched the jagged scar. "What happened?" she whispered.

"A bayonet wound during the war," he said, turning that cheek away.

She shuddered, thinking of his pain, hurting for him.

His hand suddenly fell away. "It took *me* a long time to get used to it," he said, and she suddenly realized he thought she was repelled by it.

"I think it's very . . . handsome."

He suddenly grinned. "No one's ever called it *that* before."

"You got it honorably. You should be proud of it," Nicky blurted out. Amusement flickered in his eyes and she felt like twelve instead of twenty-two. One of his eyebrows raised again, and he truly did look like the devil. Still, she felt no fear.

"And I haven't done an honorable thing since, Miss Thompson."

"Why?" It was a foolish question, particularly posed to an outlaw as notorious as Diablo. But she wanted to know.

"Being honorable is not what it's touted to be," he said with that crooked smile. "Believe me on that."

"*Why* did you go to war?"

A curtain suddenly dropped over his eyes. "I'll probably never understand that myself, Miss Thompson."

"Nicky," she said. "Everyone calls me Nicky." She knew she shouldn't invite that new intimacy, but suddenly it seemed as if they were friends.

"Nicky?"

"It's short for Nicole." Nicky held her breath as she watched his reaction. Nicole was a name for a lady, not a woman who wore her hair as short as a man's and dressed in trousers.

But he didn't laugh. "And how did Miss Nicole Thompson come to be at Sanctuary? Why isn't she married or entertaining a long line of beaus?"

Nicky snapped her mouth shut. She had already said too much. Her uncle's life, as well as hers and Robin's, depended on the image of Nat Thompson's infallibility. She couldn't tell him how much she wanted to leave, how often she'd thought about it.

She shrugged. "My uncle took us in when my father ... was killed. My mother had died a year earlier when Robin was born. Uncle Nat's been very good to us."

Some emotion crossed his face. It came and went so quickly, she couldn't place it. But his shoulders seemed to stiffen, and tension radiated from his body.

"Don't you think you'd better be getting along home?" It was as if he'd slammed a door in her face. The impact hurt. She whirled around so he wouldn't see it. Confusion flooded her, confusion and hurt and a need to strike back.

"This is *my* home, Mr. O'Brien. *My* hill. You're the intruder."

"I would think my gold makes me a very welcome intruder." There was a sudden coldness in his eyes that made her shiver. Why had she thought, even for a moment, that he was different? He was only a chameleon, a man who used charm better than most.

"It doesn't. You're paying for protection, that's all. For extending your life. Maybe you forgot my uncle's rules."

"Staying away from you? Fate keeps interfering. I had no idea you would be riding this morning."

"Or that anyone else would be," she observed acidly. "I wonder what my uncle would think of you inspecting the walls of the canyon."

"I didn't realize I was exchanging one jail for another," he replied, his jaw setting. The scar stood out as he did so, and the aura of danger heightened. An almost imperceptible shudder seemed to run through his body, as if he were trying, and failing, to maintain that rigid control she saw in him. "But I'm sorry to have disturbed your morning ride."

His tone said he wasn't sorry at all. He was angry, and she didn't understand why. She had more reason to be angry than he. He *had* disturbed her morning, had se-

duced her into liking him and then had thrown it in her
face.

Even worse, he had made her feel things she'd never
felt before. She didn't want to feel them, not for him, not
for an outlaw. Loving an outlaw had killed her mother,
had kept her from a doctor who might have saved her.
And her uncle, for all the comforts here, was an exile. As
were she and her brother.

She often ached for normalcy, for an end to fear. Fear
for her uncle, for her brother. Fear over leaving here, the
only place she really knew, and fear over staying and
never knowing anything else. She'd always been able to
push these fears aside before, but now they smothered her.

She stiffened her back, lifted her chin defiantly and
walked over to her horse.

"I'll help you," Kane O'Brien said.

She didn't want his hands on her again. She couldn't
stand that melting sensation, the yearning anguish that
settled in the pit of her stomach. "No," she said sharply
and walked Molly over to the log where she'd been sitting
when she'd first seen him. Nicky stepped onto the log,
then threw her leg over Molly's back. She knew she wasn't
graceful, but at the moment flight was more important.
Without looking back, she kicked Molly's sides and felt
the mare bolt in protest. The wild, uncontrolled ride was
fine with her. She leaned down on Molly's neck and raced
down the hill.

Kane's first instinct was to go after her, but he saw
immediately that she had control of the horse. His second
emotion was admiration. He'd never seen a woman ride
as well. She rode like she was a part of the horse. He
watched them until they disappeared, his thoughts in tur-
moil.

He should never have touched her. But she'd looked so
appealing, with curiosity darting in her eyes, her wide
mouth in a slight, wondering smile, and the sun touching
her hair like specks of gold. She had the oddest combination of innocence and toughness, and it touched him in
surprising ways. He'd felt her shiver when he touched her,
and he'd known instinctively that no man had touched

her before, not with any kind of intimacy. She was like a rosebud, so ready to open and yet fragile.

He sighed heavily, feeling every inch the villain he was said to be. There was an honesty and openness about her that made him hurt, had made him wrench his fingers away from her petal-soft cheek before he did anything to crush her spirit.

My uncle took us in when my father died, she'd said. So she wasn't here by choice. But why didn't she leave? She couldn't have much of a life here.

She's not your problem. Davy is, a hard, cold voice in his head spoke in warning.

Kane's mouth tightened into a grim line as his gaze scanned the canyon walls one more time. So far he'd found no hint of an unguarded exit. How could he pinpoint Sanctuary's location without getting outside? Without a blindfold.

Nicky. Nicky was the answer. She must know where they were. She couldn't have stayed locked in this valley all her life. The thought of using her sickened him. But he didn't have any choice, not if he was to save the man who was as close to him as his brother.

He should never have come home from the war. He'd never understood how or why he had survived when other men, better men, had died around him. Bullets caught those next to him, but always missed him. The bayonet had missed its real target, his throat, and had merely ripped into his cheek. Even in the Yank prison camp, he'd thrown off diseases that killed so many others. He'd started thinking he lived a charmed life until he'd returned to Texas, and carpetbaggers had ridden up to Davy's ranch. Hell, even then, he hadn't minded the outlaw life so much. His one regret was that he'd pulled Davy deeper and deeper into trouble.

He mounted his gray. He wondered whether Nicky Thompson would mention his explorations to her uncle. Kane wouldn't be surprised if Thompson already knew. Kane thought there was little that happened in the valley that Thompson didn't know.

• • •

NAT Thompson stared at Mitch Evers through hooded eyes. Since the episode a few days ago with Yancy, he'd asked Mitch to keep an eye on Nicky.

"She met O'Brien?" Thompson said, his voice rising ever so slightly.

Evers nodded. "I don't think it was planned."

"What in the devil was he doing riding at that time of the morning?"

"Andy says he does a lot of riding."

"Then why in the hell didn't he stay on the run instead of coming here?"

Evers shrugged. "We checked him out real good."

"Well, he'd been in prison a few months. Maybe he's just restless. But I think we should watch him."

"He'll have a shadow wherever he goes."

Pain struck Nat's stomach. He'd come to expect it now, yet he wasn't prepared for its growing fierceness. He tried to keep his face blank. He didn't want even Mitch to know how bad the pain was getting. In a moment, it faded. Not entirely, but enough so that he could straighten up. "I have another idea," he said. "I think I'll invite him for supper."

He almost grinned at Evers's surprised face. He would have, had not the pain continued to nag him.

"You've never—"

"I know," Nat said. "There's something, though, that puzzles me about Diablo."

"Nicky . . ."

Worry etched even deeper in Nat. "She's never shown any interest in anyone before. Damn, I wish I could send her out of here, but I don't have everything ready yet. A few more months . . . just a few more months."

Chapter Six

Kane finished shaving and gave himself a wry look in the mirror, trying to see deeper than the image that stared back at him, searching for the man inside. He didn't know why he even bothered with a razor, except that it separated him from many of the other guests. He didn't know why he cared about that, either. He wasn't much better than the worst of them. The law sure as hell didn't think so.

At least he'd never killed for fun. And the faces of those he had killed haunted him. All but one had been men in uniform, many little more than boys who were fighting for their country, just as he was. He hadn't felt anger toward them, nor any pride in killing them.

He had been here nearly ten days now, and he knew the others better than he'd like to. Most of them reveled in their kills. Their boasts sickened him, but there had been little else to do in Sanctuary other than share tales of banditry. Especially since he was avoiding Miss Thompson and, therefore, limiting his rides. Gambling, boasting, and whoring were the order of the day, not necessarily in that order. He knew he was considered odd because he did little of the last. So he gambled a lot, drank sufficiently, and listened appreciatively. He hoped his own lack of stories made him appear more discreet than reluctant.

But Davy was never far from his mind. As he looked in the mirror, he sometimes thought he saw his friend standing next to him. Davy had been his savior when he was a child, smuggling food to him and ointments for the bruises and cuts from frequent beatings. Davy had even taught him to read, since Kane's father considered it a waste of time and money to send him to school. Later, when the Carson family took Kane in after his father's death, Davy had helped him catch up on other studies so he wouldn't be so far behind in school. He owed Davy everything, including his life.

He remembered his friend's face when they'd been condemned together. Davy's face was anguished as he'd turned toward his wife and child. Kane would never forget that look. And he would never stop blaming himself for the incident that forced both of them into the life of outlaws. . . .

Kane had just arrived home from the war after traveling three months across half a continent without horse or money. He'd never had many dreams before the war, but after three years of war and a year in a prison camp, he dreamed of a ranch of his own, of a family like Davy's. He'd stopped at Davy's ranch to see him, his wife, and his boy, Alex, before joining a trail drive north. He'd hoped to earn enough money to buy a small ranch.

Alex, at twelve, had hungered after stories of war, and Kane had reluctantly told several, trying to keep them free from the actual horror. Kane grew cold thinking about it. He'd always felt it had been those stories that prompted young Alex to aim a rifle at land-grabbing government officials hours after the telling. . . .

A knock came at the door, jolting Kane out of the past and back to the present. He opened the door to find Mitch Evers standing there, an uncomfortable look on his face.

"Nat wants you to come to dinner tonight," Evers said. "Seven."

Surprised and wary, Kane asked, "Why?"

Evers shrugged. "I don't usually ask him why he does anything."

Kane pondered the invitation almost insolently. He was damnably tired of being pushed and manipulated.

"He would like an answer," Mitch said.

"Do I have a choice?" Kane said.

"Depends on whether you want to live," Evers said.

"That's a real gracious invitation."

Mitch Evers smiled. "Nat might have put it better. Besides you'll enjoy it. Nicky's a good cook."

"Am I supposed to enjoy it?" Kane asked suspiciously. "I thought I was to stay away from her and the kid."

"I think Nat just wants to thank you for yesterday," Evers said, not answering the implied question.

Kane wiped the soap from his face. "I'll be there, but I don't like summonses, not when I'm paying a king's ransom to be left alone."

"An invitation," Evers insisted.

Kane was in no mood to argue semantics. He didn't know what Nat Thompson wanted, but he suspected it wasn't the joy of his company. He nodded curtly.

"Seven," Mitch Evers reached for the doorknob, got halfway out and turned back. "Don't be late."

Kane swore at the closing door.

John Yancy rubbed his sore wrists. They were bloody from the tight ropes. He'd awakened in an alley with an aching head, an empty stomach, and a fierce hatred. An hour later he sat in a crowded bar in a godforsaken border town nursing his third shot of whiskey and an enormous grudge.

He'd kept trying to make sense of the series of events that brought him here. Back in Sanctuary, two men with guns had escorted him to Thompson's office after he'd just seen Diablo ride in with that brat Robin. He'd been told his brother tried to rape the Thompson girl and was dead. He was told he was damn lucky to leave Sanctuary alive. It had taken him a few minutes to understand, and then he'd thrown himself at Thompson. The two hired hands had subdued him, tied and blindfolded him, and thrown him on a horse.

Cobb was the only person he'd ever cared two hoots

about. They'd been raised in a one-room cabin by a father who'd terrorized both his wife and children. They had run off when he was eleven and Cobb was twelve and they had been together ever since. John couldn't believe his brother was dead.

It had been the bitch—and Diablo—who'd caused his death.

Both would pay. He would find Sanctuary. He knew some of the guides. He would keep looking until he found one, then follow him. He knew what to look for: a man with a steep price on his head.

John Yancy didn't care how long it took. He would find—and kill—the Thompson bitch, though he might enjoy her first. Then Thompson, and finally Diablo. He would kill them. He would do it for Cobb.

NICKY cleaned the house. She scrubbed the floors and the pots and pans. She scrubbed them until her hands were red and raw. She wanted to scrub the image of Diablo from her mind, but all the soap and water in the world wouldn't do that.

He was the most infuriating man she'd ever met. The most contradictory. Hell's bells.

She scrubbed harder, ignoring her brother's sideways glances. Her uncle had left this morning and had not returned, but he'd left a message telling her to plan on five for supper tonight. He had probably invited Jeb over.

Nicky had cooked for Nat and Robin and often Mitch for as long as she could remember. She usually enjoyed it. Her mother had taught her a little, and she had picked up the rest catch-as-catch-can. She associated cooking with smiles, and she liked feeling useful. There was little to feel useful about in Sanctuary, little her uncle approved of her doing. The encounter with Cobb Yancy had proved his dire warnings right. So had her recent experience with Kane O'Brien.

She still smarted from his dismissal, still tingled when she remembered his touch.

She wished he would leave. Until he did, she would

take no more rides to her hill. She suspected that he would be there. She could take a gun, but she feared a gun wouldn't give her the kind of protection she needed.

With effort, she turned her mind to other thoughts, like what to fix for supper that night. She heard a door opening and turned to see Robin coming into the room, his good arm carrying a box with the baby hawk in it.

"Can you help me feed him, Sis?"

She nodded. "How do you feel?"

"Real good. I want to go over and see Diablo. Maybe he can tell me something about hawks."

"It's Mr. O'Brien," Nicky said irritably. "And I don't think he wants to be bothered."

"But he brought him to me."

"You know Uncle Nat's rules. You know what happened last time you broke them."

"Diablo ain't nothing like Cobb Yancy." Hero worship was in his eyes.

"Seems I remember you liked Cobb Yancy a few days ago."

Robin's face turned bright red, and guilt surged through Nicky. She had been as deceived by Kane O'Brien's charm as Robin had been by Cobb Yancy's interest. Damn O'Brien. He had an easy way, a quick warm smile when he cared to use it. *Don't even think about it.*

If only she could stop.

"He's an outlaw, a killer, just like all the others," she said curtly.

"Uncle Nat's an outlaw, and you like him."

"And he can't go any place without being hunted. Is that what you want?"

"No one could catch Uncle Nat, and no one could catch me."

"They caught Diablo," she said, even as she realized reason wasn't working. It never did. She would talk to Uncle Nat tonight, try to convince him to go to Mexico with her, or some other place where the law couldn't find him. Now. Not six months from now.

"Yeah," Robin said, "but they couldn't keep Diablo in

jail. They couldn't keep me, either." A gleam came into his eyes. "You think he would tell me how he escaped?"

Real fear snaked through her. She leaned over and put her hand on Robin's shoulder, but he shook it off impatiently. She sighed. He was still so young. She wanted him to have a good life, a family and children. She wanted . . .

She wanted those same things for herself. But what decent man—and she would have no other kind—would want the daughter and niece of notorious outlaws?

She kept remembering her mother. A Kentucky belle who had fallen in love with an outlaw and run off with him. She'd died by pieces as she waited for him in dirty boarding houses, never knowing whether he was dead or alive. And when Robin came early, they were on the run again, and there had been no doctor. Nicky and her pa had watched her die in a dirty, cold cave. Her pa was never the same again.

Then Sanctuary had become her home, and she'd felt a measure of safety here.

She didn't feel safe any longer.

KANE arrived at Thompson's house precisely at seven. He'd had a few drinks first, though he'd been careful not to have too many. He needed all his wits tonight.

Nat Thompson opened the door when he knocked. "O'Brien," he acknowledged. "Good of you to come."

Kane had to rein in his temper and his mouth. He'd had damn little choice. He simply nodded.

Thompson had studied him before—when they'd first met—but that had been nothing to the perusal now. Kane felt like a specimen pinned to a board as the outlaw's dark eyes seemed to penetrate his very soul. He shook off the notion. It was intimidation only. Damn good intimidation.

Thompson finally moved. "Like a drink?"

Hell yes. But Kane made sure his eyes revealed nothing as he moved inside the house, his gaze taking in the gingham curtains, the bouquet of wild flowers in a painted jar on the table. Small homey touches he hadn't noticed during that other brief visit.

Nicole? Where was she? His gaze went to the partially opened door of what he guessed was the kitchen, his nose twitching as he smelled something very nice wafting through the doorway.

A drink was thrust in his hand, and he sipped it carefully, turning his attention back to Nat Thompson, who was still watching him with cagey eyes.

"Good whiskey," he remarked with casual indifference.

A gleam of appreciation shown in Thompson's eyes. "I'm glad you approve." There was a tiny bite of sarcasm in the words, and Kane reminded himself not to underestimate the man.

Thompson gestured him to a chair, and Kane sat. So did Thompson, who took a couple of sips himself before speaking again. "My nephew is real taken with that bird. I wanted to thank you for that."

Kane fought to contain his surprise. Thompson had made him aware of his proprietary view of his family, but the warm huskiness of the man's voice revealed a deep caring. Kane felt his gut constrict. He didn't want Thompson's thanks or appreciation or any other damn thing. He wanted to get his job done and get the hell out of here.

"My niece said she met you the other morning." It was spoken as a question, and Kane wondered what else Nicole had said. *Nicky. Remember, her name is Nicky.* He didn't think Nat Thompson would appreciate the fact that Kane knew her as Nicole.

"I ride a lot," he said.

"So I hear," Thompson said. "How did you like Rosita's?"

Was there anything Thompson didn't know? Probably even how well he did in bed. The idea didn't sit at all well with Kane. He didn't like being spied on. But then that was exactly what he was doing to Thompson. He shrugged.

Thompson played with his glass a moment. "How long you planning to stay?"

"Until I run out of money."

"Then what?"

"Maybe then there won't be so many posses after me. I'll make my way north."

"Planning a job?"

Kane narrowed his eyes. He knew his own suspicion was showing now, but he didn't care. In his role, he should be suspicious. "I thought questions weren't asked here."

Thompson grinned suddenly. It was the first time he'd shown as much as a glimmer of a smile. "You're right, of course," he said. He held out the bottle, and Kane offered his glass for a refill.

He was taking another drink when Nicole walked into the room. Surprise flitted across her face, then a deep flush settled in her cheeks. She turned to her uncle, her eyes asking a question even while she obviously ignored Kane. It was a deliberate slight.

"Uncle Nat?"

Nat Thompson, Kane noted, was watching both of them carefully, too carefully. He couldn't miss the red in Nicky's cheeks. Kane hoped his own face registered only indifference, even while he felt his pulse race.

"You know Mr. O'Brien, of course," Thompson said casually to his niece. Kane knew the comment wasn't casual at all, though.

She glared at Kane, acknowledging his presence for the first time. "Is he your guest?"

Nat nodded. "I wanted to thank him for what he did the other afternoon."

"I don't think . . ." She stopped suddenly.

"You don't think what?" Thompson asked.

"That he's a good influence on Robin," she blurted out, not caring whether he heard or not.

Thompson studied her for several moments. "And I am?"

Nicky bit her lip, chewed on it for a moment, and Kane felt a moment's sympathy for her. She obviously didn't want to hurt her uncle. Just as obviously, she didn't want Kane here, and he knew why. He'd been purposely rude the other day, as much for his own protection as hers.

"I thought you wanted your 'guests' away from us," she finally said defensively, her eyes avoiding Kane's.

"You saw him the other morning," Thompson said. There was the slightest question in his voice, so slight she could choose to answer or not.

"That was accidental." She bit off the words. "It won't happen again."

Warily, Kane watched the exchange. He had the oddest feeling of being the center of a tableau and yet not having the slightest hint of the story. Or more importantly, he felt as he had in prison when Ben Masters approached him: like a puppet in someone else's hands. It made him damn angry. He turned toward his host. "Thank you for the invitation," he said stiffly, trying to contain that anger. "I don't want to cause problems in your family. I'll have supper at the hotel."

"No," Thompson said. "There are no problems. My niece was just surprised. I think dinner is ready. We eat in the kitchen. Nicky, get your brother."

Kane didn't miss the look of astonishment that passed over Nicky's face. Either she was unused to being admonished, or she was still startled at her uncle's invitation. Well, so was he. His first instinct was to leave, despite Thompson's order. But then his better judgment overtook his anger. He was in Sanctuary for one reason; this supper might help him accomplish his goal. It still galled him, though, to sit at a man's table with every intention of betraying him. Even if that man was Nat Thompson.

But Thompson was already steering him toward the open door, and he was following. He sat in the chair indicated by Thompson, and Nicky returned minutes later, Robin following in her wake. If his sister hadn't been enthusiastic about his presence, Robin obviously was. His eyes lit like a candle's first darting flame.

"Diablo," he exclaimed with pleasure, and something inside Kane shriveled at the boy's obvious pleasure. "I named the hawk after you. Nicky agreed."

Kane darted a glance at Nicky, who was putting food on the table. She avoided his glance, but her cheeks flushed again, and he thought how pretty she was. Her hair was like a curly cap, golden tendrils framing the elfin face. Her eyes suddenly met his, and for a moment he thought of a startled fawn. They were so large, so brown, so . . . defenseless. That wasn't true, of course. She had killed a man. She had lived among outlaws all her life. Yet there was something so innocent about her.

He smiled. He smiled often, and he was good at it, but for the last few years his heart hadn't been in it. This time it was. He wanted to reach out to her, to wipe away the worried frown that didn't fit the face.

"Thank you," he said as she placed a platter of steaks near him.

She spared him a glance then, and her face softened, as if she hadn't been thanked much. But then she turned and was placing other platters on the table, this time fried potatoes and a bowl of tomatoes. Finally, she took a chair herself, the last empty one, across from her uncle and next to himself.

He tried not to watch her as he ate. Nat Thompson lapsed into silence, shoveling food into his mouth as if he'd never had a meal. Robin ate in a similar fashion.

The steak was better than the one at the hotel, and the potatoes were the best he'd ever had. As uncomfortable as he was at the table, as uncertain as to Thompson's intent, Kane enjoyed every bite.

Still, uneasiness gnawed at him. Although Thompson had thanked him for the hawk, Kane didn't believe for one second that was the real reason for the invite. Nor, he suspected, had it been the pleasure of his company.

Nicky was silent during the first part of the meal. She finally looked at him, and their eyes clashed. The side of her mouth curled up in a slight smile. "And how do you like Sanctuary, Mr. O'Brien?" she asked sweetly. It was a voice he decided he didn't trust. "Are you still restless, or have you found some . . . more solace?"

"Just being alive is solace," he said, noticing that Nat Thompson had stiffened in his chair.

"You escaped the day before they were going to hang

you," she noted conversationally, and a challenge was in her eyes. "What did you think about?"

"Escaping," he said with some humor.

"How did you do it?" Robin said eagerly as Nicky gave him a censorious look that had absolutely no effect.

"By the grace of God," Kane replied.

Robin looked puzzled.

"A priest," Kane explained. "A man of God who wanted me to repent. I knocked him out and took his clothes. The rest was easy." Nicky appeared taken aback, Robin incredulous, Thompson delighted.

"I'll have to remember that," Thompson said.

"I think they'll be searching priests more thoroughly," Kane said dryly.

Thompson laughed, but his gaze was thoughtful as he watched Kane.

"Will you teach me something about hawks?" Robin said eagerly, unaware of the tension in the room.

"What little I know," Kane said. "You will have to teach him to hunt on his own, since his mother can't."

"When?"

"When he can fly. And once he learns to hunt, you should let him go free."

"But I want to keep him."

"Birds are born to be free," Kane said. "Just as men are." He heard the hard edge in his own voice, a trace of the pain that lingered from his various imprisonments.

"Is that why you fought for the South?" The question came from Thompson. After the past hour, it wasn't entirely unexpected. Like a boy playing with a fly, Nat Thompson had been picking away at him since he arrived.

"Not particularly," Kane answered carelessly, keeping his gaze on Thompson's. He didn't want to see the expression on Nicky's face, not as he was about to say words that would kick her in the stomach. "I thought there might be chances of making money. Booty, so to speak. Turned out I was the booty."

"That's a hard way to make a fortune."

"Not if you didn't have anything, never had anything." He looked at Robin. "I was orphaned when I was real young. My father was a dirt farmer, had lost everything, and he put a bullet in his own head. A neighboring family took me in, but nothing was mine, not even the clothes I wore." Like all good lies, it had a foundation of truth.

But Nat Thompson nodded, as if he understood. He rose, and Kane rose with him. "Mighty good meal, Miss Thompson," Kane said formally. "I do thank you."

She stood and lifted her head, her chin sticking out. He saw disillusionment in her eyes. Good. She hadn't liked that bit about the war, nor the priest. He remembered the way she'd looked earlier today when she'd told him he'd received his scar honorably. He'd felt a moment of pride then. Now he felt like the fraud he was.

"You're welcome, Mr. O'Brien," she said, her voice icy. It had warmed a little during supper, but now he felt the chill through and through.

He followed Nat through the door to the main room, Robin falling in next to him. "You will show me how to teach Diablo to hunt, won't you?"

Remembering the rules, Kane looked at Thompson for approval. Thompson leaned over and put his hand on his nephew's shoulder. It was an affectionate gesture, the first Kane had seen pass between the outlaw leader and his wards.

"If Mr. O'Brien doesn't mind," Thompson said mildly. "Remember he's a guest here."

"You don't mind, do you, Diablo?" Robin said.

Diablo did. He didn't want to get closer to any of these people. Yet taking Robin out and teaching him about the hawk would give him more freedom. Robin might even let something slip, might know something that would help. *Think of Davy.* Davy sitting in that damn cell, not knowing when he would die, not even knowing he had a slim chance at freedom—a chance that hinged on Kane.

"No," he said. "I don't mind." It had been a night for lies.

He told still another one when he left several minutes later. "It was a fine meal, and a fine evening." As before, there was a foundation of truth.

Thompson didn't offer to shake his hand. He simply

showed Kane the door, leaving Kane as puzzled as before as to why he'd been singled out. Puzzled and filled with apprehension. Not for himself, but for Davy. Thompson had something on his mind. He'd been testing Kane, probing insistently. What did he know? Or think he knew?

Chapter Seven

GOODEN, TEXAS

Ben Masters hated to wait. It was always the hardest part of his job.

This, though, was the worst wait of his life. He'd never liked owing anyone. And the debt to Kane O'Brien was larger than any other he'd ever incurred. If it hadn't been for O'Brien, he would be dead.

Christ, he wished he could quiet his doubts about O'Brien. Masters had lost him in the small trading town on the Texas border and he was stuck here now. Diablo had said he would try to get word to Masters, but nearly a month had passed and no word had come. Diablo had just disappeared off the face of the earth, he and his horse.

And the government's money.

Masters had stuck his neck way out on this one. If he'd misjudged Kane O'Brien, he was through as a marshal. If he were a praying man he'd be on his knees right now. But he had little faith in prayers. God helped those who helped themselves. He wondered how—or even if—Kane O'Brien was helping himself, or if he were destroying them both.

• • •

KANE settled into a routine, hating every minute of it but considering it necessary. He couldn't afford to be different, not with Nat Thompson's eyes on him. So he drank more than he should, played poker nightly, even visited Rosita's one more evening with the same result as before.

Kane rode several afternoons, avoiding his usual morning rides because he didn't want to see Nicole. She was simply too dangerous to him. He made his rides seem as innocent as possible, never going toward the cliffs but always looking for a way out.

No matter how many times he went over the problem in his mind, it came down to the same solution. The kid. Robin Thompson had to know something of value. He'd decided Nicky wasn't the answer. She was too wary. But Robin—Robin was just waiting to be milked. Kane hadn't been able to force himself to act on that knowledge yet, but he would. He had to. Time was running out.

After nights of playing poker with the other residents of Sanctuary, he'd decided they knew less than he did, and cared nothing about knowing more. That lack of curiosity made it even more dangerous to ask questions; he had assumed others would also want to know where they were, curiosity being a natural part of him. But it seemed enough to the other guests that they were safe and had all the vices important to them available.

In the afternoons, he was eager to escape. Escape the town that was little more than a mirage, the men who turned his stomach, the knowledge that he had to do something that went against every grain of decency he had.

He kneed the gray into a gallop. He hadn't named the horse; he'd stopped naming horses during the war. Too many died. If you named them, they were friends and it hurt worse.

The gray was his temporarily. It had been given to him by Masters, and it was a damn good horse. His own horse had disappeared into the hills when he was taken by the Texas authorities.

Ten years, and he was back to borrowed things: borrowed horse, borrowed clothes, borrowed money.

Borrowed time.

He rode alongside the creek, wondering where it went through the hills. It had been hot and dry this summer, and the creek was shallow. He dismounted and watered his horse, then leaned against a tree. Davy increasingly invaded his thoughts now. They used to go fishing together when they were only a couple of tadpoles. Sometimes he'd walked over to Davy's house; there was always food there, and sometimes it was the only food he got that day. His disappearances always meant a beating, but they were worth a full belly and a few hours away from hatred.

When his father died, Davy's family took him in, and Davy became Kane's brother in all the ways that mattered. But Kane had never forgotten that he didn't really belong. That was one reason he'd enlisted in the Confederate Army. Another was the anger he had toward his father, an anger that his father's death hadn't erased.

That anger had died in the inferno of war. Kane soon discovered it held no adventure and offered no place to hide from his past. The closeness of death, of dying, only made the past more real. And battle did strange things to men. Some became better for it, some worse. Some took comfort in camaraderie, others became loners, afraid of loss.

He'd been one of those who pulled away from people. Afraid to care. Afraid to love. Afraid to feel. He'd wanted to die himself after the first big battle, when he'd seen a field full of dying and dead men, heard the calls for help, and been unable to do anything. He'd tried to steel himself then against caring, had succeeded to some degree until that day at Shiloh when Ben Masters's weak plea had reached him.

God damn it all, he couldn't afford that kind of weakness. Not then, not now. It was time to get to work, to do what he'd set out to do today. Another step toward damnation.

He took a folding knife from a pocket inside the custom-made boots Ben Masters had given him. Kane looked carefully for exactly the right tree and finally found a thick cottonwood. He selected a sturdy branch and started cutting.

FOR several days, Nicky used her brother as an excuse to stay inside the house at the times she usually chose to ride. Her uncle didn't say anything, although she knew he was studying her with more than his usual interest.

She still didn't know why he'd invited Kane O'Brien to supper a week earlier, but the implications worried her. She knew exactly how devious—and ruthless—he could be. She didn't like Kane O'Brien—she kept telling herself that—but neither did she want anything to happen to him on her account.

On the sixth day after O'Brien's visit, she almost went riding during the early morning hours, and not entirely because she wanted the morning air. Her body and her thoughts both betrayed her. They kept reaching toward something she knew could destroy her. Only sheer will-power had kept her in the house. Kane O'Brien was a charlatan, a man obviously used to getting what he wanted, and he didn't mind how. Yet she found herself shivering every time she thought of his touch, the finger that had wandered over her cheek. He had known exactly what he was doing, even as he'd turned away from her. He'd made her want, then mocked that yearning.

Still, she wanted to see him. Wanted to see whether that touch would create those same trembling feelings . . .

Hell's bells. She threw a pan down on the floor. She'd been making pies as if there were no tomorrow, and Robin was in glutton's heaven. She was always seized by a frenzy of activity when she was angry or sad or lonely. And now she admitted to all three.

She was staring at the offending pan when a knock came at the door.

She brushed her flour-coated hands on her trousers and went to open it, going still with surprise when she stood face to face with the unwanted subject of her thoughts. He looked just as startled, as though he hadn't expected her. That irritated her. Everything, in fact, irritated her, particularly her racing pulse. O'Brien smiled, that strangely endearing twist of lips, made unique by the crook of the scar, and held out something in his hands.

"A perch," he said in response to her puzzlement. "For . . . Diablo." The mouth crooked even further in wry amusement.

She was so mesmerized by the smile that it took a moment to understand. The hawk!

"Will you give it to him?" he said, and Nicky realized she was still standing in front of the door, barring him from the interior.

She opened it a little wider. "Robin would probably like to get it himself," she said. "He's been asking about you. My uncle thought it best he stay in bed a few more days, but . . ."

"Wounds heal fast in a boy."

"Did yours?" She hadn't meant to prolong the conversation, to ask more questions when the last one she asked on the hill had turned him cold.

"Not fast enough," he said, but this time his eyes didn't freeze. They were watching her instead, and the gray seemed to be smoldering. Heat reached out from him, singeing her. She stepped back as if she could avoid the flames, but they went with her, darting through her body, settling in the core of her.

He stepped back, as if he too wanted to escape those sudden fires, but his eyes remained on hers, and she felt fixed by them, nailed in place by the dark gray, burning intensity.

"Sis?"

Robin's voice jarred her from paralysis, the sense of being consumed alive. She wiped her hands again on her trousers and moved from the door. "Mr. O'Brien brought you something." She didn't look at her brother. She didn't want to see the light in his eyes, didn't want him to see the pained confusion in hers.

"Diablo," he said, and Nicky didn't miss the excitement in his voice.

As she hurried to the kitchen, she heard his low, deep voice. "I brought you a perch for the hawk. It's the first step in training him. First the perch, then your hand. You'll need a heavy glove."

"Come see him." Robin's voice was so eager it hurt her.

Diablo would leave in a few days, like they all did. He would also die, like they all did. A month. A year. But he would die young. A bullet. A rope. She would read it in a newspaper or hear it from one of her uncle's acquaintances. She wished the thought weren't so painful. There was so much strength and energy and arrogance in Kane O'Brien; it was nearly impossible to think of him dead.

She sniffed the aroma from the stove and checked the two pies in the oven. Bent over the open oven door, she welcomed the heat that rushed out to overwhelm the other heat inside her. Almost blindly, she reached for another piece of wood to place in the bottom of the stove. A flicker of flame from the stove reached out, igniting the sleeve of her shirt. She screamed as the flame crept up. In the next second, the door burst open, and she was being thrown to the floor, her body smothered by a larger, heavier one.

Pain mixed with awareness. Her arm felt on fire, though she saw that the flames were gone, leaving black singed cloth and a reddened arm. She couldn't stop the whimper that was part pain, part fear.

"It's all right." His voice was low and soothing. He rolled off her, ignoring obvious burns of his own and knelt next to her, his hands gently running over her arm. "Not too bad," he said.

Nicky reveled in his care, in the safety and comfort of that confident voice. She hadn't been touched with such gentleness since her mother died. She looked at his hand, the small blisters already forming where his hand had smothered the flames on her shirt.

"Nicky?" Her brother's voice was frantic. "What can I do?"

"Andy," she said. "Get Andy. Hurry."

Her gaze hadn't moved from her rescuer, but she heard Robin's racing footsteps. "Thank you," she said in a wavery voice she couldn't quite control. "You're hurt."

"Darlin', I've had a lot worse." He spoke the words lightly, but pain flitted across his face as he moved slightly. "I think we'd better get some water on those burns."

He stood and offered her his good hand. She took it, feeling the strength in it. Then she noticed his gaze had dropped, and she looked down. Her shirt was partly off, the sleeve tattered. She wore a camisole underneath, but it had slipped slightly, showing the swell of one of her breasts and outlining the other. They weren't large. Lemon size, she'd always thought, compared to the women at Rosita's who sported ones of more melon proportions. There had been no one to talk to about such things, and she wasn't sure which was normal—lemons or melons.

She felt herself growing hot again under O'Brien's intense regard. She'd blushed more around him in the past month than in her whole life. She tried to pull her shirt back together, wincing at the pain any movement of her arm caused.

"You shouldn't hide such a pretty body," he said lazily, as if he weren't feeling any pain at all.

"My uncle . . ."

His gray eyes, which had been warm and comforting, changed suddenly. Although he didn't move, she could feel his withdrawal, see that curtain fall over his eyes. He turned away, toward the sink, and with his gun hand used the pump to draw water. "Come here," he said, but the warmth in his voice was gone. It was an order, impersonally made.

She wanted to rebel against it. But his lips were clenched tight, his jaw set. His dark hair was wet with sweat, and she knew he was hurting.

Nicky moved over to him, allowed him to take her arm and hold it under the pump. The water felt good on the now-throbbing burns. She finally pulled her hand away, and took his burned arm, guiding it under the water as gently as he had hers. She looked up at his face, and saw a number of emotions dart over it before he schooled his expression into blankness. There was a second of vulnerability. No more than that. An instant of recognition between them. Raw need exchanged. Need that had nothing to do with the more sensual feelings she'd experienced before.

"The kitchen." Nicky heard Robin's voice. Then Robin, her uncle and Andy crowded into the kitchen, and Kane O'Brien stepped away from her.

"What happened?" her uncle asked, even as Andy took her arm to study the burns.

"Mr. . . . O'Brien was burned, too, worse than I was," she said. "He smothered the flames. Look to him first."

Andy nodded and stepped toward Diablo.

"No," Kane said impatiently, almost angrily. "I'm all right. Just give me some salve and I'll go to the hotel."

Andy shook his head. "Take off your shirt."

Kane did so reluctantly. It was only then that Nicky noticed the extensive raw, red splotches across his back, and she realized he must have hit the side of the stove as he'd pushed her to the floor. "Dear God," she whispered as Andy studied the burns. He had to be in agony.

Andy shook his head as he looked at Kane's back. "Those burns could get infected if they're not treated. You need someone looking after them."

"Damn it, I can do it myself." O'Brien's voice was low but emphatic.

"You can't reach your own back," Andy retorted reasonably.

"Do I have to get Mitch in here and tie you down?" Nat interceded, glaring at Kane. "You're not leaving till Andy gets through with you. You can bunk in Robin's room."

"Damn it," O'Brien exploded. "I don't . . . need . . ."

Nicky heard the sudden waver in his voice, saw him reach for a chair to steady himself. Then in an act of pure will that left her speechless, she saw him literally shake the weakness away. He straightened, obviously prepared to do more battle.

"Go get Mitch," Nat Thompson told an avidly watching Robin. "And you'll have to go through me to leave," he told Kane O'Brien. "I don't take debts lightly, and I owe you for my niece."

"You owe me nothing," Kane said, his eyes angry. But he didn't try to move. Nicky felt chilled by his cold rage though she didn't understand it. "I'm sorry," she said. "It was . . . my fault."

For the briefest moment, his eyes softened. Then he shrugged. "I'll stay if you take care of Miss Thompson first."

Thompson nodded. "Andy, look after Nicky first. O'Brien will be in Robin's room." He motioned to Kane. "This way."

Nicky watched them go, then saw Andy's eyes on her. "He'll be all right," Andy said. "A few minutes won't matter. Now sit down."

Nicky nearly screamed as Andy washed the burns with some solution from the box of medicines he'd brought with him, then gently applied a cool salve. She kept remembering, though, Kane's fixed expression, his cool dismissal of pain, and she bore Andy's ministration silently, willing him to hurry so he could get to Kane. Kane with the murderer's name. Kane, who had somehow become her guardian angel and who obviously bitterly resented being so.

"I'm not going to wrap it," Andy was telling her. "But be careful. Keep that arm clean."

"I'm fine. Go see about Mr. O'Brien."

He looked at her curiously, then smiled slowly. "I'll take good care of him." He gave her a bottle. "Here's some laudanum. If you start hurting too badly, take it. Give some to Diablo. Disguise it if you must. He's going to hurt a lot, and he doesn't seem the type of man to make it easy on himself." He went out the door and left her sitting at the table.

KANE tried to open his eyes, but they resisted his every effort to do so. Pain throbbed in his arm and back, particularly when he moved. His head felt thick, his eyes sticky and uncooperative. He struggled to remember where he was.

Then, slowly, it came back through a drugged mind.

Sanctuary. Nat Thompson. Nicky. Nicole. Fire. A quiet panic swept him.

"He's awake."

Robin's voice broke through his haze. He tried to open his eyes again and this time managed to get one partly open.

"How long . . . have I been asleep?"

"Day and a half," Robin said. "I'll get my sis."

"No," Kane tried to say, but the boy was already out the door. He'd been lying on his side. He tried to sit and discovered he was naked, except for the underwear on the lower half of his body. As he heard footsteps, he tugged a cover over him. His arm and chest throbbed. His mouth felt like cotton. He rubbed his good hand over his cheeks, finding them rough with bristle.

What in the hell did it matter, anyway? Nicky Thompson had been nothing but trouble. She was an obstacle to him, nothing more. He should be in the hotel, damn it. Not here. He didn't want her gratitude, nor her uncle's. But he kept getting sucked more and more into the lives of the Thompson family when his goal was to destroy them.

The door opened again and Nicky—Nicole—came in. She was still in a loose shirt and trousers, but femininity radiated from her. Her smile was tentative, painfully wary, and he realized how many times he'd rebuffed her. Mainly for his own protection. Guilt throbbed even more than the burns.

"I thought you might want some fresh water," she said. "And something to eat."

"You're not cooking again?" he said gruffly.

Embarrassment flooded her face. "No, Uncle Nat won't let me near the stove. Jeb sent over some soup."

He tried to sit, pulling the blanket up with him, but its roughness rubbed against his raw skin, and he winced. Her eyes shone with sympathy. They were so damned brown. He moved his gaze to her arm. It was still red, oozing with the same salve, he imagined, that pasted his arm and back.

"Are you all right?" he said roughly.

"Thanks to you."

He liked her anger better than gratitude. He muttered to himself.

"What?" she said, coming closer. He pulled the blanket up higher. Damn but he felt something stirring inside, and it wasn't his brain.

"Don't thank me. I just happened to be there. I tripped." It was a hell of a stupid thing to say. He knew it the minute amusement started dancing in her eyes. Her face changed, and she grinned. Then laughed. He'd never heard her laugh before, and it sounded like a chorus of bells. The smile was beautiful. He hadn't seen that one before, either. It had always been tentative, cautious.

"I thought desperadoes liked to claim deeds of valor." The last words were right from a book, and Kane understood something else. No wonder Miss Nicole Thompson was such a combination of innocence and sometimes startling wisdom. She must live in books. He'd noticed several bookcases earlier, but hadn't paid much attention to them, thinking they were probably for show like so many other things in Sanctuary: an attempt at normalcy.

He muttered again to himself, barely muzzling the curses that wanted to flow from his mouth. Damn, he should be pleased. Robin and Nicky were pawns in his hands now. He had Nat Thompson's gratitude, the run of his house. And he'd seldom felt lower in his entire life.

But he took the glass of water Nicky held out to him, and the man part of him tensed and hardened as her good hand touched his and lingered a moment longer than necessary. He forced his gaze away from her and started to drink, then hesitated. It tasted strange. Drugged again?

Nicky seemed to understand. She shook her head. "Andy said the pain would be bad the first few days. But I won't give you any more laudanum unless you ask for it."

"I only have a few more days at Sanctuary," he said. "I have to be strong enough to leave."

"Uncle Nat said you can stay as long as you want. No charge."

Kane was stunned. He knew Thompson had been

grateful, but the man was notorious about money. He'd heard tales from the other residents of Sanctuary about his no-credit policy. No matter how wanted a man was, he was escorted out once his money was gone, which was one reason poker was so popular. Winning could mean a few days extra. Kane had already won enough money for several more days. But he didn't have the luxury of time. He had to learn the location of Sanctuary and get out.

"I have other plans," he said curtly and watched the smile disappear from Nicky's face. Robin's face also seemed to crumple. "But you haven't taught me anything about Diablo."

"That's a hell of a name for that hawk," Kane said.

Robin's face flushed. "I didn't mean to insult you."

Kane felt he was kicking a litter of puppies. "That's not what I meant," he said, making his voice less harsh. "You shouldn't name a wild thing. You're going to have to give him back to nature. Don't get too attached. Don't let it get too attached." As he had years ago with his own baby hawk.

He finished drinking the water and handed it back to Nicky. "Thank you," he said. He wanted to say he would move back to the hotel. That's what he wanted. But if he stayed here, he might have a chance to check Nat Thompson's room and the desk he'd seen in the main room. Then he wouldn't have to get the information he needed from Nicky or Robin, he told himself. The result would be the same, though. Lawmen would ride through the valley, shooting everything in sight.

Christ, his head hurt. Every damn part of him hurt. Including his heart. If he ever got his hands on Masters, he'd kill him.

"Some soup?" Nicky asked, like that same puppy expecting a kick in the stomach.

He nodded. He'd eat the damn soup, pretend sleep, and hope everyone left. The sooner he discovered what he came for, the sooner he could leave, the sooner Davy would be released. He wouldn't, couldn't, think about the other result.

Chapter Eight

The house seemed immeasurably smaller with Kane O'Brien in it. *Diablo,* Nicky kept warning herself. But warnings didn't do any good now. She kept reminding herself that he was a killer and outlaw, but she saw only the man who'd risked himself for her.

Always watch your back, her uncle had taught her. He'd never told her what to do if a man sneaked up on her blind side and wriggled into places he ought not be.

She went riding the morning after Kane woke up. She knew she must or she would find herself hovering outside his door, wanting to go in. Afraid to go in. Afraid of all those feelings that were eating her up inside.

She rode to her hill to watch the sun tip the mountain, but some of the joy was gone. Her private place was suddenly a lonely place. It seemed to echo with his voice, and she remembered every word he said, every touch, every emotion she'd felt when she was with him, even the humiliation, the anger. She tried to bring both back, but the impact was gone. He had risked his life for her without thought. He was suffering because of her. That hurt most of all.

Who was he? What was he? He was so contradictory she no longer knew. He would turn from kind to cruel in an instant, from warm to cold, from tender to indifferent. She only knew that her heart jumped through hoops when he was near, that her blood warmed and her skin tingled. Even now, she ached for that touch again, for even more. For a kiss. She tried to imagine it but couldn't. Several men had tried a kiss, despite her uncle's warning. Two had been dirty and repulsive, and she'd scooted away; one had been seen and caught. Nat Thompson had had him tied, and he'd beat him with an old bullwhip. The third had been a young bandit, and she'd been quite willing to meet him behind the barn, ready to test her womanhood, hungry to explore this thing called a kiss. But the charm had disappeared when his lips touched hers, and the kiss had been savage and frightening and possessive without tenderness. He'd tried to force her mouth open and finally she'd kicked him in the crotch and run. She hadn't said anything to her uncle, because she'd felt it was her fault, but she'd never been interested in a kiss again.

Not until now.

She was a freak. She realized that. She'd read enough to know that a twenty-two-year-old woman didn't dress in pants. They were courted and kissed and married and had children. Why would someone like Kane O'Brien be interested in her? Not even a killer and outlaw would want a woman who knew more about shooting than kissing, a half-woman. Her eyes burned, and she felt consumed by a vast loneliness. Her gaze swept the empty valley, the stunted trees and arroyos. This was her prison. Barren and lonely. In a week, Kane O'Brien—the only color—would be gone.

But she would get her kiss first. One way or another, she would get a kiss to remember.

THEY were gone. All of them. Kane struggled to his feet, fighting off pain. Every move seemed to stretch and irritate the raw places on his back and arm. Nat Thompson had gone to his "mayor's office." Nicky had gone for a ride, and Robin had disappeared with Andy to hunt rabbits. The hawk needed fresh meat, Kane had told him, after Robin reported that the small bird was not eating well.

He touched his face. It was more stubbled than ever. He found his pants on a chair and pulled them on, wincing again at the throbbing inherent in every movement. Damn. He had to ride out of here in a few days. Kane pushed a lock of hair out of his face and headed toward the other room, and the desk. There had to be a map someplace.

His eyes searched the room, the bookcase, the desk. He went to the window and looked out. It was still early, and he didn't see anyone on the street. Sanctuary never really came to life until the late afternoon.

Kane studied the books and finally selected one, laying it on a chair near the desk. If anyone came, he would quickly drop into the chair and claim to be reading. He then went over to the desk and tried the drawers. They were locked. He swore out loud, then started checking the other rooms. One was immediately recognizable as Nicky's, though it was nearly as plain as the others.

A pleasant smell lingered from a nearly-dried-out arrangement of wildflowers on a table. The curtains were a cheery gingham, and an old worn-out doll, its china face now chipped and missing one eye, sat on a trunk. He stood in the door a moment, wondering about the doll, about the girl Nicky apparently had never been allowed to be. She'd mothered her brother, she said. Who had mothered her? No one, from the look of things.

It was a rather lonely room, with none of the feminine doodads he imagined most women liked. He could almost feel the emptiness of the room. *My uncle took us in when my father was killed.* Now Kane was trying to take one of the few things she had left.

Kane wondered about her dreams. He wondered whether she had any. She said little about dreams, less about a future. Was she satisfied to stay here? Or was it loyalty that tied her to Sanctuary? He didn't think he wanted to know.

He started looking for a hairpin. Kane could open most locks with a hairpin; it was a skill he'd learned in the past two years. Surely, there must be some kind of pin, although Nicky wore her hair short. But there wasn't one. He swore again. Feeling like the worst kind of voyeur and spy, he went through drawers until he found a sewing box and, from that, extracted a thick needle.

Kane stepped outside the room, took another look through the window, then went to work at the desk drawer. The lock was intricate, and it took him several minutes to work his way through it. He held his breath as he felt the lock move, click, and he slid the drawer open.

One more glance at the window. Still no movement outside. He carefully riffled through the papers in the desk. On top of the pile, he found his own Wanted poster along with some clippings of robberies he'd either committed or that had been credited to him. If he'd committed even half of what he'd been charged with, he wouldn't have had time to sleep or eat, he thought ruefully. And he would be a very rich man. He searched deeper and found a book. He flipped through it. Names and sums. He recognized many of them. Jesse and Frank James. John Ringo. The Cole Brothers. Captain John Jarrett. John Wesley Hardin. No wonder the law wanted Nat Thompson.

But there was no map. Not in that drawer. He closed and locked it again with the needle, then started on another drawer. The lock had just moved when he heard the back door open.

Damn it. He moved quickly to the chair and picked up the book. He knew it was either Nicky or her brother from the lightness of the steps. He pushed the needle down into the cushion of the chair and hoped like hell Nicky didn't want to do any sewing today. Needles would be precious in this little town in the middle of nowhere.

He looked up as he felt a presence entering the room. He already knew who it was. The smell of wildflowers entered with her. Kane saw her eyes light momentarily.

"You're up," she exclaimed. Her hair was windblown, a mass of taffy brown curls. Her cheeks were flushed by the wind and sun, and her eyes seemed to glow. She looked prettier every time he saw her.

"I'm not good at staying still," he said.

"I'm not, either," she said a little shyly. "It must have been very hard for you in prison."

"I don't relish going back," he said shortly. But he would. Masters had said as much. He had bargained for Davy's life alone. He would be back in jail, probably waiting for another hanging.

"My uncle said you will be leaving soon?" She moved closer, looking at the title of the book he'd chosen. *Oliver Twist* by Charles Dickens. "Learning something useful from the artful Dodger?" she asked with a slightly mischievous grin.

" 'The law is a ass,' " he said, glad that his eyes had fallen on something appropriate. "But then, I already knew that."

She laughed. It was the second time he'd heard the sound, and he wanted to hear it more often. But he couldn't afford the crack her laughter created in his heart.

Nicky tipped her head. "How did you get outside the law? You're not like the others."

He shrugged. "Like I said, it's an easier way to make a living."

"Is it?" Her question was skeptical.

"It can be," he replied cautiously.

"If you don't get caught. You got caught."

"A slight miscalculation."

"It doesn't take many slight calculations to get hung."

"No," he said seriously. "It doesn't. Why does your uncle continue?"

"Like you, I suppose," she sighed. "He was wanted. He had two kids to take care of. He figured this was the safest way to stay alive and keep us."

"Don't you ever think about leaving?"

"Of course I do," she said. "I want to take Robin away. He's altogether too impressed by the . . ." She stopped suddenly, apparently realizing she was about to insult him.

He grinned. "By renegades like me."

"You're . . . different."

"You didn't think so at first."

"I didn't know you at first."

"You don't know me now." The light teasing in his voice faded.

"You don't let me know you."

"No," he said softly. "It's not wise or healthy to know me. I'm trouble, Miss Thompson. I'm trouble for everyone who meets me."

"You saved my life."

"Maybe," he said. "It was instinct, nothing else."

She swallowed. He was warning her again, just as he had on the rise. She changed the subject. "Can I get you something to eat?"

"Not if it takes you near the stove," he retorted.

"I'm usually very good around the stove. I had ... something else on my mind."

"I told you I'm trouble," he said. "If I hadn't been here ..."

That blush came back to her cheeks. "I didn't mean ... you."

"Didn't you?" Kane said, deliberately trying to provoke her now. He didn't want to like her. He couldn't like her, damn it. He couldn't feel anything toward her.

"I'm not going to let you do it again," she said softly.

"Do what?"

"Chase me off like a child. I'm not, you know."

He gave her that off-center grin. "I know," he said wryly. "I also know what your uncle said." What her uncle said didn't make a whit of difference to him. It was of growing concern, though, that what *she* felt did.

"He likes you."

Kane's grin grew more crooked. "How can you tell? He's always so grim."

"He wants you to stay here."

"Because he feels he owes me. That's it. It doesn't change the rules. You're still untouchable, Miss Thompson."

"I didn't think you were the kind of man to follow rules." It was a challenge.

"I'm not," he said flatly. "But on occasions, it seems a wise thing to do."

She seemed to think about that for a moment, then asked warily, "And if I weren't . . . untouchable?"

Kane saw she was holding her breath, that it had taken a measure of bravery to ask the question, probably even more than shooting that coyote the other day. He had to be careful. He couldn't encourage her. Yet he didn't want to hurt her as he had before. "I have no future, Miss Thompson," he said gently. "I'll be leaving in a few days, and I'll be chased by posses all over the country."

"You can stay here," she said. "Like Andy and Jeb."

"I don't have the money."

"My uncle will find something—"

"This would be another kind of prison, Nicole." The name slipped out. He'd been thinking about it all too often. About her, about the lonely room, the solitary rides, about the way her nose crinkled up, and how her eyes sometimes sparkled with life, and the way her mouth smiled. He realized he wanted to make her laugh, to keep the sparkle in those eyes.

Remember. Remember why you're here. This is the time to ask. He swallowed his own protest. "I don't even know where we are."

"Is that important?"

Damned important. A man's life depends on it. He shrugged indifferently, though, while choosing his words carefully. "I like to know where I am. . . ."

"Indian Territory," she said, her head tipping over slightly in that inquisitive way.

One tiny piece solved, but he'd already suspected that much. But Indian Territory was a big area. How many questions could he ask without suspicion?

"You don't have to worry about being found here," she said. "Sanctuary is protected by Indians. My uncle trades with them."

Kane's mind went over the various maps he had studied during the few weeks he was with Ben Masters. Wichita Mountains? Glass Mountains? Black Mesa?

"You didn't answer my question." Nicky's voice broke into his thoughts.

He raised an eyebrow.

"If I . . . weren't untouchable?"

"But you are," he said. Her eyes were watching him with unwavering concentration. They seemed to grow larger and deeper and darker.

She swallowed hard and ran a hand through her short hair. "I know I'm not very pretty."

Dear God, how could she not know how pretty she was? How much he wanted to touch her? How much he wanted to feel her against him?

He stood and walked over to her. His good hand touched her hair, feeling the softness of the curls. "You are very pretty, Miss Thompson," he said huskily. "Which is why I've been doing my damnedest to stay away from you."

She leaned into him, whether consciously or unconsciously, and he felt a certain stiffening in his lower regions. She fitted there, against him. She felt soft and natural and . . . as if she belonged. His arm went around her, and her face lifted up toward him.

Against every ounce of sense he'd ever had, he bent his head and touched his lips to hers. It was like no other kiss in his life. Sweet as honey. So sweet he wanted to forget everything else.

He did. For a few insane minutes, he did. Even the pressure of her against his raw skin didn't matter. The pain was swallowed in an entirely different kind of torture, the kind that ached from the inside. He knew it would only worsen; already a certain part of him was straining against his trousers. He wanted her. He wanted her more than he ever remembered wanting a woman.

For a moment, reason was drowned in sensations. The need to be needed. The warmth of another human being. She reached out to him, and something he didn't know existed inside him reached back. His world rocked, the world he thought he knew so well. Their lips melded into one another, and then her mouth opened slightly. He knew her well enough to know she was reacting instinctively and not out of knowledge, and he felt as if he was being given a gift of inestimable value. Trust. Complete trust. He didn't deserve it. He should step away, but he couldn't. She had filtered into his soul.

Davy faded away.

His kiss deepened with desperation, the need to capture the moon, the rainbow, and enjoy them before they fled with the sun. But her body was more real than the sun, more substantial than a rainbow, and it pressed against his with an innocent wonder far more enticing than experience had ever been.

His tongue started a gentle exploration of her mouth, and he heard her gasp slightly. Then she purred like a young kitten as her tongue met his, took lessons, and graduated, playing and teasing as he had. His hand moved up from her waist to her neck, played there a moment while he felt her tremble, then moved up to lose itself in the tangle of her silken curls. Every woman should have short hair, he thought for the brief moment he could still think. Then he couldn't think. He was consumed by sensation—sweet and hot and needy. Her body fit so well into his; despite their clothes they were almost a part of each other, each inching more and more into the other. He started to reach for the top buttons of her shirt when he heard a noise on the porch. It was a miracle he heard anything. Everything but his immediate need was eclipsed in fog. Deadly fog.

He thought later it must have been his instinct for survival, pure and simple. He had just stepped away when he heard the sound of heavy boots and jiggling spurs on the floor.

"O'Brien?" Nat Thompson's voice was deep, suspicious. His glance went from Kane to Nicky and back again.

Kane took another step back. He wasn't sure whether he would prefer being caught going through Thompson's desk or embracing his niece. Neither held much future. His manhood ached, and he knew its need must be very evident. His mind, though, was too numbed, too shocked by his own lack of control, to respond.

"Feeling better, I see," Thompson continued when he received no answer.

"Thanks to you," Kane said.

"I have the feeling I had nothing to do with it," Thompson said roughly. "Nicky, would you go see after your brother?" It wasn't a question.

Nicky hesitated, her eyes on Kane.

"I have some business with O'Brien."

Still, she didn't move.

"Go," Kane said.

Nicky's gaze went from her uncle to Kane and back again. Nat Thompson suddenly smiled. "I'm not going to do a damn thing to him. I promise."

Kane stiffened. He was being talked about again as if he weren't there. And he damn well didn't need a woman's protection. His eyes bore into her, willing her to leave.

Obviously distressed, she bit her lip and ran her hand through that tangled taffy-colored hair. "He didn't do anything."

Kane fought a battle between his pride and the knowledge of her isolation. He hadn't realized she feared her uncle this much; she'd been far too defensive toward him. Kane moved toward her protectively.

Something glinted in Thompson's eyes. They were so cold, Kane could only surmise it was menace. But suddenly he smiled at Nicky, and his hard face softened to reveal not only affection, but love. Kane was astounded as he watched the expression change. The years didn't fall away from the face; they were deeply engraved like wagon ruts in a much-used road, but Thompson's whole demeanor changed to that of an indulgent uncle. Kane wouldn't have thought it possible of the man he knew was a killer. Not only a killer, but one who could control a town full of other killers. That demanded a ruthlessness that allowed no weaknesses. Kane had learned from Nicky that she and Robin were obligations; he hadn't realized they were also great weaknesses. He suspected Nat Thompson seldom showed that weakness to anyone. They'd been part of his rules, like any other rules in this town, but he doubted any of his guests realized how much he cared for them.

Kane wondered whether Thompson really meant to reveal that soft underbelly now.

"Leave us," Thompson said to Nicky again, and this time his voice was gentle. His body, though, suddenly went rigid. He reached out for a chair, and his hand grabbed for its support.

"Uncle Nat . . . ?" Nicky moved quickly toward him, but he waved her away with his other hand. "It's nothing. Just a cramp. Now fetch your brother." Again, Nicky hesitated, then her gaze rested on her uncle's face. Kane, feeling again like an invisible onlooker or an audience at a play, saw understanding pass between them. She turned without another word and left.

Thompson didn't move for a moment, then slowly he seemed to relax and he turned to Kane. "I hear you play a mean hand of poker."

"You seem to hear everything."

"I try."

Thompson walked over to his desk and sat down. Gratefully, it seemed to Kane. "Take a chair, O'Brien."

Kane, still wary, did so. He hadn't had time to relock that second desk drawer. He hoped like hell Thompson wouldn't try it.

"What do you think of Nicky?" The question was so unexpected that Kane blinked, and he knew his surprise was obvious.

"I don't think she should be here," he replied bluntly. "Her or the boy."

"You're right, of course," Thompson said, hunching forward in his chair. "But that wasn't my question."

A trap? Kane wasn't sure. Whenever he thought he had a handle on Thompson, the man changed abruptly. The chill was back in his eyes. There was no weakness now unless it lay deep inside the man across the desk. Thompson's eyes drilled into him, looking for the vein of truth or lies. Kane had to force himself not to blink again.

"I'm not sure what you want me to say," he said finally.

Thompson's eyes became even more intense. "You're not afraid of me, are you, Diablo?" Kane was so thrown off balance, he almost missed the last word. It was the first time Thompson had used his outlaw name. He'd always been O'Brien. His instincts started ringing like church bells.

"Only a fool wouldn't be afraid of Nat Thompson."

"And you aren't a fool?"

Kane grinned. "I certainly hope not."

"Then what are you, O'Brien? You're no ordinary outlaw."

"I hope not."

Thompson smiled at the rejoinder, but the expression had little real warmth in it. Kane wished to hell he knew what Thompson wanted. What game he was playing.

"Are you interested in my niece?" The questions reminded him of enemy cannon during the war. Kane had felt then that the balls were coming directly toward him. He had that same feeling now.

He shrugged. "You said she's out of bounds."

"That doesn't stop some men."

Now Kane smiled and, like Thompson, there was no humor in his smile. "I heard. I also heard what happens. I don't need more trouble."

"You don't think she's worth it?"

Damn the man. No matter which way Kane answered, he was trapped. "It doesn't matter what I think, does it?" Kane finally replied.

"Do you ever answer a question directly?"

"When it makes sense," Kane challenged, tired of the game. "I don't like being baited."

"I'm not baiting you, Diablo. I'm interested in you."

"Why?"

Thompson smiled again. It was no longer menacing but neither was it warm. "I'm not sure yet. Maybe because you might have saved my niece's life. Maybe because I might have need of a man like you."

"I don't understand."

"Mitch is getting old. I can trust Andy and Jeb, but neither of them have the steel it takes to run this place."

Kane didn't believe what he was hearing. It must be a test of some kind.

But Thompson was continuing. "I need someone who can think, not just shoot. I need someone with brains as well as grit. You survived two years as one of the most hunted men in Texas, and you broke out of gallows row. I haven't heard of anyone doing that before. Problem is I'm not sure of you. How come a man like you went to the other side of the law? An officer and gentleman?" There was some mockery in the last, an obvious distaste for the respectable.

"Killing's killing," Kane said. "There's not a whole lot of law in war, or even afterward, not if you're on the winning side."

"Trouble back home?"

"You could say that. I don't feel obliged to give you my life story."

Thompson hesitated. "I started Sanctuary twelve years ago. First off I just wanted a safe place for my brother's kids, a shack far enough away from the law that they couldn't find me. But it grew. First Mitch, then Jeb. I had kind of an arrangement with the Comanches. They didn't bother me, I didn't bother them. And I could offer them a few ... items they wanted."

Guns, Kane thought instantly. And whiskey. Nothing else would protect Thompson. He swallowed the distaste rising in him.

Thompson continued. "Sanctuary just kind of grew. Slow at first, then faster as it gained a reputation as a safe haven. It became important to make it secure, and I did. Those first visitors are either part of Sanctuary ... or dead." He hesitated a moment, then continued. "I've been safe here. You can be safe here." There was the slightest hint of desperation in his voice.

"Why me?"

"I told you. You have brains. More than that, I think you care something about my niece and nephew. There's ... Christ, I don't know, but most men here wouldn't have troubled themselves with a boy nor risk their own hides to help Nicky."

"Why don't you just send Nicky and Robin away?"

"To where? Neither have been more than fifty miles outside this valley in twelve years. Robin is only fifteen. Nicky ... well, Nicky can take care of herself in some ways, but . . ." His voice trailed off. "Damn, it's just not easy for a woman alone . . . and a boy."

Something was not being said. Kane felt it. Like a ghost hovering in the room.

"Think about staying here, O'Brien. At least for a while. I'll make it worth your while." Thompson rose, placed a hand on his desk and rested for a moment, then made for the door. He was gone before Kane could ask another question.

Kane continued to sit and stare at the desk. He was being offered Sanctuary. Safety. Probably even Nicky. Why?

Another trick? Another manipulation?

He swallowed hard. If it hadn't been for Davy, he knew he would consider it. He really didn't want to die, particularly not at the end of a noose. Kane looked around at the books, the comfort of the room. Nat Thompson had apparently lived very comfortably here for twelve years. Could he . . . if his life depended on it? With Nicky? Damn it, Nicky was the joker in the deck. She had been since he'd first set eyes on her.

She can take care of herself in some ways. But . . .

Kane knew. By God, he knew. She was so damnably innocent in some ways; she had been enticed by *him*, for God's sake, a man who wanted to use her. The thought of anyone else's using her, and for a different, more intimate reason, scorched him. The thought of anyone's laying a hand on her hurt more than he would have thought possible.

He could have her. He could have her and his freedom, and Sanctuary's protection. He could have it all if he surrendered what honor he had and gave up the life of the man who was closer to him than a brother.

Kane thought about the drawer, the unlocked drawer. Two options. Both of which led straight to hell.

And he knew his namesake—the devil—was probably doubled up laughing.

Chapter Nine

Nicky found her brother at the blacksmith's. He and Andy had just returned from hunting rabbits, and Robin held up one clean carcass with pride.

"Diablo gets some," he said. "You can have the rest for stew."

Somehow the leavings of a hawk didn't sound too appetizing to Nicky, but then she thought little would. She was still worried sick about the other Diablo.

She kept telling herself she shouldn't be. Her uncle had never lied to her, not once. He was usually brutally honest. But she had also knew what he'd done to the one man he'd found pestering her.

Kane O'Brien hadn't been pestering her. She had wanted everything he'd done. And more. Even now, she remembered the pure, joyous sensation that had galloped through her body at the touch of his lips.

She wondered what her uncle had wanted with him.

She tried to hurry Robin, but he was bragging about shooting the rabbit.

"First shot, wasn't it, Andy? Even with my bad arm."

Andy grinned and nodded, oblivious to her scowl. She didn't want Robin to be proud of his shooting ability. She wanted him to read more and write better and maybe even go to a university and be something. Nicky wasn't sure how she could manage that, not now that her uncle seemed ill, no matter how hard he tried to hide it.

Unexpectedly, a feeling of desolation struck her, settling in her heart.

"Your hawk's going to be hungry," she finally said.

"You mean Diablo?"

She scowled again. She didn't want to be reminded that Kane O'Brien was Diablo. She wanted him to be like he was in the kitchen. She wanted to remember his gentleness, not the lawlessness.

"I mean he's your responsibility," she said sharply, and he looked at her oddly. She was rarely short with him, and he'd always been able to get around her. He had been her world for a very long time; she still remembered how he had clutched her finger in his tiny fist when he was first born, when their mother was dying of childbirth. She had promised then to take care of him. It had seemed easy to an eight-year-old, particularly with the "housekeepers" Nat had hired until she was twelve. He had always been a good baby, then a good child. But now he was growing into a man, and she didn't know what to do about that. She didn't know how to help him. Most of all, she didn't know how to teach him right from wrong, when she didn't know herself.

All she knew about the outside world was what she read in books. Honor meant loyalty and fidelity. Her uncle deserved that for all he had given up for them. And he had given up much for them. She hadn't missed the longing glances he sometimes gave the mountains, nor the intensity with which he read clippings of exploits. He was a born bandit, a hawk like the one Kane O'Brien had found. She and Robin had clipped their uncle's wings, and he'd never expressed a word of regret to them.

And now he was sick. She knew it deep in her bones, and she couldn't leave him, not even for Robin's sake. There was also another reason. Kane O'Brien was here. Sanctuary was linked to him, and he to Sanctuary. He would leave—they all left eventually. But at least remnants of him would remain in this valley. Memories. A touch. A kiss. Her first real kiss. She didn't want to think how sad that was.

The thought left her cold and lonely.

She shook the melancholy away. She wanted to get back. She wanted to make sure Kane O'Brien was all right. Her tongue touched her lips, remembering the way he tasted. She hadn't known a man could taste so good.

"Come on, Robin," she said impatiently. "Mr. O'Brien is up. Maybe he could tell you more about how he raised his hawk."

Robin's eyes suddenly lit like a candle in the dark. He grabbed the dressed rabbit. "Thanks, Andy," he tossed back over his shoulder as he dashed toward the house.

Andy grinned. "He's found another hero."

"Better than the last, I hope," she said, remembering the Yancy brothers.

Andy's grin faded, but he didn't say anything. He just went back to his forge and started a fire. "Have some horseshoes ordered."

"What do you think of him?" Nicky asked.

"Diablo?"

She nodded.

"I'm not sure," he said thoughtfully. "Your uncle asked me the same thing. He doesn't quite fit the reputation he has, and that worries me."

Horror suddenly rushed through Nicky. "You don't think he's a law dog." That's what her uncle called them, the marshals and sheriffs. Two had already tried to infiltrate Sanctuary. She hadn't known about them until days after they had disappeared. Nicky didn't know for sure exactly what had happened to them, but deep in her heart she knew they were dead. Neither had stood a chance, since they didn't have guns. That was a part of her uncle she tried not to think about.

Andy shook his head. "No. After that last one, Nat's been particularly cautious. Diablo is who he says he is, all right, but he ain't like the others, and that troubles me some."

"Why? You aren't like the others, either."

Andy frowned. "Maybe more than you would like to

think. But I had a healthy case of the carefuls where the law was concerned. I don't think Mr. Diablo does. I think he enjoyed sticking his foot up their ..." He stopped a moment, his face going red. "Noses," he finally completed.

Nicky chuckled, delighted at Andy's embarrassment. She was used to rather colorful language, but Andy and Jeb and Mitch all tried to be circumspect. They didn't always succeed. "I don't think that's what you meant."

"What I'm sayin' ... he's not the kind of man to run and hide." Andy's face went even more crimson, if that were possible, but he was trying to explain something that was obviously sticking in his craw.

The chuckle died in her throat. Now that Andy mentioned it, she knew he was right. "Then ... why ... ?"

"Could be lots of reasons, I guess. A woman, maybe. Hell, I don't know. Just seems odd, that's all."

A woman? Nicky fought the impulse to run her fingers through her hair. She didn't want Andy to see that small vanity, that sign of nervousness. Of course, there would be a woman. Probably more than one. Kane O'Brien was a handsome man, despite the scar, or maybe because of it. And he was a bold and daring one, the kind she supposed attracted women.

"Am I pretty, Andy?" She didn't know why she blurted out the telltale question. It was stupid. What was he to say? No, you're an ugly hag. She wanted to run away and hide, like she had sometimes as a child. Instead, she lowered her eyes so she couldn't see his expression.

"Aye," he said softly. "You've always been as pretty as a buttercup, and your smile lights the skies."

His voice wasn't just kind. The ring of honesty gave her courage. "I wish I had a dress," she said wistfully.

"Because of Diablo?"

She looked up, met his worried, honest eyes. "Yes."

"Be careful, little one. There's layers and layers to that one."

"I know," she whispered but she turned before he could say anything else, before there were any more warnings she didn't want to hear. She had too many in her head already.

• • •

KANE didn't have a decision to make. Just as he reached for the drawer to lock it, he checked the window and saw Robin approaching the house. He had all of a minute to turn the lock and move away from the desk. Damn it.

Still, he felt a momentary relief that the decision had been taken from him, at least for the time being.

Robin held up his catch. "Shot 'im myself," he said with a pride Kane remembered all too well.

"Takes some doing to shoot a running rabbit," Kane observed, and the boy's chest puffed out even farther.

"I'm gonna be a gunfighter someday. Like you."

Kane winced at the description. He would never have called himself a gunfighter. He sure as hell never wanted to be one. "I'm not a gunfighter," he said bluntly. "I'm a thief, and not a very good one, since I got caught."

The glow of admiration in the boy's eyes didn't falter. "But you got away."

"This time," he said. "I won't always."

"Uncle Nat . . ."

"Your Uncle Nat is safe because he stays put here. But he's in prison, just the same as I was. He can't go anywhere without being hunted, and neither can I. It's no way to live, boy."

"People respect you," Rob said stubbornly.

"People like Yancy?" Kane said with contempt. "Think about it, Robin."

Robin stared at him, confused. "Then why did you become an outlaw?"

Kane shrugged and lied. He didn't want to give young Robin any excuse to admire him. "It was easier than workin'. At least I thought so then. I don't now. Hanging isn't easy, boy. Neither is a bullet in the gut, and that's what I have to look forward to."

"I don't believe you," Robin said. "You aren't afraid of anything."

"Only a fool isn't afraid of dying," Kane said. "Especially dying alone." He felt infinitely tired. Drained. Like he'd been sucked of all life. Everyone wanted something from him: Masters, Nat Thompson, Robin. Even Nicky. They all wanted him to be something he wasn't. Masters wanted a traitor, Thompson a man as ruthless as he, Robin a gunfighter to emulate. And Nicky . . . Nicky wanted a hero. She'd mistaken his actions in the kitchen for those of a knight in a book. He had the world's sorriest armor, as tarnished as it got.

His voice suddenly softened as he saw Robin's face fall. "Come on, we'll go feed your hawk. You'll need a heavy glove. . . ."

KANE moved back to the hotel that night. It wasn't entirely his doing, but he wasn't regretful about it. Andy had pronounced him free of infection and well enough to move around. The blacksmith had been carefully neutral, but Kane had sensed a reserve that hadn't been there earlier.

Kane knew he'd lost his chance to explore the drawers further, but it had been damned risky in the first place. And staying in the same house as Nicole Thompson was like putting a match to dynamite. It made the other risk comparable to a child playing in the sand.

If he'd had no feeling for her, he could probably have controlled his more lustful longings. At least, he thought he could. But he *did* have other feelings. His body responded to her in the damnedest ways. He couldn't seem to take his eyes from her, from that tentative smile, or from the depth of her eyes, the way her body moved under the ill-fitting clothes that only hinted at something fine beneath. His blood started racing, and his throat felt as if it were weighed with stone. He didn't even want to think about the other parts of his body.

Worse, though, was the passion and energy that radiated from her, that had so entrapped him earlier in the day. Despite the accident with the stove, he'd discovered she was an excellent cook. She was also a fine rider and markswoman, according to Robin. Nicole Thompson evidently had the determination and intelligence to do many things well, and a passion for life that promised . . . paradise as a lover. The fact she'd had so little experience with being a woman had only spurred her to be more bold and adventuresome.

He tried to tell himself that was all it was. That physical magnetism, and her complexity, was the sum of his attraction. But then his gaze would meet hers, and that wistful, almost fragile vulnerability reached out and struck a part of his heart.

Kane jerked himself back to reality. She was as fragile as a rattlesnake. He'd seen her stand over Yancy. She must know what her uncle had been doing all these years. She must know about the lawmen that had disappeared, just as he knew he would disappear if he weren't more careful. He'd been self-indulgent, playing with fire that was far more dangerous than that in the kitchen, and whose burns could prove far more deadly.

Still, as he walked over to the hotel, acknowledging the curious nods of the other guests, he knew he would miss her presence, and that of young Robin, who reminded him so much of himself years ago. He'd planned to conquer the world, too. Show it exactly how tough he was.

He'd shown it all right, all the way to a hangman's noose.

Sam Hildebrand stopped him before he reached the hotel. "Heard tell you've been staying with Thompson." He eyed the blistered skin on Kane's hand avidly.

Kane nodded.

"Ain't no one done that before."

"Maybe no one got burned in his kitchen before." The last thing Kane needed now was resentment from the other guests. God knew he had enough people on his back.

Sam absorbed that piece of information, then nodded. "Poker game tonight. You in?"

Hell, why not? It was better than sitting in his room, staring at walls and wondering what in the devil's name he was going to do now. "Yeah."

Sam hesitated a moment. "You been with Thompson's daughter? We all been real curious about her."

Kane wanted to hit him. There was a leering curiosity in his eyes, a knowing smirk on his lips. He knew one thing about these kind of men, though: Show one sign of weakness and you're dead. Maybe not immediately, but it would be stored for future reference. Soft men didn't survive long among this company.

Kane shook his head. "You know Thompson's rules. No woman's worth getting killed for. Or hung. I don't fancy leaving yet."

Damn, he hated explaining himself to the likes of Hildebrand.

"We don't want you to," said Hildebrand. "You've won too much of our damned money."

Kane relaxed slightly. "You'll have a chance to even things tonight."

"Rosita's later?" A question lingered in Hildebrand's eyes, and Kane knew he hadn't really given up the subject of Nicky. In fact, he was probably sent as emissary from the others to pry.

Kane shook his head. "My back hurts too bad for the kind of activity I like."

"Burned that bad?"

"Bad enough."

"You really save the girl?"

Damn, but this place was a sieve of information. Andy? He doubted it. It was more likely Robin. "You hear that from the boy?"

"Yep. He was braggin' 'bout his friend, Diablo." There was derision in his voice, a dangerous edge of jealousy.

"Well, forget it. He's a kid. He exaggerates everything. I was just getting some water when the fire flamed. It caught both of us."

Hildebrand smiled slyly, then shrugged. "See you later."

Kane swore again as he made his way up to his room. He hadn't liked the look in Hildebrand's eyes. He was up to something, and Kane had the sinking feeling that he, Kane, was part of it. He was a fly caught in a web, and the number of spiders was increasing. The question was whether they were going to destroy each other before they got to him.

• • • •

Nicky debated with herself all night before she visited Andy's wife, Juanita. She didn't own a dress, hadn't owned a dress since the day after her father died, when Uncle Nat had taken her and her brother and fled Austin, Texas. Nicky had been tending Robin in a rented room while their father had "gone out on business."

Her uncle had returned alone, and she'd known instantly that her father wasn't coming back. She'd known even then he was a robber, that she had to be careful about what she said to the various housekeepers and what few people she met.

Uncle Nat had taken her dress and given her trousers instead, said it would be easier riding that way. It was, and he'd never seen the need to buy her anything else. Neither had she. She had loved the freedom of trousers. Later, when she realized men were looking at her differently, she was grateful for the almost shapeless clothes.

But now she wanted to wear a dress. She wanted Kane O'Brien to notice she was a woman. She wanted to be pretty for him. She swallowed hard, remembering those long-ago vows that she would never care for an outlaw, never suffer what her mother suffered.

Kane was different, though. She longed to see that too-rare smile. She yearned to see admiration in his eyes. Juanita, she knew, could help her. Juanita would loan her a dress and help her do something with her hair, short as it was.

Then she would ask Kane O'Brien to dinner tomorrow night. She didn't think her uncle would object, not now. She had seen Kane leave, whole and well, and her uncle had been expansive after their meeting. He was interested in Kane for some reason of his own, a reason that Nicky no longer believed spelled danger for her outlaw. Nat Thompson didn't like many people, but he apparently liked Kane O'Brien.

She picked up her pace, even as her stomach quaked in uncertainty. She had made a decision. A fatal one, maybe, but inevitable. She couldn't say she loved Kane O'Brien. She didn't know that much about love. What she felt might be gratitude, or attraction, or curiosity.

Need. Desperation. Or just plain lust. She didn't know. She only knew she had to find out.

GOODEN, TEXAS

Mary May Hamilton's gaze went to the tall, lean drifter who had become a frequent customer at the Blazing Star Saloon. She'd watched him for the past month. He came in, took a seat by a wall, ordered two glasses of whiskey, never more, and left. He was always alone, but his eyes never stopped moving, watching.

She'd approached him several times and was rebuffed gently. So were the other girls at the Blazing Star. "Nothing personal," he would say. "Just prefer my own company."

It was her job to cozy up to patrons, get them to drink more, buy her fancy concoctions that were little more than water. It was up to her whether she wanted to take things further. Sometimes she did; more likely she didn't. Mary May didn't consider herself a whore. She didn't take money for loving; she just enjoyed it if the man was right. And she was very particular. The man had to be clean, attractive, and gentlemanly. The stranger fit all those qualifications. He didn't try to grab her backside or make ribald remarks, and he had steady eyes, not cruel ones.

It had been a long time since last she'd been pleasured, and she was feeling that familiar ache that plagued her after a long abstinence.

She had another reason to want to know the stranger better. She had a sideline business: information. She provided tidbits now and then to a man called Calico who paid her handsomely. That money, and most of the dollars she earned at the Blazing Star, went to Mrs. Culworthy in another town. Mrs. Culworthy cared for Mary May's three-year-old daughter, Sarah Ann.

So the stranger interested her in more ways than one. Calico wanted information on strangers. He wanted information on anyone who asked about a place called Sanctuary. He wanted to know about anyone who seemed to be running from the law, or anyone who *was* the law. Mary May suspected the stranger was one of the two.

She had given Calico the name of a man with a scarred face weeks earlier, and had earned a good sum of money for it. She had seen that same man talking in the alley to this one. Mary May hadn't voiced that particular observation to Calico, though she wasn't sure why. Maybe because more information would mean more money. Or maybe because the stranger intrigued her. She usually had any man she wanted; men took great pride in being selected by her. But not this one. So far.

Though he wore no badge, she had a nagging suspicion he had something to do with the law. He had a military bearing: straight back and confident tilt of his head. There was something always alert about him despite the lazy pose he affected in the saloon and the slight limp that would be imperceptible to most. There were certain things a man couldn't hide. Not from her. She knew men far too well. Because she enjoyed most men and had an honest fear of others, she'd learned to sniff danger.

The stranger smelled of exactly that. He had the assurance of a man who had faced death and won, and who was comfortable with decisions he'd made. He fascinated her. He had from the day he'd first declined her company.

Mary May had few illusions about herself. She was not beautiful, but she loved a good joke and laughed easily, and had learned to turn aside unwanted overtures with a good nature that defused trouble. When she dealt cards, she did it well and honestly, determined not to make her husband's mistakes. He'd been a gambler, and had caught a bullet when found cheating, leaving her a pregnant widow with few skills. Her only assets had been her smile and body.

It wasn't a bad life at the Blazing Star. The owner, Dan Calhoun, watched out for his girls. If they attracted gamblers and sold enough liquor for him, he didn't care whether they sold more than liquor.

Her gaze wandered over to the tall stranger again. He had finished his first glass of whiskey. His feet were stretched out, as if he hadn't a care in the world. Yet she had the impression of a coiled rattlesnake. Not the menace, exactly, but the striking power.

She turned to the bartender. "Tom, I'll take him the second glass."

He shrugged. "Gonna try again?"

"Hell, why not?" she said.

He grinned. "There's a bet over which one of you girls will break him down."

"You and Dan doing the betting?"

"Yep."

"What's the stakes?"

"Ten greenbacks."

"Who bet on me?"

"I wouldn't bet against you, love."

"Why, that two-faced, no-good . . ."

"Aw, come on, Mary, we tossed for you and he lost. He took all the others."

She felt better. She checked the stranger from under lightly painted eyelids. He was looking ruefully at his empty glass, waiting patiently for a refill. She got the feeling he did a lot of waiting. Question was why. Two kinds of men waited: outlaws waiting on a job, and law dogs waiting to catch them.

She took the glass of whiskey to his table. Ordinarily when she wanted a man's attention, she'd put a hand on his shoulder or wink at him. She didn't think either approach would work in this case. Instead, she stood silently, forcing him to acknowledge her.

"You waiting for someone?" she finally said, still not setting the glass down in front of him.

Those watching eyes slid over her, noted every detail. She felt naked.

"I'm waiting for that," he said, indicating the glass in her hand.

"You've been in here every day." It was a dumb observation. Of course, he knew he'd been in every day, but she was at a loss as to how to continue the conversation. She wasn't going to ask him whether he wanted company. He would say no, and that would be the end of that.

His eyes were a slate gray-blue like first dawn. Clear.

No sign of whiskey blur. She hadn't seen him smile, but suddenly he did, and her knees went weak. The smile transformed the hard face. "An astute observation," he said.

She flushed for the first time in years, yet his words were said with humor, not contempt. "I suppose it was," she said, suddenly smiling back. "But my pride's at stake."

One brow questioned her.

"There's a bet," she said to the unuttered question.

His brow raised higher. "About me?"

She nodded. "Who will break you down."

"Not much to do in this town?" His question was wry, and she immediately liked him.

"Well, you don't gamble, you don't drink much, and you don't want company. That sorta makes you... strange."

"Strange?" he said with a small chuckle that rumbled across the table.

"Different," she said, afraid she'd insulted him.

"Then I have to remedy that," he said formally, and she knew suddenly he'd been well-raised though he was dressed like any drifter. "May I buy you a drink?"

She grinned then. "I thought you would never ask." She handed him the glass and sat down. "I'm Mary May."

"I know," he said, and she realized he hadn't been as indifferent as he seemed. "I'm Ben."

"Ben what?"

"Ben Smith."

"You have a lot of kin out here."

He smiled. Slow and lazy again. "Yep, guess I do."

"Waiting for one of them?"

"Could be."

"Ex-military?"

He looked startled for the first time. For a moment, he looked as if he would deny the assumption, then his body relaxed. "That obvious?"

"To me, it is."

"Why?"

"Your hair's shorter than most, for one thing. Most military men wear it that way. Also, the way you hold yourself. And the discipline. Always two drinks, never more."

He shrugged. "The military and I took leave of each other long ago by mutual agreement. But some habits die hard." For the first time his expression darkened. She'd intruded some place she shouldn't have. But relief flooded her. She didn't think he was a lawman. He didn't have that . . . arrogance about him.

He gestured to the bartender for a drink for her. Tom grinned and gave her a sign of victory. For the next thirty minutes, she sipped the watered drink, and found herself saying things she hadn't mentioned in years.

It wasn't until later, when she was in her room, unhappily alone, that she realized he hadn't said anything at all about himself, except that one bitter comment about the military.

BEN Masters glared at himself in the mirror. He ought to be concentrating on Diablo. He'd been crazy to start going to the saloon, but he'd hoped to learn something; it was at the Blazing Star that Diablo had made his first contact. And Ben was damned tired of waiting.

Ben had noticed the woman right off. Hell, he'd have to be blind not to notice. She brimmed with life. She was as unlike his former fiancée as night from day, or the sun from the moon. Clara had been a pale beauty, blond and fragile. Too fragile for a man torn apart by pain and guilt, and who was trying to bury both in whiskey.

He didn't want to think of that now. He needed to keep his mind on Diablo, not on some saloon woman, no matter how she smiled or laughed. For a few moments, Mary May had helped him to forget the worry. He knew her reputation, but he liked her honesty, her smile. He liked being with a woman again.

He went to the window and looked out again, as he had every night for the past several weeks, and wondered how Kane O'Brien was faring.

Chapter Ten

This time the dinner invitation came from Nicky. And to Kane, it was even more alarming than the one from her uncle. It also came via a more deceptively benign messenger—Robin.

"Sis wants you to come for supper," he said from the doorway. "So do I."

Kane didn't even ask whether their uncle did. Nat Thompson's offer had haunted him during the past few days. No matter what Thompson was, he had made an offer in good faith, and Kane detested his role of spy and betrayer. Deception had never come easily to him. Even when he was on the run, he had been openly defying the law.

And, damn it, temptation deviled him. Thompson was offering him something of his own for the first time in his life, even if it was not what he would have chosen. But any brief mental flirtation with the offer reminded him of the lawmen who had disappeared, and he knew he could never be a part of that. He also knew he could never profit at Davy's expense.

As he looked at Robin, though, he realized he had no obvious reason for refusing the invitation for dinner, even though everything within him rebelled against getting more involved with the Thompson family.

Yet, he still had to discover the location of Sanctuary. And Nicky and Robin were still his best hope.

Robin, his face eager, stood at the door, waiting for an answer.

"Tell your sister I look forward to it," Kane lied. He hesitated, reluctant to prolong the boy's stay. "How's your hawk?"

Robin grinned. "He's making little whistling noises, and he ate that rabbit real good. I'm going out hunting again. You wanta go?" he asked hopefully.

"I don't have a gun."

"That's all right. Andy has one, and he can loan you one while we're hunting."

Kane hated the anticipation in Robin's eyes. It had been a mistake bringing the boy the hawk. The more Robin came to admire him, the more disillusioned and hurt he'd be when he discovered he had been used to destroy his uncle, his home, possibly his sister.

"I don't think so," Kane said in a voice harsher than he'd intended.

Robin's grin faded.

"I don't like hunting," Kane said, his voice gentling slightly. "I've been hunted too long myself."

"Oh," Robin said, clearly not understanding at all. The thought of being hunted apparently seemed adventure-some, not bleak, hellishly uncomfortable, and often terri-fying. Kane thought of the two years he'd spent as a fugitive—always on the move, poor food, little shelter. He thought of the hopelessness that last time when his horse simply couldn't run any longer, and he'd stood helpless as a posse surrounded him.

There had been nothing glamorous about the handcuffs that rubbed his skin raw, or the leg irons that forced him to hobble to the courthouse and back. There had been nothing adventuresome about his cell or the prospect of hanging.

If only Robin understood. But he didn't, and he was headed straight in the same direction.

He wanted to shake some sense into the boy, to warn him what to expect if he continued to admire the "guests" at Sanctuary. But he couldn't. He could only try to convince him slowly, all the time trying to extract information from him. Some example of law and order he was.

"What time is supper?" he asked.

Robin's grin was a little tentative, some of his enthusiasm obviously ebbing at Kane's curt answer about being hunted. "Six," the boy said, still hesitating, obviously reluctant to leave.

Kane internally counted the days he had left before Davy died, damned Masters yet another time, and stopped the boy as he started to turn around. "Instead of hunting," he said, "what about fishing? I'm pretty fair at that."

Robin nodded eagerly. "Tomorrow?"

Feeling all sorts of a knave and damned beyond redemption, Kane forced a smile. "Sounds good."

"I'll see you tonight. You can see Diablo," Robin offered hopefully.

The name made Kane flinch. "How is he doing?"

"He's sitting on that perch you brought." The words kept rushing out.

"You get that glove I told you about?"

"Yep," Robin said happily. "Had one over at the store. Real heavy riding glove."

"That should work well," Kane said.

"How long before I can start teaching him to hunt?"

"He's probably ready now," Kane said. "You'll have to make him a tether."

"You'll show me, won't you?"

"I won't be here that long."

"Uncle Nat said you might be staying. I heard him talk to Mitch."

Kane was trapped again. "He said *might,* Robin. I have . . . other matters to see to."

"You'll stay. I just know you will," Robin said, then turned and fled before Kane could say anything.

NICKY looked in the mirror at herself and didn't quite believe the reflection that stared back. She *was* pretty.

Juanita had given her a dress and helped her stitch here

and there to make it fit. Juanita's breasts and hips were larger than her own, but their waists were the same. Nicky thought the rich deep blue color very pretty and, once altered, the dress flattered her slender figure.

Juanita brushed Nicky's hair until it fairly shimmered with gold, and then pinned a blue flower behind her ear. She used a little of her paints to deepen Nicky's eyes and put a faint blush in her sun-darkened cheeks. Nicky, who'd never paid much attention to her appearance and often merely ran her fingers through her hair to comb it, was amazed, pleased, and terribly uncertain. *She* thought she looked nice, but would Kane? He was probably used to more . . . experienced women. Prettier women.

But her uncle's eyes had widened when she entered the main room from her bedroom, and he stood for her. He'd never done that before.

"You look lovely, Nicky," he said.

A warm feeling enveloped her. "Thank you," she said shyly.

"Is that you?" Robin said, his eyes squinched up mischievously. "Is that really you, Sis?"

"No," she said. "It's your wicked stepmother who will make you sweep out the fireplace if you don't behave."

He grinned happily. "I bet Diablo will think you're real pretty, too."

"The man or the hawk?" her uncle teased in rare good humor. Nicky knew he was pleased by her invitation.

"Both," Robin said, red suddenly darkening his cheeks. He wasn't used to giving compliments, not any more than Nicky was to receiving them.

Nicky bit her lips, hoping that what he said was true. She went into the kitchen to check on the chicken that was cooking in its own juices. She'd already roasted potatoes and made biscuits and an apple pie.

She looked down at her dress. It wasn't nearly as comfortable as her trousers. Besides which it made her feel different in ways that were not all pleasant. She was scared. Just plain scared. Scared he would . . . be amused, afraid she would trip over her skirts or do something silly. She was afraid of seeing him—and of not seeing him.

But most of all, she was expectant. She couldn't tamp that part of her that hoped, dreamed, ached to be touched and loved and wanted.

Even by a man who was an outlaw. For the first time, she understood her mother, and why she had followed her husband to the ends of nowhere, dragging a child behind her and expecting another.

Nicky was still in the kitchen when she heard the knock on the door, then male voices. Kane O'Brien's and her uncle's. There would only be the four of them tonight. Mitch, who often ate with them, had left Sanctuary on some business.

Her uncle's voice was hearty, strong. She wondered whether she had imagined the spells, those moments when he appeared to be in pain. Maybe, as he claimed, they had been caused by something he'd eaten that disagreed with him. She smoothed the front of the dress, wishing she didn't feel so awkward in it, then checked the flower in her hair. She felt odd, even a little ridiculous, pretending to be a lady. What if Kane laughed? She couldn't bear to see derision in his eyes. Or even worse, pity.

Suddenly, she had an urge to hide in the kitchen or sneak through the back and climb in the window of her room.

"Nicky?"

She turned away from the stove toward Robin, who was standing in the door. "Diablo's here."

Diablo. She hated that name. It didn't fit him. Not now.

"Here," she said. "You can help carry some food in."

"That's woman's work."

"It's Robin's work, too, if he wants to eat," she retorted.

"I have a bad arm," he protested. It was the first time he'd complained about it, and she suddenly realized he didn't want Diablo to see him doing what Robin considered "women's work." In his mind, gunslingers evidently didn't do that.

"You were able to shoot that rabbit," she said. "You can carry in a dish."

"Aw, Sis."

"And I have a bad arm, too," she said.

"But . . ."

"But you're going to let your Diablo starve if you keep arguing with me."

"Just wait till he sees you," Robin said, changing the subject and inching out the door.

"Robin!"

Balefully, he returned and took a platter.

Nicky waited a moment until he disappeared, bit her lip and transferred the chicken onto a platter, then headed for the main room. A glass in his hand, Kane was standing, leaning against a wall, his gaze on the food Robin had fetched, until he obviously sensed her presence and looked up. Nicky saw the surprise dart across his face as he straightened, then something akin to pleasure, slow and lazy and appreciative, took its place. The crooked mouth smiled, the dent in his cheek deepening.

He put down his glass and moved quickly over to her, taking the platter from her hands and placing it on the table. Nicky wanted to shoot a triumphant gaze over to her brother, but she couldn't take her gaze away from Kane's. His eyes had deepened, and there was no ridicule or pity in them. They were, rather, smoldering in a way she'd never seen before.

"Miss Thompson," he said. "You look very . . . pretty."

Her heart felt squeezed, trapped by her ribcage. It wasn't so much his words as the admiration in his eyes. "Thank you," she said and turned, seeking the kitchen again, a shelter to hide the blush in her cheeks. She wished she didn't always do that with him, feel so vulnerable. Why couldn't she just accept a compliment? Her throat felt like it was weighed with stone.

Robin, after seeing his hero take the plate from her, needed no more urging in delivering several more plates as Nicky placed the pie on top of the stove to keep it warm. She heard the voices in the next room and leaned against the wall next to the door, listening for a moment and enjoying the sound of Kane O'Brien's deep, confident tone.

He was asking questions about Sanctuary. Perhaps he really was thinking about staying. He wouldn't be on the run, then. Sanctuary was safe. It was just . . . lonely. *Please*, she said to whomever listened to people like her. *Please let him stay*. But then she thought about her brother, his need to leave this place.

Had her mother been faced with choices like the ones she faced?

Nicky desperately wished that her mother were alive, that she could ask these questions. She remembered her mother's softness, her gentleness. She remembered whispered words between her mother and father, and the way they had touched all the time. She remembered her father's grief when her mother had died. Still, he had continued his outlaw ways, finally leaving two orphans. She had loved him dearly, but she'd never forgiven him for that. How could she even think about loving a man like her father?

Her hands knotted into fists. It's Robin who's important, she thought. Robin. Remember that.

"Sis." Robin was back in the kitchen. "We're waiting for you."

She nodded, wiped her hands on a towel.

Remember Robin, she kept telling herself as she took the few steps toward temptation.

KANE tried to hide his astonishment. Nicole Thompson was not only pretty, she was enchanting. The blue of her dress emphasized the gold highlights in her tousled hair, and the small wildflower behind her ear was perfect for her delicate gamine face. Her eyes seemed enormous, and her cheeks were slightly flushed, either from some rouge or heat from the oven. If it was the former, it had been very artfully applied.

He'd known she had a nice figure. Even the masculine clothes hadn't been able to completely disguise the slender but soft body, and his hands had confirmed that opinion. But the dress enhanced every curve, including the smallness of her waist. He wanted to put his hands around it, and he wanted to pull her against him. Even more appealing, though, was her uncertainty, her unawareness of her own desirability. Kane had not felt humbled often in his life, but he felt both humbled and despairing that she had gone to this trouble for him.

He was only too aware that Nat Thompson was studying his face every couple of seconds, and Kane had tried not to show his interest, his own vulnerability where Nicole Thompson was concerned. When she'd disappeared so quickly, he'd tried to turn his attention to his job, prying information from Nat Thompson.

The man had a damnably self-satisfied smile on his face. For some reason Kane didn't understand, he had been selected as heir apparent, and it seemed he'd been correct in assuming that the position included Nicole Thompson. How much had her uncle had to do with gussying her up tonight? He was suddenly furious at Nat Thompson.

"Tell me more about Sanctuary," he said after Nicole left the room. "Exactly how safe is it?"

"Thinking about what I said?"

"Maybe," Kane said. "But some people have to know where Sanctuary is. Your guides, for instance. And those who trade with the Indians, and whoever brings in the supplies. How can you be sure they won't talk?"

Nat shrugged. "I have too much on them for one thing. Another thing, I pay well. There's something else they remember, too," Nat said. "A number of dangerous men like this place. They wouldn't appreciate its exposure."

"The Indians? What if they make a treaty?"

"I deal with renegades who hate the army. Most of them are wanted themselves."

"What about the army?"

Nat grinned at him. "They have no authority over civilians here."

"Supply routes?"

Nat's grin grew wider. "If you decide to stay, I'll share some of our secrets. You thinking about it?"

"Who wouldn't?" Kane countered. "But why me?"

"Like I said, you use your head. Like now. You don't just accept; you ask questions. You want to know everything about the situation. Most men would jump at the opportunity to take over Sanctuary."

Kane hesitated a moment. "I appreciate the offer."

"But?"

"I told you before. I get restless. I don't know if I could stay in this valley for months, much less years."

"It has its benefits, Diablo," Thompson said.

Just then Nicky entered the room and Kane stood up. Thompson and Robin stared at him in amazement.

"My army training," he said as he waited for Nicky to sit, her gaze fastened on him. Even with her brother and uncle present, electricity rippled between them. Kane felt singed by it as he slowly sat after she had seated herself. "One of the few things I picked up as an officer and gentleman," he added with self-derision.

But Nicole looked pleased, and that ripple of electricity turned into a stream of warm pleasure that ran through his blood.

Robin looked disgusted, but Nat Thompson didn't. He appeared pleased again. "What else did you learn?"

"Stay toward the back," he answered with a smile. Unfortunately, he hadn't learned that until it was too late.

"And tactics?" Thompson obviously wasn't through with his constant probing.

"I wasn't ever asked for an opinion," he said. "I was more cannon fodder."

"It took some damn good tactics to survive as long as you did in Texas. How many robberies?"

"I didn't count," Kane said.

"How many men did you have?"

He was being interrogated by the best of them, Kane thought. Marshal Ben Masters didn't come close. But then Masters hadn't been interested in Diablo; he only wanted Sanctuary.

Kane shrugged. "It varied." He took a piece of chicken and put a piece in his mouth. It was tender enough to melt there. His eyes went back to Nicky.

Nat Thompson chuckled. "There are definite advantages at Sanctuary," he said, then started eating himself. The interrogation was over, at least temporarily.

Throughout the rest of the meal, little conversation took place, although Kane noticed Nicky's gaze wandering toward him. He was having a hard time keeping his eyes off her, too. He had the ugly feeling that Nat Thompson was noting and enjoying his weakness.

Kane could scarcely eat the apple pie, as good as it was. Every bite stuck in his throat. Nicky's eyes were glowing, her smile both sweet and endearing. There was a directness about her, especially her kiss, even in her uncertainty, in the shyness born of inexperience. She had been so damn direct in that kiss, the kiss he kept remembering. Feeling. Wanting.

When he'd taken the last bite, Nat Thompson looked at him speculatively. "I asked Andy to get the buggy ready, since my niece is wearing a dress," he said. "I thought you might like a spell of fresh air after dinner."

Kane hesitated. God knew a breath of fresh air would be welcome. Gulps of it. A skyful of it. He wanted it with Nicky, but he *needed* it alone. He needed to think, and he couldn't do that when Nicky was anywhere nearby. And he was being manipulated again. He resented it like hell that Nat Thompson was using his niece as a lever to get what he wanted. The thing that so confounded him, though, was why. Why had *he* had been chosen?

He still wasn't sure, despite Nat Thompson's earlier explanation. Thompson had run Sanctuary all these years. Why change now? Why use someone he obviously loved to get his way? None of it made sense to Kane.

His hesitancy was apparently obvious. Nicky was rising, her face a little more colored that it had been. "I can't go, Uncle Nat," she said. "I have to clean the kitchen and . . ."

Thompson glared at Kane. "Nonsense," he said. "It's nothing that can't wait."

Kane realized his hesitation had been interpreted as reluctance. Nicky, who had met his gaze all evening, was now avoiding it, bowing her head ever so slightly even as her back stiffened. Against hurt? Against humiliation? His chest constricted, anguish striking at his heart. Of everyone involved in this unholy mess, she and Robin were the most innocent and would be hurt the most.

His unwilling but growing liking for Nat Thompson plummeted. One thing he couldn't do was humiliate Nicky in front of her family.

"You're right," he said to Thompson. "A buggy ride sounds just fine."

Nicky was halfway out of her chair, and she stopped, turning to look at him directly again. "You don't have to take me," she said in a tight voice. "I don't even want to go."

"Please," he said. It had been a long time since he'd last said please. He couldn't even remember when. The word sounded rusty on his lips.

Her eyes were suddenly confused, uncertain, and the constriction in his chest grew tighter. He could barely breathe, waiting for her answer. He wanted her to say yes. He longed to erase the hurt she tried so hard to keep from her face, repair the pride that kept her body so stiff. Kane knew about injured pride, how much it ate at the insides. God, he knew.

What will happen to her pride when she discovers you were only using her to ruin her uncle?

Damn, he couldn't think of that now. Three pairs of eyes were on him, judging him.

Kane stood and walked over to Nicky, holding out his hand. After a moment, she took it, but the stiffness didn't go away. He felt her tension in her slender fingers. Her hand seemed small in his, fragile, hardly strong enough to pull a trigger. He reminded himself that she was stronger than she appeared, that those fingers *had* pulled a trigger and killed a man. He tried to equate that woman with this one: soft and pretty and so easily wounded. He couldn't.

"Come with me," he said, hearing the seduction in his own voice, knowing he himself was being seduced.

She took a step and another, and then they were at the door. He opened it. There was one last hesitation on her part, a question in her eyes.

"I want you," Kane heard himself say softly, so softly he didn't think the others could hear. He hadn't meant to say it that way. He'd meant to say he would like her company. Both were true. Her hand moved in his, her fingers wrapping themselves around his. A gesture of trust. The anguish inside him deepened. So did the want. The need.

And the self-disgust.

They didn't say anything on the way to Andy's livery. They didn't have to. The air was alive with sparks, with words unsaid, emotions too raw and new to explain.

Andy had the buggy ready. What's more, Andy showed him the rifle that lay in the back. Kane wondered what the blacksmith thought about this change in rules. His face was inscrutable, though, and Kane wasn't sure he wanted to know. There was something tight about his mouth, as if he didn't approve. Kane wondered whether the blacksmith was aware of Nat Thompson's offer.

Kane helped Nicky up into the buggy, his hand hesitating before releasing hers. Heat radiated between them. He was reluctant to let it go.

Andy cleared his throat, and Kane dropped her hand and stepped up into the driver's seat. He tried not to think of her just inches away, but it was damn difficult when she smelled of flowers. The awareness between them seemed to reverberate like the echo of church bells. He tried to concentrate on the buggy instead. He hadn't seen this vehicle before and guessed it had been in the back of the barn. Sanctuary apparently had every little comfort, even this absurd buggy in the middle of nowhere. It was black and red. Obviously new, or rarely used. Kane snapped the reins and the horses moved ahead.

He headed for the river, away from town. He didn't particularly want any of the "guests" speculating, though he knew the news would probably permeate Sanctuary in a matter of minutes. He was courting the forbidden niece of Nat Thompson, obviously with Thompson's approval.

Kane snapped the reins again, pushing the horses into a faster pace toward the creekbed and trees and whatever limited privacy there was in Sanctuary.

Sanctuary? He thought he'd been in hell in the Yank prison camp. That place had been a nursery next to this one.

"Kane?"

His name was said softly, and he was suddenly very aware it was the first time she'd used it. It was also the first time he hadn't hated it. Kane sounded somehow soft in her voice, on her lips. Not harsh. Not murderous.

He turned and looked at her. Her face was visible in the light of an almost full moon. Her features appeared luminous, and altogether too appealing.

"I'm sorry my uncle . . . forced you . . ."

"He didn't force me to do anything," he said shortly. "I only hesitated because I'm so wrong for you. I don't have a future, Nicky. You deserve better."

There was a long silence. He didn't know whether she accepted his explanation or not. But they rode in silence along the ruts that apparently served as the road for supplies. He chucked the horses several times, just to pretend a concentration on driving that he didn't feel. He was too aware of her presence. God, how he wanted her in his arms.

There was a slight pull on his arm, and he looked toward her. She pointed to a stand of trees along the creek, and he made for it, though the buggy bumped and groaned. When he reached it, he stopped the horses. She jumped down without his help, and he had no choice but to follow. Then he cursed himself for a liar. He did have a choice. He could stay in the seat and be safe. Safe from her, safe from what he knew was coming.

He stepped down.

He looked at the pale silver of the moon, at the stars sprinkled like dust across the sky, and then his gaze turned to Nicky. She stood shadowed by the trees, a lonely, lovely figure. He didn't move, thinking of the first time he'd seen her and the moments after she'd shot Yancy. She'd been so defensive, so full of prickles and fight. It had all been a sham, just like so much of him was a sham. They were both lost, she through no fault of her own, and he through self-inflicted mistakes. But he saw his own loneliness reflected in her, a loneliness he'd denied for years and that now shouted out for acknowledgment.

Kane moved toward her, propelled by a need so strong it denied anything else. He held out his hand. She took the several steps to him, and her fingers curled around his. She moved even closer until they were only inches apart.

He leaned down and rested his cheek on her hair. It was newly washed and smelled fresh and sweet. For a moment, his loneliness eased.

Neither of them spoke. She was unlike most women that way, he'd noticed. She was content with silence, satisfied just to be with him. He swallowed hard, knowing this was a rare peek at heaven.

He felt her every breath, her every heartbeat. Her body melded into his as if it were made to fit there. Her fingers intertwined with his, locking them gently but firmly to her. And then she moved slightly to face him, her expression full of both wonder and question.

"I never knew," she said softly, "that I could feel so . . . like this."

She obviously couldn't find the words, and neither could he. Maybe it was something like belonging. He wasn't sure because he'd never belonged to anyone or anything. But he knew it was something extraordinary, this flow between them, these currents of wonder and contentment and anticipation, and . . .

He never finished the thought. She was reaching on tiptoe, and her mouth was an inch away. Her lips met his, and his world seemed to explode, and all caution exploded with it. His mind couldn't absorb anything but sensation.

Chapter Eleven

The kiss was beyond all of Nicky's expectations. It was beyond anything she'd ever even imagined, and she savored every taste, feeling, and touch. She wanted to hold it to her heart forever.

Kane's hands touched her with infinite care, with a restrained tenderness that made her soul bleed. She knew then that he hadn't lied when he said he wanted her, hadn't taken her buggy-riding because of her uncle. He cared in the same special way that she cared.

The kiss said so, and she never wanted to let it go.

The kiss was enough for a few moments, and then a new wanting started gnawing at her. She knew he felt it, too, because his kiss deepened and his tongue sought out hers. She knew now what to do, and her response was as fevered as his. Her body moved closer, so close she felt his heart beat against hers. His hand moved to the back of her neck, one of his fingers stroking the tender, sensitive skin there with increasingly powerful effect. She felt his body change beneath the confining trousers and heard the quickening urgency of his breath. Her body ached to move into his, to explore the sweet craving that was so irresistible.

I want you. She kept remembering those words, and the intensity with which he'd said them. They echoed in her mind, her heart. They wouldn't go away. *I want you.*

Soul-wrenching words jerked unwillingly from him. And now she knew why. She knew the full meaning of the word *want*.

She felt his hunger and she wondered at her own. How could she lust so after something she'd never had? Her hands went up around his neck, entwining her fingers in the dark thick hair. His mouth released hers then, and he just held her as if she were the most precious thing on earth.

It felt wonderful to be precious to someone. To be wanted. To be loved.

She would have died for him in that moment. She'd never understood her mother so well. She moved her right hand from his neck and traced the angles of his face, her finger resting on the scar. A tremor ran through his body, and she felt that, too, as if she were part of him. Her finger moved down to his mouth, to the side twisted slightly. He stiffened against her, but the want was still there. She felt that want. She felt it grow, just as that odd intolerable craving was expanding inside her.

She wanted to say love words, endearments. But she was afraid. She felt his hesitancy even though she didn't understand it. He had gone to Rosita's, hadn't he? All the men did. Why then did he hesitate to do with her whatever men did? He virtually had her uncle's permission, maybe not for this, but to be with her. And he wasn't afraid of her uncle. She knew that.

Something, though, was stopping him. Did he possibly think she was unwilling?

"I want you, too," she blurted out suddenly, and only then did he look back down at her. The moon was bright, but not bright enough to show her his thoughts. It was never that bright. Even the sun wasn't that bright. His gray eyes were dark and unfathomable. But she heard a harsh moan. It came from deep inside his throat like an animal in pain.

His mouth went down to her neck, and he kissed her throat. Then she knew why he'd moaned. She heard herself whimper with the need fomenting inside.

"Nicole," he whispered, and the sound of her name on

his lips was like a song sung low. Nicole, not Nicky. The name of a woman. She felt every inch that woman.

His head lifted from where it had been nuzzling her throat, and his eyes met hers as his hands moved to her dress. There was a question in them now. A question and something else: fire. There was no other way to describe the glowing glitter in them. She swallowed hard. They had started a blaze together, and even in her inexperience she knew it would be hard to quench.

She didn't want to quench it. She knew that when their eyes dueled. He was almost daring her to back away, and a part of her wanted to. The part that was afraid. She felt the fear running almost as hot as her blood. She wasn't afraid *of* him as much as she was afraid of caring *for* him. But she might as well try to stop breathing. He had already worked his way into her very being.

So much seemed clear at that moment. She hadn't known whether she believed in the kind of love she had read about in books. She had wanted to believe. It had always sounded so marvelous for two souls to join, even easy. But her only experience with man-woman love had been tragedy. Her mother always waiting. The tears. Finally the terrible, wrenching pain of childbirth in a cold cave. And then her father's pain. How could anything be worth that?

Now she knew. She knew as Kane held her. She knew as he kissed her. She knew as he unbuttoned her dress and his finger caressed her skin. She knew as he picked her up and carried her to a protected place under the trees, as he knelt beside her, as his arms moved up and down hers, ever so gently over the recent burns. She knew as he finished undressing her, hesitating at every step, waiting for a protest that couldn't make its way from her lips. She knew as her own hands unbuttoned his shirt, and she touched the dark hair on his chest, ran her fingers over the muscles and bone.

And she knew when his body bent to hers, when his reluctance was still so strong that she became the seducer.

Kane had always longed for something of his own. Now he was being given that gift, and it was too strong a need to deny. He knew Nicky was a virgin. She couldn't be anything else and respond to his kisses with such amazed wonder. It was all the more reason to pull away, to run like hell, but he couldn't. God help him, he couldn't.

He needed her as much as she needed him. He needed that innocence and wonder as much as he'd needed anything in his life. He needed *her* like he'd never needed anything. Life had always been little more than a bad joke until now. He'd stumbled from one mistake to another. Even now he feared he was about to make the worst one in his life. Yet he couldn't stop himself.

Nicole's fingers crawled up his chest. Nothing in his past, no experience with women, had prepared him for this: the sweet explosion, the overwhelming hunger, the excruciating desire that hardened his body. His mouth found hers, pressed hard, his tongue urging her lips to open to him. They so readily, so eagerly, did. Her smallest touch was like a torch to him, her slightest movements firing new blazes until the ache inside him was unbearable.

He touched her breasts, then moved his mouth down to them, caressing, tasting, nibbling until they hardened and she cried out—a purr of anticipation as her body writhed with reaction to his slightest touch. His hands moved down, drawing the rest of her dress from her. She was wearing drawers and a camisole and nothing more. He thought of all she hadn't had these years—all the womanly gewgaws that seemed to mean so much to other women. He wanted to give them all to her. He wanted to put them on, and take them off, slowly. He took a deep shuddering breath. It wasn't too late to stop.

But then her hands went around his neck and drew him down to her, and he couldn't stop. He was still wearing his trousers and he felt the hard throbbing demand against the cloth, seeking freedom. His hands went down, quickly unbuttoning, and his sex sprang free against her. She stilled for a moment, and he could no longer feel her breath against the skin of his chest.

Stop. He heard that voice inside but he couldn't obey,

particularly when he again felt her soft, sweet breath, and her body started reacting to his, straining and trembling and reaching. He started kissing her everywhere, his lips savoring every part of her—eyes, nose, cheeks, the curve of her neck. He felt her pulse, the quickening of it as her hands faltered where they'd been touching the back of his neck. Her entire body was trembling with feeling, with its reaction to him. He'd never known this kind of passion—a fierce tenderness that assaulted every barrier he'd ever erected inside himself. He'd never loved a woman like this, and he'd never known the rewards, the incredible sweetness of it, the exquisite longing that was more than hunger. For the first time, he felt a need to give more than to take.

But he *wasn't* giving. He was taking a part of her forever. He was making promises he couldn't keep.

With a groan of pure anguish, Kane pulled himself away and lay beside her, closing his eyes and trying to steady his breathing.

He felt Nicky's hand on him, on his chest. Seeking. Questioning. Her body moved next to his, cuddling as close as she could, placing her head on his shoulder. "What's wrong?" she finally whispered, and his soul cried at the wretchedness and confusion in her voice.

He lay there for a moment, saying nothing, hoping the breeze would cool the heat in his body, the fever in his head. He'd never wanted anything so much in his life, and he'd wanted a lot. He was experienced in not getting what he wanted, but this time the pain ate into his gut as it never had before.

There weren't many more days now, not for him. But she had so many. He couldn't bear to leave her the legacy of the worst kind of betrayal. What in the hell had he been thinking?

He hadn't. He had only been feeling. He felt now. He felt her body next to his. Ready. Wanting. Like his. His manhood throbbed with need. So easy to roll over and take her. He'd never allowed himself to think of hell, but it couldn't be worse than this. Except perhaps knowing for the rest of his days, however few they might be, that he had destroyed her.

"Kane?" Nicky's voice, soft and questioning, quivered slightly.

He swallowed hard. "You're a virgin, aren't you?" he finally asked, already knowing the answer. No one could fake the wonder, the awakening of her body.

"Does it matter?" she said, and he knew she was prepared to lie. She was so inexperienced that she wasn't aware he would know the difference, that he already did.

"Your uncle said a buggy ride," Kane said harshly. "I don't think he meant for me to . . . ruin you."

"I don't think I would be ruined," she said in a small tentative voice.

"A man wants a virgin for a wife," he said cruelly, "not damaged goods."

There was a long silence. She'd flinched at the words. He felt her body stiffen for the tiniest moment. He was making it very clear he didn't want her as a wife.

"It doesn't matter," she said after a long, agonizing moment, but the indifference she tried to feign sounded hollow. "No one would want the niece of Nat Thompson, anyway."

Anyone would want her. Anyone with any sense. But she believed what she was saying. Her acceptance of what she believed was truth, her bravado, touched him deeply.

He rolled over so he could face her. "I want you, Nicky. I want you worse than any damn thing in my life. But you're worth more than me. You deserve a hell of a lot better."

"No," she said. That simple, fervent denial was like an arrow in his heart.

"I'm not going to risk your uncle's anger," he said, trying another tack. "I've heard what happens."

"You aren't afraid of him," she said. "That's why he likes you."

"I want him to keep on liking me." Kane tried to keep his voice impassive, even indifferent.

"Then why did you bring me here?"

"Because he suggested it, but I don't figure he had this

in mind," he said, hating that cruelty he was forcing into his voice again. "A buggy ride, that's all." He rolled away from her, grabbing his trousers that had slipped down to his ankles. He pulled them up, turning so she couldn't see his arousal, his difficulty in covering it.

He couldn't see her face. He didn't want to see her face. He couldn't bear to see it, nor that long-limbed slender body that still sent quakes through him. He'd never prayed before, not even when he thought he would hang. But he prayed now. He prayed for the strength to keep from touching her. She couldn't be allowed to see how hard this was for him.

Most of all, she couldn't know that he was falling in love with her.

Kane walked to the shadows of some trees and waited. He waited for some sound to indicate she was dressing. He waited in an agony of self-disgust over what he had almost done. What he still wanted to do. Like his namesake, he seemed destined to destroy those closest to him: his mother, Davy, and now Nicky.

How many days did he have left? How many to save Davy? How many before he had to destroy Sanctuary and everyone in it?

Christ! He hit the bark of the tree with his fist. The jarring force stretched the burned places on his back, but he welcomed the pain.

"Kane?" Her voice again. Tentative.

He swung around, expecting to see her dressed. She was, but only in his shirt. It hung way below her hips, and expanded seductively across her breasts. Long, shapely legs seemed to tremble slightly as she rose to stand. Her hair was tousled, a few pine needles clinging to the curls that framed her face. She was the most enchanting sight he'd ever seen.

"Get dressed," he said in a strangled voice.

"Not until you tell me what's . . . wrong," she said. "If you're so damn worried about my uncle, he won't care much for you leaving me out here." There was anger in her voice now, as well as a plea.

"I can carry you back."

"Like this?"

"I can dress you."

"I'll just take it back off."

Despite his frustration, his lips cracked slightly. She would, too. He could always tear a piece of cloth from his shirt and tie her, but he imagined she would be a wildcat on the way home. He supposed that was one of the things that he liked about her. She didn't give an inch. She hadn't the first time they met, or when she was defending her brother against Yancy. Just like tonight. She simply didn't know how to do anything halfway.

The mere thought made his blood run hot again. She would be as passionate in lovemaking as she had been in defending her brother. And then he felt that splash of ice-cold water again. He was worse than Yancy. At least Yancy had been honest about what he wanted.

"I told you," he said finally. "I'm no good for you. I can't offer you a damn thing. Not a future. Not a day beyond tonight."

"I didn't ask you to offer anything."

"Your uncle would," he said wryly. "He's not a man who would take . . . this lightly."

"My uncle has nothing to do with this."

"He has everything to do with it. He loves you, Nicky."

"He wants you to stay. He would approve."

"And you? Do you want to stay here forever?"

She was silent for a moment, and he knew then she had also thought of escape.

"If you were here," she said, "I would."

He felt humbled again. He remembered her that first day on the hill, how she had gazed toward the mountains. There had been longing in that look.

"The law's going to find this place one of these days," he said flatly.

"Uncle Nat doesn't think so. If they do come, we can get away," she countered. She hesitated. "There's a way out only a few know about."

Kane's heart stopped. "Where?"

"I'll show you one day," she said. "But no one could

find us. We could go to somewhere far north. Maybe even Canada. Uncle Nat's talked about that . . . and California."

"I travel light," he said curtly.

"I can, too."

"What about Robin?"

She paused then, bowed her head. "I can't leave Robin."

"No," he said softly. *And I can't leave Davy.*

"He can go with us." Hope enriched her voice.

"And be an outlaw? On the run?" He heard the weariness in his own voice. He saw her head droop slightly.

"You're not going to take Uncle Nat's offer, are you?"

He couldn't answer her truthfully. If he turned down the offer, Nat Thompson would wonder why. He had to lead Thompson on and the only way to do that was to lead Nicky on. His stomach turned at the thought.

"I have some obligations to take care of," he said.

"A . . . woman?"

"Yes," he replied and watched her face crumple. He couldn't do it. He just couldn't. "The wife of a man who rode with me. I told him I would make sure she was taken care of."

"He's dead?"

Kane didn't answer for a moment. "He's in prison," he said gruffly. Christ, why did he say that?

"I'm sorry," she said. "He must . . . mean a lot to you."

"He's like a brother," Kane said. "His family took me in when my father died."

"When was that?" she asked softly.

He shrugged, not wanting to even think back to those days.

"That must have been terrible," she said. "I remember when my father died."

He stared down at her. "It was the best day of my life," he said emotionlessly.

Nicky's eyes opened wide with questions.

Kane shrugged again. "He hated me from the day I was born, because my ma died, just like Robin's. He meant to name me after the Cain in the Bible, but he couldn't read or write, and the preacher who prayed over my mother wrote it wrong in the Bible. He told someone

later he didn't think it right that a boy be named Cain."
He shrugged. "Diablo's not all that far from Cain, is it?
So maybe my father was right all those years ago."

She moved against his chest. He felt her through the
cloth of his shirt. Her light scent mingled with his. "He
wasn't right," she whispered, lifting her mouth to his. Her
eyes were full of empathy. Understanding. Love. He'd
been able to deny it minutes earlier, but now . . .

His lips crushed down on hers, trying to prove she was
wrong. He *was* the devil. He was *her* devil. Goddammit,
he was his own devil.

The kiss was punishing, rough, desperate. But she
didn't move. She only seemed to absorb that anger, to take
it on herself. He tore his mouth from hers. "Run," he
rasped out. "Run like hell."

She shook her head. "I can't."

"Then we're both damned," he said and crushed her
to him, no longer able to deny his need for her. The fires
were out of control.

Nicky knew the moment he surrendered. She knew
how he felt. She felt the same hopelessness of inevitably,
irresistibly, sliding into a sea of disaster and pain. Despite
her earlier brave words about not caring about the future,
a small child's voice inside warned her; how could she
pass on the fear and grief and loneliness she'd felt most
of her life? One time, she assured herself. One time to
explore these feelings, to know what it was to be a
woman. Just one time.

And when his hands touched the back of her neck and
his lips caressed the throbbing pulse in her neck, she was
as helpless as he to stop. If she were damned, then so be
it.

His hands were gentle as he lowered her to the ground
again, as fingers eased her shirt back, and his hands slid
along her body with a possessiveness that thrilled her. Anticipation throbbed deep inside her, and his gentleness
turned to urgency as his hands touched her woman place.

Her body arched up at the unfamiliar touch, at the
unexpected sensations his fingers aroused. She felt a wetness, then waves of exquisite desire. Her hand went to his

chest, touching the hair with fascination. Her fingers seemed to be drawn downward to where his trousers were bulging. They undid the buttons, even as her body was writhing with his increasingly intimate touches.

"Nicole," he groaned as she touched the man part with wonder.

So large. So smooth. So mysterious. As she felt his hand doing exotic things to her, she caressed him, wondering whether their feelings were the same, whether he felt this . . . building of pleasure, the promise of something so splendid she heard her own spontaneous sounds.

He moved, his hands leaving her private place and his body hovering over her. The tension in his body seem to vibrate in the air as his man part touched her, teased until she whimpered with a need she didn't entirely understand.

And then there was pain, sharp, excruciating pain, but it didn't stop the want, the overwhelming need in her. The pain faded, as did the strangeness of his body becoming part of hers. Her body started responding, reacting on its own, singing its own song as if it had been made specifically for him.

As waves upon waves of new sensations washed over her, she was amazed at the instinctive knowledge of her body, the pure beauty of their mating. He penetrated deeper and deeper into her, and her body started moving with his. He was reaching so far inside, becoming so much a part of her, she imagined their souls touching.

And then she couldn't think at all. She was soaring like a hawk toward the sky, reaching for the sun. And then the explosion came, the splendid explosion that erupted inside her, sending sensation after sensation roaring through her like great fireballs. She went still, in awe of her body, in awe of him.

Kane rolled her on top of him, his hands going around her protectively. "Did I hurt you?" he asked in an anguished whisper. She answered with a kiss, one that handed her heart over to him.

He was silent for a long time, just holding her, her heart against his heart. And then he eased her over and rose slowly. She was still wearing his shirt, but he was naked, the two of them having pulled off his trousers. She slowly got to her feet, aware of his gaze on her.

"You are so lovely," he said. "I'll always remember you like this."

She took his hand and nibbled on it. He sounded as if it were good-bye. It couldn't be good-bye. She wouldn't allow it to be good-bye. She wouldn't let him say the words, because then they wouldn't be real.

"Nicole—"

"No," she said. "I don't want to talk now. I just want to feel."

He was silent again, but she felt the tension in him again. She didn't know why it was so strong. She knew he wasn't afraid of her uncle, no matter what he said. She knew he didn't feel he had much of a future, but she didn't care.

That was a lie. She did care. Desperately. The very possibility of losing him was agonizing. *We're both dammed*: his words just minutes ago. Why? He wished she understood some of his secrets. She wished he would share some of his demons with her, that she could share hers with him.

She tried to shake away her sudden apprehension, push away her own doubts. She knew she loved him. She also knew he cared about her. But did he love her? Enough to stay at Sanctuary? He was in grave danger anywhere else. And if he did stay, what would happen to any children they might have? To Robin?

Nicky leaned her body against him, her head against his chest so he wouldn't see a tear she felt sneaking from her eyes. Her fingers wandered across his chest, entwining themselves in the dark hair that angled down toward his stomach. Feeling him tremble under her touch, she turned her head up and looked at him, hoping the tear had disappeared against his skin. "I love you," she said simply.

Pure anguish ripped across his face. She couldn't see his eyes in the shadows, but she felt his pulse move in his neck. Her fingers went up and touched his eyes, and she felt a wetness there.

And she knew. She knew he loved her, too, even if he wouldn't admit it. She moved slightly so her lips could touch his, and she tried to tell him what was in her heart. But the anguish didn't leave his eyes, nor did the tension leave his body.

That anguish seeped into her, building on her own apprehension, her own fears. The silence was suddenly heartrending. And ominous.

Kane didn't say anything, though. He held her for a moment, then gently disengaged her. He helped her dress, then assisted her into the buggy. He didn't touch her on the way back to Sanctuary, but her hand moved to his leg, and he didn't try to remove it.

When they reached the stable, Andy was waiting there, his face carefully composed. "Hear you might be staying," he said as he took the reins as Kane helped Nicky down. She held her breath.

"I might," Kane said, and Nicky's heart swelled with a bittersweet mixture of hope and anxiety. It was the first indication he'd given that he was considering Uncle Nat's offer. What then of Robin?

She wished she could wipe away that nagging worry as Kane took her hand and led her to the porch of her house. He leaned down and kissed her lips. Lightly.

Then he straightened. She couldn't read his eyes in the dark of the evening. She couldn't read his heart, either. She suddenly felt cold. She wanted assurances. She needed them. But his mouth was set in a grim line. She could see that, and she wished she hadn't.

"Kane?"

His hand touched her cheek. Briefly. "Thank you," he said simply, then turned and strode away.

Chapter Twelve

Ben Masters looked forward, now, to his visits to the Blazing Star. More specifically, he looked forward to seeing Mary May Hamilton. He told himself she was a good contact. She must know everything that transpired in the saloon, and he was reasonably sure the saloon was where Kane O'Brien had made contact with Sanctuary.

He had avoided asking many questions, particularly any pertaining to Sanctuary. Questions raised suspicions. He'd hoped that simply keeping his ears open would accomplish the same result. It hadn't. No one spoke of Sanctuary. But Mary May's interest in him gave him an excuse for questions. He'd made them impersonal, at first. During the next weeks, they had become increasingly more personal.

Ben had never been a lady's man. His father had been a lawyer in Chicago and had wanted him to be a lawyer. Because Ben had sought his father's approval, he'd studied law and joined the family practice. He'd never had time to court, and it wasn't until he was nearly thirty that he'd taken the time to fall in love. Clara Schaffer had been beautiful, deceptively so, and Ben had fallen miserably in love. He became engaged a few days before the war started. At the urging of Clara but against his father's wishes, he enlisted. Most of all, though, he joined because of principle. He detested slavery and held those who owned slaves, and those who fought for slavery, in contempt.

In the three years that followed, he developed a new respect for his opponents' courage. The day Kane O'Brien had saved him, he realized his lifelong belief in black and white, good and evil, didn't work in the real world.

His wounds had been severe. He'd returned to Chicago to recuperate; he'd been on crutches then, and the doctors didn't know how, or if, his leg would heal. He drank too much to forget the pain, the death, the blood, and he'd had terrible nightmares and an even worse temper. Clara finally eloped with a banker who'd safely spent the war in Chicago. Two months later, his father died of a heart attack, and his leg had healed enough for him to return to duty.

After the war, there was no reason to return to Chicago. Nor did Ben wish to return to the practice of law. And he owed a debt, a powerful debt that wouldn't let him go. So he set out to find Kane O'Brien, and became a marshal along the way. It was a wandering life, free and uncomplicated, and it gave him room to pursue his search.

He wanted no ties, not after Clara. Mary May Hamilton was just a diversion, one he found himself bedding by the end of their first week of acquaintance. He never forgot, though, the reason he was in Gooden, Texas.

As each day went by, Ben's concern grew, both for O'Brien's safety and for his reliability. He could be in Canada now, living on the U.S. government's money. Still, Ben's gut feeling kept telling him he'd been right about O'Brien.

Ben had spent the morning in his hotel room, watching below, watching for a man with a scar on his face and for a man in a bright calico shirt. He'd heard the name Calico whispered in the same breath as Sanctuary once, and several days later he'd mentioned to Mary May that a friend had asked him to look up a man named Calico.

Mary May had looked at him curiously. "I know a man named Calico," she said. "Wears a colorful calico shirt. No one knows any other name."

"He been around?"

"Not lately," she'd said, her green eyes growing cautious.

Ben hadn't missed that sudden alertness that passed across her face. Apprehension had struck him then, a curious foreboding he didn't like. He'd dropped the subject.

Now, as he watched below, he wondered about that again. Did Mary May have anything to do with Sanctuary? He didn't like the notion, but he knew he would have to find out.

His leg ached. It usually did when the weather changed or when he abused it, staying on it too long. He sat down and rubbed it, reminded again of that day O'Brien had stopped long enough to apply a tourniquet. *Where are you, O'Brien?*

And what in the hell does Mary May know about Sanctuary?

Both questions haunted him.

Christ, he was driving himself crazy in this room. He pulled on his boots, buckled on his gunbelt and left for the Blazing Star.

MARY May watched Ben Smith enter the saloon. He was limping more than usual. She felt her blood quicken and grow thick and warm. There was even a feeling of giddiness that she'd never felt before, not even with her husband. She was terribly afraid she was falling in love with the man named Smith.

Nothing, she knew, could be worse. The more time she spent with the tall, quiet man, the more she realized he was much more than a saddle tramp. He was waiting for something. And it scared the hell out of her. She couldn't forget seeing him talking secretively with the scarred man in the alley, nor could she forget his interest when someone once mentioned Sanctuary. Now Calico.

She was slowly coming to the realization that he must be a lawman, after all. She could make one hell of a lot of money by passing the word on to Calico, probably enough to insure Sarah Ann's future.

And Ben Smith would end up dead behind the saloon.

She watched as he went toward his usual seat, backing up to the wall. He remained standing, a slight smile on his face. His eyes warmed as she neared, and she wondered how she'd ever thought them cold.

The bartender was already on his way with the "usual": Ben's glass of bourbon, her watered-down one. She slipped into a chair opposite Ben.

"You're late today," she said.

"I'm that predictable?"

She grinned. "Maybe I just missed you."

Her smile slipped when she saw that he was more tense than usual.

"How long will you be staying?" she asked. It was the first question she'd asked him, the first meaningful one.

"I'm not sure," he said. "Until I get restless again."

"You get restless often?"

He shrugged. "Often enough."

"What about tonight?"

He hesitated.

"Dinner? In my room?"

His slate-blue eyes studied her for a moment. "Sounds good."

"After the Blazing Star closes."

He nodded.

Mary May reached out a hand to him. "Want some advice?"

He looked at her quizzically.

"Don't ask questions," she said, softly enough that no one else could hear.

He waited, without saying anything.

"Especially about Sanctuary."

His hand tightened around hers. "What do you know about Sanctuary?"

"Why do you want to know?"

"I have a friend there."

"Like Calico?" There was disbelief in her voice this time.

"No," he said. "Not like Calico."

"Someone you're after or care about?"

"Why do you ask?"

They were dueling now, their voices low.

"Because it's dangerous to ask questions about that place. I don't want you to get hurt."

He grinned suddenly. "I take good care of myself." He tossed down the rest of the drink. "I think I'll save the other one for tonight."

She watched him stand. He obviously didn't want any more questions. She didn't think she did either. She'd warned him; that was all she could do. And keep her mouth shut when Calico appeared again.

NICKY studied herself in the mirror, trying to identify certain changes. It had been two days since she had made love. Since she and Kane had made love. She felt years older in some ways; younger in others.

She kept dismissing his rather abrupt departure that night, choosing, instead, to remember his gentleness and those splendid, remarkable feelings and sensations he'd awakened in her.

Nicky had seen him several times since, twice in meetings with her uncle. And he was coming again this afternoon. Her uncle felt confident that Kane O'Brien—Diablo—would accept his offer.

So she studied herself in the mirror with great care. She wished her hair were long and feminine, that she had more than the one dress. The next time her uncle sent out an order, she'd ask for some dresses.

And if Kane did decide to stay? What then? How could she persuade Robin to leave alone? How could she allow him to stay? And her uncle? He needed a doctor. Maybe they could all go to Canada or Mexico. Some place where Kane wasn't wanted. They could start a ranch or a farm, or . . . anything. Hope bubbled up inside her.

She looked in her pile of books and found one of her old favorites. Sir Walter Scott. She had dreamed dreams of his heroes, but she'd never thought to have one, and finally she'd set the book aside. But now she believed in dreams again. She leafed through the pages to her favorite poem, "Lochinvar."

Oh! young Lochinvar is come out of the west
Through all the wide Border his steed was the best . . .

And then:

So faithful in love and so dauntless in war,
There never was knight like the young Lochinvar

Her gaze fell to the ending:

With a smile on her lips and a tear in her eye . . .

Kane O'Brien might be a rather tarnished knight, but he had become *her* knight.

TIME was running out!

Kane ran a comb through his hair and regarded himself in the mirror with disgust. For the past two days, he'd played with the idea of staying. Nicky's heart, his own heart, against Davy's life.

But there really was no choice. There had never been one. He had made a promise, given his word, and he would keep it. But he had frantically been searching for a way out of this mess that wouldn't destroy Nicky. After two days of hell, he'd come up with one. It wasn't a great plan, but it was the best he could do. As for himself, he didn't deserve any consideration. He deserved the hangman's noose and to roast in hell for what he'd done to Nicky. He'd just needed her so badly, had needed the warmth and belonging. He'd needed to love and be loved. Just once in his life.

He'd wished Nat Thompson had exacted his usual punishment on those who trifled with his family. But he hadn't. The lights had been off when he'd returned Nicky, and the next day Thompson had talked to him again about Sanctuary. It was then that Kane started grabbing for a lifeline.

It came when Thompson doubled over and grabbed his desk. His teeth clenched tightly together, and Kane had no doubt that the man was seriously ill. His face was pale, bathed in sweat, and Kane remembered another time when Thompson had suffered a similar attack.

"Can I do anything?" he asked.

Thompson nodded. "Glass of water," he replied as he fumbled in his desk for something.

Everything started coming clear to Kane then: the offer, the urgency of it. Thompson was sick, the kind of sick that was fatal, and he needed someone to look after both Sanctuary and his family. Kane wondered whether Nicky had any idea.

The more he thought about that conclusion, the more it made sense. Mitch Evers was growing old, and none of the other permanent residents seemed capable of controlling Sanctuary. Kane's offer to take responsibility for Yancy's death, as spontaneous as it was, had evidently convinced the outlaw leader that he had the stomach for the job.

Which meant Sanctuary would shortly be a thing of the past.

If only he could keep Masters at bay long enough. Perhaps he could plead for another three months. He could be in control of Sanctuary then and close it down himself. He realized that wouldn't be easy. The lair was altogether too important to those who used it, which was probably why Thompson hadn't moved in that direction himself. Any sign of weakness on his part, and the others would turn on him like a pack of wolves.

Time was what he needed. Time to get Nicky and Robin out of here before the whole thing blew to hell.

He had to get to Masters, somehow convince him. It wouldn't be easy. Masters was as hard-nosed as they came, and he obviously hadn't had the slightest reservation about sending Kane to what could be a very painful death. Damn, but he hated being under the marshal's thumb, detested the thought of begging him for more time. But at this moment, he would get down on his hands and knees and grovel if he had to.

So many lives were teetering on the precipice. Davy. Nicky. Robin. Even Thompson, whom he was learning to respect if not particularly like. And Masters held the rope that could save them all. The question was, would he?

First, though, he had to find a way to leave Sanctuary. He had to accept Thompson's offer, but convince him he had some personal business to handle first. Perhaps Thompson would give him the directions in and out of Sanctuary. But Kane doubted it. The man was too careful. He wouldn't reveal the secrets of Sanctuary until he was absolutely sure of Diablo.

How much time did he have left? Less than a month before Sanctuary was taken, if Davy was to live. Kane had little more information on Sanctuary's location than he did on that first day. He knew it was in Indian Territory and probably the Wichita Mountains, but posses could comb that area for months and never find anything.

And Nicky. He tried not to think about that. He'd committed some stupid acts in his life, but none as reckless and damaging as taking her virginity and, he feared, her heart. He deserved any damn thing the U.S. government wanted to do to him. But Davy didn't. Nicky didn't. Young Robin didn't.

Christ, he felt sick. He was sick of himself. He would walk from here and lie to Thompson, just as he had lied to Nicky and Robin. He would lie and lie and lie to save a friend he'd led to the gallows. He would betray a girl who'd laid her heart in his hands, and a boy who had handed him trust. Disgust at himself and pure hatred toward Masters made him want to retch.

He would see Nicky again today when he went to Thompson's. She would look at him with those soft deer eyes as if he were God instead of the snake he was. He had to convince Thompson to let him go, and he had to convince Masters to give him more time.

Kane O'Brien wasn't at all sure he could do either.

•   •   •

JOHN Yancy had been to several towns, looking for the scouts who directed clients to Sanctuary. The towns were small, lawless crossroads in Texas where questions could be asked easier than in towns with strict law-and-order sheriffs. The last place he stopped was Gooden, Texas.

He and his brother had been there before. It was where they had negotiated their last stay at Sanctuary through a man named Calico. There was also a woman who Yancy suspected was connected with Sanctuary in some way. He remembered that woman. Both he and Cobb had tried to take her to bed, but she'd turned them down flat. Like they were nothing.

Perhaps he could get some information from her, find out when Calico was returning to Gooden. Then he could follow the man to Sanctuary. Once he knew the location, he could find others to help him wrest the hideout from Thompson. He and Cobb had already talked to Hildebrand about the possibility.

Gooden was just as he remembered. Dusty, dirty, and small except for the number of saloons. He was running out of money, so he took a room in the cheapest hotel, spruced up a bit, and made for the Blazing Star.

With any luck, Calico would be there. Or the woman might be persuaded to talk, one way or another.

Gooden didn't have any law, not even a sheriff. The last one had been killed, and no one had wanted to take his place, not for the few dollars a month the town offered. Yancy felt safe enough here.

The saloon was full, the gambling tables were crowded and so was the bar. He looked for a bright calico shirt but didn't find it, then his gaze went to the women. They were all pretty at the Blazing Star. The owner, Dan Calhoun, took pride in that. He also took pride in protecting them, so Yancy knew he had to be careful.

He saw four, all dressed in low-cut blouses and skirts that barely reached the calves of their black-silk-covered legs. He saw the woman he sought immediately. She stood out from the others, not only by the number of men that surrounded her, but by the dark red hair that fell in curls down her bare back. She was some woman, all right, though too damn haughty for her own good. He and Cobb had talked about taking her down a peg.

The thought of Cobb stirred the hot anger inside him. Hot anger and thoughts of revenge. She would pay for rejecting them, *after* she told Yancy what he wanted to know. Perhaps even tonight. He grew hard thinking about it.

He moved over to the faro table where she stood. Her green eyes saw him, and she nodded, but it was only a small nod and had little welcome. "A drink?" he offered.

"Sorry," she said. "I promised these gentlemen I would bring them luck."

"Yeah," one said. "Can't take her now. Got a hundred dollars riding on this."

Yancy tried a smile. He saw her eyes turn cool, and he knew he hadn't succeeded. "Maybe later," he said.

"Maybe," she allowed.

He spent the rest of the evening watching her, hearing her laugh. Her eyes kept wandering to the door, and Yancy wondered why.

It was hours and several drinks later before he finally got a minute with her. She was walking past, and he grabbed her arm.

She pulled away, but stopped. "Sorry," she said, "but I'm off now."

"Just a minute," he said. "I'm looking for Calico."

Her eyes changed slightly. "So are a lot of people," she said noncommittally.

"I'll make it worth your while."

"I never know when Calico comes," she said.

"I want to get to Sanctuary."

"I don't know what you're talking about," she said, turning away and looking toward the door. A tall, lean figure was entering. The newcomer hesitated at the door, his gaze moving around the room before stopping when it found the woman. Yancy could feel heat vibrating between them, and the anger grew in him. The stranger was just another trail bum from the looks of him, yet the woman had eyes for no one else once he entered the room.

Damn it, John swore silently, she was with *him,* John Yancy.

"Excuse me," she said politely, and without waiting for an answer moved over to the newcomer and gave him a radiant smile. Yancy studied the stranger again, readjusting his first impression. There was a quality of danger about the man, an assuredness of movement that marked him as a man who knew how to take care of himself. Also there was something familiar about him that nagged.

Yancy went to the bar. "Who's that cowpoke?"

"Smith," the bartender said. "Ben Smith."

"Been here long?"

The barkeep stared at him, hostility gleaming in his eyes. "Folks around here mind their own business. Mr. Smith does. You best do the same."

Yancy shrugged, though he took offense. Deep offense. He wasn't used being talked to that way. "You know who I am?"

"Don't know, don't care," the barkeep said. "You want a drink or not?"

Yancy felt like going for his gun. But the bar was full, and this was a popular place. There may not be a sheriff, but most of these towns had a lynch law of their own. "Just asking," he said soothingly. "I'll take a bottle."

The barkeep handed him a not very clean glass and a bottle already opened. Watered, Yancy guessed. Not like Sanctuary, where the whiskey was good. Where his brother had been killed. Where he had been run out like a common beggar. They would pay. They would all pay, including this insolent barkeep.

He took the bottle and found a table, keeping his eyes on the man named Smith and the woman. They talked for a few moments, then left together out the back. He wanted to go after them, kill them both, but first things first. He would bide his time for a few days, wait for Calico. Calico was a surer thing than the woman. If the guide didn't show in the next week, Yancy decided, then he would go after the woman.

He filled his glass and gulped it down, then another. *I'll get them for you, Cobb. I swear.*

Chapter Thirteen

"So you've decided to accept my offer?" Nat Thompson leaned back in his chair and puffed on a thin cigar.

"I need at least two weeks first," Kane said. "I have a promise to keep."

"That's what I like about you," Thompson said. "You're reliable."

Kane shrugged the comment aside. "I don't make many promises. I try to keep the few I do."

"And I have your promise you'll return."

"You have my promise I'll try. My picture's still on a number of posters."

"I can help you with that," Thompson said.

"How?"

"Our barber used to work for a theatrical company before he fell in love with the leading lady and killed her husband," Thompson said with a wry smile. "There isn't anything he doesn't know about changing appearances."

"With my scar?"

"He can fix that, too. He's a magician, which is one reason I kept him," Thompson said.

Kane nodded. "When can I leave?"

"When a guide returns," Thompson said. "Should be a couple of days or so. He's bringing in a new guest."

"You don't trust me?" It turned Kane's stomach to ask the question.

"Step by step," Thompson said. "I'm a careful man. Maybe in a few months."

A few months. Kane didn't have a few months. Neither, he thought as he looked at Thompson's pasty complexion, did Thompson.

Kane shrugged. "It's your deal."

"You might keep your ears open while you're out there," Thompson said. "I like to hear anything that's said about Sanctuary."

"I will."

Thompson offered him his hand. Kane inwardly winced as he took it.

"Why don't you and Nicky take a ride, a picnic this afternoon. It's a fine day."

Kane had no excuse, no reason to say no. He knew now that Thompson was playing cupid, that he hoped Nicky would insure Kane's loyalty. But spending hours alone with Nicky was sheer hell.

He tried to sidestep the torture. "Promised some men I'd let them try to get their money back."

"Plenty of time for that later tonight," Thompson said. "You're still winning, I hear."

"Nothing else to do in prison," Kane said ruefully. "One of the other prisoners was a professional gambler. I learned a lot in a year."

Thompson raised an eyebrow. "In Texas?"

Kane shook his head. "The Yank prison camp," he said. "They didn't let anyone close to me in the Texas jail."

"Except that priest."

"I doubt the guards will make that mistake again," Kane replied dryly.

Thompson smiled, but it was a strained smile, laced with pain. "I would have liked to have seen their faces when they discovered your absence."

"There was one man in particular," Kane said, watching Thompson's face grow pale despite the determined set smile. "I wish he'd been there that night. I owed him a few blows."

"Maybe you'll have your chance at him some day."

"Maybe," Kane said. "I found out a long time ago, though, revenge isn't usually worth the trouble it brings."

"Is revenge why you crossed over the law?"

"One reason," Kane said. "I've never been real good at rules."

"Then how did you survive the army?"

"More like the army survived me," Kane replied.

Thompson stood. "About . . . Nicky . . . ?"

"Are my intentions honorable?" Kane asked. "Isn't it a little late to be asking?"

Thompson stared at him. "I'm usually a good judge of character. I hope I'm not wrong this time."

A plea was in Thompson's eyes, and Kane knew the time for fencing was over. He still wasn't sure whether he liked Thompson or not, but his respect for the man was growing.

"I told her," Kane said, "I'm a lousy candidate for a future. But I care about her."

Thompson smiled. Nodded. Kane had the feeling that his comment was better received than declarations of love would have been.

"Go on," Thompson said. "I asked Juanita to fix a little something for you."

Kane turned to go, then stopped to look back at Thompson. "I'll try to look out for both of them—for Nicky and Robin."

"You wouldn't be here if I didn't think that was true," Thompson said. His face suddenly contorted again. "Get out."

Kane closed the door softly, held on to the knob for a moment. He swore softly, then went in search of Nicky.

KANE watched Robin race ahead as he and Nicky followed more sedately behind. He kept his eyes straight ahead, avoiding Nicky's searching looks.

He didn't know how long he could keep his eyes from her, could keep her from realizing how much he wanted her. Robin's presence was the only reason he was controlling himself now. Nicky had looked so pretty in the kitchen where he'd found both her and Robin. He'd wanted to grab her, to kiss her, to just simply hold her. He longed to tell her he needed—and wanted—her more than he'd ever wanted anything in his life. He'd wanted to tell her how much she had given him.

But none of that was possible, not until he worked out his problem, not until he knew he wouldn't harm her even more than he already had.

And so he had asked Robin to accompany them on the picnic.

"Bring the hawk," he said to Robin, "and some meat."

Robin didn't even try to hide his pleasure with manly indifference. He grinned. "Andy took the sling off my arm for good."

"I see," Kane said, then changed the subject. "You need a tether for the bird," Kane said. "Go ask Andy to fix you one. About fifty feet at first."

Robin grinned. "I already did. I'll get Diablo."

Robin was out the door before he could say anything else. Nicky looked at him with both gratitude and disappointment. She was back in her man's shirt and trousers. As he watched, she ran a hand through her hair. It was now an endearingly familiar gesture.

"Thank you for inviting Robin," she said. "But . . ."

"I know," he said softly. And he *did* know. God, how he knew. He wanted to be alone with her as much as she obviously did him. But then he really would lose his soul. "But I need to keep my hands off you."

"Why?"

That damned honesty again. He loved it. He hated it. Christ, it always made him feel lower than a worm. He wanted to be just as honest, but for Davy's sake he was only allowed lies. "I'll be leaving in a few days."

"But you'll be back."

"I'll *try* to come back."

Her mouth creased in a wonderful smile. "Then you'll stay?"

Kane swallowed hard. "For a while."

She studied his face, the smile disappearing. "Something's wrong, isn't it?"

Kane shrugged. "A lot of things can happen. Pictures of my face are all over the place, and it's too damned distinctive."

Her eyes looked puzzled, and he knew she hadn't accepted the explanation. "If I know your uncle," he said, "Andy will have our horses saddled and ready."

"Is that it?" she asked with sudden insight. "Did Uncle Nat say anything about me? He isn't forcing you . . . ?" Her voice trailed off as a stricken look permeated her eyes.

"No one forces me to do anything," Kane said. Which was a lie. Everyone seemed to be forcing him to do something, all of which went against every instinct he had. But for once he was glad he had lied. Her eyes cleared slightly, only a small spark of doubt remaining.

He wanted to lean over and touch her, to wipe away that doubt, to bring the mischief back into her eyes. He had just started to reach out his hand when Robin bounded back in the room, the hawk on his wrist.

"See," he said. "I've already trained him to sit on my wrist. He eats from my fist. He'll be able to fly in no time."

"And go back home to the cliffs," Kane said.

Robin nodded eagerly. He had transferred his desire from keeping the bird to teaching it to fly and hunt. He had a new purpose now, and Kane realized that at least part of it stemmed from a wish to please Kane. The other part—the best part—was finally having a goal of his own.

His eyes met Nicky's, and she smiled. He remembered her saying how she had raised Robin almost by herself. He knew how worried she'd been about his attraction to gunfighters.

"Let's go," he said, unable to meet her eyes any longer, and the three of them walked over to the stable, where Andy had two horses saddled. Kane quickly saddled his own gray. Only once did the blacksmith glance toward Kane, and it was a worried look. Kane knew in his bones that the blacksmith smelled trouble.

The three of them trotted out of the stable, Nicky carrying a basket of food. Robin and his horse exuberantly moved ahead, as Kane and Nicky rode more leisurely.

"Thank you," she said. "Thank you for giving him the hawk. I haven't seen him so interested in anything since he lost our dog."

"He's a natural with animals," Kane said. "He would make a good horse doctor."

"If I could get him away from this valley," Nicky said wistfully, and he knew then what she'd hinted at but never said: She, too, wanted to leave Sanctuary.

Her face suddenly flushed, and he knew she was reminded that he'd just said that he'd decided to stay. Once again, pain drove through him. She had been willing to stay for him, to give up whatever dreams she'd had of leaving. He made a vow to himself then. No matter what happened to him, he would make sure Robin and Nicky did leave. He still had people back in Texas who owed him, and he would do something he'd never done before: call in a debt.

But the day was too fine to worry. The sun was bright and the sky too blue to describe. They stopped at what Kane now considered Nicky's hill. He watched Robin slide down from his horse, the young hawk still on his arm. For the next hour, Kane worked with Robin as they patiently tried to teach the hawk to take short jumps, moving a piece of meat farther away each time. One foot, two feet. It needed to gain strength and confidence before it could fly.

Kane turned around frequently and looked at Nicky. She seemed very content sitting and watching. The sun sent shimmers of gold through the light brown hair and a warm breeze ruffled it like so many fingers. Even in the shirt and trousers, she looked incredibly feminine. And desirable.

When the hawk tired, Robin put the bird on a small branch that served as a perch, and the three of them opened the package of food Juanita had prepared. Bread and cheese and chicken, and a bottle of very fine wine. Nat Thompson was reinforcing his offer, making sure that Kane knew exactly what Sanctuary had to offer. The wine might as well have been poison.

But Kane kept his voice light as he and Robin discussed

the hawk and the next steps in its training. Kane promised to help fashion a lure. When the hawk was strong enough, Robin would throw the lure and hope the hawk would go after it.

Despite all his worry, Kane enjoyed the day. It was one of the few really pleasant days he'd had since before the war. He enjoyed Robin and was warmed by Nicky's presence. For a few hours, he allowed himself to forget everything else.

It was only when they started to leave that he thought about how few the hours had been, how few days he had left with her. When would Sanctuary's guide return? Three days? Four? And then he would leave for Gooden and try to make the deal with Masters. If he couldn't convince Masters to give him more time, he wasn't sure whether Masters would allow him to return. And if he was allowed to come back, exactly what he would do?

When he helped Nicky into the saddle, she looked down at him. "Thank you for a wonderful day."

It *had* been a wonderful day. He only hoped that she could remember it this way.

KANE started losing at the poker table that night. He didn't try to lose. His luck just seemed to ebb away.

Hildebrand was sitting at the table. So were Curry and Parker. And one other man he hadn't met yet.

"Been busy, I noticed," Hildebrand said.

"Yeah," Curry echoed, a sneer on his lips. "We keep seeing you with Thompson's niece. How do you manage that?"

Kane shrugged. "Right place at the right time."

"When you planning to leave?" Hildebrand asked.

"I thought no one asked questions here," Kane said as he dealt a new hand.

Hildebrand chortled. "No need to answer. I was just wondering about that little job I mentioned."

"You'll have to find someone else," Kane said. "I have other business."

"Couldn't have anything to do with Sanctuary?"

Kane stared at him with unblinking eyes. In a minute, the man's own gaze fell. "Just asking."

"It's your bet," Kane said.

The game went on, but Kane felt everyone's eyes on him, not only at the table but throughout the saloon. He was losing, and badly, and he hated that. He always hated to lose, but he particularly hated losing to Hildebrand and his friends. By the end of the night, he was down five hundred dollars. His only satisfaction was that he still had fifteen hundred he'd won in earlier games, and the stake had come from Marshal Masters. He hoped the son of a bitch was wondering where in the hell his money was. He hoped like hell Masters was worried sick his pet dog wouldn't return home.

Kane lost the next two hands and called it a night.

GOODEN, TEXAS

Ben Masters ran a comb through his hair and put on the leather vest. Mary May said she would be free tonight. He'd asked about Sunday—tomorrow—but the brightness had left her eyes and she'd looked away as she shook her head. Later, someone told him she always disappeared on Sunday. A man? He hadn't liked the jealous resentment that explanation birthed. She was a saloon woman. Why should he care?

He found his hat, jammed it on his head, and left for the Blazing Star, trying not to wonder what he wanted most: Mary May or information.

MARY May tried to concentrate on listening to the cowpoke next to her. But her mind was like a pit of hot coals. Whenever she leapfrogged one, she landed on another.

The note from Mrs. Culworthy was burning straight through her dress. The woman could no longer take care of Sarah Ann. She was leaving for Boston at the end of the month to care for her ill brother.

Mary May didn't know what to do. It had taken a long

time to find someone she could trust to take care of her daughter. Mrs. Culworthy was one of very few "good" women who would agree to take the child of a fallen woman. And she did want Sarah Ann raised to be respectable.

She was also determined that her little girl would never be sent to an orphanage, as she herself had been. Mary May figured that if she hadn't been so starved for love, she might not have run away with Ian Hamilton. She might have seen past the handsome face and pretentions to the weak character behind them.

Sarah Ann was the light of Mary May's life, the one pure thing that made her life mean something. She would have loved having her daughter live with her, but it simply wasn't possible. She couldn't raise the child in the back of a saloon, and she had no other occupation.

What to do? She would go to Cove Springs on Sunday as she always did. Perhaps Mrs. Culworthy would have some suggestions. She would miss seeing Ben, but nothing was more important than Sarah Ann. Nothing.

Her mind was still jumping between her daughter and Ben when he sauntered in with a deceptively lazy smile on his lips. He was anything but lazy, particularly in bed. She only wished she knew more about him, that he talked more. Most men couldn't stop talking, but she had to pry every word out of Ben Smith.

She smiled at him and was trying to figure out how she could leave the man who had just bought her a drink when she saw another familiar face—that of the thin, dangerous-looking man who had been asking about Calico. That man's attention had also gone right to Ben, searching his features as if they were familiar to him. She remembered the ugly stranger from months ago, when he and his brother had been looking for someone to guide them to Sanctuary. Yancy, that was it. She remembered the name, the reputation. Where was the other one?

She didn't like the way he was looking at Ben. She didn't like it at all.

She almost gulped her drink, thanked the cowboy who had bought it with a few tactful words and a reminder that her job required her to move around. She gave a sign to the bartender for another drink and walked over to Ben's table. "Want company, cowboy?"

Ben looked a little surprised. "If you're it," he said, a slow smile forming in his eyes. She had not thought him particularly handsome the first time he'd walked into the Blazing Star. He'd been, in fact, rather ordinary-looking, with light brown hair and blue eyes. The only distinguishing feature had been a catlike alertness.

She sat down, waited until the bartender brought them both a drink, and then leaned over. "A man's been studying you ever since you walked in. He was looking at you yesterday, too."

Ben's eyes didn't flicker. "What does he look like?"

"He's over in the corner: thin, ugly."

Ben nodded, but his eyes didn't seem to move. Mary May was becoming more and more suspicious that he was a lawman. She had to wonder what he would do if he knew she was connected, even in a small way, to Sanctuary. She could go to prison, and then what would happen to Sarah Ann?

He was watching her, and suddenly she had the strange feeling he knew every thought in her head.

They hadn't discussed Sanctuary since that one time when he'd asked about Calico and said that he had a friend in Sanctuary. It was as if they both had silently agreed not to mention the place again.

She was worried, though. Worried about Yancy, whom she knew was a gunfighter with a fearsome reputation. Ben Smith looked like he could take care of himself, but Yancy had the look of a backshooter.

"Do you know who he is?" Ben asked.

"Don't you?" she retorted. He would if he was who she thought he was. She hated the game. Neither wanted to admit how much instinct they had about the other.

He shook his head negatively.

"John Yancy," she said. "And he's mean as a devil."

Ben shrugged. "I don't know the man except by reputation."

"He looks like he knows you. Be careful."

"I think he's just looking at you," Ben said. "And mad as hell that it's me with you." He hadn't moved his head one bit, yet somehow he had taken note, catalogued and discarded the threat.

"No," she said sharply, sharper than she intended. "He's seen you before. He just doesn't know where. I've seen that look before."

"You're imagining things," Ben said. "I'll miss you Sunday."

She didn't like the way he'd changed the subject and she knew he didn't believe what he'd said for a minute. There was a slight awareness in his body movement, like a wild stallion who sniffed danger.

She bit her lip. "Me too, but I have to make a little trip."

He shrugged as if it didn't matter, and Mary May felt unexpected pain. She'd been in control of her life for a long time, choosing the men and choosing the times, but she was losing that control. She wanted to be with Ben Smith. She wanted to be with him now, tonight, Sunday. She didn't think beyond that. She wasn't the kind of woman a man married, not any longer.

Suddenly, she didn't want him to think there was another man. She wanted him to think well of her, and that hadn't been important for a long time.

"I'm going to see my daughter," she said, one of her hands clawing into a fist in her lap. She waited for him to laugh.

He didn't. His light blue eyes almost smiled. "Is she as pretty as you?"

"I hope not," she said. "All it ever got me is trouble."

He ignored that comment. "Where is she?"

"A little town twenty miles from here."

"How old is she?" He seemed curiously intense.

"Three," Mary May said, and she heard the softening in her own voice. She'd never told anyone about Sarah Ann before, not here in the saloon. She'd been afraid they would use it in some way. When she'd discovered she was pregnant two weeks after her husband died, the owner of the Blazing Star had provided funds for her to go away until the baby was born. She'd returned to repay him, then stayed. But neither of them had ever told anyone about Sarah Ann. That was her own secret, her own treasure.

Why was she telling this man?

"Can I go with you?" His question was so unexpected she was stunned for a moment.

It was a long ride, more than twenty miles each way. She usually left at daybreak on horseback because a buggy would take too long. It was a killing ride for both her and her horse.

She looked at Ben Smith from under her lashes, trying to understand him. She didn't, at all. He seemed to be waiting for something, somebody, yet he was willing to spend an entire day on horseback.

"If you wish," she said. "It's a long ride."

A shadow crossed his face for a moment, then disappeared. "When do you want to leave?"

"At daybreak," she said, then catching the saloon owner's signal, she stood. She gave Ben one last, long look, and turned away.

THAT had been a damn fool thing to do, Ben told himself as he finished his second drink by himself. The words had popped out of his mouth before he could stop them. There had been something so wistful in her face. And sad. Totally unlike the smart-talking, laughing woman he had come to like.

He tried to justify that impulse: Maybe she would talk more about Sanctuary. But then his conscience stepped in: What if Kane O'Brien came looking for him? Hell, he'd been waiting nearly six weeks now. One day wouldn't matter.

Chapter Fourteen

Time seemed to rush by like a flock of geese heading south for the winter.

Nicky watched just such a flock as the sun rose in the eastern sky. It was early, way early, for geese to be heading south, and she wondered whether their migration meant an early winter. She had hoped Kane would join her this morning, but he hadn't. Not this morning nor any of the others. Six now since the night they'd made love.

She knew he was avoiding her. She also knew he would be leaving tomorrow. Her uncle had said he'd finally agreed to stay at Sanctuary after he took care of some personal business. The guide, Calico, had returned the previous night with a new guest. He would need a day's rest, and then be ready for the return trip.

Her uncle was sure that Kane would be coming back. Nicky wasn't so sure. For one thing, the whole state of Texas was after him. Besides that, he seemed to be hiding something. There was a part of him she could never quite reach; it scared her, that secretive man inside the facade.

She had watched him with Robin. Even his smile held secrets. It never seemed heartfelt, though she didn't think it deliberately false. There was an emptiness about him, a loneliness that no one else seemed to see. Her uncle was pleased—no, more than pleased. He seemed happier about the prospect of Kane O'Brien joining him than he had been about anything or anyone in a number of years. And Robin was tagging along with Kane at every opportunity.

She wondered why they didn't see what she did: the despair. Why? What haunted him? The question ate at her.

Though they were seldom alone now, she saw him often, several times a day, particularly now that her uncle invited him to supper every night. Kane spent every afternoon with Robin and the hawk. Sometimes she would go with them, but yesterday she'd declined. She couldn't stand being so close to him, being touched by him as he helped her on and off a saddle, and feeling him draw back.

Every day—every moment—she felt him inching further and further away.

Ironically, her feelings for him grew each day. She tried not to love him, but she couldn't keep her pulse from racing nor her heart from tumbling every time she saw him. She loved watching him with Robin in particular. He never talked down to her brother as so many of the guests did; instead he spurred Robin's interest in animals, in the life around him. He never romanticized gunfighting or bragged about exploits. And to her everlasting shame, she had watched him after he left the house. He sometimes went to the saloon, sometimes to the hotel, sometimes to the livery, but she didn't see him go to Rosita's again.

When he went to the livery, he would ride out moments later, racing his horse like a bat out of hell.

Tonight, if he went, she was determined to go after him. It might be her last chance to see him alone, to feel his hands on her, to know the magic of his kiss. She'd thought she would have more time, but he would be gone tomorrow, and she had only a few hours left to convince him to come back. Not only for her sake, she told herself, but for her uncle's and Robin's as well.

Nicky returned home to learn from a grim-faced Mitch that her uncle was still in his bedroom. That worried her. He never stayed in bed this late. But she also saw an opportunity to do some snooping without Uncle Nat looking over her shoulder.

After Mitch left, Nicky went into her uncle's study and found the key under the rug where he kept it. She started to unlock the second drawer of his desk, but to her surprise it wasn't locked. He always kept it locked. Always. She swallowed hard. It was another sign that he was much more ill than he admitted. She bit her lip as she pulled the drawer open and took out a leather pouch filled with maps.

Her uncle had shown her the maps of the territories around Sanctuary a long time ago, "just in case" anything happened to him. She also knew the route through caves known only by Uncle Nat, Mitch, her and Robin, and perhaps Andy. She wasn't sure about that.

Nicky studied the maps for a long time. She knew Kane had come from Texas, that he'd contacted Sanctuary from a little town named Gooden. As far as anyone knew, he hadn't been outside Texas since the war and could be expected to head back down that way. Any "obligation" he had would be there.

Nicky hesitated a moment, then rolled up one of the maps and stuck it inside her shirt. She closed the drawer and locked it, returning the key to its usual place. Her uncle was a careful man; when he'd told his niece and nephew about the routes to follow out of Sanctuary—a dry stream bed, an odd rock formation, waterholes—he had also given both her and Robin an oddly carved piece of rock on a leather thong. It would protect them, he'd said, if they ran into the Comanches that often roamed these mountains and occasionally provided protection.

She hugged the map against her chest. She hated not telling her uncle that she was taking it, but neither could she tell him of her thought about Kane . . . the inexplicable intuitive fear that he was in grave danger.

The questions kept pounding at her as she waited for Kane's usual afternoon appearance. She decided to bake some bread as a way of keeping herself from going crazy, and was just starting when Robin came into the kitchen.

"Where's Diablo?" he asked, as the other Diablo—the hawk—squealed from its perch on his arm.

"I don't know," she said.

"Uncle Nat says he's leaving tomorrow, but he'll be back in three weeks."

"Three weeks?" That was more than Kane had told her.

"I was listening," Robin said, completely unabashed. "Calico's supposed to take him to some town, then meet up with him again in two and a half weeks."

Robin certainly believed in Kane O'Brien, believed his friend would certainly try to return. Why didn't she?

Because of those few unguarded comments he'd made about Sanctuary being a prison in itself? She wasn't sure. She was sure, though, that Robin would be bitterly disillusioned if Kane didn't return, that probably everything that Kane had done with and for him would be rejected. She wondered whether Kane realized that, whether he understood the impact he'd had on Robin—and her—during the time he'd been at Sanctuary.

Robin shifted impatiently from foot to foot. "Then where do you think he might be?" he asked anxiously.

"Probably the barber's," she replied.

"Yeah," Robin replied with disappointment. Many of the guests went to the barber's before leaving.

"I'm going to try to teach Diablo to hunt today. Why don't you go with me, Sis?"

She shook her head. "You go alone," she said. "I have bread in the oven."

"I *will* see Kane before he goes, won't I?"

"I'm sure you will," she said. And she was. Kane truly liked Robin. She wished she were as sure of his feelings toward her.

Kane arrived a few minutes before supper, but she almost didn't recognize him. Gray tinged the hair around his face, and he sported a moustache and beard. Stage paint had blended the scar almost to oblivion. The barber hadn't been able to change Kane's eyes, though, the gray eyes that sometimes lit with amusement but more frequently clouded with shadows.

Amusement hovered in them now as he studied her reaction to his new appearance. "Think I'll pass?"

"For what?"

"A grizzly old prospector, of course."

"A few more wrinkles," she said, tipping her head as she examined him. "A limp. Dirtier clothes."

"By the time your uncle's guide drags me across the prairie, I'm sure I'll look just like that," he replied with a grin. The rare instance of lightheartedness melted her heart.

He reached up and tugged off the beard. "Sid gave me some hardier glue for later," he said.

She grinned. "That was kind of him. I would hate to look at that beard over the table."

He looked insulted. "I thought it rather handsome, myself," he said, then changed the subject. "Does your uncle arrange this for everyone who leaves Sanctuary?"

"Everyone who wants or needs it," she said. "For a price."

"Everything in Sanctuary is for a price," Kane replied dryly.

"It's worth it. I don't think anyone would recognize you," she said comfortingly.

"You did."

But she was in love with him. Nicky knew she would recognize those eyes, that walk, that lean body anywhere. What she said though, was, "I was expecting you, and I know what Sid can do."

He grinned. "No more Diablo?"

"You'll never lose a bit of that devil," she said, "but I haven't thought of you as Diablo since the second day."

His eyes twinkled. "But you did think so that first day."

"You looked . . ." She hesitated in midsentence.

"Like a desperado," he finished. Then his voice softened. "And you looked so damned pretty."

Nicky's heart warmed at the tone, at the look in his eyes. They weren't shadowed now. They were full of emotion. "Robin wants to say good-bye. He should be back soon."

"I'm sorry I missed going with him this afternoon. As you see, I was otherwise occupied."

She smiled wistfully. "I wanted to see you before you left, too," she said quietly.

They both knew what she meant. Her heart—and desire—was in her face.

"That's not a good idea, Nicole," he said, and she noticed the use of her proper name. He had used it rarely, only the evening he'd made love to her. His eyes, his expression were saying he cared. She wondered whether he realized it.

"Why not?"

"Because a lot can happen in the next few weeks. I don't want to leave you with child."

A child. She hadn't even thought of that. The idea was startling. A child with Kane. "I would like that," she said softly.

"Out here? In the middle of nowhere? A bastard?" His voice grew harsh. "The son or daughter of a condemned convict."

"My father was wanted," Nicky said with as much dignity as she could muster. His words hurt, as they were meant to hurt. "My uncle is wanted."

"And I wouldn't wish this life on my worst enemy, much less a daughter or son," he said. "Hell, after all you've seen, would you want to raise another child the way you've had to raise Robin?"

Hurt balled inside her like a tight fist. *I wouldn't wish this life on my worst enemy.* Did he really hate Sanctuary so? Then why had he agreed to stay? Was it that he cared about her? Or was she merely a way to get to Nat Thompson?

She backed away. "My uncle said you were going to stay."

Regret flickered in his face, and then his eyes turned cold, as cold as those of some of the other guests at Sanctuary. "It was an offer I couldn't refuse at this particular time," he said. "It's not one I would accept if I had any other choices."

"And me?" she said, hating the strain in her voice. "Was I an offer you couldn't refuse at this particular time, not one you would take if you had other choices?"

His face froze. But before he could speak, they were interrupted by heavy footsteps.

"Is that Diablo?" her uncle said from the other room.

"Yes," she said, but her voice was very small.

"It is," Kane called out.

Then her uncle was in the room. "Glad you could come tonight," he said to Kane.

"It was good of you to ask."

"I have a couple of things I would like you to do for me," her uncle continued, oblivious to the tension between her and Kane and to the hurt she was sure must be stamped on her features.

He took Kane by the arm and propelled him toward his office. "Someone I want you to see in Gooden. A woman. She's been real valuable to us, and I want you to get to know her."

The door closed behind them, and Nicky leaned against the doorjamb. Gooden. So he would be going to Gooden, as she'd thought. The map was in her room, now buried among her clothes in a trunk.

Almost in a daze, she moved toward the kitchen and the stove that held their supper. A stew tonight, along with the freshly baked bread. She remained in a foggy state as Robin came in, as the two men and boy sat down to eat. She kept hearing his words in her mind. *I wouldn't wish this life on my worst enemy.* Then: *It's an offer I couldn't refuse. It's not one I would accept if I had any other choices.* She felt as if she'd been whipped by rawhide, only the wounds were all inside.

"Nicky?" her uncle said. "Aren't you going to eat with us?" She was about to say no, when she decided not to give Diablo the satisfaction. He was Diablo again, not Kane O'Brien, the gentler of the two men who inhabited one striking body.

She sat down before he could stand to hold out her

chair for her. "Why don't I go with Mr. O'Brien?" she said suddenly. She wasn't sure where the idea came from. Or exactly what motivated it. The need for a reaction? The desire to be with him? A longing for assurance?

Both Diablo and Uncle Nat stared at her.

"Why?" Nat Thompson said, his eyes wary.

"I should know more about Sanctuary," she said.

"Me, too," Robin said, his eyes sparkling.

"What do you think, Diablo?" her uncle asked. The fact that he deferred to Kane startled Nicky even more than the question had.

Kane's gray eyes went even flatter than usual, but she saw a muscle in his cheek move. "No," he said.

"Why?" she demanded. "It's time that I saw some place other than—"

"It's dangerous," Kane said curtly. "It's dangerous going out, and it will be even more dangerous where I'm going."

"I can shoot," Nicky said.

"So can I," chimed in Robin.

"Not with me," Kane said and looked toward Nat Thompson for reinforcement.

Thompson nodded. "When Diablo returns, you two can make the trip with Calico. Nicky's right. She and Robin should become more familiar with the routes." As if the subject were closed, he looked at Kane again. "Calico wants to leave before dawn."

Kane nodded.

Thompson looked as if he wanted to say something else, but instead started eating. Nicky noticed he wasn't eating as well as he had a month ago, but was only picking at his food. He excused himself early.

"Good luck," he said to Kane as he hesitated a moment at the entrance of the hall to his bedroom.

"Luck usually doesn't have a lot to do with it," Kane replied.

"Then be careful."

"I'm always careful."

"I'm counting on it," Thompson said and disappeared through the door.

Kane left minutes later. Thompson's last words echoing in his mind. The man was playing straight with him, offering him his most precious possessions for safekeeping: his family, his life. He sensed Thompson didn't trust often, and probably was trusting now only out of necessity, but that didn't make him feel better. Judas, liar, cheat. He was all of that. And more.

He headed for the saloon. And oblivion. Anything to erase the words and faces of tonight. Anything to keep him from thinking about his choices, which were really no choices at all. Christ, he felt sick. Sick and wanting, and so damned alone. He'd been alone before in his life, plenty of times, but he'd never felt this goddamn alone.

He had no one—no family, no friends other than Davy. There was no one to turn to, no one who really knew him, to whom he could tell the truth. Yet, through some hideous twist of fate, he'd been made responsible for so many people's lives.

He wanted to trust Nicky, yet he couldn't. She'd said she loved him, but would she still if she knew he'd come to destroy her uncle? Not a chance!

Kane had no hope—none at all—of having a future with Nicky, couldn't even let himself consider what it would be like. But he knew he had to find a way to satisfy his obligation to Davy without ruining Nicky's life or die trying.

Christ, but he needed that drink.

The saloon was full, every man jack of the guests there. He saw a new face, probably the man who'd ridden in with Calico. He had that weary look. His face was still unshaven, and he obviously hadn't been as eager for a bath as he himself had been. The stranger was smelling up his end of the bar.

Kane went to the other end. He didn't care for conversation. "Whiskey," he said. "A bottle."

The barkeep looked at his changed hair and barely visible scar. "On the way out?"

Kane nodded.

Hildebrand approached him. "Couple of poker hands first?"

Kane shrugged. Anything to get his mind off Nicky. He'd been losing steadily, but he didn't give much of a damn. It was Masters's money. He knew he'd been throwing the games away, but it had been useful in cultivating some of the other guests. Losers were liked. Winners weren't. On the other hand, winners usually became more and more effusive.

Perhaps the more information he could provide Masters, the more slack the man would give him. A couple of months. Just a couple of damned months and he could probably hand over Sanctuary without a shot.

Hildebrand picked three other men for the game, and they found a table. Kane discovered that his luck had returned. His cards were not just good, they were a gambler's dream. No matter what he did, what risks he took, he won and kept on winning. One by one, grumbling men left the table, everyone but Hildebrand.

"All or nothing?" the man said, his eyes as cold as a snake's. "Turn of a card?"

Kane was developing a real dislike for Hildebrand, but he didn't need another enemy—God knew he had enough of them—and his intuition told him that he would win again. He always did when he ran a streak. In cards, anyway. "You're crazy," he said. "I can't lose tonight."

"I want to see how much guts you have," Hildebrand said. "Scared?"

"There must be two thousand dollars there," Kane said. "You got money to throw away?"

"I got enough. I'm going to get more," Hildebrand said. "What's the matter, Diablo? I thought you were a man who liked taking risks."

It was a taunt. Kane was being baited and he knew it. He also suspected he knew why. No one had said anything about his visits to Thompson's home, but he'd sensed a growing resentment in the past few days. The other guests might not know for certain, but they suspected he'd been chosen to stay at Sanctuary. And they didn't like it.

"It's your risk," Kane shrugged.

Hildebrand lowered his voice slightly. "I take it you decided to refuse my offer?"

"I don't like banks," Kane said, remembering Hildebrand's earlier proposal.

"I changed my mind," Hildebrand said. "I have something closer in mind."

Those warning bells started ringing in Kane's head again. They were getting real familiar. Too damn familiar. He felt like a man running through a battlefield targeted by a thousand cannons. Every time he dodged one ball, he was running straight toward another incoming one.

Kane shrugged his indifference. "I have plans of my own."

"Mind saying what they are?"

"Yeah," he said. "You want this deal or not?"

Hildebrand smiled. It was a cold smile. "Go ahead. I trust you."

He didn't, not worth a owl's hoot, but Kane didn't care. He shuffled and laid the deck on the table. "You first."

Hildebrand put his fingers on the deck, then lifted about a third of it, showing a king of hearts at the bottom. He grinned.

Kane studied the deck for a moment, then lifted a few cards of the remaining two-thirds. They both saw it at the same time. Ace of spades.

"You have the devil's own luck," Hildebrand said.

"Sometimes." Kane gathered in the pot of money and asked the barkeep to send it to the hotel for him. Six months ago, he would have been elated. Now he didn't care. It wasn't going to do him a damn bit of good where he was going. But he wouldn't let Hildebrand know that. He smiled, and he knew it was every bit as cold a movement of lips as Hildebrand's own.

They were surrounded now, the other "guests" drawn by the high stakes. Kane moved, pushing his chair out and getting to his feet. "It was a pleasure, Hildebrand."

Hildebrand smiled. It wasn't pleasant. "Have a nice trip, Diablo."

Kane nodded and moved toward the door. It had been

a mistake coming here. Despite the glasses of whiskey he'd consumed during the game, he felt as sober as a teetotaler. Something was happening. He could feel it. He'd been tested for some reason, and he wasn't sure whether he had passed or failed.

He ran over his options for the rest of the evening— there were damned few—and headed toward the stable. At least, he could control his horse. And that seemed about the only thing he could control.

Andy was gone, and as he saddled the gray, he thought about how he would lose him soon, too. The horse belonged to Masters, just as he did.

The horse needed no urging to move into a gallop, obviously as restless as Kane felt. Together, they rode away from Sanctuary and, Kane hoped, toward a few hours of comparative peace. He was only too aware that he might be back in a cell in a few days, waiting again, along with Davy, for a rope. He hadn't succeeded in the task given him; he still didn't know the exact location of Sanctuary. He was risking everything on the chance that Masters would give him more time, and Masters had not seemed like a man prone to lengthening a chain once he had a man on it.

NICKY watched from her window. She'd almost given up. Kane had been in the saloon for hours. Just as she was about to give up and close the curtains, she saw him. He didn't even look toward the house, nor toward Rosita's, but moved with that lean grace toward the livery.

She waited until she saw him ride out, then quietly left her room. The main room was dark and empty. Her uncle had not appeared after leaving the table, and she imagined Robin was in bed. Wherever they were, she was grateful she didn't have to make explanations.

Nicky hurried down to the livery. She didn't bother to saddle her mare, but led the horse out, closed the door, and, gripping the horse's mane, she vaulted up on Molly's back. Kane had headed toward the stream. To where they had made love? Without looking backward, she headed after him.

HILDEBRAND watched Diablo leave the saloon. He still wasn't sure whether the outlaw was a possible ally. He did know two things: the man had guts and was lucky. Those were two commodities Hildebrand valued.

He didn't mind losing the money. His life had been spent finding and losing large sums of money. The challenge was what appealed to him.

Right now, the challenge was taking over Sanctuary.

He had discussed the possibility with the Yancy brothers. Unfortunately, one had acted precipitously. Damn fool. Hildebrand didn't trust too many men at Sanctuary. Hell, he didn't trust anyone. He needed, though, someone smart and ambitious but perhaps not as smart and ambitious as himself. He wasn't sure whether Diablo fit in that space.

Hildebrand knew, though, that he couldn't take Sanctuary by himself. He just wondered what Diablo's motives were, the way he had been bootlicking Thompson. Hildebrand went to the door of the saloon and looked out, wondering whether Diablo was going to Rosita's. Instead, he saw Diablo ride out of the livery. Just as he was pondering that, he saw Miss High-and-Mighty Thompson slip from her house and make for the livery. Several minutes later, she rode out.

Was that it? Was she going to meet Diablo? Was that Diablo's interest? Or did he have more—like Sanctuary itself? If so, the two of them were going to clash. He reminded himself that Diablo was leaving, but that just didn't ring true, not with all his visits to Thompson's house and the girl riding out to meet him.

He immediately made a decision. He went to the livery, saddled his horse and rode out in the same direction the girl had taken. If she wasn't meeting Diablo, maybe she might be interested in a little play. If she *was* meeting the outlaw, perhaps he could learn exactly what was going on between Diablo and Nat Thompson.

KANE trotted alongside the stream for a while. He paused at the place where he and Nicky had made love, remembering, wishing. But not hoping. He had few hopes now, and none for himself.

In his mind's eye, he saw her there in his shirt: lithe and young and lovely, her brown eyes misty with wonder and her mouth crooked in a delighted smile. God, he'd wanted her. He still wanted her. He would always want her. He hadn't realized he could love like this, that the longing could run so deep.

Davy loved his Martha like that. He remembered the looks they exchanged, the touches between them. But Kane had never thought he would have anything like that kind of . . . belonging. Of giving.

Kane shook away the memory. He turned away from the spot, unable to bear even another minute of memories. He was just turning back toward Sanctuary when a sudden thought brought him to a halt. He remembered what Nicky said about a secret way in and out of Sanctuary. This was his last chance to find it.

He guided the horse toward the wall of the valley. He had searched it before and found nothing, but he hadn't known then that there was a secret way through the mountains. It had to be a cave. He'd found no other breaks in the mountains other than those already heavily guarded. He knew he was engaged in a fool's task. He could probably search for months, even years, without finding the hidden path. But he had to try.

Kane circled the north part of the valley wall. The moon was laced by clouds and only occasionally lit the earth beneath. He stayed carefully in the shadows, looking for anything unusual: a bush that shouldn't exist, a trail so faint none but the best tracker could find it. But where the dim moonlight protected him, it also protected the secrets of Sanctuary.

He started back, the trail taking him close to the stream, too close. He couldn't afford sentimentality. He couldn't endure the lacerations it tore in his heart. Still, he found himself heading back to that spot as if driven by some invisible force.

Chapter Fifteen

Nicky approached the clearing alongside the stream cautiously. She had lived at Sanctuary long enough to know it wasn't wise to sneak up on a gunslinger. She didn't see Kane, but the trees provided some shelter, and the night was dark. It was really too dark, she knew, to be riding safely.

She dismounted and walked Molly to the spot where she and Kane had made love, dropping the mare's reins, knowing that she wouldn't wander far. Nicky stood listening for a moment, trying to stave off disappointment that Kane wasn't there. She had hoped, rather than expected, that this was the place she would find him. And now she felt a bitter disappointment that she was wrong. Did she know him at all?

She simply had to see him before he left, even if she had to sneak into the hotel. She had to know if she meant anything at all to him—or if she had imagined that, too.

"Where are you?" she whispered to the night.

As if in answer, she heard Molly neigh a welcome, and she knew a rider was approaching. Then she heard the soft clump of hoofbeats against the earth. Her pulse quickened. She went totally still. But no one rode here at night except Kane; the others were too busy whoring, gambling, and drinking. Still, an edge of fear ran down her spine, and she realized how foolish she had been. She hadn't brought a rifle. She hadn't even stopped long enough to grab the tiny derringer.

A figure materialized out of the night and instantly she knew it wasn't Kane. Another man—he sat a horse well enough, but his silhouette against the dark sky was heavier than Kane's and he rode slumped in the saddle. Molly was several feet away, and Nicky took the few steps to her side. Just as she started for the reins, the mare backed a few steps away.

"Waiting for someone?" the man on horseback said. Just then a cloud moved to reveal the moon, and in the sudden shaft of light, she identified the newcomer.

"Mr. Hildebrand." She moved toward the horse again, the encounter with Yancy still fresh in her mind. This time, though, she had no weapons.

He wouldn't dare try anything, she told herself. But Yancy had. Something was happening in Sanctuary. The myth of Nat Thompson was fading. Refusing to let her apprehension show, she moved deliberately toward Molly, crooning softly to quiet her.

She kept her voice low, her movements slow—not only because she didn't want to scare off the mare, but because to show fear to a man like Hildebrand was to invite attack. The realization that he must have followed her only made the fear grow stronger.

She reached out her hand and, this time, she gripped Molly's mane. Moving to the horse's side, she got ready to leap to her back.

"Can I help you, Miss Thompson?" Hildebrand had dismounted and was moving toward her.

"No," she said shortly, not wanting Hildebrand's hands on her. He wasn't an ugly man, yet there was something reptilian about him.

"But I insist," he said, his voice low and threatening. He was close enough to touch her.

Nicky shuddered involuntarily. She knew she had been incredibly foolish to come out here without a weapon. But she'd not been thinking about anything but Kane, and she'd expected to meet him here. Now she was alone, without a weapon, with a very dangerous man.

"All right," she said, knowing she wouldn't win this contest by denying the fact that his strength was greater than hers. And once on Molly, she could make a run for it. "Thank you," she added, trying to keep her voice calm.

But he didn't move. "Do you come here often, Miss Thompson—Nicky?"

"Often enough," she replied.

"Meeting someone?"

"No."

"It's dangerous to go riding at night." His voice was a purr, but there was nothing soft about it.

"I have a gun," she bluffed.

His hand went to her waist and moved along her trousers, then her shirt. "I don't think so," he said. "Maybe you wanted someone to come riding after you. I suppose you get lonely here."

"No," she said, cringing from his touch.

"Not even for Diablo?"

Her heart slammed against her ribcage. There was a malevolent edge to the question. "No," she said. "My uncle would kill anyone who touched me."

"Maybe once upon a time," he said. "I think he's slowing down."

"Keep thinking that," she said, "and I'll dance at your funeral."

Hildebrand's hand came up and touched her cheek. The action was meant to be provocative, but it wasn't. It was . . . abhorrent.

She stood absolutely still, afraid to move, afraid to give him cause to continue. "My uncle is expecting me home. I would be grateful if you help me mount."

"Tell me more about Diablo first," he said.

She turned and wrapped her fingers in Molly's mane, ready to try to mount herself, but his hands went around her waist and jerked her to him. "Now that's not polite," he complained. "I bet you don't run from Diablo."

Instinct told her to be careful. She couldn't throw Kane in his face. She heard the jealousy in his voice, the competitiveness. "There's nothing to run from," she said, forcing a coolness into her voice. "Now, let me go," she added, finally letting her anger take form, unable to do anything else. He was too strong, and although his hands had released her waist, one had fastened around her arm.

His grip tightened. "Tell me about Diablo," he said again. "Why is he at your uncle's so much?"

She stopped struggling. If he would loosen his hold, perhaps she could mount and race for home. *Where was Kane?* "They play cards," she said. "Why are you so interested?"

"Everything about Sanctuary interests me, and the others," he said. "We pay enough."

"And you're protected," she spat back. "That's all you need to know."

"Some of us think your uncle is losing his grip," Hildebrand said harshly.

"You think you can do better?"

"He needs help."

"You?" she asked, unable to control the contempt in her voice even though she knew it was a mistake. It was.

He swung her around, and bent his face toward her. She tried to avoid his kiss, but she couldn't. His lips fastened on hers angrily, and his mouth and tongue tried to force her mouth open. One hand went around her neck, holding her so she couldn't free herself.

She opened her lips and when his tongue entered, she bit down hard. He jerked away, cursing, but his hand stayed around her neck.

"You'll pay for that," he said as he pushed her to the ground. She tried to kick him, but he pinioned her body and started tearing at her shirt.

"My uncle will kill you," she gasped.

"I don't think so," Hildebrand said coldly. "I'm not the only one who thinks it's time for a change. We're all tired of his damn rules."

His lips came down again on hers, rough and punishing, and this time he didn't give her a chance to bite. She struggled beneath him, reaching out to grab a fistful of hair, yanking as hard as she could. He jerked back, cursing, and the instant her mouth was free, she screamed.

Hildebrand reared back and slapped her, dazing her for a moment. She felt him rip at her shirt again and knew the material had given way. Then he started on her trousers. . . .

KANE heard the scream. He was upstream, near the place where he and Nicky had made love, and he knew immediately it was she. He spurred his horse into a gallop, wishing he had a gun with him.

The first things he saw as he approached the clearing were the silhouettes of two horses, then, an instant later, he could make out two figures struggling on the ground. One, he knew, was Nicky. And the other . . .

He slid down from the horse, just as the man twisted from his position on top of Nicky. Kane didn't stop to think. Fury roiled through him as he tore into the larger figure, his fist ramming into a hard-muscled abdomen. He heard the grunt, saw the man double over, and he turned toward Nicky.

"Watch out," Nicky cried.

Kane turned just as a fist came at him. He was too late to avoid a blow to his face, but he moved with it, and then both of them were on the ground. His opponent's face was close enough now to see: Hildebrand.

Hildebrand was wiry and strong. They rolled over and over, vying for an advantage and neither winning. Hildebrand landed a blow on his shoulder, leaving an opening to his stomach. Kane hit as hard as he could, heard the whistle of Hildebrand's breath as it expelled, then hit him again—harder. Then he landed a crunching blow to the jaw, and one more in the stomach. Hildebrand rolled over in pain, clutching his midsection. He was finished. For the moment, at least.

Kane slowly got to his knees, watching the outlaw closely. Kane had a knife in his boot, and he itched to pull it out and slit Hildebrand's throat, but he didn't. He was damn sick of killing, even scum like Hildebrand.

Kane waited until Hildebrand got to his knees. "Enough," the outlaw said.

Kane didn't take his eyes from the man. "Nicky?"

"I'm all right," she said.

"He didn't . . ."

"No." Her voice was barely audible.

Kane still didn't allow himself to look at her. Keeping his attention focused on Hildebrand, he said, "Nicky, come here."

He heard the rustle of grass as Nicky moved beside him. Unlike most women, she didn't demand his comfort or attention. She stood quietly next to him, waiting.

Kane wanted to kill Hildebrand, and what was more, he knew he should. He probably could do it with his bare hands—or with a word to Nat Thompson. He could ask for his guns and shoot the bastard himself, and he knew Thompson would approve.

But he was reluctant to do either. He knew the burden of killing, and Nicky already had one death on her hands. He didn't want to put the responsibility of another on her.

"When are you planning to leave?" he asked Hildebrand.

The man was still holding his stomach, but he managed to get to his feet. "A week or two."

"Wrong answer," Kane said. "You go tomorrow with me, and I won't mention this to Thompson."

"What about her? Will she say anything?"

"Nicky?" Kane's gaze flashed briefly to her.

"No," she agreed.

Hildebrand's teeth shone in the darkness. "I guess I'm leaving tomorrow then."

"Get the hell out of here," Kane said.

Hildebrand took slow steps to his horse, hesitated, then swung into the saddle, spurred the horse and rode out of sight.

Kane waited until the sound of hoofbeats faded. Nicky hadn't moved. She still stood next to him, and he put a hand on her shoulder. He felt her shiver, and he knew it was reaction rather than desire. "Are you all right?" he asked.

"Yes," she replied, then, in a small voice, added, "He'll try to kill you now."

"I don't think so," Kane said. "He doesn't have a gun, and he discovered I'm better than him at fighting."

"What about later? When he does get a gun?"

Kane wanted to laugh. He didn't have any later. No, Hildebrand was the least of his worries.

"I can take care of myself," he said.

"That's what I thought about myself," she said ruefully, moving closer to him.

"Where's that derringer?"

"I left it at home."

His hand felt her skin where the shirt had been torn away. He thought of Hildebrand's rough hands on her, terrifying her, and for a moment he had to struggle to bring the rage inside him back under control. He felt her tremble again, and all the resistance he might have felt about touching her, holding her, disintegrated. With a murmured sound of comfort, he took her in his arms, holding her tight. Her heart was racing, her whole body trembling.

She looked up at him. "What if he comes back?"

"He won't. He's going to be hurting real bad tonight. And he can't get a gun." His voice turned harder. "What in the hell are you doing here without one?"

Her hand went up to his face, touching him in the darkness as if she were blind and needed to reassure herself that he was familiar. "I wanted to see you. I saw you headed this way," she said with characteristic honesty. Kane was both pleased and appalled. She had taken a terrible risk only to see him. Damn it, he wasn't worth it.

"I wasn't planning to stop here," he lied. "I was out riding, and I heard your scream."

But she seemed not to hear as she moved even closer to him, and their bodies began to react to each other. Her trembling had stopped, and it had been replaced by a warm and pliant softness. He felt himself grow hard. He'd been aching for days, every time he saw her, or even thought of her. The urgency became nearly unbearable as she stood there in his arms. Still, he forced himself to be gentle, afraid of reminding her of the violence she'd been victim of only minutes ago.

"I wish I had killed him," he muttered, half to himself.

"No," she said. "Then I could never remember this place as I want to."

"How do you want to remember it?"

"Full of magic," she said. "Magic and wonder."

The answer touched him. She'd asked so little of him, had offered so much. He leaned down and kissed her cheek. "Don't let me spoil you on magic," he said softly. "Or wonder. They are much too rare."

She was silent for a moment, the silence a communion between them, a sweetness that beggared the first fresh smell of flowers in spring. She was so warm, huddled against him. He felt raw, unable to guard himself.

Finally she said, "You weren't going to say good-bye."

"No," he said. He was glad it was too dark for her to see his eyes. She might see altogether too much. "I don't like good-byes."

Her breath hit his throat, soft and tempting, coming in short, soft sighs. Her hand was touching his face. She had started trembling again lightly, but he didn't want to think it had to do with fear. He wanted to make her safe, forever. His arms tightened around her, and her body melded into his. Her breasts were almost bare, and he felt their softness against his chest. His hand went down to one. He thought maybe she would shy away, especially after Hildebrand's rough handling, and he made his touch tender as he felt her nipple swell and grow taut.

Her hands went around his neck, played with his hair with an intimate possessiveness that stirred him. The ache in his lower regions grew stronger. Don't, he told himself. Run like hell. But her mouth was reaching toward him, and he couldn't move away. He lowered his head slightly, and his lips touched hers, and then the fire exploded between them.

There were remnants of fear in her. He sensed it. It should have cooled him, but it didn't. He wanted to wipe away every memory of any man's touch but his own.

She had said she wanted to remember this place as

being full of magic and wonder. He wanted to give both to her. Yet he feared he would also rob her of both.

"I love you," Nicky whispered.

The words were like a sword through his gut. Yet another part of him rejoiced in them. He had never been loved before. Exquisite agony filled him, and his hands became tentative, uncertain. He knew what he should do. He wasn't sure he could.

"Don't go away," she said. "I need you."

He knew instantly that she wasn't referring to his leaving tomorrow. She meant now. But what about tomorrow? And next week? Next month? Damn it to hell, he would work out something with Masters. He had to. He couldn't, wouldn't, give Nicky up.

"Oh God, Nicole," he said. "I need you, too." He meant everything the word meant. He'd said it to her a week ago, but then he'd tried to deny that the need was anything but physical. Now he knew how deep it ran.

Her hands touched his face again, but really they were touching his heart. And his heart was woefully in need. He wanted to give her everything she was giving to him.

His kiss deepened as his hands fumbled at her trousers, and then they were loose. Seconds later, his were also off. She lay on the grass, waiting for him. So open. So exquisite. He lowered himself over her, letting his manhood tease her until she cried out, and then he went into her. He felt her arms around him, and then her legs. She knew what to expect now, and any shyness was gone. She was as honest in her passion as she was in all else.

He filled her and felt the tremors, the great shocks of desire rolling through him, but more than that he felt the two of them joining in every way.

I love you. The words rolled over and over in his consciousness. *I love you, too.* But the words stayed locked within him because he didn't have the right to speak them. Still, he tried to convey his love in every other way.

Nicky was drowning in a sea of sensations. Kane had been infinitely gentle until he entered her. And then they both were savage in their needs, in taking and giving. He pushed deep inside her, filling her, and her body moved instinctively in rhythmic circles until they were lost in a primitive dance that was wild and fierce and free. Tremors of ecstasy shook her universe. He *was* her universe. She didn't know anything else except the oneness with him, the incredible expectations that throbbed through her body. His hands moved up and down her hips as his lips devoured hers.

She soared to the heavens and beyond, lost in a sea of emotions and feelings and sensations that tumbled her over and over. And then the heavens exploded, and she felt like a shooting star streaking across the sky, glowing, radiant, free.

She felt his body collapse on her, the sweat that suddenly chilled with the night, the lovely perfume of lovemaking. She felt all that, and painted it into her mind for all time.

He stilled, and they both lay there, afraid to pierce the quiet and beauty of the night with words—to tarnish the last few seconds with a reality that neither wanted. He was leaving the next morning.

A cool breeze swept over them, drying the dampness of their bodies, and he very carefully rolled away from her and handed her shirt to her. She put it on but didn't button it. Instead, she snuggled down in the crook of his arm and let her fingers crawl over his chest and the dark arrow of hair that led downward. It was fine, that chest. Hard and supple at the same time. She leaned over and trailed her tongue along the outlined muscles, feeling his body tense again.

"Nicole," he said warningly, but she ignored it.

She couldn't get enough of him. Not now. Not ever. There was still so much exploring to do. "You taste good," she said.

He chuckled, and she loved the feel of his body rumbling. He didn't chuckle enough. He didn't smile enough. He never laughed. She suddenly wanted to hear him laugh and, feeling inspired, she started playing with the tufts of hair on his chest, tickling, exciting.

"Nicole," he warned again, but his chest was rumbling even more—and something else was happening a bit lower. She watched with fascination. She had felt him grow hard before, but she'd never actually watched it happen. The wisps of clouds had passed the moon again, leaving her enough dim light to see, and she reached out her hand and touched, feeling the strength of his arousal.

"It's very interesting," she said, her hand exploring.

He groaned. "Interesting?"

"Splendid," she amended.

"That's better," he said, and there was definitely laughter in his voice.

"Better than splendid," she said. "What makes it grow?"

"You do," he said mirthfully. No wariness now, no sarcasm, no caution.

She was encouraged. "Why?"

"You have to ask God," he said.

"Do you believe in God?"

"Sometimes," he said. "Especially when someone asks a question like that one."

She pondered his answer. "I don't know much about God."

Kane didn't suppose she did, growing up as she had. Well, he hadn't known much himself until he went to live with Davy's family. His own father's God was a vengeful, hateful one who wreaked destruction on all who sinned, and even those who didn't. The Carsons' God was a gentler one, of whom one asked for blessings., He hadn't thought about either God in a long time, not since he went to war. It had been hard to believe in any but a vengeful God during those years of blood and destruction.

But now, with Nicky in his arms, he wondered. He wondered how such sweetness and passion had come to him, wondered if there was indeed a God that blessed.

Or was his vengeful God merely setting him up for a long, hard fall?

And would Nicky fall with him?

He wanted to protect her always. He wanted to hold her like this, and feel her wonder and innocence. He wanted to build something with her, like Davy and Martha had built a family, and he wanted to believe in happy ever after. He didn't want to think about Masters, or the death sentence hanging over his head, or Davy sitting in prison. He groaned, his arm tightening around her as if he could close out the rest of the world. If only he could.

She was still watching the progress of his erection, her fingers tracing the small veins on his manhood, cradling its smooth tip until he thought he was going to explode.

"How big does it get?" she asked.

It was about as big as it could get. He was literally vibrating with need. And she was rolling onto him, spurred apparently by curiosity and instinct. "Sit up," he said and guided her body until she sat astride him, and he felt himself swelling even larger as he went into her.

"Oh," she gasped. "Oh, oh."

And suddenly she was riding him, and he felt a joyous rapture he'd never known in lovemaking. She sheathed him tightly, moving in ways that made his blood boil and every nerve tingle. And all the time, great rolling waves of sensation washed through him. He heard her whimper. He exploded in her, and she cried out, low and throaty.

She leaned down and kissed him, long and savoring, and then she collapsed on him.

"Hell's bells," she sighed.

As exhausted as he was, he felt his chest rumbling again, and a smile form on his lips.

Chapter Sixteen

Reality did not return to Kane until they started to dress. His departure was hanging between them like a curtain, creating a certain awkwardness. Kane knew that Nicky had no idea how thick the curtain was, but awareness keep picking at his mind like a steady current of water eating away banks of a river bed.

"It won't be long," she said, touching his face with such gentleness that he wanted to take her up on his horse and ride away, away from Sanctuary, away from obligations and lies and death.

"You look so sad," she said.

Damn that slice of moon. He swallowed. Whatever he said would be a lie. His life was a lie. He'd even lied to himself. It had been easy with her in his arms. He'd sought justification for loving her, and it had come easily when his blood was hot. He'd told himself everything would be all right, that Masters would give him time; but now that the wind was cooling him, and common sense was returning, he knew it had been nothing more than wishful thinking.

Masters wasn't going to let him off the hook, and Nicky would discover his perfidy. He had used her as Masters was using him. His breath caught in his throat. What in the hell was he doing? To her? To himself?

"Kane?"

He looked down at her. Her face was turned upward toward his. He took her in his arms and held her, one hand soothing that short, curly hair. "Always know I cared," he said.

Her body stiffened, and he knew he'd made a mistake. *Cared.* Not care. His words sounded like a good-bye— and most likely were exactly that.

"You are coming back?" she asked, her voice uncertain.

"I'm going to try," he said. A long silence passed. He had said that before, but there was a warning now that hadn't been there before.

He knew she heard it as he watched her bite her lip, her body sliding closer to his. "Promise you'll be back."

"I can't," he replied.

"Why?"

"There's a price on my head, remember?"

"Then don't go. And don't go with Sam Hildebrand."

"I won't leave him here with you."

"My uncle will take care of him."

He shook his head. "The other men here, your 'guests,' didn't like Yancy being ejected. Hildebrand's respected. Your uncle would be asking for trouble if he killed Hildebrand now."

"Mitch . . . ?"

"Nicky, you have a powder keg here," he said. "Your uncle has been able to control it through sheer will, but that will isn't so strong anymore, and the others suspect it."

"What's so important that you have to leave?"

"A friend," he said simply. "The best friend I ever had. I owe him everything, including my life. Remember that, Nicole, if I can't return. Nothing else could make me leave you."

She was shivering. He needed to let her go before he said more, before he forgot his other obligation, the one pledge he'd made in his life, and meant to keep.

He laid his cheek on her head for a moment. "If for some reason I don't return in three weeks," he finally said, "get yourself out of here. As soon as you can. And take

Robin. I have some money. I'll leave it with Andy in the morning."

"My . . . uncle."

"Listen to me—you will have done everything you could for him. You've paid back any debt you might have owed him. If not for your own sake, leave for Robin's."

"It's not a debt," she protested. "I love him."

Kane closed his eyes for a moment against a new onslaught of pain. "I know," he finally said softly. "But he wants you and Robin safe. That's why he invited me to stay. You won't be doing him any favors by endangering yourself. Go, if I'm not back in three weeks. Promise me."

"You expect trouble," she said hesitantly. "There's something you're not telling me."

Damn her intuition.

"No," he lied. "I just think it's time for you to leave Sanctuary. For good. It's too dangerous. They smell blood, damn it."

"When you come back . . ."

"Even if I do return," he said, "and, God help me, I'll try, Sanctuary is still no place for you or Robin."

"I won't go without you."

"What about Robin? What about his future?"

She hesitated, obviously torn. "Can't we go somewhere with you?"

"I don't have any place to go, Nicky."

"Why . . . ?" Her question trailed off. Then a minute later, she said simply, "I would go anyplace with you. I love you."

His jaw clenched. He didn't want her to love him. He didn't want to be the cause of her destruction, as he had been the cause of Davy's. Hell, he'd never been good for anyone.

"Don't," he ordered.

"I can't help it," Nicky said. "It just happened."

"I can't marry," he said. "I'm a convicted murderer. There's a rope with my name on it. I've been disaster for everyone I've ever cared about, and I'm not adding you to that list." Or had he already?

"Have you ever been in love?" she asked.

He knew he should say yes, knew he should scare her away. "No," he said. *Not before Nicky*.

A brief pause, then: "Andy said there are layers and layers to you."

Layers and layers of deceit, of lies. The blacksmith was too perceptive.

"I'll take you home," he said, letting the implied question die.

"I don't want to go yet."

His hand touched her hair, ran through the silky curls. "It's late, and I'm leaving at dawn. I won't leave you here alone." He heard the hollowness of his own voice, and he hoped she didn't detect the anguish filling him.

Her hand caught his and brought it to her lips. "Come back to me," she said. "To Robin and me." His hand trembled.

"If anything happens, if I don't come back," he said, "don't mourn me. Just take the money and go to San Antonio. I have friends there. A blacksmith named Harry Clayton. He'll see to it that you're all right."

She didn't say anything, just held his hand.

"Promise me," he said.

"I can't," Nicky replied. "Not until I can get Uncle Nat to a doctor."

"It might be too late," Kane said, feeling her body stiffen. "And if he goes, you won't be safe. Promise me. If I'm not back in three weeks, swear you'll leave. For Robin." He knew nothing else would work.

"Yes," she finally whispered in surrender.

He sighed. He'd won one battle. One small battle. If only he could win the larger one with Masters and get two more months of time, maybe even three....

"Let's go back," he said, leading her to her horse and helping her mount.

But she hesitated. "Be careful."

He felt himself smiling. "I will. I don't think anyone will recognize me through the beard."

"Except Sam Hildebrand."

"I can take care of him."

She finally allowed him to help her mount. She didn't

say good-bye, and he was grateful. He didn't think his crumbling defenses could stand it.

NICKY stalked the confines of her room as dawn approached. She kept returning to the window until she saw the silhouettes of three men on horseback, moving slowly from the livery. She recognized Kane's back. She would recognize him anywhere. Kane. Hildebrand. Calico. She watched until they were out of sight, a sense of foreboding filling her. Though her body was sated and tired from his lovemaking, her mind was restless, seeking answers that kept evading her.

A friend. He was going back for a friend. But who was it? And what was the debt that Kane owed this person? Was it really so strong that he had to leave the relative safety of Sanctuary to honor it? Clearly, the answer was yes, and she hated not knowing more.

What she did know was that terrifying finality in Kane's tone and demeanor, an anguish that went beyond the mere words of his explanations, such as they were.

Are you coming back? she'd asked. And he'd replied, *I'm going to try.* She believed he would. But she also believed he didn't feel he had a hope in the world that he would succeed.

And then there was Hildebrand. Nicky thought about telling her uncle what had happened. He would probably wonder why Hildebrand had chosen to leave so abruptly. But she couldn't bother her uncle now, not when he was feeling so poorly. She worried that Kane might not be able to control him, but surely he and Calico, together, could.

Unable to stay in the room another moment, Nicky found her small derringer, slipped out of the house and headed toward the livery stable. She would give Molly a few oats. Maybe that would give her a respite from the worries building like blocks, one upon the other, in her mind.

The door to the barn opened easily. Theft was not a

problem in Sanctuary. No one dared, knowing there was no way out other than through a gauntlet of guards.

She went inside, knowing that Kane had been here moments earlier, remembering his face only a few hours before when they'd unsaddled their horses together. He had touched her face with such tenderness, with such a melancholy sadness etched into his features, that she'd been sure he was saying good-bye forever. She shuddered once, then wiped the thought away.

Molly caught her scent and whinnied from her stall. Nicky grabbed a handful of oats and allowed the mare to nibble from her fingers. The other hand twisted in the horse's mane. A moment later, she heard a noise—and the sound of voices. Hunkering down in the corner of the stall, she wished Andy were here. A month ago, she wouldn't have been frightened, but things had changed. Her own home was no longer safe. She recalled Kane's words. *They smell blood.*

A voice: "That goddamned blacksmith isn't here."

Another: "Good. I'll look around, see if I can't find any weapons in the back room. There has to be at least a knife somewhere."

"Any ideas where Thompson keeps the guns?"

"Hell, no. If we knew that, we could take them now."

"I feel damn naked without a gun."

"Sam said to find any weapons we can. He'll take care of Diablo."

"You sure he can?"

"Sam says Calico owes him real big. And Calico has a gun. Between the two of them, they can take Diablo, all right. Sam says he approached Diablo about a job, even hinted about this one, and the man backed off. Seems he's turned yellow. Either that, or he's in Thompson's pocket. Now get to looking. Make sure the rifles aren't here."

Nicky heard the harsh music of spurs, then the banging of several drawers along with some curses. She moved into the back of the stall and tried to fade into the hay. Her hand grasped the derringer; but there were two of them, and she only had one bullet.

There was another loud curse. "Nothing here."

"Must be in Thompson's house then. Have a man watch the house, and when they're all away, search it."

"I'm not too sure about this."

"Hell, Sam has friends. He'll come riding back with them, and we have to be able to help him from inside. We'll have ourselves a nice little town with rules *we* make for a change."

"Thompson ain't no pushover."

"He didn't *used* to be. But I agree with Sam. Thompson and Evers are old. That's why they need Diablo. I heard them talking about it. I don't think Evers likes it much, though."

"And the girl?"

"Hell, she seems sweet on him. Sam thinks she's part of the deal with Diablo. I wouldn't mind tasting her myself."

"We'll all have that chance when Sam gets back."

"Mebbe we shouldn't wait for Sam."

"That's fool's talk," one of the men said derisively. "Ain't no one going to join us till Hildebrand gets back and we get those guns."

"His leaving's pretty sudden."

"It's his chance to get Diablo before he can bring men back here."

"Wonder if that's the only reason. Hildebrand didn't look too good when he came in last night."

"Sam can take care of himself. I worked with him on other jobs. He's a good planner."

The footsteps and spurs retreated, and Nicky stood, leaning against the wall of the stall. She waited what seemed ages, enough time for the men to disappear from sight. Then, keeping herself close to the buildings, she headed for home. Home. She wondered whether Sanctuary would ever be that again.

When she reached the house, she went immediately to her uncle's room and knocked lightly. A grunt answered, and she went inside. He was in bed, his face even paler than before, but he tried to smile. The old confidence was gone, though, and for the first time she realized how truly ill he was.

"Nicky, what is it?"

She wanted to tell him, started to tell him. He had always been the epitome of strength and infallibility. Her protector, hers and Robin's. But he looked so old. She couldn't tell him about the threat. He would go after Calico and Hildebrand himself, and she knew he wouldn't make it.

Mitch. She would go to Mitch.

Nicky tried a smile and went over to her uncle, reaching over to take his hand. "I think we should get a doctor. A good doctor."

"I'm all right," he said, sitting. He tried not to reveal the effort it took him, but he couldn't.

"You stay here," she said. "You deserve some rest." She hurried out. Mitch had a small house next to theirs. She knocked on the door and waited, but he didn't answer. She thought about Andy, but Andy wasn't a gunhand. She thought about the guards over the passes into Sanctuary, but if Calico had turned traitor, then she couldn't be sure of their loyalty either.

Ain't no one going to join us until Hildebrand gets back.

Kane was her one hope, and Kane was also in danger. She couldn't wait until Mitch returned. He might be out looking for supply wagons, or meeting with their Indian allies.

She went to her room, scribbled out two notes, one for Mitch and one for Andy, warning them of trouble, telling them of the plot and that she would go after Kane. She didn't want to talk to Andy. He would try to talk her out of going.

She would leave the one for Mitch in his house, and the one for Andy in the stable. If he were there when she went to get Molly, she would leave it in Molly's stall where he would find it but not soon enough to stop her.

She took the map she'd found in her uncle's drawer, tucked the derringer in her trousers, and took her rifle out of its locked cabinet. Shoving an old hat on her head, she then packed one change of clothes in her saddlebags, some candles, and some bread she'd baked the previous day.

She knew she would have to hurry, and she knew she would take the entrance through the caves. She didn't want anyone to know she'd left, no one who might have an interest in those leaving and approaching Sanctuary.

Nicky walked swiftly to the stable. She saw smoke rising from the blacksmith shop next to the stable and knew Andy was there. At least, she wouldn't have to lie to him. She hurriedly saddled Molly and fitted the rifle into the scabbard. She left the note, telling Andy she'd gone after Kane and asking Juanita to look after her uncle and brother. Then she mounted and walked Molly out. A man was loitering outside the hotel, his gaze on the Thompson house. Nicky doubted whether her uncle would leave the house, not until he felt better, but even if he did no one would find the guns and rifles. They were locked away in a room under the house. The entrance was covered by what looked like flooring, then carpet. Unless someone knew the exact location, they would never find it.

Nicky walked Molly slowly out of town, but once out of sight of the buildings, she gave the mare her head. They had a lot of miles to make up.

GOODEN, TEXAS

Ben Masters was looking forward to his outing with Mary May. In the first place, he enjoyed her company. In the second, he needed the exercise. He dismissed the part of his conscience that said he had no business leaving Gooden now.

"I thought you might decide against this," she said, when he met her at five in the morning at the town livery.

It was still dark, but she had told the liveryman to expect them, and he had already saddled her horse. She was wearing a green riding outfit, a jacket and split skirt, and she looked elegant and lovely. The liveryman stood grinning stupidly at her, and Ben wondered whether she had that effect on all men. Hell, he'd thought himself immune to just about any woman alive, but she had him looking forward to every meeting, even a public one in a saloon. He felt like grinning stupidly himself.

It scared the hell out of him.

Especially since he knew she had knowledge of Sanctuary. He had come to believe that Gooden was probably an important piece in the Sanctuary puzzle. The fact that Diablo had disappeared from this town was not accidental. And it made sense. There was probably one town in each adjacent state or territory that was an entrance to Sanctuary. And the lack of law in Gooden made it a prime candidate.

He'd thought about it all night. He'd thought about Mary May and Kane O'Brien, and he wondered how the two interconnected. Perhaps Mary May would slip and tell him something useful.

"I wouldn't miss a chance of being with you all day for the world," he told her with unaccustomed gallantry. She made him feel gallant.

She gave him a beguiling smile. "You may be sorry for that in the wee hours of tomorrow morning, Mr. Smith."

He helped her mount, much to the disappointment of the liveryman. "I don't think so," he said.

In minutes, he had saddled his own horse and was riding alongside her. Fall was approaching, and there was just the slightest chill in the air. The sky was clear, and the moon was only a sliver sinking close to the horizon. There were still a million stars in the sky.

Mary May set a good pace, and he enjoyed the quiet companionship as they passed through the town, then through the slightly rolling prairie. They stopped briefly at a creek as the sun started to show over the eastern horizon, showering streams of light across the grass, turning the dry spikes into a carpet of gold.

They dismounted and watered the horses, allowing them a few moments of rest. "Tell me about your daughter," Ben asked.

She smiled, her eyes glowing, not beguilingly or with wit, but with a softness that went straight to Ben's heart. "Her name is Sarah Ann, and I love her more than life itself."

"Why don't you raise her yourself?"

"As the daughter of a saloon hostess or worse? You know what kind of life she would have. Other children laughing at her, taunting. I want her to be a lady. A real lady."

"Have you thought about leaving the Blazing Star?"

She shrugged. "What else would I do? I can entertain men. I can deal cards." She looked away. "I could also marry. I know that. But the first time was a disaster. Besides, we get three kinds of men in the Blazing Star, and I wouldn't want any of them for Sarah Ann's father."

"What are the three kinds?" he asked.

"The drinker, the gambler, and the bully."

"Which of the three am I?" he asked, only a shade of humor in his voice.

She turned and stared at him. "You don't fit any of them, and that worries me." Her gaze intensified. "*Why* are you here?"

"I told you I'm waiting for a friend."

"Must be a good friend."

"He saved my life." Ben didn't add that O'Brien sure as hell didn't consider *him* a friend.

Mary May looked up at him, those bright green eyes meeting his directly. "Are you a lawman?"

He stood there, stunned. He thought about lying for about three seconds, but there was something about her that kept him from doing that. In the past few weeks, a kind of trust had developed between him and Mary May and he was damned if he could break it. She wouldn't betray him, not a man she was taking to meet her daughter. Not unless he was more wrong than he'd ever been in his life.

"Yes," he said.

She drew a deep breath and expelled it slowly. "Why are you here?"

He shook his head. "I can't tell you that."

"Something to do with Sanctuary," she said, almost to herself. It wasn't even a question.

He didn't reply.

"Be careful," she said, and he knew for certain, then,

that she wouldn't betray him. She turned away from him and went to her horse. She didn't wait for him to help her, but swung into the saddle herself. He followed suit.

He moved his horse alongside hers. "Are you connected to Sanctuary?"

She didn't say anything for a few moments. Then, without looking at him, asked, "Is that why you came with me today?"

"No. I came because I wanted to come."

"You're a different kind of law dog," she observed with puzzlement in her voice.

He'd heard that expression before. It wasn't complimentary. He grinned suddenly. "I've been told that before."

"Why?" She was looking at him now.

"I don't know," he said. "Perhaps because I was once a lawyer. I was raised on the idea that there are many sides to any one question."

"A lawyer?" she said with surprise. "Why . . . ?"

He shrugged. "It seemed . . . too dull after the war. I couldn't seem to stay in an office."

She shook her head. "I don't understand you."

He grinned. "No one does, including my superiors."

"You said you were waiting for a friend?"

His mouth suddenly tightened. He knew he had said too much already. But Mary May was so very good at listening.

"Will you tell me about your connection with Sanctuary?" he countered.

She stared at him, as if trying to decide whether she could trust him. The mutual knowledge that he had entrusted to her a secret that could get him killed hung between them.

Finally, she sighed. "Nothing much. I just pass on information. It helps pay for my daughter's care."

"You don't know where it is?"

She hesitated, then evaded the question. "That kind of knowledge gets people killed." She paused. "So do questions about it."

"What if someone wants to go there? How can they tell the outlaws from the curious drifter?"

"They have their ways," she said.

"How?" he asked.

She looked at him chidingly and spurred her horse into a canter, making any additional questions impossible. He smiled at her tactic. He'd already learned more from her than he thought possible, yet she'd very carefully skirted around the really vital information he needed.

Still, he knew he wouldn't get more. Not now. And it was a beautiful day, bright and clear. The sky was vividly blue and endless, the sun a glowing ball that bestowed a gentle warmth rather than parching heat. Despite the conversation, he felt an odd sense of well-being.

And the day had only begun.

Chapter Seventeen

After a long, frightening trek through a narrow, musty cave, Nicky quickly found the trail of Calico, Hildebrand, and Kane. She knew a little about tracking, had the map, and Calico had little reason to hide his trail on this end.

She doubted Hildebrand or Calico would make their move until night, when Kane was tired. She had to catch up to them before then.

Nicky knew there were Comanches in these parts who tolerated, and even protected, Sanctuary for a price. She had met some when they came into Sanctuary for food or liquor, and she had her talisman with her. But she didn't see another human being throughout the day, nor any sign of one, other than the horse tracks she followed.

She hurried the pace. She couldn't afford to lose them when it fell dark. Yet her quarry was moving fast, too. The droppings continued to be slightly baked by the late summer sun. She wondered whether she was close enough to hear gunshots, swallowing hard at the thought. She wasn't sure at all that she could handle this on her own.

Sometime around late morning, she'd had left the mountains and entered the plains. The terrain made following easy. Grass was bent, and the odor of horses was strong. Nicky knew Molly was tired. The mare was wheezing, but Nicky realized she couldn't stop. "A few more miles," she whispered to the mare. "You have to keep going."

The sky grew a deeper blue as dusk hurried along. The sun dipped, and the sky was suddenly painted with brilliant colors. Ordinarily, she would have enjoyed the scene, but at the moment she begrudged every slipping inch of the sun. There were more droppings ahead, and she slipped from the horse to test them. This time, they were slightly warm. Success battled apprehension. Another thirty minutes and she would barely be able to see anything, much less a trail. She dug her heels into Molly's back, whispering a slight apology.

Minutes later, it was dark, almost black. The stars were out, and the moon was rising in the east. Although she could see its full silhouette, only a tiny sliver gave light.

Molly stumbled, and Nicky dismounted. She would have to lead Molly from there. She didn't know what to do. She could no longer follow the tracks. Yet she couldn't stop. She had to warn Kane. Every step, though, only made her more aware of the hopelessness of her chase. She felt ridiculously foolish, riding alone in a territory she didn't know after three men who, among them, had been chased by more posses than she could possibly count.

And she had hopes of catching them?

Nicky searched the darkness around her, trying to find one of the landmarks on the map. At least it would help to know if she was going in the right way. But nothing was familiar. She kept walking in the direction she'd been traveling until, suddenly, rising from the darkness on the horizon, she saw the silhouette of a rock formation she remembered from the map. She said a brief prayer—not that she was all that familiar with the process, but she would try anything at this point.

Nothing.

Feeling a deepening frustration and fear, she moved forward, still leading Molly. She was suddenly aware of the mare halting, her ears cocking forward, her nostrils blowing harder than they had. Clearly, Molly heard, or smelled, other animals.

Nicky looked around desperately for a place to tie the

mare. She didn't dare take the horse farther. If Molly detected other horses, those other horses could also smell her. The last thing Nicky figured she needed was a noisy horse reunion. She finally found a struggling mesquite, and tied the reins to its base. She took the rifle from its scabbard and touched the derringer in her belt.

There were horses around, but where?

They had been moving south. She looked up at the sky, wished she knew more about the stars, more about direction. She could only stumble around, hoping for luck. She went in the direction she had been traveling, keeping the rock formation to her right. Minutes seemed like hours. And then she saw a flickering of a light. A campfire.

Nicky sat for a moment, trying to gain her breath . . . and her wits. She was as jumpy as a grasshopper in a fire. She wasn't a fool; she knew she had one chance at best. Both Hildebrand and Calico were very dangerous men. The only thing she had on her side was surprise. Surprise, and Kane. If he were still alive.

He had to be! She'd seen no body, no shallow grave. She'd heard no shots. And she knew in her heart he still lived.

After several moments, she had forced her breathing to calm. Her heart wasn't pounding quite so hard. She stood again and moved as quietly as she could toward the fire. Calico had no reason to expect a trespasser. The Comanches wouldn't attack a party from Sanctuary, and no one else was likely to be roaming their territory.

But as she moved closer to the fire, she dropped to a crouch, listening for conversation. There was none, but she did see figures moving around. If the men she heard in the barn were right—if Calico and Hildebrand were together—Hildebrand might have a gun by now. Both were fast gunhands. She couldn't simply walk up with the rifle in her hand. She could, but it would be chancy, and too much depended on this. Kane's life. Her uncle's life and possibly Robin's.

It would be better to wait, she decided, until the fire had died low and the men had turned in for the night— though she thought the wait might possibly drive her to madness. She lay on the ground silently. Kane was several hundred feet away, but at the moment it might be a thousand miles. She tried to ignore her discomfort. Sore and exhausted from riding so long, she was also scared. Nicky hated to admit to that last, but she was.

Nicky rolled over on her back and looked at the sky. She didn't know how long she lay there before she heard a mumbling of voices, a brief nicker from one of the men's horses, then silence. The glow from the fire was gone. The prairie was silent. She waited for another half hour or so, then started moving toward the dying fire. If they were going to try to take Kane, it would be now, when he should be asleep. Urgency clawed at her belly, making her sweat. She crawled closer toward the barely glowing embers. To her right, a horse stomped nervously.

She reached a stand of tall grass where she could see three blanket-clad forms. Which one was Kane's? She decided it was probably the one farthest from the other two. Kane was a loner, and he certainly didn't like Hildebrand. Not only that, he would be on the watch for Hildebrand, if not for Calico. And then she recognized the gray near the lone form.

On the premise that a man—particularly an outlaw on the run—would sleep near his horse, Nicky began to move toward the direction of the gray. She crawled a few feet, stopped to listen for movement, a sign that she was being discovered, and when there was none, she moved again. Seven times, she repeated the pattern until she was within a few feet of the lone figure, and she knew she had been right. It was Kane. To arouse him without disturbing anyone else, Nicky had to let go of the rifle, but the derringer was in her hand as she reached out to touch Kane. Suddenly her own wrist was grabbed. She fought to keep from crying out as Kane turned over. It was too dark to see an expression, but she felt his body relax. She put a finger to his lips and tried to move from the hold. He let her go. She watched him look around. As she started crawling away, picking up her rifle as she did, he followed.

They kept moving. A hundred feet, two hundred,

three. Then he leaned toward her. "What in the hell are you doing here?," he asked in a rough whisper.

"Calico has thrown in with Hildebrand," she whispered. "They planned to kill you, recruit some men, and take Sanctuary."

"How do you know?"

"I overheard two men in the stable."

"Your uncle?"

"He's real sick. I couldn't tell him and I couldn't find Mitch. There wasn't anyone else I could trust. Except you."

He was silent for a moment. "Do you know how many are involved?"

"I only heard two men. They said they wouldn't do anything until Hildebrand returned. They were looking for guns, though."

Kane swore. "I knew something was wrong," he said. "Hildebrand was too damned accommodating."

"We have to go back," she said urgently.

"I can't," he said, then a moment later, asked, "You sure they won't move without Hildebrand?"

"That's what they said."

"Then we have nearly a week before he would be expected back, he and Calico."

"But . . ."

"There's something I have do in Gooden," he said implacably.

"Can't that wait?"

"No." Kane's voice was flat, uncompromising.

She waited as minutes went by. She knew he was thinking. "What will we do about Calico and Hildebrand?" she finally asked.

"We?"

"I can use a gun. I got you out of there, didn't I?"

"And I have a whole lot of questions about that," Kane said, "but there's no time now. I have to take care of those two."

Nicky felt a chill go down her spine. "Kill them?"

"I should," Kane said coldly. "But I'll try another way first. You have something other than that rifle?"

"The derringer."

"No six-shooter?" He muttered, then sighed. "You like living dangerously, don't you?"

"I . . . don't have one, and there wasn't time—"

"It's all right." His voice softened. He put a hand on her cheek. "You did really well. Thank you."

She nodded.

"Give me the derringer. You stay here with the rifle. I'll try to take them one at a time."

She started to protest and he leaned over and kissed her, quieting her protest.

"Do it," he said in a low but adamant voice. "I know what I'm doing."

Nicky believed him. She gave him the derringer, then took out the knife she'd brought and handed it to him.

"No need," he said, reaching into his boot to pull out a knife of his own. He put a finger to her lips to stop questions, then started crawling away toward the fire.

She watched as he hesitated, as if searching for something, and then he moved ahead again. A horde of grasshoppers seemed to take up residence in her stomach as she watched him crawl off into the darkness.

Despite her promise, she moved behind him, although she maintained a distance between them. She stopped about seventy feet away and clutched the rifle. Nicky saw Kane's silhouette reach the side of one of the men. She saw him lift his hand, then strike downward.

Another silhouette started to move, and Nicky grabbed the rifle, pointing it in the man's direction. She heard voices.

"What in the hell . . . ?"

The figure leaped for Kane, and both men fell to the ground. The sound of scuffling, punctuated by loud grunts, traveled clearly in the air. Kane had told her to stay, but she couldn't. Clutching the rifle with her two hands, she moved rapidly to within feet of the two men. In the moonlight, she saw the brightly patterned shirt. *Calico.* She also saw a knife; it was in Calico's hand, but Kane was keeping it away from his body. They rolled over once, then again, as Nicky tried to aim. Then there was a grunt, and the men stropped rolling. Kane was astride Calico. His fist rammed into the man's head. Once, twice, a third time. Then Calico was still.

He rose wearily. "Calico has rope on his saddle. Get it."

She handed him the rifle and rushed to get the rope. She watched as he tied both men, hands behind them, feet together. Both were still unconscious.

Then Kane sunk down on the ground, obviously exhausted. She knelt next to him, wanting to make sure he was all right. He wasn't. Her fingers found a dampness in his shirt. "You've been cut," she said.

"It's nothing," he said, but he didn't move, and the dampness was spreading. She looked frantically around, wishing there were more wood for a fire so she could see better. There were a few mesquite trees, and she broke up a few branches. She stirred what remained of the old fire, finding only a few embers, but those caught the new wood and flamed for a moment. She pulled the tail of her shirt from her trousers and tore off a piece, pushing his shirt up till she found the cut and held the cloth to it. In a moment, he took it himself. "It really isn't much," he said. "Not more than skin-deep."

She sat next to him, drained. She knew he was right, but still she felt herself trembling with fear for him. Leftover fear. "Damn you," she said illogically. "I told you to be careful."

He chuckled, and she could have killed him. Right after she kissed him. After she kissed every part of his body, after . . .

His hand reached for hers. "Thank you," he said simply.

The words were so simple, yet they sounded so eloquent on his lips.

She leaned into him, careful to avoid the wound. Her hand felt his where he pressed cloth against the tear in his chest. He removed it and investigated. "It's almost stopped bleeding already," he said.

Nicky wasn't sure she believed him, but she realized he

didn't want her to fuss over it. "What are you going to do with them?" she asked of the two trussed men.

"That's a damned good question," he replied.

An answer hovered between them. They could kill the two. *Kane* could kill the two. After all, they had planned to kill him and Nat Thompson and, probably, her and Robin. But he would have to do it in cold blood, and something in her rebelled at that. She waited, afraid of his answer, afraid of being disappointed. Afraid he was not what she had come to think he was.

DAMN it all to hell. Every one of his opportunities was disappearing down the sewer of someone else's greed.

Kane knew Nicky was waiting on an answer, that she would probably agree to whatever he suggested—and if he suggested the obvious, he would make her into what he was.

He debated his new set of limited options. He felt he was in a chess game, constantly being checked, his available moves getting fewer and fewer. He couldn't spare the time taking Calico and Hildebrand back to Sanctuary. Neither could he take them into Gooden to Masters; he had to get some rest, and he couldn't afford hauling two dangerous men along with him.

But he did have one weapon. Fear.

"You did leave messages for your uncle?" he asked.

She nodded. "I left them with both Mitch and Andy."

"You mentioned Calico."

She nodded. "I included everything I heard."

"Without guns, the others can't do anything," he said. "And I expect Hildebrand's and Calico's plan depended completely on surprise. How sick is your uncle?"

"I don't know," she said wretchedly. "He wouldn't get a doctor, but . . ."

That now-familiar tightening in his gut tugged at him. He was betraying not only a man who trusted him, but a dying one. If he kept Nicky from returning to be with him, she would never forgive him or herself.

"You go back," he said. "I'll take care of these two."

"No," she said simply. "I can help. You don't know the way."

His senses sharpened. "You do?"

"I studied the map, and Uncle Nat explained the land-marks to both Robin and me, in case . . ."

"You can tell them to me," he said tightly. She had what he needed in her head. She had Davy's freedom, her uncle's death warrant. God help him.

She shook her head. "It'll save time if I go with you. You can get to Gooden, do whatever you must and we can come back together."

He started to argue, but her face was set, her chin tilted determinedly. She wasn't going to change her mind, and he knew he didn't have time to argue. He would learn the rest of the route through her—although he still wouldn't know how he'd gotten to where they were now. Calico had kept him and Hildebrand blindfolded during the daylight hours. At least, he'd thought Hildebrand was blindfolded.

He wondered now why they had waited before killing him. Worried about the sound of gunfire? That it might bring riders from Sanctuary or the Indians he kept hearing about? It would be easier to plunge a knife into his back at night. No sound.

Whatever the reason was, that guardian angel—or devil—that had seen him through years of war apparently remained with him.

He didn't know that route of one day, but Nicky did. She had traveled over it alone. Admiration and appreciation rushed like waves through him. And something else. She had risked her life for him. For a man who was doing his damnedest to betray her. He so sickened himself, he wanted to retch.

"Kane?" Her voice was soft, and a hand reached out, touching his shoulder lightly.

His father had been right. He was appropriately named, and the damned preacher should have spelled it right, warning everyone away.

"Go home," he said harshly again.

"I won't go without you," she said in a stubborn voice,

and he knew she detected the anger, the hopelessness in his tone. He also knew they tied her closer to him. She was a caretaker. Regardless of where she lived and how she was raised, she was as compelled to care for those she loved as he was to destroy them.

He caught her hand. "Don't care for me," he said. "I'm not worth it."

She practically threw herself into his arms. It took all the strength he had not to wrap them around her and hold her tight. She had more courage in her little finger than he had in his whole body. He felt so damned humbled by her. And she was kissing him. Kissing him on every bare spot he had. She was trying to tell him he was worth caring about, damn it, and he didn't know how to convince her otherwise without telling her the truth.

He gently disentangled her, ending the gentle rain of kisses, though it took every ounce of his self-discipline to do it. She felt so good. Being *loved* felt so good, or it would if his conscience weren't a roaring furnace.

"We'd better go," he said, knowing now any efforts to send her home would be futile.

She slowly backed away and stood. She knew she had won. He had to smile. She was always so determined, so damned full of guts combined with that rare gentleness that always attacked him at precisely the wrong time. He had no weapon or shield against either.

"What about Calico and Hildebrand?" she asked, back to being practical.

"We're going to scare the hell out of them," he said.

He stood. He knew he shouldn't do it, but he couldn't help himself. He took her in his arms and just held her for a moment. Then he let her go and strode to where the two men were tied. Hildebrand was conscious. Calico was not. Kane swiftly dealt with the unconscious man first, taking his gunbelt and buckling it around his own waist. He untied the man's feet and pulled off his boots, then his trousers to reveal the long underwear underneath. He then untied Calico's hands and took his shirt, quickly binding the hands together again.

He made sure there were no hidden weapons. Then he approached Hildebrand, who stiffened.

"I'm going to untie you, friend," he said coldly. "And you're going to take off your shirt and trousers."

"Hell I am."

"You have an alternative. You can die," Kane said coldly. "You would, in fact, were Miss Thompson not here." He looked over at Nicky, who'd dumped Calico's clothes several feet away and now held her rifle again. "Kill him if he makes a wrong move," he said. "And, just in case she doesn't, I have your friend's six-shooter, and I would take great pleasure in blowing you to hell."

"You should," Hildebrand said defiantly, and Kane admired his courage. "I'll get you for this."

"You might." Kane leaned over and untied his hands. "Take off that shirt, then untie your ankles."

Hildebrand hesitated, and Kane cocked the pistol in his hand. Hildebrand slowly did as he was told. When he was down to his underdrawers, Kane looped a prepared rope around Hildebrand's hands and tied it, taking the end and tying it to Calico.

He approached Nicky. "Where's your horse?"

"Not far," she said. "I didn't want her to warn them."

He grinned. Damn, but she was smart. He nodded toward her rifle. "Hold it on them. If either makes a move, shoot him." Kane took the bundle of clothes to where the three horses were tethered. He packed them in a saddlebag, then saddled his own horse, putting the other two on a tether.

He mounted and rode over to the two men and Nicky. He offered her his hand.

"You're not leaving us?" Hildebrand asked, his voice rising slightly. Calico started stirring. "Tied like this? We'll die."

"No great loss," Kane said, "but I didn't tie you that tightly. You can get free in an hour or so ... if you try hard enough."

"We'll die without a horse or weapons, damn you."

"You have a chance. It's a better one than you were going to give me," Kane said coldly. "Just don't even think about returning to Sanctuary. Ever. Nat Thompson knows about your plans. He'll kill you on sight. If he doesn't, he has a lot of friends who can."

Calico was now trying to sit up. "As for your friend here," Kane said, glancing over toward the guide, "his life won't be worth a damn any place in this territory. You both will be wise to make tracks north. Far north."

"Damn you," Hildebrand said.

"If you do survive," Kane said conversationally, "I wouldn't suggest you sell any information to the law, either. If you don't hang, Thompson or his friends will hunt you down wherever you go."

He turned the horses and started going.

"Diablo," Hildebrand yelled. "You can't leave us like this."

But the devil could, and did.

MARY May's daughter was a miniature version of her mother, with ringlets of auburn hair and bright green eyes and the same raw energy. The minute the child saw Mary May she ran and hurled herself into her mother's arms, and Mary May swung her around as Sarah Ann screamed with delight.

Ben watched with bemusement, as Mary May then pressed the child's cheek to her own and just held it there for a moment before planting a big kiss on her face.

"I missed you, lovebug," Mary May said, her eyes brighter than Ben had ever seen them. Perhaps it was the sheen of something wet that made them so luminous.

"Love you too, Mama," the little girl said clearly, her hand clinging to Mary May's as she was lowered to the ground. Then Mary May led her over to Ben, and Ben watched as the little girl's eyes kept moving up and up and up. He must seem a giant to her.

"This is my friend," Mary May said. "I told him how pretty you were, and he wanted to meet you."

Sarah Ann curtsied, then looked at the woman who stood in the doorway of the neat bungalow for approval. She won a smile and a nod for her efforts and beamed.

Ben was enchanted. He knelt down so he wouldn't be quite so big, so frightening, and held out his hand. "It's very nice to meet you, Sarah Ann."

"Pweasure," she replied, looking this time to Mary May for approval. Mary May knelt, too, and swooped the girl into her arms again.

"Now where did you learn that, lovebug?"

"Cuwwy," Sarah Ann mumbled happily as she buried herself in Mary May's arms.

Ben grinned. Mary May had said the lady taking care of Sarah Ann was Mrs. Culworthy. "Cuwwy" was evidently Sarah Ann's version of "Cully." But even happily sheltered in her mother's arms, Sarah Ann grinned over at him. She was as natural a flirt as her mother.

Mary May finally let go and stood again. "I brought you something," she said.

If a beaming smile could get any brighter, it did, and Mary May smiled happily back. She looked years younger, almost like a girl herself. "You stay here with Ben while I get it," she said. "Is that okay?"

Sarah Ann turned to Ben. "Are you my papa?"

Ben nearly choked. He looked up at Mary May, who shrugged slightly, but he didn't miss a momentary sadness that washed over her eyes. She knelt again. "Your papa died, lovebug. He's in heaven, looking down after you."

Sarah Ann's face set stubbornly. "I want a papa *here*, like Lizzy has."

Mary May looked helplessly at Mrs. Culworthy.

Sarah Ann turned back to Ben and cocked her head as if she was considering him for the post. It was an impossibly grown-up gesture, and Ben wondered whether she was mimicking her mother or whether it was just plain female instinct. He also felt as helpless as Mary May looked. He didn't know much about children, hadn't even been around one in years.

Then Mrs. Culworthy stepped in. "I think we'd better see what your mama brought," she said, and Sarah Ann's curiosity was suddenly captured.

The stubborn look became expectant. "What is it?"

"You'll see in a minute," Mary May said. "Mrs. Culworthy?"

The older woman went to take Sarah Ann's hand but the child went to Ben instead. "I want to stay with him."

Mary May looked helpless again, and Ben felt his heart turn to butter. Mary May was usually anything but helpless. Sarah Ann obviously was her one vulnerability. He leaned down. "And I would like you to stay with me," he said gallantly, winning a giggle.

Mary May threw him a grateful look, then hurried to her horse.

Ben went inside with Mrs. Culworthy and took the chair the woman indicated. Sarah Ann crawled up on his knee without so much as a by-your-leave and her hand touched his face as if exploring it. Her fingers were soft and chubby, as she was, and even through his awkwardness he was quite aware of falling under her spell.

"Do you know a story?" she asked.

He didn't. Not one. He felt terribly inadequate.

"No," he said.

Her face fell, and he felt totally unfit to hold a child. God, it had been so long since he'd been a boy, and even then he didn't remember being told stories. His mother was always sick, his father was either tending her or at his law offices.

"Can you play market?" Sarah Ann persisted.

Feeling even more inept, he raised an eyebrow to Mrs. Culworthy, who looked at him with pity.

"We'll teach you," she said.

"To market, to market," Sarah Ann said in a singsong voice, then stopped expectantly. After a moment of silence, she turned to him in disgust. "You're the horse. You go clip-clop."

Mrs. Culworthy signaled with her leg what he was to do. He experimentally moved his leg up and down like a horse and was rewarded with a giggle.

"To market, to market to buy a fat pig," Mrs. Culworthy and Sarah Ann responded, "Home again, home again, jiggidy jig jig."

At that particularly vulnerable moment, Mary May returned, a package in her hand. She looked at Sarah Ann, then Ben, and he felt an odd and very unfamiliar warmth. Sarah Ann tumbled off his knee and made for the package.

It was a doll, a beautiful doll with red hair and green eyes, and Ben watched as Sarah Ann cradled it just as her mother had cradled her.

"Thank you," she said solemnly, all grown-up again. "She's beautiful."

"She looks like you, lovebug."

Sarah Ann looked at Ben, obviously fascinated with him. "You name her." It was such a transference of trust that Ben felt his heart quake. But he was utterly out of his field. He was competent enough at capturing bad men; he had no idea what to name a doll. Yet, she looked at him so expectantly, he searched his mind for names until he found one he hoped would do. "Susannah," he said. "Like in the song, 'Oh, Susannah.' "

Sarah Ann looked not quite sure. She deferred to her mother, who nodded. "I think it's a wonderful name."

Satisfied, Sarah Ann's gaze went back to the doll. "Zuanna," she mispronounced happily.

Ben felt proud. As proud as if he'd captured an outlaw. Prouder, in fact. He saw Mary May's gratitude, the sheen in her eyes again, and he felt ten feet tall. He didn't think he would ever feel quite like this again.

He watched as Sarah Ann introduced the doll to Mrs. Culworthy and then cuddled it, whispering motherly things to Suzanna. Then she brought the doll back to him. "You hold her," she demanded.

Ben took the doll, not quite sure what was expected of him. "She needs a daddy, too," Sarah Ann told him solemnly. "Even just for a little while."

He swallowed hard. He was thirty-eight years old, and until that moment he'd never realized what he'd missed in allowing his job to consume him.

But now he wondered if he hadn't missed a sweetness every man should know.

Chapter Eighteen

Ben and Mary May were on their way an hour later. Sarah Ann had cried, saying she wanted to go, too. Mary May had leaned down and kissed the tears away. "I'll be back next week," she promised.

While Ben had learned the rest of "To Market," Mary May had talked to Mrs. Culworthy. Worry puckered his companion's face as she left the house, this time carrying a bag of food prepared by Mrs. Culworthy.

Ben helped Mary May mount. He was close enough to see the tears in her eyes, though she tried to hide them with a smile. Seeing she was unsuccessful, she turned away.

Ben didn't say anything, waiting for Mary May to talk, and finally, after an hour she did.

"I don't know what to do," she said. "I tried to dissuade Mrs. Culworthy from leaving, but she has to go, and she hasn't found anyone to care for Sarah Ann."

"Why don't you?" he asked frankly.

"I don't want her shamed," she said, her mouth frowning.

"She knows you're her mama," he said. "What does she think you do?"

"I don't know," Mary May said with anguish. "I thought about letting her think Mrs. Culworthy was her mother, but I couldn't. I couldn't stand her calling someone else Mama. And then there was always this possibility, that Mrs. Culworthy would leave. She told everyone my husband died, and that I had remarried and my new husband wouldn't take the child. At least, it's kept me respectable enough that other children would play with Sarah Ann. But I've always feared someone would recognize me. Mrs. Culworthy was a godsend. She protected me and Sarah."

"And now?"

"I don't know," she said. "I don't know how to do anything else, not well enough to support a child. I haven't been able to save much because I've been sending it to Mrs. Culworthy." Her back was straight, her chin set, just like Sarah Ann's had been when she'd announced she wanted a father *now*.

Ben was silent for several moments. "Her father?"

"My husband," she said with just a trace of bitterness. "He died before I knew Sarah Ann was on the way. Killed in a poker game for cheating. I was surprised it hadn't happened sooner. He didn't cheat well."

"He has no family?"

She shrugged. "He said he came from some . . . wealthy family in Scotland, but he lied a lot. I never knew what was true and what wasn't, though he did have a Scottish accent. And he spoke well. He just couldn't stay away from gambling. Once when he was drunk, he told me he'd been disowned for gambling something away." She grimaced. "He was real bitter."

"Have you thought about contacting them?"

She laughed humorlessly. "I don't know where they live, who they are, or even if they exist. I certainly can't turn up on their doorstep, even if he had told the truth for once, or especially if he had."

"Maybe," Ben said, "I can help."

"I don't take charity," Mary May said sharply. "That's not why I brought you."

"*Why* did you bring me?"

"I don't know. It's just a long ride, and I . . . " Her voice broke and she looked away.

Ben wanted to say everything would be all right. But

he didn't make promises he couldn't keep. And he didn't know what could be done about little Sarah Ann. He was certainly in no position to marry, even if he were of the inclination. And he wasn't. He'd decided years ago, after his broken engagement, that he wouldn't marry. He told himself it was because of the kind of life he had: wandering to hell and back in pursuit of lawbreakers. But the truth was, he knew deep inside, he was just plain scared. After his broken engagement, he'd never really trusted a woman again.

They stopped at dusk to water the horses. The wind was blowing up and clouds were rushing across the sky, which meant there might be rain.

Ben had been thinking hard about Mary May's problem. And Sarah Ann's future. He broached a solution as they ate the sandwiches Mrs. Culworthy made.

"There's a reward," he said, "for outlaws in Sanctuary, for anyone who helps us find the location. It could be a nest egg, a start for you and Sarah Ann. You can find a boardinghouse someplace, or . . ."

He stopped at the look on her face.

"You think I would take money from someone and turn around and betray them?" Fury filled her eyes. Fury and disappointment. Disappointment in him.

"You didn't tell them about me," he countered.

"I wasn't sure," she said, not even trying to deny her connection. She'd already said too much. He'd heard too much.

"And now that you are?"

"I wouldn't tell them about you any more than I would tell you about them," her voice breaking again. "I wouldn't take your blood money."

Ben stood there, thoroughly shamed. He had become accustomed to using people for his own ends. Wasn't that what he was doing with Kane O'Brien, no matter what his motives were? When had he become so hardened, so indifferent to feelings? When he'd seen so many people do exactly what Mary May refused to do. Sell out their friends, their relatives, for a pouch of gold? Except O'Brien hadn't done that. He'd agreed to Ben's offer only to save his friend. And here was a saloon girl refusing to take an easy way out of her dilemma. What kind of man was he to use either of them?

"I'm sorry," he said lamely.

"Don't be," she said bitterly. "Why should you think I would do anything different? You found me in a saloon." All the old confidence and spirit were gone. There was only wretchedness in her voice.

He put a hand on her shoulder, and she jerked away. But he wouldn't let her. His hand caught her arm and spun her around. He saw the naked hurt in her eyes, and knew he had disappointed her by his offer. He lowered his head and touched her lips, the lips that had so welcomed him during the last few weeks. They were cold at first, unyielding, but then they responded, just as her body responded.

"Damn you," she whispered.

He raised the hand and wiped away a tear. "I'm sorry," he said. "I was ... trying to find a way to help. I didn't think...."

"I know," she said. "There's no reason you should think well of me."

"I think very well of you," he whispered. "You're the most honest, *truly* honest, woman I've ever met."

She stared at him with disbelief.

His rough, callused hand touched her cheekbones gently. "We really should go."

"Yes," she agreed, but neither made a move toward the horses. Instead, their lips met, and their tongues exchanged fire and then they were on the ground, spending the hurt and anger and worry in a fury of lovemaking.

NICKY didn't know why she didn't give Kane the map she carried. She trusted him, but some instinct, a basic caution she'd learned at Sanctuary, kept her from sharing it. She also knew that if he had the map, he wouldn't need her, that he would try to send her back to Sanctuary. So she only told him of the landmarks her uncle had mentioned, one by one as if she were remembering them. He didn't question her, and that made her feel guilty.

He pushed hard, and that was fine with her. She wanted to get back to Sanctuary as soon as possible. She couldn't help but worry about her uncle and Robin. Kane was also quiet. He was usually quiet, but now there was a tight, private expression on his face, as if he were lost in some troubled world.

They stopped for the night at a stream, though it hardly justified that label. Only a trickle of water flowed along a muddy bottom. It wasn't fit for washing, but provided enough water for the horses. Nicky felt dirty and grimy and not at all seductive.

She wanted to be seductive. As tired as she was after nearly two days in the saddle, she wanted the intimacy and security of feeling Kane inside her. She sensed him moving farther and farther away from her with every mile they rode. He seldom looked at her. He certainly didn't smile at her. He definitely didn't laugh with her. He was sharing none of himself, but instead seemed to be pushing her farther and farther away.

His remoteness and preoccupation frightened her, and perhaps that was why she didn't tell him she had a map. She also thought he might send her back.

When they stopped for the night, they investigated the contents of the saddlebags on the other two horses. Calico's held a bottle of whiskey as well as a handful of coffee, jerky, and hardtack. Neither of the latter was appetizing, but they were practical.

It was cool but not cold, and Kane made no attempt to start a fire. After the past few days, she didn't question that decision. She no longer knew who was friend or foe.

After they'd watered the four horses and Kane had established a line for them, he'd offered her what food she wanted, then spread out their blankets, obviously making a conscious effort to separate them. Which was, after the past two nights, preposterous to her way of thinking. Still, she watched as he tipped Calico's canteen several times, diverting his gaze from her.

The clouds had fled with the winds, leaving a black

canvas sprinkled with stardust and a bright chunk of moon. She was tired, weary almost to the point of not being able to function, yet too tired to sleep. She wanted him to hold her, she wanted to go to sleep in his arms with her gaze directed skyward. She wanted to wish on all those stars and know that Kane O'Brien would make all those wishes come true. She wanted all of that, and she wanted it desperately.

And he obviously only wanted her a safe distance away.

She scooted over to him. He looked like he wanted to scoot away. He didn't. He just looked at her warily. Now that they were well away from Sanctuary, he had attached the beard and a moustache which made his emotions even more difficult to decipher than before. She yearned to touch the uncovered places of his face. She craved the feel of his hands.

She scooted again and held out her hand. "May I have some of that?"

He went stock-still. "You don't drink."

True enough, she didn't. At least, she never had. Her uncle had been adamant about it. Drinking women, he'd often said, were not attractive. But then she'd done a lot of things for the first time since she'd met Kane O'Brien. She'd made love; she'd worn a dress for the first time since she was a child; she'd killed a man; she'd left Sanctuary on her own; she'd saved Kane's life, not that he seemed all that grateful. She'd even lied a little, or at least withheld information. Drinking whiskey didn't seem all that great a leap toward perdition's flame.

"How do you know I don't drink?" she challenged.

That stopped him. She watched him ponder the question for a moment, then he handed the canteen to her. She took a long gulp, as he had, and instantly her throat caught on fire, then her insides. She coughed, and most of the contents caught between her mouth and throat came spewing back out. She had never been more mortified in her life.

She'd also dropped the bottle, and its contents were seeping out onto the ground.

She was sick, tired, and so humiliated that she felt unfamiliar tears rush to her eyes. She started to rise, but his hand on her wrist held her back, and when she finally had the courage to look at him he held out his arms and she dove into them. With his damnable beard disguising and hiding his mouth, she hadn't been able to fathom his expression: pity or disgust or sympathy. She didn't want any of those. She wanted him to care about her like she cared about him. But at the moment, his arms were safe haven, particularly to a body as tired as hers and a mind as completely besotted with the events of the past night and day.

He held her tight, and she felt herself shiver, then felt tears running unchecked down her face. She hiccuped, and he held her tighter.

"I shouldn't have given that to you," he said softly.

"You were right," she hiccuped. "I've never had a drink of whiskey before."

"I could tell," he said with a wry smile.

"And I'm tired," she complained.

"I know that too, little one," he said softly. "We should have stopped much sooner, but you didn't let me know. You have too much heart for your own good."

She snuggled in his arms. They felt so good. He felt so good. Heart. He thought she had heart. The words warmed her all the way through. She felt his arms tighten around her. She looked up at the sky. At least one of her wishes was coming true.

Nicky closed her eyes and felt loved, and wanted, as sleep closed in like a welcome friend.

KANE didn't move for a long time. She smelled of whiskey and sweat and dirt, and he thought he'd never smelled anything so sweet and noble in his life.

He had tried so hard to keep her at a distance. He should have known it would be impossible, especially after his weakness two nights ago. She'd look at him with those solemn brown eyes, and damn it, he was like clay in the hands of a potter.

You can't even see her eyes in the dark, he told himself.

But he did see them, every minute of every day, they were vivid in his mind. He knew the second she fell asleep, the way her body relaxed, completely trusting.

He kept trying to fit Nicky, who had killed Yancy and who had followed him all night long and risked her life to warn him about Hildebrand and Calico, with the Nicole, who was a soft and trusting woman, who'd never tasted whiskey or made love, and who hadn't left the confines of a small outlaw hideout for years. She was such a rare combination of utter innocence and raw, determined courage.

She deserved so much better than him, better than what the future held. If she ever found out about his deception . . .

No, make that *when* she found out.

He couldn't bear thinking about it. He had pushed that aspect of his mission aside over and over again, pretending to himself that he could prevent disaster. Hell, he'd never prevented disaster in his life, and all those failures were crashing down on any hope dwelling in him now.

Why should Masters listen to him? Believe him? He hadn't really accomplished a damn thing yet, not anything he could show Masters.

Part of him wanted to run away with Nicky. Now. He wanted it more than anything in his life: Return to Sanctuary, take Robin, and go to any damn place away from here—Mexico, even Canada. He would never have to tell her of his lies, of what he'd planned to do.

Then he thought of Davy, of an afternoon so long ago. Kane had been eight, Davy nine, when his father found him reading with Davy. Rufus O'Brien had started hitting him, then Davy had torn into the large man. Kane's father turned his anger from his son to Davy, almost killing him. His arm was broken, along with two ribs. Kane would never forget that beating, nor the aftermath. Davy's father had threatened to kill O'Brien if he ever hit either boy again. The beatings had stopped, and Kane's father had killed himself a month later. . . .

No, he couldn't abandon Davy and live with himself.

Nicky squirmed in his arms. The breath drained from

him as he felt her body fit more firmly into his, though she was still obviously asleep. Her breathing was soft, natural. His body was in sheer agony, and it got worse as his hand swept across the short curls. He hurt because he loved her. He'd never loved a woman before, and the sheer intensity and yearning and need were so painful he wondered how anyone loved and survived.

But then, he supposed, most men didn't plan to betray the woman they loved.

Christ, how could he?

He tried damned hard to rationalize. Nicky was young. She would find love again. She was too fine a person not to. Whereas Davy's life was at stake. He would have no second chances.

Kane had to weigh the two: a life against trust. It was the devil's own choice, and he'd made a devil's bargain. He wanted to crawl under a rock, where it was dark. Where he belonged. Instead he lay there, holding her, hurting, he supposed, as much as a man could hurt.

When the sky began to brighten, night giving way to a rosy-gray dawn, Kane was still awake.

I love you. He thought the words as she squirmed in his embrace, as long, dark brown eyelashes started to flutter, and she stretched, igniting a reaction in his own body. She opened her eyes and smiled at him lazily, happily, and his heart thudded wildly.

She reached up and touched his lips. "I don't think I like that beard," she said.

His hand went up to it, to where the scar was usually so visible.

"I like the scar," she said, her fingers moving up to where the faintest edge showed.

"So do the law and bounty hunters," he said. "It makes me very easy to identify."

"It won't matter when we get back to Sanctuary," she said, stretching again before snuggling back into his arms and lifting her face for a kiss.

He leaned down and gave her a light one, but she protested. "That's not very satisfactory."

"We have to go."

"Not yet," she said, and he wondered whether she had any idea how seductive, how completely appealing she was with those lazy sleep-filled eyes and inviting mouth. Too appealing. He couldn't help but lean down and do a more satisfactory job of kissing her.

Her arms went around his neck, and he couldn't think of anything but how he needed her. Her lips were so sweet on his, so expectant. His lower regions became molten as her breasts touched his shirt and her rounded bottom sat exactly where it shouldn't.

He wanted her. He wanted her with every fiber of his being. But Gooden was close now. Masters was close. Betrayal was close, and he simply couldn't do this to her again. He couldn't let her believe they had a future. He couldn't take another chance on making a child.

He ripped his mouth away and stood, keeping a hand on her arm so she wouldn't fall, ignoring her mutter of protest. "We have to go," he said again.

She looked at him with such profound disappointment that his heart pounded against his rib cage. If only he didn't want her so much and know that she wanted him just as badly. That was the real hell of it. That would always be the hell of it. He stood there for a moment, fighting himself, fighting that fierce need inside for something soft and warm and sweet and miraculous. Fighting against being loved when that was all he'd wanted his entire life. He fought against tears in his own eyes. He couldn't ever remember crying. Ever. But now the rush of grief was so strong, he could barely control it.

He turned abruptly away, so she couldn't see, and put a hand to his face as if trying to wipe away any outward pain. He looked around at the plains, where there seemed to be no end and no beginning.

God, he would sell his soul for a map. If he hadn't already sold that particular commodity for Davy's pardon. The sun was rising in the east; all he knew was they were headed south.

Convinced that he had mastered his emotions, he turned back to her. She was watching him with that steady, searching gaze of hers. He couldn't figure why she hadn't already guessed at his purpose, at his motives, that she hadn't sensed he was a wolf in sheep's clothing or, more accurately, a coyote in wolf's clothing.

"Kane?"

"Do you have any idea how far Gooden is?" he asked.

"A day, maybe," she said slowly. "Uncle Nat said it was two days' hard riding."

That was shorter than his journey to Sanctuary, but he'd thought then that Calico might have doubled back several times. But she was going on hearsay, on guesswork herself.

"Where do we go from here?" he asked, and he knew his voice was harsh.

"Follow the stream bed to a river," she said as if reciting a litany. "The river should take us into a road."

He nodded and went to the saddles on the ground, taking some jerky from the saddlebags and handing it to her. "I'll fill the canteens upstream, and then we'll start." He didn't look at her again as he turned and trudged upstream. The water wouldn't be much better there, but at least it wouldn't be soiled by the horses.

Don't think. Keep moving. Whatever you do, don't think. If you think, you'll return her to Sanctuary and forget about Davy. But you won't forget about Davy. Not ever.

Christ, why wouldn't his mind quit? A dozen devils were pounding at his brain, each with a torture of his own.

He filled the canteens with muddy water, then he waited about ten minutes. He wanted to give her time to take care of any private needs. There wasn't much cover here.

Were they in Texas yet? He had no idea. They hadn't seen any Indians, but that didn't mean there weren't some out there somewhere. He'd welcome a good honest scalping at the moment. He saw to his own needs. It would be a long ride today. Kane tried to think what day it was. Sunday? Monday? He'd lost track. He only knew time was running short for his friend. Too short to feel sorry for himself.

He turned around and hurried back to the horses, ignoring Nicky's puzzled, worried look. He wished to hell she'd complain, whine, faint, anything he thought most women would do under the circumstances. She didn't. She merely gave him a tentative smile when he went over to help her mount.

He tried one last time. "The stream bed to the river," he repeated her directions. "I can find it. You should return to Sanctuary. Your uncle will be worried."

She shook her head. "He knew I would be with you. He trusts you."

The words only added to his guilt. He should send her back, at least try, but he knew her well enough now to realize she wouldn't go. She would only follow. And he couldn't leave her like he left the two men, tied and nearly naked. He had no choice but to take her with him to Gooden, to the man who wanted to hang her uncle so badly.

BEN Masters woke up in Mary May's soft feather bed. They'd arrived back just before dawn. He had checked at his hotel, but a sleepy clerk said no one had asked for him. He'd already seen Mary May to her room, and suddenly he felt unbearably alone. He also wanted to apologize to her. He walked back along the lonely street to the steps behind the saloon. It led up to a row of rooms that the girls rented.

He'd been in Mary May's room several times, and he knocked at her door lightly. She had already undressed and was wearing a light green nightdress that was little more than gauze. She looked at him for a moment with those green eyes, then opened the door wide. "I'm glad you came," she said in a voice husky with feeling.

Ben had stepped in, closed the door behind and taken her in his arms. They were both tired, yet when she leaned into him, their bodies responded just as they had that afternoon. He quickly pulled off his boots and then his trousers and underdrawers. He hadn't bothered with his shirt. . . .

His shirt was still on, and Mary May was lying naked and asleep next to him. The smell of lovemaking still hovered in the room. He thought of yesterday. Of Sarah Ann, of their argument, of the fiery aftermath. A saloon woman with scruples. It was just his damn luck. Yet he liked her even more for it. And he'd liked the way her face had looked as she'd held her daughter. His left hand ran down the smooth skin of her arm, and he felt her body react. Her eyes opened slowly, then widened as they saw him, then became hazy again with desire.

"Good morning," she said huskily.

"More like afternoon," he said.

"It's morning to me," she retorted with a smile. "And I'm hungry."

He started reluctantly to rise, but she stopped him. "Not that kind of hungry," she said in what was almost a purr. He leaned down and kissed her, hard and wanting, and then she was wrapped around him. Ben came hard and fast into her, her soft moans like an aphrodisiac. He kissed her cheek and realized he had never done that before while making love. He'd never engaged in the small endearments, in the affectionate touches.

A deep shudder ran through him as he realized that for the first time since Clara, he cared. He really cared. Even as satisfaction surged through him, he felt a new and strange kind of fear.

Chapter Nineteen

Nicky and Kane reached Gooden at dusk. The town was just as miserable as Kane had remembered it. He had spent several anxious days there—nearly a week, in fact—waiting to be contacted prior to his journey to Sanctuary.

He had asked them how Gooden had come by its name. One drunk told him merrily that another drunk had found the place. He had built a cabin alongside a stream that was dry half the year and flooded the other half. He lived off the land and sold some animal skins for his whiskey. He was well into one bottle when a wagon train of settlers passed by. An inexperienced guide had asked the name of the place, and the drunk misunderstood. He thought they were asking about his whiskey. "Good 'un," he mumbled.

A flood kept the settlers camped there, and several of them decided to stay. Gooden was born. Kane had asked what happened to the founder and had been told he'd drowned the next time the flood came. As far as Kane was concerned, the whole town could well be swept away. It was dirty and dusty and violent.

But Nicky, who had been silent all afternoon, was looking at it like a kid at a circus. Her eyes were lit up like Robin's had been when he'd given him the hawk.

Kane was reminded again of her lonely childhood. She had been in Sanctuary so long, everything outside those valley walls must be new and exciting to her. She'd known no other children, had no playmates. For all the agonies of his own childhood, he'd had Davy. They'd fought and teased and adventured. Nicky's life had been a town of outlaws.

He suddenly wanted to show her a fine city: New Orleans or San Francisco. He'd seen New Orleans during the early days of the war, and he'd heard about San Francisco. He wanted to show her the ocean and big cities and green mountain valleys. He wanted to show her an entirely different world than the one she knew, one barred by cliffs and filled with violence and sudden death. He wanted that for Robin, too.

"It's grand, isn't it?" she said of the dilapidated buildings and dirt streets and fading signs. A drunk lurched out of one of the saloons and fell in the middle of the street.

"Grand," he echoed wryly.

"Where are we going?" Her brown eyes were alive with interest. He turned and looked at her. He had decided she would do better as a boy in Gooden. A new woman was always big news in a small male-dominated town. He had trimmed her hair again with his knife and pulled her hat down to shade the face. She was wearing her usual shapeless trousers and shirt, and he'd added his jacket.

"A hotel," he said. "Traveler's Rest." It wasn't the hotel he'd stayed at before, and it wasn't the one where he should find Ben Masters. It was, however, the more respectable of the two hotels. "You can get a bath there."

She looked at him, questions in her eyes, but as usual she was cautious in asking them. He wished she would ask. He wished she would keep asking until he told her the truth. But she ventured only one shy question, "How long will we be here?"

"A day or two, no longer."

"And then we'll go back to Sanctuary?"

She was worried sick about her uncle, about Robin. How much more worried would she be if she knew his purpose in coming here?

At the hotel, he helped her dismount and together they went into the hotel. It didn't have much of a lobby, just a reception area with a desk. A man behind it eyed their trail dust disdainfully.

"Two rooms next to each other," Kane said, "For my brother and myself."

Through the corner of his right eye, he saw Nicky's startled expression as the clerk cleared his throat and asked insultingly, "You got money?"

Kane flipped a twenty-dollar gold piece on the counter. "That enough?"

"More than enough, Mr. . . . ?"

"Jones."

Not very imaginative, Kane thought, but it usually stopped any additional questions. The names Smith and Jones in this town usually translated into gunmen. Sure enough, the man nodded and shoved the register over to him. "How long will you be staying?"

"I'm not sure. Two, three days. And I want enough water for a bath sent to my brother's room."

"Yes, *sir*." The gold piece had obviously done its job. Either that or the name Jones.

"And some wash water for me."

Kane led the way to the rooms, made sure the key worked in the lock of Nicky's room. It did. He admonished her not to open it to anyone but him and the clerk and to stay in the room while he stabled the horses.

"Kane?" she said, as he turned to leave. Her voice was small and miserable. The excitement was gone from her face, her voice, her eyes.

He went over to her. "What is it, Nicky?"

"You will be back?"

Since the first moment he'd met her she'd been brave and bold and defiant and determined. But now he saw fear in her eyes. Self-loathing rushed through him. He'd hardly spoken to her all day, and now, when she was in a place alien to all she knew, he was leaving her with the sole purpose of betraying her.

His hand went to her cheek. "I'll be back. I promise."

She swallowed hard. "Can I go with you?"

He touched her face with all the tenderness he felt welling up inside him. "I'm just going to see about the horses," he said, hating the lie, hating everything he was doing, everything he was. "You get some rest."

Something flickered, then died in her eyes. She turned away from him.

He hesitated a moment, reluctant to leave. He knew she sensed something was wrong. But the sooner he saw Masters, the sooner he could present his offer.

"I'll be back soon," he said and left, closing the door before he could change his mind.

He took the horses to the livery, then went the few steps to the Longhorn Inn where he'd last seen Masters before the guide to Sanctuary had knocked at his door. That had been their bargain: Masters would wait at the place he'd last seen Kane.

Kane hurried his steps. He didn't want to be gone longer than necessary. Gooden was a hellhole of a town and though he knew Nicky could shoot, he couldn't help worrying about her, nor could he forget the lost, sad look on her face as if she knew something bad was happening.

There was no one at the desk of the hotel, and Kane turned the register to see that Ben Smith was staying in Room Five. He took the steps two at a time and knocked at the door. He swore when there was no answer.

Had Masters given up? Was Davy already dead?

He tried to quiet his rising panic; he couldn't expect Masters to stay in his room every moment. Reassuring himself that the man was still checked into the hotel, Kane headed for the saloons. Christ, the town was full of them. He would try the Blazing Star first. He remembered it from his first visit, and Thompson had asked him to look up a woman there.

It was dark, but the saloons were well lit. He remembered the Blazing Star as the best of the lot; its girls were younger and prettier than most. He tried to remember the one called Mary May, but he couldn't. On his last visit, he'd been too concerned with finding Sanctuary.

He looked back toward the room where he'd left Nicky. How long had it been? Damn. Yet he was as compelled to reach some agreement to his plan as he was to return to Nicky. Where in the hell was Masters?

The Blazing Star was full. Men took up nearly every inch of the bar, and all the tables were taken. He glanced around quickly. Last time, he'd seen Masters, the marshal had been wearing a dark sweat-stained hat and leather vest. Then he stopped looking for a moment, his gaze settling on a tall, thin man who was watching the door. John Yancy! He'd seen him briefly at the hotel in Sanctuary before his expulsion.

Kane hesitated, wondering exactly how good his disguise was. He wouldn't have recognized himself in the mirror, but surely Yancy was familiar with all of Sanctuary's offerings, including disguises. Yet there wasn't a flicker of recognition, or even interest. Kane took a deep breath and surveyed the women, wondering which was Mary May Hamilton.

With Yancy in the room, he hesitated to ask questions. His voice wasn't disguised, and now he felt an urgency to get back to the hotel. Nicky was unpredictable. He had to let her know that Yancy was here.

He had turned and was going back through the swinging doors to the street when he saw Masters approaching. Now was as good a time as any to test the beard. Kane sauntered drunkenly forward and stumbled into Marshal Ben Masters.

Masters backed up, looked at him in disgust and started to go on his way—then stopped short. Slowly, he turned and stared at Kane's eyes. Even in the dim light, Kane saw the recognition dawning in his face. The disguise was good, but Masters was more observant than most.

"You're late," he said in a low voice.

Kane shrugged. "I'm here."

"My room. Ten minutes. You know the hotel. Room Five.

Kane nodded. "Make it thirty."

"You keep trying to change the rules, don't you?"

"You want to keep discussing it here?"

The marshal conceded. "All right," he said in a lower

voice. And then in a louder one, "Watch where you're going from now on."

"Then don't get in my way, you clumsy bastard," Kane retorted in a voice loud enough for everyone in the saloon to hear. The obscenity wasn't all for effect.

Kane hurried back to the hotel. Food, damn it. Nicky needed some food; so did he, for that matter. But there was no time. He took the steps two at a time and knocked at her door. "Nicky," he called.

It opened almost immediately.

She stood there, looking wonderful. She had evidently taken that bath and washed her hair. The short curls were damp and soft-looking. Her eyes were cautious, though she wore a tentative smile on her lips. He cursed himself again. She couldn't know what to expect from him next; in trying to stay away from her, in trying to limit the injury, he was causing more injury. If only he didn't face stone walls wherever he turned.

He held out his arms, and she went into them, snuggling against his chest.

"I thought maybe . . ." Her voice trailed off.

"Thought what?" he asked.

"You might not come back," she whispered.

"I wouldn't leave you . . . not alone like this," Kane said in a choked voice. Hoping she didn't understand the full meaning of words he hadn't intended, he tightened his grip around her. He kissed the top of her hair, smelling the freshness of soap, and feeling every inch of the dust on his own body. He moved away slightly and frowned. "John Yancy is in town."

Her eyes opened wide. "Yancy? Why would he be here?"

"Your uncle said he's vowed revenge. Maybe he's trying to find out how to get to Sanctuary."

"He didn't recognize you?"

"No." He shook his head.

Nicky relaxed slightly. "No one would, except me."

Someone would—and had, but he couldn't tell her that. "You can't leave this room," he said. "I don't want Yancy to see you. *You* are very recognizable."

"I'll stay with you," she said.

"I have to go out again," he said. "Alone. I won't be long, and I'll bring us both back some food."

Nicky nodded, but her eyes were suddenly different. They had been hard to read when he'd first met her, but ever since he'd taken the hawk to Robin, they had been as open and honest as those of a child. Or a woman in love. It was as if she'd had no reason to hide any thoughts. Trust. It had been trust, pure and simple, and now he was watching it seep away slowly because of his own contradictory, inexplicable actions. He hoped to hell he could work out his problem tonight, come back and even tell her the entire truth.

If only Masters would listen.

Christ, he wanted to wash and clean up, but the dirt did as much to disguise him as the beard. His hair color was indistinguishable under the grime. But when he returned . . .

He put a finger to her cheek. "I should be back soon," he said softly.

Doubt filled her eyes. Her mouth was pursed so solemnly, he wanted to lean down and kiss it, but there was no time for that now. He would do it later. He would kiss away the doubt and caution. Later . . . There had to be a later.

Before he said any more, he left, going down the stairs as rapidly as he'd gone up them. He would convince Masters of his plan. He had to.

BEN Masters entered the Blazing Star. He'd told Mary May he would meet her there at eight, and he didn't want her to come looking for him and finding Diablo.

There was a new lightness in his steps, even his bad leg felt agile. O'Brien *had* come back. Ben hadn't liked putting him off, for even a few moments, but neither of them could afford to be seen with the other. O'Brien must have the long-awaited information. Ben congratulated himself about being right about the man; he couldn't wait to tell him that he'd talked the governor into giving him a pardon as well as Carson.

There was a posse awaiting word in a nearby town. Perhaps in another week or two, this whole job would be wrapped up and he could start thinking ahead.

Ahead to what? Another job in another town? Tracking, moving, always moving? He thought about Sarah Ann, her laugh, her delighted smile upon seeing her mother. He thought how nice it would be to have someone welcome him. He even caught himself thinking about marriage, but then he drove the idea away. Mary May always made it clear she liked being independent.

Ben looked around for Mary May and found her dealing cards in a corner. He paused for a moment before going to her table. The man she'd pointed out to him several days earlier was standing by her, his gaze moving from Mary May to the game. Damn. He had to talk to her. Deciding to risk reviving the man's memory—if Mary May was right—he trod carefully over to the table.

One man got up. "Too rich for me," he said.

Ben quickly slid into the chair before anyone else could. Only by a flicker of eyelashes did Mary May give any indication he was more to her than any of the other customers. He'd not played at one of her tables before, but he wasn't surprised at her dexterity or mastery of the game. He lost two hands and purposely lost a third he knew he could win. "The man was right," he said. "It's too rich for my blood, too."

"Losers can buy me a drink later," she said lightly as she often did.

He hesitated. "I'm not sure I can make it."

She nodded and smiled neutrally. The owner of the Blazing Star and the bartenders, as well as the other girls, were quite aware that Ben Smith was special to Mary May. But taking a favorite wasn't something she advertised among the customers. It could make some think she was something she wasn't—a woman available to any comer—and that would invariably start trouble.

He rose lazily, tipped his hat, knowing she understood. He would return when he could. His eyes momentarily caught Yancy's. God, they were reptilian. Because Ben didn't want to seem too interested, he turned and walked away. But he felt as if the man's gaze was following him every step of the way.

NICKY went to the side of the window and looked out. She saw Kane striding purposefully across the street.

He had been strung as tightly as a string on a fine fiddle, closing himself off as thoroughly as if he were still in that prison cell, surrounded by iron and brick and rock. She couldn't figure what was bothering him so much that he couldn't tell her.

A friend, he'd said. A debt to a friend. But then why was he so tense? A vendetta? A robbery? Nothing made sense. He didn't seem the type for vendettas, or he surely would have killed the two men who planned to kill him. A robbery? He didn't need money. She knew how much he'd won in the games of chance at Sanctuary, and her uncle was offering him something of far more value than the proceeds of a simple robbery.

Something to do with her uncle? A woman? The worries wouldn't go away. Jealousy and fear loomed like great vultures on the ledge of her heart. She had to know. She watched him walk down the street and go into another hotel. A light went on in one of the rooms. Then the shades closed.

The vulture spread its wings wider.

She clutched the edge of the window. Yancy was down there somewhere. Or was Kane lying about that? She immediately dismissed that possibility. She knew there were things Kane hadn't told her, but he wouldn't lie about something like that.

Nicky couldn't stand it any longer. She had to know, had to get answers to so many questions pounding in her head and in her heart.

She put her hat on, pulling it low on her forehead, and quickly put her arms through Kane's jacket. She thought about Yancy briefly, but she remembered that he had stayed in the saloon at Sanctuary even more than the others. She would keep a safe distance from the town's drinking establishments. She went down the steps, saw the clerk glance at her, then back down to the newspaper he was reading. This new world was strange, and the freedom it offered would have been exhilarating if she were not so worried about Kane.

She couldn't help looking at everything. Sanctuary was a miniature version of this place, but there was so much more activity here. She walked quickly, sticking to the walls, trying to keep to the shadows, avoiding the lights of the saloons, and then she was at the hotel she'd seen Kane enter.

Nicky really didn't know what to do. She thought Kane was probably in one of the front rooms, but maybe the lighting had been coincidental. And what would she do if she found him? Burst in? Doubt filled her. Still, she was here.

There was no one behind the clerk's desk, and she hurriedly ascended the stairs that, as at her hotel, probably led to most of the rooms. The hallway of the second floor was empty. She figured out which door led to the room with the lit window and walked there as quietly as she could. Every footstep seemed to echo in the hall. Down the way, she heard a man and woman yelling at each other. She hoped the doors were as thin as the walls seemed to be. She felt like a sneak, and she hated herself for it, but she had to know. Nicky stopped outside the door she had chosen and huddled next to it, trying to hear something, anything.

KANE tried to keep his expression neutral, his resentment toward Masters hidden. It galled him to ask a favor of the man, who was so ruthlessly trying to use him. Except for that time in the Yank prison camp, he'd bent to no one, not since his father died. Even in the Yank prison, he had resisted authority with every ounce of his being. Now he was being manipulated into doing something that went against every one of the few decent qualities he had. He wanted to slam his fist into Masters's gut.

But he couldn't afford that. He had to present his bargain coolly, with confidence. Still, he found himself swearing when no one answered the door to Masters's room, glaring at the marshal when he appeared several minutes later.

Once they were both inside and the door firmly closed, Masters stared at him for a long time. "That's damn good," he said. "Where did you get the beard?"

"Sanctuary," Kane said shortly. "You can get anything there for a price."

Masters went over and studied it again. "I wouldn't have recognized you except for the eyes, and the fact I was expecting you. Days ago," he added with an edge to his voice.

"Worried?" Kane couldn't resist the taunt.

Masters's hard face didn't change. "About your friend, maybe."

"I doubt it," Kane said bitterly, acknowledging the reminder, the reason he was here.

"You have what I need?"

Kane took a long breath. "I have something better."

Masters raised an eyebrow in question.

"What if you can take Sanctuary with no loss of life?"

The question hung there in the air for a moment. Masters's face didn't change. There wasn't the slightest hint of interest. But Kane knew men. He knew that Masters was listening.

Kane went over to the window and looked out. He could see the Traveler's Rest down the street, and he looked for Nicky's window. The room was still lit. Thank God, she was finally doing as he asked.

"Spit it out," Masters said abruptly after a silence of several minutes.

"You ride in there with a posse, and at least half of them will die," Kane said. "It's a natural fortress guarded by sharpshooters. It's also protected by hostile Indians."

Masters sighed. "Where is it?"

That was a question Kane wanted to avoid for a few more moments. He damn well didn't want to tell Masters he didn't know.

"Indian Territory," Kane said.

"Where in Indian Territory?" Masters persisted with single-minded persistence.

Kane silently damned him in every way he knew. "You want to hear my proposal?"

Masters shrugged. "Go ahead."

"The man who runs it is dying. He's offered Sanctuary to me. In two, three months, I can just turn it over to you."

For the first time, Kane got a reaction. Masters's eyes narrowed, his lips thinned. Kane watched as the implications of his offer were weighed, found wanting.

"You don't have two or three months," Masters finally said.

"You can give them to me."

"I'm not the governor. He made the terms."

"*You* proposed them. It was your idea to use me," Kane said heatedly.

Masters hesitated. He'd never told Kane that.

"It was you, wasn't it?" Kane persisted, finally receiving a curt nod from Masters. "Now I can give you even more than you wanted. You can be a hero," he added sarcastically.

Masters studied him. "Who runs Sanctuary?"

"A man named Nat Thompson."

"Thompson?" Masters said with surprise.

"You know him?"

"I know of him. He was a bank robber. And a killer. Disappeared about twelve years ago. He's still wanted." One of Masters's eyebrows lifted. "He's dying?"

Kane nodded.

"Why you? Why single you out?" Masters asked suspiciously.

"Damned if I know," Kane lied, not wanting to mention Nicky or the boy. "I just know he asked me if I wanted to join him."

"You're lying."

Kane felt his hope draining. Masters was too good a judge of men. There had to be a reason Thompson would make his offer. Kane hadn't been in Sanctuary long enough to win the confidence of a man wily enough to keep his hideout secret for so long. He balled his fists. How much could he tell Masters? How little? He had to make Masters believe he could do exactly as he promised.

"I did him a favor," he said shortly.

"What?" Masters asked.

Kane knew he had to answer. He had to make a case for more time, damn it, but he hated explaining himself to the marshal. "The 'guests,' as Thompson calls them, smell blood. They know something's wrong with him, and they want Sanctuary for themselves. One of them made a move and . . . I happened to help someone close to Thompson. He was, well, appreciative."

Masters was staring at him with a strange expression. "Another error in judgment?"

Kane wondered what he meant for a moment, then remembered their first conversation when he'd said his rescue of Masters had been an error in judgment. "Something like that."

Masters was silent for a moment. "I want to know where Sanctuary is."

"I can't tell you."

"Can't or won't?"

Kane didn't know how far he could tantalize Masters. He needed the marshal as much as Masters needed him. The trick was not to show it, but play to his strength. He had—almost had—what Masters wanted.

"I can give you part of the route," he said tightly. "Not all of it. They blindfold you coming and going."

Masters stared, disbelief punctuating the features. "Surely if Thompson offered you . . . an interest in Sanctuary, he would tell you where it is."

"Thompson is a very cautious man," Kane said. "You must realize that, or you would have found him a long time ago. He said he would tell me when I returned—when, I guess, he was sure of me."

"What excuse did you give him for leaving?"

"Just personal business," Kane said. "A matter I had to clear up."

"He accepted that?"

"No reason not to. I have a reputation, remember. That's why you wanted me."

Masters paced the floor. "Carson's to be executed in ten days. I can't stop it without Sanctuary."

"Then you don't get Sanctuary," Kane bluffed. "Not now, not in two months, not ever."

"How far is it?" Masters asked.

Kane was stubbornly silent. He was gambling everything now.

Masters swore softly. "You knew what the arrangement was. I can't change it now, even if I wanted to. . . ."

"Damn it, don't you realize this is a better one? Think about it, Masters."

"It's not my decision," the marshal retorted, a muscle throbbing in his cheek. "And if you won't give me more information, I'll have to take you back to prison."

"Not without one hell of a fight." Kane's hand went to his six-shooter.

"You gave your word."

"I made you an offer, a damn good one," Kane said angrily. He lowered his voice then. "A few weeks in exchange for one hell of a lot of lives."

"On your word alone. The governor won't take that."

"Make him."

"Goddamn it, I would if I could." Masters raised his voice in frustration. "I can't. You give us Sanctuary. That was the deal. That's still the deal."

Kane stared at him incredulously. "I can't."

"You must know enough to make some good guesses."

"If you want to hunt in a hundred-mile radius with hostile Indians," Kane said defiantly. "That's the best I can do."

"Then you have to go back to Sanctuary."

"There's not enough time."

Masters lowered his voice. "I might be able to get you a week or two. Nothing like months," Masters said. "How were you supposed to get back? Meet someone? I could follow."

No, there's a woman in my hotel room who knows the

way. Kane felt the familiar sickness. Only now it was worse than at any other time.

"No," Kane said. "They take precautions."

There was a creak outside the door, but Kane was too preoccupied with his task to pay much attention. There were lots of creaks in the floors of these hotels. But he took care to lower his voice as he humbled himself. "Will you at least wire the governor for more time?"

"Why do I think you know more about Sanctuary than you're telling me? A lot more." Masters attacked.

"You have a suspicious mind," Kane replied.

"You don't do a damn thing to help quiet it, either," Masters said. "Damn it, O'Brien, I want to help you."

"You want to help yourself. Don't get hypocritical on me."

"I know you don't like me, but—"

Kane cut him off. "That's real intuitive of you. You can use all those brains to find Sanctuary."

Masters frowned. "Goddamn it, get past your dislike. Think about Carson. Yourself. Tell me everything you know about Sanctuary. I can use it as leverage for a little more time. But two or three months is—"

Kane heard another creak outside the door, along with a muffled cry. He turned at the sound. So did the marshal. They stared at each other for a moment, then Kane took several quick strides toward the door and flung it opened. The hall was empty, but he heard boots going down the steps. He knew that cry. He knew the owner of the light steps.

"Nicky," he called after the retreating steps. He started out the door, but Masters put a hand on his arm, restraining him. Kane tried to shake loose, but Masters's grip tightened.

"You know who it was," Masters accused.

"Get out of my way," Kane said with deadly intent.

"Damn it, O'Brien, I can't help you unless—"

Kane tried to shrug away again, but the hand was like a vise around his left arm. Swinging around, he sunk his right fist in Masters's gut as hard as he could. He didn't take time for satisfaction as the lawman doubled over. He landed another punch on Masters's cheek, and Masters landed on the floor. Kane ripped off his bandanna and jerked the man's hands behind him, tying them before Masters could recover from the blows.

Masters groaned, tried to struggle to his feet. "Don't run, O'Brien."

But Kane was already out the door, taking the steps two at a time. Just as he pulled open the front door of the hotel, he saw someone riding hellbent down the center of town. He recognized the mare, then the slight rider in the saddle. He also recognized the gray following behind on a lead.

"Nicky," he yelled and darted to intercept, but she only swerved past him with a new surge of speed.

Chapter Twenty

Nicky rode as if all the demons in hell were after her. Fierce, unbelieving fury had initially numbed the betrayal, the humiliation. But grief wasn't long in coming. Deep, all-consuming grief that was tearing her apart.

Tears ran and dried in the wind. Her heart dried, too, shriveling up in the hot windstorm of treachery.

I made you an offer, a damn good one. Kane's voice.

Then a stranger's: *You give us Sanctuary. That was the deal.*

Those were the only words she was able to hear. The others were muffled by the door. They were all she'd needed, though she tried to hear more.

The truth was obvious. Kane had made a deal with the law. He had been playing a part: spy, traitor, betrayer. Nicky couldn't believe how stupid she'd been to believe he really liked her. He was trying to save his own skin by sacrificing her uncle, Robin, herself. No wonder he'd asked so many questions about Sanctuary. Why hadn't she guessed?

She'd heard his voice in the hallway and realized he'd heard that barely muffled sob. She knew she had to get away, had to reach Sanctuary and warn her uncle. Keeping her hand on her derringer, she had raced for the stable, intent on escaping Kane O'Brien and his lies. Praying for a few extra moments, she'd saddled Molly in record time and had bridled Kane's gray; the gray would go with her, so he couldn't follow. She'd used the derringer when the liveryman had protested, forcing him into the tack room and locking him there after taking his keys. Kane wouldn't easily get another horse unless he stole one, and then a new posse would be after him. After leading out the two horses, she'd locked the livery door, then mounted and raced out of town, barely missing Kane....

She doubted it would take him long to find a new mount, but long enough for her to escape, for her tracks to be lost with so many others.

With every mile, her heart hardened, became more brittle, her sense of betrayal stronger, her grief deeper, her belief in herself smaller. If she stopped, she would die. She couldn't stand the pain. It would shatter her. *Give us Sanctuary. Give us Sanctuary. Give us Sanctuary.* The words kept echoing in her mind over and over again.

She had to warn her uncle. Kane still didn't know the exact location. He would have been blindfolded that first day out. But he could make some good guesses now, narrow the area for a posse, and eventually Sanctuary would be found. At least, some small measure of caution had kept her from giving him the map.

Diablo. She had tried not to think of him that way. But that was exactly what he was. A devil. The worst kind of devil. Cain, who had killed his brother. He was killing her now. The tears came faster as she thought of his touch, his gentleness, his lying, betraying gentleness.

She could barely see the road for the tears. She angrily wiped them away, and when she put her hand back down on Molly's mane she felt the horse heave. Dear God, what was she doing? She would kill Molly if she kept going like this. She leaned down, burying her head in the mare's mane, feeling the sweat on the horse's body. "I'm sorry, Molly," she said with anguish. "I'm sorry."

She guided the horse off the road at a walk, moving toward a series of gulches. She dismounted after a distance and stood there in the dark, shattered and alone.

Molly whinnied, nudging her as if understanding. But she couldn't possibly understand. Through the leaden grief, the hopelessness of feeling so betrayed, she tried to think. She would change horses, ride the gray bareback and lead Molly for a while.

Kane would come after her. He had money, and once he got into the livery, he could purchase another horse. It would take time, but not much. Therefore, she had to avoid the exact route she had taken here. She had to get home. She had to warn her uncle. And, ill or not, he would put his own reward on Kane O'Brien. Every cutthroat in the territory would be gunning for him. The thought made her sick. She sank to the ground and emptied what little contents were in her stomach. Aching despair immobilized her. She couldn't move. She couldn't think.

Molly nudged her again as if asking a question. But Nicky had no answers. None at all as she bent her head and wept until there weren't any tears left.

ANGUISHED and desperate, Kane ran to the livery, found it locked, and broke open the door. It took him only a few minutes to break a second lock on the tack room door, negotiate for a new horse, and saddle it. The new mount didn't look as fast or as sturdy as his gray, and Nicky's mare, for all its small size, was swift.

God help him, what had he done?

Kane should have known Nicky wouldn't have waited in her room. She had been tense, uncertain, and he had done and said nothing to change that, except coldly leave her. And now she was running for her life, and probably for her uncle's without food or clothes or money.

And she was the only one who could help him save Davy. He should have told her everything. He could only imagine what she thought now. What in the hell had she heard?

Perhaps he could catch her. At least, he had to try. He knew a day and a half of the route now. If only he could catch up with her before reaching that rock formation that signaled the end of his knowledge.

Self-loathing poured though his veins as he thought of

her out there, thinking he had lied to her, used her. He had to convince her it wasn't true. He didn't know how in the hell he could do that. Not now. "Nicky," he whispered as he saddled his new horse, swung up into its seat and galloped out of town. "Christ, what have I done to you?"

JOHN Yancy had watched the tall, blue-eyed man leave the saloon after exchanging glances with the saloon woman. It wasn't the first time he'd seen those intimate exchanges, and jealousy and envy ate into him. The woman had ignored every one of his own overtures, and he wasn't used to that. What right did any saloon whore have to reject him?

The man bothered him, too. He had an air of authority, though he was doing his best to disguise it. He also wore a gun as if he knew how to use it. Yancy would bet his last dollar that the man wasn't an outlaw. That left one likely alternative.

But what interested him most was the woman's connection to Sanctuary. Yancy was tired of waiting for one of Sanctuary's guides to appear. He had planned to follow the man back to Sanctuary, then ambush Thompson. But perhaps there was another way, a faster way. Mary May Hamilton probably knew Sanctuary's location. She also probably knew who—and what—her lover was.

He wanted to know the answers to both questions.

He slipped into the seat left by the man who so interested him and started fishing. "That gent didn't stay long," he observed.

"Smith?" said one of the other players. "He doesn't play much."

"Smith?" Yancy grinned. "Real fashionable name."

"Ben Smith," said another loquacious player.

Yancy didn't miss the sharp glance the woman sent him. It was a "mind your own business" warning, and the player shut up. But it was enough. Ben. Suddenly, he knew where the familiar feeling came from. Fort Smith. He'd been holding over in Fort Smith when a U.S. marshal brought in a prisoner. Yancy had only gotten a quick look at the lawman, who was dirty and bearded, but he remembered the name, Ben Masters, and the cut of him. Wouldn't Thompson be interested in knowing someone who worked for him was whoring with a U.S. marshal?

He won the poker hand, lost another, and called it a night. He went outside and looked around until he found what he wanted. A drunk who wouldn't remember much. "Tell Mary May that Ben Smith is waiting for her at his hotel," he told the man, giving him enough money for several drinks.

"Yes, *sir*."

Yancy knew where Smith was staying. He'd watched him cross from the hotel to the saloon often enough. There was an alley, a dark path between buildings she would have to pass through. And then he would find out everything he needed to know.

MARY May received the message with a smile. She had missed her usual afternoon drink with Ben. He had never asked her to his room before. They had always used hers, and she was pleased to be invited into his private quarters.

She was also hungry for him. She was always hungry for him. No one had ever satisfied her as he did, perhaps because she liked him so much. No man had ever treated her as an equal before, had listened, had really seemed to care about her beyond the sensuality they shared.

And he had been so good with Sarah Ann. She could still see him sitting in the neat bungalow, Sarah Ann giggling on his lap. The memory warmed her.

But then she went cold as she thought once more about her problem. What to do with Sarah Ann? How to find a decent home for her? Part of her mind went to Ben, but what man would want a woman like her for more than what they already shared?

She hurried toward his hotel. She always felt good with Ben, as if everything would work out. Even if he was a lawman, he was unlike any other she'd ever met. He hadn't used her, he hadn't threatened, and he had accepted her refusal to help him with equanimity.

Mary May was thinking about his eyes—the way they had warmed when he had looked at her daughter—when she heard someone behind her. She started to turn, and she felt a knife at her throat and an arm around her waist, pulling her to the dark alley between buildings. Then pain erupted in her head, and everything went black.

She woke to blinding agony. Her head was pounding fiercely, and when she tried to move, she couldn't. Water splashed on her, and she felt a rough hand slapping her face. She opened her eyes.

John Yancy's face was inches from hers. A long, narrow candle cast just enough light for her to see the malevolence in his eyes. Fear filled her, almost suffocating her. She feared for her own life, but even more for Sarah Ann's. What would happen to her daughter if she died?

She tried to stay calm. What did he want? And where was she?

She tried to look around but she was hogtied, her hands bound in front with a rope that led to another binding her ankles. Her dress was up around her hips. She was in some kind of abandoned building, lying on a dirt floor.

"What do you want?" she said finally, forcing boldness into her voice.

"The whereabouts of Sanctuary."

"I don't know what you're talking about," she bluffed.

His expression grew uglier, and he backhanded her across the mouth. The blow split her lip and she tasted blood. "Let's try that question again," he said. "Where's Sanctuary?"

Mary May knew the general vicinity of Sanctuary for a variety of reasons, mostly by keeping her ears open. Calico had dropped several bits of information over the past several years, and she'd once met Nat Thompson fifty miles north of Gooden. But she didn't know the exact location. She thought about giving Yancy directions to nowhere. But she knew she couldn't do it too soon or he would be suspicious. "Thompson will kill you for this."

"So you know Thompson, do you? He one of your lovers, too? Like that lawman you're whoring for?"

The fear deepened, seeping through every pore of her body. She saw in that instant that he wasn't just after Sanctuary; he was furious that she had refused his offers. "I only pass on messages," she said.

"You're a liar," Yancy said, taking a knife from his belt and touching it to her cheek, pressing it downward just enough to draw blood. "If you know Thompson, you've been there. He never leaves Sanctuary."

"You're wrong," she said. "We met at a rendezvous in Indian Territory three years ago. I've never been to Sanctuary."

"I think you're lying," he said, the knife pressing deeper into her skin.

"I can't tell you what I don't know," she said, panic coloring her voice.

"What about Smith?" he said. "Were you planning to betray Thompson?"

"I don't know what you mean."

The knife moved to her clothes and Yancy sliced away at them, uncaring when the blade cut her. She heard herself whimpering.

"You must think I'm stupid," he said.

"No," she said, her voice rising now, part of it a scream as the knife moved down to her stomach. She felt blood flow from her cheek and shuddered. What had he done to her face? "I would tell you if I knew. I don't owe either of them anything."

"I saw the way you looked at that marshal. I remembered his name, and it ain't Smith. It's Masters." He watched her face. "What is he after?"

"Could be you," she said spitefully, and the knife bit into her abdomen.

"Could be I'll slice you wide open, too," Yancy said.

Mary May tried to think. She could scream, but then no one in Gooden paid much attention to noises like screams, or shouts, or gunfire. Where was Ben? Dear God, *where was he*?

"No smart reply to that?" Yancy taunted, and the knife started tearing at the top of her dress.

Time. She needed time. Maybe Ben would come looking for her. She already felt blood leaking from her body in a number of places, and she felt lightheaded. "Indian Territory," she said, hearing her own voice weaken, almost break.

"You have to do better than that, whore."

"I only know part of the way."

His knife stopped biting into her. She closed her eyes and pictured Sarah Ann, the curly red hair and bright green eyes. She heard her daughter's deep giggle, and felt warm arms around her neck. *You have to survive*, she told herself. For Sarah's sake. *Ben will come. I know he will come.* She didn't know why she was so sure of that. She hadn't relied on a man since her husband died, but now she was bone-sure Ben would find her. The question was whether it would be too late.

"Start talking," Yancy said as his knife pressed deeper into her abdomen.

"The Glass Mountains," she lied. If she told the truth, then Thompson would come after her. "Arkansas River."

"Where in the Glass Mountains?"

"Map. There's a map in my room."

"If you're lying . . ."

As if to punctuate his threat, the knife pressed farther into her stomach. Mary May was feeling faint now. She had always been a fast bleeder, her small cuts producing copious amounts of blood. "Not lying . . ."

"I'll be back if it isn't." Yancy put the gag back in her mouth.

Mary May watched him leave. He wouldn't find a map. But she had some time now. A little. She fought to keep awake. She had to keep awake. For Sarah Ann. But her eyelids were so heavy and everything was going gray.

Then she saw Sarah Ann. She was standing there just feet away. She tried to reach out, but she couldn't. "Sarah," she whispered. "Sarah . . ."

• • •

IT took Ben thirty minutes of intense effort to free himself. O'Brien had been too much in a hurry to do an expert job of tying him.

What in the hell had prompted O'Brien's attack? Or who?

Ben had seen the horror in his face, then the anguish. It had been so stark that his blows had been totally unexpected. Ben wished like hell the man trusted him, but then he really had no reason to do so. As far as O'Brien knew, Ben Masters wanted only to use him, and had dangled a life in front of him to accomplish that aim. Ben wouldn't trust a man who'd done the same to him, but it had seemed the best way at the time to accomplish two very difficult and different objectives.

Now O'Brien was gone, and Ben doubted seriously that he would return. O'Brien would be hunted and his friend would die. As for his own career, it would be ruined, but he really didn't care at this point. He had one chance to salvage things, and that was Mary May. She knew something. If she could only guide him in the right direction, he might be able to find O'Brien before it was too late.

He rubbed his wrists as he made his way to the Blazing Star. Mary May wasn't there. He asked Sam, the bartender, who looked at him with amazement.

"She went to see you. Right after you sent the message."

Ben went rigid. "I didn't send a message."

"Somebody did, and she lit up like she always does when she sees you. Said she would be gone a few hours."

"Upstairs?"

"She went out the front in a real hurry."

"Who brought the message?"

"Sandy . . . you know the old drunk that waits outside hoping someone will buy him a drink. Well, someone paid him to bring the message, 'cause he bought two drinks. He's down at the end of the bar now."

Ben saw the man and went directly to him. "You brought a message for Mary May," he said abruptly. "Who gave it to you?"

Sandy looked at him through bleary eyes. "What business is it of yourn?"

Ben fought to keep his temper. He dug in his pocket and brought out a five-dollar piece. "What about this?"

"Sounds like your business all right," the man said with a drunken grin. "Tall, thin gent. Been hanging around the last few days. Pale blue eyes. Real gent, though."

Ben felt sick. Yancy! He'd bet anything he had on that. But why? Unless he wanted information, and Mary May knew about both him and Sanctuary. "Where did he go?" he asked the old man.

Sandy shrugged indifferently.

Christ, how could everything be going so wrong? First O'Brien. Now Mary May.

He would try Mary May's room first. He made for the stairs and walked swiftly to her room, stopping abruptly as he heard noises inside. He drew his six-shooter and tried the door. It was unlocked. Ben threw it open and stared at Yancy, who was tearing the bed apart. Yancy turned, saw Ben and went for his gun. Ben shot, aiming for the shoulder. He didn't want Yancy dead, not yet.

Yancy dropped his gun, his hand going to his shoulder, as he swore a string of oaths. Ben moved next to him, and put a gun to his chin. "Where's Mary May?"

Yancy spit at him, and Ben hooked a leg around Yancy's, tumbling him to the floor. Then he quickly went over and closed the door and locked it. "Don't care about dying, huh?" Ben said when he returned. "What about something real sensitive?" He lowered the gun, aiming it at Yancy's crotch.

"You won't. You're a lawman."

"Hell, I won't. You're wanted dead or alive. I don't mind taking you back in pieces. Where is she?"

Yancy's face turned pale. Ben meant every word, and Yancy heard the ring of conviction in it. "The old livery at the end of town. She's all right."

Ben knew the building; it had been partially burned, and what remained was none too solid. He heard voices outside the door, a crowd drawn apparently by the shot. Moving toward Yancy, he used the butt of his pistol on the back of the man's head. Yancy collapsed into unconsciousness.

Ben opened the door to face a hallway full of men. "Caught the bastard rifling Mary May's room," he said. "I suggest you take him outside of town and leave him there. I'll find Mary May."

"I say we kill him," one man said. Mary May was a real favorite. There were murmurs of assent.

Ben shook his head. "We don't want the law here. Just dump him outside town."

There was an authority to his voice that overrode the budding vigilante spirit. Several of the men nodded; they liked Gooden as it was.

Ben passed by them. He had to get out of Gooden before Yancy could tell the self-appointed vigilantes who Ben was, or they stopped long enough to listen to them. If Yancy was lying about Mary May, he would search the outlaw out and kill him, inch by inch. But now he had two other people to worry about: Mary May and O'Brien.

He had some time. Yancy would be out for a while, and then he would have to worry about that shoulder. The fact that he was caught in Mary May's room would make every explanation suspect, particularly any charge against the man who had shot him.

Ben moved as quickly as he could toward the ramshackle remains of the livery, only barely aware that other men were following him. He tore off the door, which was half on hinges. Ben lit a match and searched the large building. The roof was off and burned timbers made walking difficult, but then he saw her in a corner. Trussed and covered with blood, she looked like a broken toy. He swallowed.

"Get the doctor," he told several men who had followed him, and they disappeared out the door. He struck another match, lit a half-used candle in the corner, and knelt, cutting the ropes around Mary May's ankles and wrists. His hand felt her cheek. It was warm, but her eyes were closed and her breathing shallow. Blood was everywhere. He wished now he had killed Yancy. He knew he would in the near future.

He leaned down. "Mary May," he said softly, then again in a louder voice, his hand stroking her cheek. No response. He tried again, his voice choking. She'd lost so much blood. Even that fine, fiery red hair was covered with it.

Ben's hands smoothed back her hair, then touched her cheek. "Mary May," he said again. "Don't give up."

Her eyes flickered open then, and she tried to smile. "I knew you would come."

Ben swallowed hard. "A doctor's coming," he said. "Hold on."

She sighed, her body slowly expelling air.

"Why?" he asked. "What was he after?"

"Sanc...tuary. He wanted Sanctuary. I...didn't tell him."

"You wouldn't," he said holding her tightly.

She swallowed, and he held her tighter. He hated to ask, but he had to. "Mary May. A man who saved my life years back is in danger. He's headed to Sanctuary, and..."

"Wichita Mountains," she whispered.

Ben could barely hear her. He bent closer to her, holding her tight, wishing he could transfer his strength into her. "Sarah...," she said. "Promise you'll take...care of Sarah. Money...Dan has some money in the safe."

"You can take care of her yourself," he said.

She shook her head slightly. "Promise," she said, trying to move. More blood poured from her body. He tore off his shirt to tie some of the wounds, but there were so many. "Promise," she insisted again.

"I promise," he said softly, and she relaxed, closing her eyes.

"Mary May," he said, refusing to let her go. The very sound of her name ripped agonizingly through him.

She opened her eyes again. "Thank...you for taking care of my baby." Her hand fell away, and he heard the breath slip from her mouth and the life from her body.

"Mary May," he whispered harshly. "Damn you, Mary May. Damn you." And he sat there holding her until the others came.

Chapter Twenty-one

Broken and weary, Nicky kept moving. She didn't have food, but she didn't care. She didn't think she could eat without getting sick. She drank enough to keep her alive, all the time wondering why she bothered. Instinct, she thought dully. Instinct keeps the most miserable of creatures alive.

She had ridden all night, then stopped for several hours in the morning at a stream to rest Molly. She'd tried to sleep, with little luck at first. She kept hearing those voices. Over and over again. At some point, though, she had finally drifted off, only to wake to Molly's nuzzling.

How could she have been so wrong? Her uncle so wrong? She understood Robin's gullibility. He'd been so eager for any kind of male friendship, he'd taken up with the Yancy brothers. She had done the same with Kane O'Brien, who was worse than either of them. He just hid his snake scales better than most.

A sob escaped her. They had been escaping for the past two days, no matter how hard she tried to hold them back. The tears were gone, emptied. Dried. But the dry, racking sobs remained whenever she thought of him. She would never trust a man again. Never.

She leaned down over Molly's neck. The mare was plodding on. In a few minutes, she would change again to the gray, but she preferred riding Molly. She didn't want to be reminded of Kane. She didn't want to remember how he sat the gray. She never wanted to think of him again.

They had been traveling since that morning, but Nicky was afraid to stop, afraid that numbness and inertia would steal the last crumbs of determination that kept her going.

She pulled Kane's coat tighter around her as the sun began to set and the air grew chilly. She would have to stop soon; the horses needed rest, and her own endurance was fading fast. She'd not gone back to her room after hearing Kane, and she had neither food nor bedroll. Running like that had probably been foolish, but the hurt and shock had replaced all reason.

If only she could find an outcropping of some kind to shield her and the horses from the cold wind. She pulled out the rough map still in her pocket. She was staying away from the route she and Kane had taken from Sanctuary, deviating enough, she hoped, that he couldn't find her trail.

There should be a river nearby, and that might mean trees, something to cut the wind. Molly stumbled, and Nicky dismounted. She started to mount the gray bareback, but she was tired, so tired that she couldn't reach its back. Suddenly, the horse shied, tossed its head, and jerked away from her. Before she could grab the lead rope, the big gray galloped off back toward Gooden. She could only watch helplessly. Molly could not possibly catch him.

Swallowing hard, she took Molly's reins and led her toward the river. She and Molly would have to go on alone. It had been two days since she'd had any food. Her body needed it, but she still didn't think she could keep it down.

Walk. One step after another. She tried to push images of Kane from her mind. The crooked smile. The warmth in his dark gray eyes. The tenderness of his touch. Lies. All lies. Concentrate on getting home. Home. Lonely, lonely home.

• • •

KANE cursed as he searched the ground for tracks. Where was she?

He felt hollow, empty, desperate. He had ridden along the route he and Nicky had taken because that was the only route he knew. No sign of her. He'd stopped at the few isolated homesteads, hoping she might have stopped for supplies. But no one had seen a young boy or girl with two horses.

It was as if she'd disappeared from the face of the earth.

He tried to think as she would think. She would, of course, believe he would come after her, so she would do her best to confound him. How? Kane knew she had little experience outside Sanctuary. She had little or no money. No food. No blanket roll. She would move as fast as she could towards Sanctuary and, because she wasn't that familiar with the route, would have to stick fairly close to the trail they had taken.

Kane had mentally memorized every rock, every rut. He followed the river as long as he could and then retraced the trail he and Nicky had taken. But she wouldn't follow it exactly. She would be trying to outguess him, and that always took time.

What would he do if he were Nicky? Move parallel, about a mile distant, so she could still see the landmarks. But left or right? If he guessed wrong, he would surely miss her. He had one advantage: Nicky had the desperation of the betrayed, but he had the even greater desperation of the damned.

Kane decided he would ride as fast and hard as he could during the night, along the river, then when the trail left the waterway, he would cross left to right until he found tracks, some sign of horses. He had two days to find her. Just two days. If he didn't, Davy would die, and Nicky would always believe he used her for his own benefit. He couldn't let either happen.

NICKY decided to risk a rifle shot on the evening of the second day. She had reached the limit of her endurance.

Although she still felt too ill inside to eat, she knew she could no longer go without food.

She had stopped at a waterhole and noticed the animal tracks, some small. Whatever had made them would be back in the dark of night. She drank her fill and washed her face, then found a hiding place behind bushes, hoping the slight breeze would wash away her scent.

She lay still, warding off sleep, knowing that food was even more important. Finally, she heard a rustling. She peered around, wishing there were more light. Something moved and she aimed at it and shot. The noise seemed to echo in the vast loneliness of the place, but the movement stopped.

Nicky moved cautiously toward her target and leaned down. A rabbit. It still moved, and she closed her eyes for a moment. Dear God, how she hated this, hated to kill anything. She pulled the trigger again, and the rabbit was still.

Now a fire. A small fire. She had some matches in her trousers, put there from when she had taken several from her saddlebags to light the oil lamp in the hotel. She gathered some kindling and one fair-size branch, breaking it into pieces with her foot. Then she cleaned the rabbit, and put it on a spit she made from another branch.

She huddled close to the fire, watching grease drip from the meat and sizzle in the flames. Ordinarily the aroma would make her mouth water, but she could just stare at it. She had never gotten drunk, but she had heard curses from men who did, and she suspected she felt a little as they had. Her mouth was like cotton, her eyes strained and weak and hurting.

As soon as the rabbit was cooked, she quenched the fire, kicking dirt into it and stomping on it to smother the coals and smoke. Only then did she eat, taking big bites because she had to, because she had to get home. When she was finished, she mounted again. She didn't want to stay anywhere close to that fire and the shot that must have echoed across the plains.

She would sleep at dawn, in one of the arroyos that pitted the area.

Nicky put her head against Molly's neck. They should be back home late tomorrow. What would she tell her uncle? Robin? Could she really sign Kane's death warrant? But she had to tell them something. She had to warn them.

She would think about that tomorrow. She couldn't think now. She couldn't even feel any longer. No, that was wrong. She could feel. She *did* feel. She just wished she didn't.

KANE heard a shot. It came from a long distance away to the north. He kicked his tired horse into a gallop and wished for his gray.

It was dawn when he found the ashes of a fire. He had criss-crossed the area, finally heading for the small clump of trees that indicated a waterhole.

The ashes were cold. He knew from the small boot prints that the rider was probably Nicky. At least she was still alive. He found several bullets and one small bone, probably rabbit. So she had killed something. Thank God. His admiration for her grit—and wiliness—grew.

But now he could pick up her tracks. He was exhausted, but she must be even more so. He was used to going days without sleep, disciplining himself to stay alert, learning the art of grabbing a few minutes' rest in the saddle. He tried not to think of the feeling of betrayal that must now be pushing her. He didn't know what he would say to her when—and if—he found her. She had been a hopeless dream, and he'd been a fool to think he could ever free Davy and still have her.

She would hate him now, and he couldn't blame her. She might even kill him, and he wouldn't blame her for that, either. But before she did, he had to explain; she had to know why he acted as he had. She had to know he hadn't betrayed her and her uncle for money or to save himself.

Not that it would probably make any difference, he thought. Lies were lies, and betrayal was betrayal. No reasons—no matter how noble—changed that. An overwhelming sorrow for what might have been filled him. He ached for a passion he knew would never be repeated. He ached for an innocence that was gone forever.

Damn it, he couldn't let it all be for naught. He *had* to save Davy and still get Robin and Nicky away from Sanctuary before it was raided. He didn't know how, but he knew he had to try.

For much too long, he had allowed others to control his life: his father, the army, the prison officials, the carpetbaggers in Texas who had nudged him into banditry, and now Masters. By God, he was taking his life back— starting right now. He was goddamned tired of playing Masters's game. He would play his own from now on.

Kane watered his horse, then searched for tracks and finally found them heading north. There was only one horse now, and it wasn't the gray; he knew its hoof markings. Still, it had to be Nicky. He stayed on foot for a while, making sure they didn't change direction. Then he mounted and spurred his tired mount into a canter.

BEN Masters hesitated at the door of Mrs. Culworthy's cottage. He had some money with him. He only hoped to hell it was enough to convince Mrs. Culworthy to keep the child a few more weeks.

And then what?

He wasn't sure. He wasn't sure of anything at the moment. Grief still leadened his heart, and he functioned only on sheer will. He had lost Mary May. He wasn't going to lose Kane O'Brien, dammit. He couldn't.

And Mary May had given him the key: the Wichita Mountains.

Ben had already wired the posse to meet him twenty-five miles north of Gooden. O'Brien had been gone a day now. Something had to have gone terribly wrong, he knew, or O'Brien wouldn't have disappeared as he did, not after his plea for time, not with his obvious desire to save his friend.

He swallowed hard. After making arrangements for Mary May's funeral, he had forced himself to turn his attention to O'Brien. God knew it hadn't been easy, but he had to do something, to keep busy, and he couldn't do anything more for Mary May than keep his promise.

He had checked O'Brien's hotel and discovered a young boy had checked in with him. Both were gone now. He kept remembering the stricken look on O'Brien's face as he'd swung at him. It was a puzzle Ben didn't understand, one he had to solve. Instinct told him to go after O'Brien immediately. He couldn't wait and hope for his return.

But Ben feared leaving without contacting Mrs. Culworthy first. The child might disappear into some orphanage or God knew what.

He finally knocked at the door. Mrs. Culworthy answered, a smile wreathing her face. "You and Mrs. Hamilton come to pick up Sarah Ann?"

Feeling as cold as a January day in Alaska, Ben shook his head. "I have some bad news. Where's Sarah Ann?"

"Taking a nap," Mrs. Culworthy said, the smile changing into a frown. "Come in."

Ben moved awkwardly into the parlor. It seemed empty without Mary May. He kept remembering her laughter. Sarah Ann's laughter.

"Mrs. Hamilton was killed," he said.

Mrs. Culworthy's face paled.

"She asked . . . me to look after Sarah Ann. I have to leave for a week, maybe two. I was hoping you could keep her that long. I'll make it worth your while."

"Poor little mite," Mrs. Culworthy said. "I suppose I can postpone my trip another few weeks. But what will you . . . do?"

Ben shrugged helplessly. "I don't know. I'll think of something."

"Are you going to tell her . . . about her mother?"

Ben hesitated. "Let's wait until I get back." He hated putting off unpleasant things, but he simply didn't have the time to do it right. Kane O'Brien was out there someplace, and Ben didn't know what in the hell was going on. He just had a very bad feeling about all of it.

He took some coins from his pocket and handed them to Mrs. Culworthy. "Will twenty dollars be enough?"

"More than enough," Mrs. Culworthy said. "I liked Mrs. Hamilton. I'll pray for her."

"She'd appreciate that," Ben said, meaning it. "And I will, too."

"You be careful, Mr. Smith. That little girl needs someone."

Ben nodded. He wasn't sure Sarah Ann needed *him*. He wasn't sure anyone needed someone like him. He would have to change his ways, and he wasn't sure he could do that. Maybe he could find another Mrs. Culworthy someplace.

But he had no time to consider that now. He stared around the room once more, again seeing Mary May with her daughter, seeing their smiles. He felt a tightness behind his eyes. He didn't look forward to telling Sarah Ann her mother wouldn't be back. But neither could he ask Mrs. Culworthy to do it.

"Thank you," he said. He hesitated a moment, then handed her a letter he had written at the hotel. "If I'm not back in two weeks, contact this gentleman. He'll make provisions for the girl."

"God be with you," Mrs. Culworthy said as she took it.

"I hope so," he said fervently, not for himself but for little Sarah Ann and a man named Kane O'Brien.

NICKY rested a little after dawn. She had ridden throughout most of the night since cooking the rabbit; she'd wanted to put distance between the shot and herself. But she had to give Molly some rest.

She knew where she was now. She no longer needed the map. She took it from her pocket, then burned the parchment until the flames licked at her fingers. She dropped the remaining scrap, knowing it wasn't enough to help anyone.

If Kane did find it, he would realize she hadn't entirely

trusted him. A small, bitter victory. Somehow, it didn't make her feel any better.

SIX hours after he'd left the remnants of Nicky's fire and nighttime meal, Kane found the spot where she had rested, possibly slept. The outline of her body was obvious in the dirt behind some rocks. He also found something else: a partially burned map that he instantly knew led to Sanctuary.

So she'd had a map all along, and she hadn't shared it with him.

Enough of the map was burned to obliterate all but a few miles north of Gooden. He wondered if she'd left the remainder to tell him she'd had it, to taunt him with it, or whether she hadn't wanted it to fall into his hands and she had been too exhausted to make sure it had burned completely. Either way, she apparently hadn't trusted him as completely as he thought. Oddly, that hurt. Well, she had been right.

He rubbed a hand over his face, feeling the heavy, hot beard that was drenched in sweat. He didn't need it anymore. Sitting where Nicky had slept, imagining he still felt the heat from her body, Kane then took his knife from its holster and used it to peel the beard from his face, nicking the skin as he did so. He felt the blood running down the bristles of his own beard. At least he felt like himself. For better or worse, he was Kane O'Brien again.

And Kane O'Brien was sick of the lies and deception. After deciding earlier to be no man's pawn again, he had developed his own plan. It started with finding Nicky and telling her the truth. And then he was going into Sanctuary, confronting Nat Thompson, and convincing him to send Nicky and Robin away immediately. He would make Thompson believe a posse was on its way; the threat, at least, should be enough to make Thompson act.

It wouldn't be much of a jump from the truth. Kane would be surprised if Masters weren't hot on his trail by now; he hadn't had time to cover it, nor had Nicky.

And Davy . . . well, he had that figured, too. He remembered every word of his conversations with Masters.

I want that pardon for Davy if I'm killed.

I might be able to convince the governor . . . if we find your body.

I'll try to get killed where you can find me.

So, he would see to it that his body was found. He would goad Thompson, who was bound to kill him for his treachery, into making an example of him, to make sure his body was dumped where others—including Masters—would see it. He wasn't sure how he could accomplish that aim; he only knew he must.

It was the least he could do for Davy, the only way to try to repair the damage to Nicky. It was the only way he could accomplish both of his objectives. And, hell, he'd rather take a bullet than die by the noose any day.

Chapter Twenty-two

Only a few more hours to Sanctuary if Nicky had reckoned right. She knew she should be relieved, but she wasn't.

What was she going to do? What was she going to tell her uncle? She had to tell him at least part of the truth. He had to be warned; Kane knew much of the route now.

A hot wind blew against the dried tears on her cheek. Her body felt stiff with dirt and sweat. She was numb from weariness and hunger and heartbreak.

A few more hours. A bath. Food. Bed. Her uncle. Robin. She could see her brother's face now as he realized Diablo's betrayal. How many betrayals could a boy tolerate?

She sighed and stopped, slipped down, her legs almost giving way from sheer exhaustion. The mare's mouth was ringed with foam and had to rest. There were no more water holes, not that Nicky knew of, so she emptied the contents of her canteen into her hat and held it out to Molly.

A few minutes' rest wouldn't hurt. She didn't want to consider that she might be delaying the end of her journey because she would then have to make decisions that she still wasn't quite ready to make. Why she wasn't ready, she didn't begin to know. Kane had betrayed her, used her. She should feel nothing but hate for him. And she did hate him. But then, she also remembered the tender touch of his lips, the gentleness of his fingers. . . .

Tricks. All tricks. If only she didn't hurt so badly. If only the pain didn't seem to temper the anger rather than strengthen it.

She walked Molly until she found a small rise where she could see a long distance in every direction. She sat down, looking up at the sky, watching as clouds tripped across the sky. Light, billowy clouds. The sun shone bright, and she welcomed the warmth because there was none inside her. She stretched flat on the ground and stared upward until drowsiness crept over her, and her eyes closed.

Panic woke her. Panic and fear. Bewilderment. She didn't know where she was, but the very air seemed to crackle with danger. She fought her way out of the exhaustion-drugged sleep.

"Nicky?"

She heard his voice before she opened her eyes. Kane's voice. It was soft, questioning. New waves of pain rushed through her. He had managed to track her despite her precautions. A sob caught in her throat. Maybe she wanted him to find her. But then what did that make her?

"Nicky?"

She slowly opened her eyes. He was standing next to her. The beard was gone, replaced by dark bristle on his cheeks. His dark gray eyes were wary, all laughter, indeed any spark of life, gone from his gaze.

Her heart stopped, and for an instant she couldn't breathe. She wanted to hit him, swear at him, kill him, but she couldn't move.

A muscle in his cheek throbbed against the side of his face, making the scar more prominent. The mark of the devil. Of Cain. Why didn't she reach for the rifle lying next to her? Why couldn't she move?

He stooped down, and his hand reached toward her face. She flinched, shying away like a wounded animal would move from the thing trying to kill it. He jerked his hand back.

"You heard me and Masters, didn't you?" he asked finally.

She still couldn't speak. She was afraid what might come from her mouth if she started. His face changed, looked haggard and tortured. She knew the feeling. Chunks had been cut from her these last two days, leaving her raw and bleeding and tattered inside.

"Will you hear me out?" he finally said.

"No," she finally whispered. And the tears came again. Tears she thought she'd used up. Tears that came from somewhere so deep she couldn't stanch the flow. Like a mountain stream fed by ice and snow, they thundered from the deepest part of her, demanding an escape. She huddled on the ground, her body heaving, even as she hated those tears, that show of weakness before a man who had already used her.

"Nicole." His voice was a broken whisper, but all she heard were the lies in it. All the lies.

A hand reached out again, and once more she shied away. "Don't . . . touch me," she said in an agonized whisper, pulling her body into the tightest knot she could possibly manage. She had thought so many times about what she wanted to say to him, the words she wanted to throw at him, and all she could do was curl up in a shaking wet ball.

He waited until she stopped, until all the tears were gone, and the heaving left her body with a wretched weakness. She finally managed to still the tremors. Her hand futilely tried to wipe away the tears. Then she sat up and looked at him.

He was still, like a piece of marble, except for his eyes. If she didn't believe all the things he was or did were lies, she would have said there were real tears in them.

But it must be nothing but the glare of the setting sun, she decided, trying to regain what wits she had after that outpouring of emotion. She felt so empty, so completely hollow. "What do you want now?" she asked bitterly. "Actually, since you followed me, I guess you have what you want." She buried her face in her hands, feeling the betrayal again, just like it was new. "I was a fool all over again."

He started pacing a small imaginary line. Back and forth. The length, she supposed idly, of a prison cell, one he was so eager to leave he was ready to betray those who would befriend him, love him.

His face was like granite. No more movement of a muscle. No more emotion in his eyes. She might be looking at marble.

"I have to see your uncle."

"I won't take you," Nicky said grimly. "I don't care what you do to me."

He kneeled next to her. "God help me," he said. "You can't believe I would . . ." His voice trailed off.

"Hurt me?" she asked. She laughed, a short choking noise. "Why not? What do you think you've done? I would much prefer you inflict pain honestly. A gun. Your fists. Either would be better than your . . . sweet words."

All of a sudden, her emotions exploded. Her hand went back and she slapped him as hard and violently as she could, harder than she'd thought her ebbing strength would allow. He took it without flinching, without moving, and she saw the mark of her hand against his face, drops of blood trickling from his mouth.

She sat back, drained and empty. Awaiting retaliation. But he just continued to kneel next to her. He was like a statue, but his eyes never left her.

"Damn you," she said.

His eyes closed, and the fingers of his left hand balled into a fist. "I'm sorry," he whispered. "So damn sorry."

"That I found out before you got your blood money?" she asked, tears blinding her eyes again. She hiccuped and turned away, humiliated.

"I never lied to you," he said in a low voice.

She laughed again, and even she heard the hysteria in the sound. She was shaking. She felt the tremors roll through her. How could she hate someone so much, and still love him? Because she did. She looked at his anguished face, and she loved him. She wanted to put her hand to his cheek, to sooth away the lines around his eyes and the harsh, self-condemning set of his lips.

He stretched out a hand again. "Nicky. I didn't tell you the truth, but I didn't lie, either. Not about how I felt."

The sky was blood-red behind him. His face looked demonlike in the last dying rays of the sun. Lean, hollowed, scarred. "I trusted you," she whispered.

Kane bent his head and closed his eyes, a groan coming from deep inside him. She wished she could trust that sound of pain. She couldn't, though. She would never trust anyone again. Especially Kane O'Brien.

She wanted to hurt him again. Not physically, but like he'd hurt her. "Where's your friend?" she asked. "How far behind is he? And exactly what was your price? My uncle would have bettered it, you know. He was even willing to throw me in." The laugh came back to her as a brittle echo. "Is that what scared you off? Is that why you went looking for a better offer? And what were you going to do with me? Turn me in, too?"

He hadn't moved. Now he did, his hands reaching out and taking her arms. They were like iron bracelets. "Don't ever think that," he said, and once more his voice seemed to break. "God, I tried to stay away from you. I tried."

"But I wouldn't let you," she said. She realized now he was right. He *had* tried to stay away. She had done the chasing, the tempting. She had made a fool of herself.

"No," he said as if he read her mind. "Damn it, I . . . cared. God knows I shouldn't have, but—"

"But you still needed the map, the last few miles before you get your blood money," she finished. "Or was it just a pardon? Or both? How much did you sell yourself for?"

He stared at her for a long bleak moment. "I want you to take me there," he said woodenly. "The law knows too much. They're much too close. You and Robin have to get out. I have to make your uncle understand that."

"How far is a posse from here?" she replied dully.

"There's not a posse, damn it. I saw you ride out of town and knew you'd heard something. I came alone. But your uncle's running out of time."

"How did you find me?"

"I knew part of the way. I heard your shot, and then I was able to track you."

"Liar. Spy. Tracker. How many other talents do you have? Or have you always been a law dog?"

"No," Kane said wearily. "They were going to hang me."

"So you decided to save yourself by befriending and betraying us."

"If that was true, then I would have just accepted your uncle's offer," he said.

"Then what? What did they offer?" she asked.

"Would you believe me if I told you?"

"No," she said flatly. "I wouldn't believe anything you said."

She saw a muscle throb in his cheek.

"Then it doesn't make any difference, does it?" he finally said wearily.

But the reason did. She wished it didn't, but she had to know. What did he want so badly he would risk everything, including . . . whatever had been between them? He might lie, would probably lie, but . . . she still had to hear it from his lips.

"No . . . but I want to know," she persisted. "I want to know why."

"It has to do with a friend," he said softly. "A very good friend."

She stared at him. He had mentioned a friend before. Several times. She couldn't ask what she wanted to know. *More important than me? More important than Robin? Than your word, implied if not spoken?*

"All for a friend?" she asked softly, unable to keep a new rush of anguish from her voice. "And what were you planning for me?"

He was watching her. "I didn't bring a posse, but I suspect there will be one soon. They can track me like I tracked you. That's why I have to see your uncle."

She turned away. "He'll kill you."

"That's likely," he said.

"Then why?"

"I want him to send you and Robin away."

"No." She started to turn away.

His hands caught her shoulders, then fell to her arms, holding them captive. "Damn it, Nicky, you have to take me." He took a gun from his gunbelt and handed it to her. "Backtrack if you want. Check for yourself first. But you must get me through the entrance to Sanctuary, to your uncle."

There was a pleading note in his voice she'd never heard before. He was good. He was very, very good. She almost believed him. She wanted to believe him. The pain would be less if she thought he was protecting a friend rather than enriching himself. Or would it?

She finally stood, feeling the weakness in her legs. The torrent of tears had taken what little strength she had after so little food and so much hard riding. But she forced herself to take the gun, and she pointed it at him. "I could kill you."

"I know." His gaze met hers. His eyes were so deep in the falling dusk, so unfathomable. She wondered whether she had ever known him at all.

"Why shouldn't I?"

"For Robin," he said, "if not for yourself. I have to convince your uncle to send you out. I don't want . . . either of you hurt."

She stood straighter. "Sanctuary is my home."

"It's a nest of killers."

"And what are you, *Diablo*? I read the posters, the accounts in the newspapers." She watched him wince as she used his outlaw name. She looked at his face, the scar that marked it, the new bristles of beard that hardened it. She looked at the guarded eyes, the mouth that had once kissed her but now was strange to her. Her body felt cold and hot at the same time, warring against itself. The heart was cold; the core of womanhood, though, still remembered the feel of him.

She met his gaze. "I hate you," she said, her voice shaking. "I'll never take you through to Sanctuary, so you can take me in now. At least, you'll have something to show for your blood money."

Her hand, holding the pistol, dropped to her side. She wanted to shoot him. She wanted to hurt him like he had hurt her. But she couldn't. She couldn't pull the trigger. She could only hurl words at him, and words were meaningless.

He just stood there, not moving. His eyes were empty, his jaw set. His mouth worked for a moment and his shoulders slumped. What was left of her heart, what small fragments still existed, crumpled as she saw the defeat in him. She balled her fists in agony. She wouldn't go to him. She wouldn't trust again. Never.

He finally reached for his pistol, took it from her hand and pointed it toward the ground, firing three times in steady succession.

Nicky swallowed. She knew exactly what he was doing. He was inviting company. Her uncle's men? He had to know they would kill him. He'd admitted as much. Or was he simply calling a posse?

"There's no posse behind me," he said softly, reading her thoughts.

"Then go," she whispered. "Go before my uncle's men come."

Kane looked down at her. "I can't." His gaze seemed to bore right through her and he smiled at her. Wry. Tender. Unafraid. His hand went to her face, his knuckles brushing softly along her cheek. "Remember that black-smith I mentioned in San Antonio?"

She nodded stiffly.

"Take Robin there. He and his wife are good people; they'll help you. Don't let your feelings about me . . . keep you and Robin from going there. He'll be good for the boy." He swallowed hard for a moment, reluctance written all over his face. "I have no right to ask you for anything," he said finally, "but . . ."

Nicky couldn't take her gaze away from him. Her heart was pounding. His words sounded like a will. And they would be, if he didn't leave. Sanctuary was well within the range of the sound of gunfire.

"Leave," she ordered fiercely. Why did she still care?

He shook his head, his eyes holding hers, willing her to listen, to obey. "My friend . . . he'll die, unless . . ."

"Unless what?" She didn't want to know, but his intensity was so strong, she couldn't ignore it. He was willing her to listen, and God help her, she wasn't capable of turning away from him.

"Masters. The man in Gooden. Let him know . . ."

"Know what?" she asked when he hesitated.

"The bargain was—"

But the approach of horses interrupted his sentence, and she recognized Mitch Evers. He had three Comanches along with him. Her gaze returned to Kane's face.

"The bargain?" she prompted.

"Tell him how I died," he said, stooping down and placing his gun on the ground. He ignored Evers, who dismounted and approached. "Please," he added urgently, his will again reaching out to her, enveloping her in it. She found herself nodding.

"Ben Masters . . . or Smith," he said, lowering his voice. "Gooden." He turned to face Evers.

Nicky felt herself shaking again. Why had she agreed? What was he doing?

Mitch stopped in front of her, his curiosity frank as he looked at her, then Kane, and back again. "Thank God, you're all right," he said to Nicky. "We heard gunshots . . ."

Nicky felt her back stiffen. The truth would kill Kane. Probably slowly and painfully. Mitch might even give him to the Comanches. The thought was excruciating, even more painful than his betrayal.

Loyalty warred with loyalty. Except she owed no loyalty to Diablo. But it was there, just the same. She felt as if a civil war were raging in her head.

Mitch was obviously waiting for some explanation. "We got your note," he said finally when none came. "We found Calico dead, but no sign of Hildebrand. Are you all right?" His voice lowered as he inspected her. She knew how she must look, how the tears must have left trails on her face and a redness in her eyes. She nodded.

Mitch looked dubious, then looked toward Kane. "What happened?"

"You aren't going to like it," Kane said, and Nicky

knew instantly that he was going to sign his own death warrant. She wanted to stop him. No matter what he had done, she couldn't let him . . .

She started to open her mouth, but he stopped her with his next words. "There's a posse on its way. They know about Sanctuary." He'd just denied that to her.

"How?" Mitch asked flatly.

"I'll tell Thompson," Kane said.

Mitch looked at her in question. "What's going on, Nicky?"

"I don't know," she said. But she was beginning to, and the truth was like a dagger in her heart. For whatever reasons, Kane hadn't lied to her, but he was lying now. There was no posse—or it would already have been here upon hearing the shots—but he wanted Mitch to believe there was one. Kane *wanted* to be taken. He was inviting himself to be killed.

Mitch's eyes narrowed. "Nicky?" he said in a warning tone. "You've been gone nearly a week. Nat's been sick with worry. And why isn't O'Brien blindfolded?"

"Because I followed her," Kane interrupted. "She didn't realize—"

Nicky found herself breaking in before he could say anything else. "I found him the night I left and told him about Calico and Hildebrand. He fought them, tied them both up, and we went on into Gooden. I decided to return because I knew you would be worried, and I thought he would be another couple of days. Maybe he decided he didn't want to wait on a guide." Lies begat lies. Did they come that easily to Kane?

"Why wouldn't he just ask you, then?" Mitch asked.

Nicky wished she had Kane's glib, lying tongue. "Maybe he didn't want to be blindfolded." She hesitated, then started down another deceptive path. "Mitch, we heard some things in town. Maybe they don't know exactly where Sanctuary is, but I think they have a good idea. We . . . heard a posse's being formed." She avoided looking at Kane, even as she lied for him.

Mitch's head jerked up.

"We may not have long," she said.

Mitch's eyes went to Kane again, then back to Nicky, as if seeking a truth he wasn't being told. "Nicky?"

But she set her chin and went to Molly. "I think we'd better warn Uncle Nat."

Mitch nodded. "Let's go," he told Kane.

Kane hesitated, and Nicky finally looked up at him. She couldn't read the emotion in his eyes, but that muscle was working in his cheek again.

She turned away, realizing her efforts were in vain. He was going to tell her uncle exactly what had happened. She had given him a way out, and he wasn't going to take it. Telling herself she didn't care, she held out a hand to Mitch, avoiding any contact with Kane. Then why was she so sick at her stomach at the thought of what was going to happen? And why had she tried to help him?

Mitch helped Nicky into the saddle and muttered a few guttural instructions to the Indians with him. Two of the braves turned toward the direction of Gooden, and Nicky knew they would scout for a posse. One remained with them.

"They'll cover our trail," Mitch said as her eyes questioned him, and the small band started toward Sanctuary.

KANE's gaze fixed on Nicky, who rode just ahead of him with Evers. Why in the hell had she lied for him?

He still saw her face, tear-streaked and tired and broken. He still heard her voice. *I hate you*. Her accusations still echoed in his soul. *Liar. Traitor*. He recalled how she shied away from his touch as if he were a monster.

Yet she had lied for him, tried to protect him despite everything she knew. He supposed he should grateful. Hell, he was. Grateful and . . . touched beyond anything that had ever happened to him. But the guilt was now a burning brand on his soul. He wondered whether the pain would ever fade. She had lied for him, she who was always so agonizingly honest. She had put aside her own hurts, bitter as they were, to soften his. Why?

He wished she had run a sword through him instead. Her uncle would soon realize she was protecting a traitor.

God, he knew the agonizing cost of divided loyalties. No torture would be worse than the look on Nicky's face, than the soul-shattering tears, than the contempt that replaced them. Every one of her words—liar, traitor—kept ringing in his head. He'd been unable to counter them, unable to defend himself. He was everything she said he was. And worse. He had killed the spirit in her as much as he'd killed that sheriff's deputy two years ago.

Kane shifted in the saddle. His heart lay in torn remnants, sliced apart by the hurt he'd inflicted on one of two people he'd loved in his life, his inability to help the other. He bent his head, the muscles in his throat working convulsively. He didn't even care if anyone else heard the barely suppressed groan as waves of pain exploded throughout every feeling part of him.

NAT Thompson leaned against a post of the front porch. Lookouts had signalled the approach of riders. It had to be Nicky. She'd been gone nearly a week now, and worry had furrowed even deeper lines in his face.

She never would have taken chances like this if he'd been well.

He tried to will away the pain that kept grinding at him, then turned back to the pass where the riders would be appearing. He made out Mitch first, then Nicky, and his heart lightened. He then saw a man on a bay. Diablo. *Diablo was back.* The pain in his belly seemed to explode, and he clung to the post.

The riders drew closer. Nat looked at Nicky's face. It was pale and obviously tear-stained. She was keeping a distance from Diablo. She wouldn't even look at him. As the horsemen approached him, Nat addressed his question to Mitch. Nicky looked as if she was ready to fall apart. "What happened?" he barked, and he managed to put some of the old authority into his voice.

"Damned if I know," Mitch said. "Diablo says he has to talk to you."

Nat's eyes moved over to the subject under discussion. Diablo's face was like stone and his back as stiff as a piece of lumber. He looked like he'd aged years in the past week. The lines in his face seemed to have deepened into furrows. He looked like he'd visited hell.

Nat turned to Nicky. "Nicole?" He never used Nicole. He didn't know why he did now, except for the odd, desperate look on her face. She trembled. She never trembled. Nat had once thought it was because of all the grief she'd had as a child. Nicky seldom showed emotion. And since her father died, he'd never seen her cry.

But she *had* been crying. Nothing made dirt streaks on the face like tears. She wouldn't look at Diablo, either, which was strange. Nat hadn't been too sick to notice her eyes had seldom left the man before he left Sanctuary. If Diablo had done anything to her . . . Nat would watch him skinned alive.

Mitch dismounted in front of him. He nodded toward Diablo, who was dismounting. "He wants to talk to you."

Nat turned to Diablo, frowning. "Diablo?"

Diablo looked at Nicky, then down at Nat. "The law is headed this way," he said.

"How do you know?"

"I told them enough that they could probably figure the rest out," Kane replied.

Nat felt as if someone had dropped a giant boulder on him. His shock and surprise were too great to react for a moment.

"You might have a day," Diablo continued. "Time enough to get Robin and Nicky out."

Nat tried to recover from the surprise, from the pain roiling in his belly. "Why? Why in God's name did you tell them?"

Diablo's gray eyes darkened. "My own reasons."

Nat turned his gaze to Nicky. She had dismounted and was standing next to Evers. Her face was white, her hands knotted together. "Nicky?"

She just looked from one man to the other.

Nat turned back to Mitch. "Take him to my office. To the back and make sure he stays there. I'll be there in a few minutes."

Mitch looked at the Comanche, and the man slid from

his horse. Nat watched as the two led an unprotesting Diablo toward his office.

Nat turned to his niece. "I want to know everything you know," he said, biting off the words. Failure overwhelmed him. His instincts as well as his health were gone. A traitor, by God. He had supped and entertained a traitor. Had even offered him his valley, and his niece.

Nat took Nicky's arm. "I want to know everything," he repeated.

Just then Robin came running in, the hawk on his wrist. "Andy saw you and Diablo ... Where is Diablo?"

Nat hesitated and looked at Nicky. Nicky swallowed. "He's real tired," she finally said. "He's getting some rest. Will you take our horses and rub them down, see that they get some feed?"

"But I want to show him how Diablo can fly."

"Later," she said abruptly.

Robin looked at his uncle in mute appeal. "Look after the horses," Nat said in the tone that allowed no room for disobedience. He rarely used it with his niece and nephew—his two weak spots—so it always got results. Robin looked rebellious but headed for the door.

Nat closed it, and faced his niece. He needed to sit down. He felt so damn weak. But he needed honesty now and he knew he was more intimidating on his feet than sprawled in a chair. "What happened out there?"

Nat could almost see her mind working. She was often cool, unemotional with the guests, but her every feeling showed within the family. He saw the grief and worry, the anguish, the reluctance to hurt someone she cared about. *She still cared about him. Whatever he had done, she loved the man.* The truth was in her eyes. Pain exploded in his stomach, this time so great he doubled over, just trying to keep from falling to the floor. Nicky's hands caught him, and she helped him over to an overstuffed horsehair sofa.

He struggled against the pain, the weakness that was becoming more and more pronounced each day. How much time did he have? He thought he would have months, if not a year, but now he wondered. And perhaps

Sanctuary only had hours, if Diablo had told the truth.

Nat knew he had to get Robin and Nicky out. He had to do it now. But how? All his hopes had been pinned on Diablo. In his need, he had rushed to what apparently was a disastrous decision.

"Uncle Nat?" Nicky's worried voice snaked into his consciousness.

He tried to sit up straight, but damn the pain was bad, the worry worse. "You have to tell me about Diablo," he finally managed.

"I can't . . ." she said, and he saw her face set.

"Your brother's life might depend on it, even if you don't care about your own," he said harshly, the words grated out between clenched teeth.

Her face was an agony of indecision. Her mouth trembled, and she bit her lower lip. She was fighting herself, fighting competing loyalties. He saw it all in her eyes.

Nat tried to help. "He appears to want to talk," he said gently. "I just need to know what I can believe."

She looked up at him. "Are you going to kill him?"

"I don't know," Nat lied. Diablo had signed his own death warrant unless he came up with a damned good explanation. He hesitated. "I want you to pack whatever you need . . . and want. Robin too. I'm sending you out with Mitch. Tomorrow." He should have done it months ago, he thought regretfully. Even years. A Diablo had been bound to happen. Rage started to overtake the pain. Something had died in Nicky's eyes. Probably in her heart. He wouldn't help either her or himself by insisting she say things she couldn't bring herself to say. He would talk to Diablo. If necessary, and only as a last resort, he could always come back to her.

He conquered the pain. Temporarily. He would take some laudanum as soon as he talked to Diablo. He reached out and took Nicky's hand, holding it tight. "You've been like a daughter to me," he said and saw the surprised look in her face. He'd been protective in a hard, cold way, but seldom had he openly expressed affection. "Get some food and some rest." He tried a smile. "And a bath."

"You won't . . ."

He stood, somehow burying the pain. He had to. For her. Nicky and Robin were all he had. "No," he said gently. "I won't do anything . . . final."

Nat Thompson saw her face crumple. She was smart enough to understand the inference. "Please . . ."

But he felt his own face set. "I have to know what he knows," he said. "It's up to him. Now go pack."

"I want to go with you," she said stubbornly.

"No," he said. "If you want to keep him alive a bit longer, you'll do as I say." He forced strength into his voice. Conviction. It took every last ounce of strength he had.

She hesitated, doubt in her eyes. But her shoulders were sagging, and her eyes were almost closed with fatigue. "You swear?" she said with one last attempt.

"I swear I won't kill him."

She looked into his eyes for a long, silent moment, then turned and went to her room.

Now, he amended the promise in his head. He took a step, then another. If only he could manage the next few days, if only he could get Nicky and Robin someplace safe. He had to know how much time Sanctuary still had.

KANE had been thoroughly bound. He hadn't been surprised to see handcuffs and leg irons produced from a cabinet in Thompson's office. Nothing surprised him about Sanctuary. Why shouldn't it have all the trappings of a jail?

Neither the Comanche nor Evers had been gentle. They had pushed him in the office, roughly handcuffed his hands behind him, then hustled him into a back room. Evers had pushed him to the floor and attached the leg irons.

He was familiar with the feel of them, the bite of metal. Evers nodded to the Indian, who left. Evers then leaned against a wall and looked at Kane, who remained on the floor. Kane could probably struggle to his feet, but he saw no purpose in it. With his hands chained behind him and a very short link of chain between his ankles, he could barely move.

Kane looked around the room. It was windowless and completely empty. What light there was dribbled in from windows in Thompson's office.

"You could have had it all," Evers finally said. "You ever seen a man after the Indians get through with him?"

Kane wanted to tell Evers the Indians couldn't even come close to approaching the agony he'd suffered the last few days.

Evers's face was twisted with anger. "I want to be there, too," Evers added harshly. "Nicky ... Nicky's real special."

Kane dragged himself over to a wall and pulled himself up to lean against it. Where was Thompson? He had to talk to Thompson. Every minute was important now. "Thompson?" he asked.

"He'll be here soon enough, as soon as he knows what you did to Nicky. I wouldn't be so anxious if I were you. If there's one thing he hates more than traitors, it's someone who hurts his family. I feel the same way." Evers took several steps towards him. Suddenly, he aimed a kick at Kane's stomach, and Kane doubled over with pain. Another kick went into his ribs. He stifled his cries while fighting to stay conscious. He *had* to stay conscious. He had to talk to Thompson.

Another kick went into his chest, and his head bounced against the wall and everything went black.

Chapter Twenty-three

Kane woke to a bright light shining in his eyes and a splash of cold water in his face. Every part of his body hurt. He tried to move, and that only made the hurt worse.

"O'Brien?" The sound of his name seemed to come from a long way off. Instinctively he tried to curl up, but couldn't. It hurt too damn much.

"O'Brien!" His name again. Spoken with an urgency he didn't understand. He tried to remember. Tried to think who he was and where he was.

Another splash of water, and he tried to focus. Tried to remember. And then as he did, he wished he hadn't.

"Damn you, Mitch. Did you have to hit him so hard?" Kane heard that, too.

"I would like to kill the son of a bitch."

"Later," Thompson said. Kane knew that voice now. Everything was coming back, slowly. Christ, everyone was standing in line to kill him. The state of Texas, Hildebrand, Thompson. Probably even Nicky, now that she'd had time to think about it. Nicky had the greatest right.

Thompson's foot probed him, and he couldn't withhold a grunt of pain. Then the light shone in his eyes again. "Get up," Thompson said.

Kane tried. He managed to get to his knees, but he was too weak to stand without using his hands, and they were still chained behind him.

"Help him up," Thompson said to Evers, and Kane was roughly dragged to a standing position against a wall.

He struggled to remain upright. A lantern shone in his face, blinding him so he couldn't see Thompson's expression.

"Who are you?" Thompson said.

"O'Brien," Kane said.

"You're working for the law?"

Kane tried to straighten. "Yes," he said, offering no excuses. Any would be self-serving and make no difference to Thompson. He had to convince Thompson to send his niece and nephew away. Now. And then provoke him into killing him and leaving his body where it could be found. Just in case Nicky didn't contact Masters. He couldn't blame her if she didn't. He'd been surprised as hell when she had nodded.

How many days did Davy have left? He'd lost track.

The lamp seemed to dip slightly, as if the hand holding it faltered. He sensed, rather than saw, Evers take possession of it.

"Who?" Thompson said.

"A marshal named Masters," Kane said. There seemed no reason not to identify the bastard.

"What does he know?" Thompson cut to the most immediate problem.

Kane wondered what Nicky had told him. Not much, apparently.

"He knows most of the route to Sanctuary, and I left a clear trail for the rest of it," Kane lied. He'd covered it damn well, and it would take Masters time. "It won't be long, Thompson. You need to send Nicky and Robin out."

"Why did you come back?"

Kane debated which truth to tell him. There were several of them. He knew there was probably only one Thompson would believe. "I came after Nicky. She heard something she shouldn't have heard. I . . ."

"You wanted to stop her from telling me?"

Kane shook his head. "I don't know what I wanted." That too was a partial truth. He knew what he wanted;

he just hadn't known how to achieve it. "Just get your niece and nephew out of here," he said. "Now."

Kane saw Thompson move. He seemed bent over in the shadows. In a moment he straightened up again. "How?" Nat said bitterly. "It seems I can't trust anyone."

Kane tried to move, but it seemed only the wall was keeping him upright. He fell back against it. "Evers and you can take her."

"We both have prices on our heads. Besides, I don't know if we would make it out alive. Seems there are a few plans to take over Sanctuary." Thompson suddenly swung at Kane. It was a weak blow, but full of helpless rage. "God damn you. I trusted you."

Kane slumped against the wall.

"Why?" Thompson asked. "Why, when you could have had Sanctuary? Was it a pardon? Money?"

Kane laughed. It was a cold, ugly sound. "Not my life, and certainly not money. Hell, you offered more than the goddamn government could pay," Kane said. "You don't know how badly I wanted it."

"Then why?"

Kane suddenly wanted Nat Thompson to understand. It wouldn't affect his death sentence, nor the manner of it. He had violated Thompson's trust and every rule in Sanctuary. There could be no pardon. He didn't expect one. But he wanted Nicky to know. He couldn't bear for her to think he'd betrayed her for money. "There was another man taken two weeks after my capture. He'd been trying to free me." Kane paused, wondering whether Thompson was listening. "He was, is, the best friend I ever had. I was promised his life."

"And yours," Nat Thompson said harshly.

Kane didn't say anything. He wasn't going to reveal the real bargain. It would sound self-serving. False. Whatever credibility he had, which was damn little, would be destroyed.

Evers held the lantern closer. "You don't believe this, do you, Nat?"

There was a long silence. "You know I'm dying," Nat said to Kane. "Why didn't you just wait me out?"

"Davy Carson didn't have that long."

"And Nicky? Were you just using her to betray me?"

Kane sighed, forcing himself to refrain from saying the truth. It had been Thompson who'd thrown them together. Over and over again. He suspected the reminder wouldn't help. "I tried my damnedest to stay away. I never wanted her a part of this. Her or Robin. Christ, *I* didn't want any part of it."

"She's trying to protect you," Thompson said harshly. "Even now."

Kane groaned. No one knew better than he the gut-wrenching sickness of having to choose between people you care about. He didn't want her to go through that, not for him.

"Take her out of here," he pleaded. "You and Evers can get through with your Comanches."

"And go where?" Thompson said. "All my money's wrapped up in Sanctuary. I don't have long to live, and Mitch is wanted. What kind of life will they have on the run? No money? No protection?"

"Give yourself up," Kane said. "Meet Masters. All he wants is Sanctuary. I think you can trust him to leave Nicky and Robin out of it . . . and I have a little money, enough for them to have a grubstake."

Evers snorted.

Thompson didn't say anything for several minutes, then spoke harshly, "If I left with my family, my own men would kill me. They suspect I'm sick. They might figure I'm going to the law."

"You can't believe him," Evers broke in angrily. "He's just trying to save his own skin. Maybe no one's coming at all."

Kane straightened. "I'm a dead man now," he said. "I know it."

"What about your friend?" Thompson asked.

Kane decided to gamble everything. "If Masters finds my body, he'll release Carson. That was the deal."

There was a long silence.

"Just why should I accommodate you that way?"

Thompson finally asked. "If the Comanches take you, there'll be damn little left."

"I thought you might want an example, a warning to those who might try to come after ... what's yours," Kane said. "And you don't have anything against Carson. I'm the one who—"

"And I'm thinking now the death of your friend might be a worse punishment than your own," Thompson said thoughtfully. "Think about that, Diablo."

The lantern went out, casting the room into total blackness. Kane heard movement, the banging of the door shut, a bolt shoved into place. Then total blackness. He slid down to the floor.

He'd lost his gamble.

NAT Thompson managed to take the steps back to his house without help. Nicky wasn't there, but she would have heard him enter, and he knew she would join them soon. He headed for his desk.

"I think I should take you to the bedroom."

"The desk," Nat managed.

Mitch helped him into the chair behind the desk, and looked at him worriedly.

"Tell Andy, Jeb, and Sam that we might be moving out," Nat said. "Tell them to keep it to themselves."

Mitch nodded but hesitated. "Are you all right?"

"I just need a few minutes to rest," Nat said. "Now get out."

He watched as Mitch left, then opened his top drawer and found a small bottle. Laudanum. He would take a few drops, enough to dull the pain. Not enough to sleep. He couldn't afford that now. He unlocked the drawers to his desk and took out the clippings about Diablo.

A knock came at the door. Urgent. "Come in," he said.

Nicky had washed and changed into clean clothes. Her face wasn't splotched, but her eyes were red.

"He's still alive," Nat said without waiting for the question. "Sit down," he added as he looked back down to the clippings and read them more thoroughly. One did mention a man named Carson, who had been condemned with Diablo.

As he finished, a numbness started to creep over him. He forced himself to stay alert. "Did Diablo ever mention a man named Carson to you?"

He watched her try to remember. She finally shook her head.

"Or mention a friend?"

Nicky's eyebrows furrowed. "Why?"

"It's important, Nicky. It might just save him."

"Will anything save him?"

"It might," Nat said softly. A plan was forming in his mind. "Do you really care?"

"I don't want to," Nicky said, bending her head. "But, Uncle Nat, I don't want him to die."

"Then try to remember."

She hesitated, apparently trying to recall. "I accused him of trying to save himself. He said if that had been true he would have accepted your offer."

Nat thought for a moment. Could O'Brien have made up that story? He had no reason to think it might make a difference. But it *did* make a difference. Perhaps he hadn't been entirely wrong about the man. There had been something about him from the very beginning that had appealed to Nat, something that separated him from the others.

He closed his eyes. The laudanum was affecting his mind as well as dulling his body. He knew he didn't have much longer, maybe not more than a few weeks the way the pain was growing. What was best for his niece and nephew? That was all that mattered.

Nat had always taken care of his younger, handsome, devil-may-care brother, ever since they were children in an orphanage. He'd loved John's wife, and had promised both he would take care of the children. It was the one promise in his life he'd always kept.

Nicky loved Diablo. That was plain enough. She'd protected him as much as she could. It was also plain to him that Diablo loved Nicky. Otherwise he wouldn't have come back. He wouldn't have condemned himself by warning Nat. He'd never seen so much anguish on a man's face as he had moments ago on Diablo's face, and it wasn't for himself.

There was one thing Nat prized above all else: loyalty. He and Mitch had that kind of loyalty, and he would die for Mitch, just as he would have for John. He understood that kind of loyalty, and now he understood Diablo and why he had done what he had. He wasn't sure yet, though, whether he was going to forgive it.

"Uncle Nat?"

Nat opened his eyes. She was looking at him with undisguised worry. Worry for him. Worry for his prisoner.

"You didn't tell me everything, did you?" he said.

A red flush flooded her cheeks. "No," she said honestly. "Why?"

"I couldn't . . . I didn't . . ."

"Nicole," he sighed. "Your mother was like that. Once she fell in love with John, nothing else mattered. Not that he was an outlaw, not that he was on the run. Sometimes, I look at you and I see her. She was so damned pretty, so damned stubborn. She would never stay behind and take care of herself."

"I *don't* love him," she said, her chin jutting out ominously. "How can I when . . ."

"When you did the same thing?" he asked softly. "You were torn between him and me, and you purposely didn't tell me things about our Diablo. I think O'Brien was faced with the same dilemma. He was offered his friend's life for the location of Sanctuary. I think that's why he came after you. He did what he could for his friend, and then he was willing to face my wrath to get you away from here, you and your brother. That took guts, Nicky. He knows what happens to people who betray me. The deaths aren't easy."

She winced.

"He practically invited me to kill him. He wants me to leave his body where it can be found, so his friend will go free. Apparently that was part of the bargain he made with the law, that if he died in the attempt to find Sanctuary, the man named Carson would go free."

"No," she said with horror, then whispered, "he asked me to promise to contact a man named Masters in Gooden, begged me to tell him..."

"Tell him what?"

"How he died," Nicky said brokenly.

Nat nodded. So O'Brien had told the truth. The pain was getting stronger again. He needed more laudanum. "I'm dying, Nicky," he said suddenly. "I don't have any more time, but you do. You and Robin. *If* I can get you out of here, make sure the law understands you had nothing to do with Sanctuary."

Denial flickered across her face. "You can't be..."

"I've known it for months," he said. "That doc who stayed with us said it was cancer, said there wasn't anything to be done. I thought I had longer, long enough to see you and Robin safe someplace, but it moved faster than I thought."

"We can go someplace, find another doctor."

"I can barely stand, Nicky. I know I'm dying, just like an old dog knows."

"No," she said vehemently. "We'll find a good doctor." The passion of her caring warmed him.

"Yes," he corrected her gently. "I have a few weeks, maybe a month. No longer. Don't worry. I've had a long life, and I've had you and Robin."

Her face paled even as it continued to deny. "What are you going to do?"

"Go to the law. Give myself up. Make sure they understand you didn't have anything to do with Sanctuary. Diablo says there's a marshal..."

"Give yourself up?," she asked. "I won't let you."

"I won't live to hang," Nat said. "The only thing that's important to me now is yours and Robin's safety. If a posse finds you here, they'll consider you as guilty as me. And God knows what will happen if there's a shoot-out."

"Robin and I can leave, send a doctor."

"You don't understand. Thanks to Diablo, the law has a damn good idea where Sanctuary is. They could be here in another day, maybe a week, but our secrecy is gone. If my guests get even an inkling of that, they'll kill all of us. They'll certainly kill your Diablo."

"You won't?" she said in a small voice, asking for assurance.

"I haven't decided yet," Nat lied. "It depends on you. I need him to help us get out of here. My guests are already very jumpy, and ... greedy. If I disappear with you and Robin and Mitch, they'll know something's wrong, and I suspect they think I have a hell of a lot more cash than I do. I don't believe the guards will be much happier with me. Once they know Sanctuary's finished, they'll loot everything in sight. We might well need another gun." He looked at her for a long moment. "Do you trust him at all?"

Nicky avoided the question. "What about Andy and Jeb?"

"Neither of them are gunhands. I'm letting them know they should get out on their own. There's no sense for them to be taken, too." He needed another draught of laudanum. And rest. It was nearing midnight. If they were to leave, they had to leave before dawn. He decided to give her another push. "Can we trust him to get us safely to that marshal?"

"What about Mitch?" She was still evading his question.

"Once we're out of Sanctuary, he'll go his way. What about Diablo?"

"I don't know," she said bitterly. "I just don't know."

"Then I'll tell Mitch to kill him."

"No." The word was explosive, expelled from some deep part of her heart.

God, his belly was hurting. "Take him some water. He'll need it. Mitch hurt him some." Nat watched her pale. "Then give me an answer. Wake me up if I'm asleep."

She nodded slowly and left.

Nat swallowed some more laudanum and did something he'd never done before in his life. He prayed he was right.

• • •

NICKY closed her uncle's door, feeling that the last remnant of her world had just been shattered. Uncle Nat had looked so old, so infinitely weary.

She stopped to look in at Robin. He was asleep. The hawk was tethered on the perch Kane had made. Kane O'Brien, the traitor, the user . . . The man who'd taken time to save a hurt bird, who patiently taught a boy to care for it.

Can we trust him? Her uncle's question had astounded her, not only because he was asking her advice but because he was apparently willing to give Kane another chance.

I don't know, she had answered. And she didn't. Her world had been rocked. Her faith. Her trust. Her love.

You did the same thing. You were torn between him and me. You didn't tell me things about our Diablo. Uncle Nat's gentle admonition. Had Kane endured that same agonizing choice?

Would she ever know? *Really* know? The hurt still ran deep. Hurt and anger and emptiness all ran together, like streaks of color in a sunset, each trailing roads in the sky before melding into one burst of color.

In the kitchen, she mechanically prepared a canteen of water and some bandages and then left for her uncle's office—and Kane.

Mitch was sitting in the outer office, apparently guarding Kane. He was looking old, too. She had never thought of him that way before.

"Uncle Nat suggested I bring . . . Diablo some water," she said hesitantly. "And I want to talk to him."

He looked at her with sympathy. His lips, though, thinned in a hard line, and she knew Kane could expect no quarter from him. In fact, her uncle's oddly tolerant attitude still confounded her.

"Are you sure, Little Bit?" That had been his pet name for her years ago, though he hadn't used it since she'd turned fifteen.

She nodded.

"I'll stay with you."

She shook her head. "Alone," she insisted.

He hesitated and looked at the bundle in her hands. She smiled. "I don't have a weapon. Just a canteen and some bandages."

Mitch looked dubious.

"Uncle Nat suggested it."

Suspicion and doubt etched a frown in Mitch's face.

"He told me he was dying," Nicky said. "That he might need to use O'Brien."

Mitch's frown deepened, but he lit a lantern, handed it to her, then unbolted the door to the back room. "You call if you need anything," he said.

Nicky needed a great deal. She hesitated at the door, then went inside, closing the door behind her. The light illuminated the room, and she saw him lying on the floor, his hands pinned behind him, irons circling his ankles. He blinked several times in the sudden glow of the lantern, then tried to sit.

He looked terrible. His face was discolored and swollen, and she saw a muscle move in his cheek as he struggled to sit. His eyes continued to move, trying to see beyond the bright light. She set the lantern on the floor and went over to him with the bundle.

"Kane?"

He blinked again. "Nicky?" His voice was low and disbelieving. And raspy.

"I brought you some water."

He tried to sit straighter, and despite the anger still burning bright in her heart, she ached for him, suffered with him. She opened the canteen and offered its contents to him, holding the opening to his mouth. He drank greedily at first, then slowed. He finally withdrew his mouth from it. His eyes swept over her, traveling from her face downward over her body. She was still kneeling, fixed by those eyes.

"Thank you," he said simply.

Nicky didn't know what to say. He was so battered and bruised, and yet his eyes didn't falter, didn't look away from hers. She was the first to flinch, leaning over to take a piece of cloth from her bundle, wet it, and softly run it over his face.

"How bad did Mitch hurt you?" she asked softly.

Kane shrugged. "I probably look worse than I am." He hesitated. "You shouldn't have come here. Your uncle—"

"Uncle Nat suggested it," she said.

His partly swollen eyes flew open, then closed in a kind of resignation. "I told him everything I know."

"Your friend," she said hesitantly. "Tell me about him."

"He hangs in a week," Kane said abruptly. "Maybe less. I've . . . lost track of days."

"You must care . . . a lot."

Kane shifted against the wall uncomfortably. He took his eyes off her for the first time, and they seem to fasten on a piece of the door behind her. He didn't answer. He was slipping away from her, going someplace she couldn't follow.

"I want to understand," she tried again.

He finally focused back on her. Anguish twisted his face. "I do care about him, about you. Too damn much. Don't ever think I didn't care." The words seemed torn from his throat.

Nicky couldn't help it. She dropped the cloth and her fingers went to his face. Touching it. Sketching his mouth, the lines around his eyes, the scar. Soothing it. "I loved you," she said. It was almost a whimper.

"I know," he said. "I would have done anything to spare you this . . . I thought I could. Because I wanted it so damn badly, I thought I could serve two masters," he added bitterly. "I was a fool."

"If you'd told me—"

"And what would you have done?" he asked. "Telling you would only have given you the same damnable choice I had. I couldn't do that to you."

"But you *did* give me that kind of choice," she whispered. "I couldn't tell my uncle what you told me. He knows that."

Kane cursed quietly, so quietly she couldn't make out

many of the words. She sensed their meaning, though. "And Robin, what does he know?"

"Nothing. Yet."

A muscle throbbed in his cheek again. "Is your uncle sending you away?"

"Yes."

"Good," he said, then turned his face. "Thank you for the water. You'd better go."

"What about you?" she asked.

He shrugged. "I'm not worth worrying about. Just take care of Robin. Don't let him . . . go against the law."

"He says his hawk has learned to hunt," she said desperately.

Kane smiled. It was a flicker of one of the early smiles she remembered. Slow and lazy and affectionate. Her heart whirled again. She warned it to stop, but it wouldn't.

"What would you do if Uncle Nat lets you go?"

His eyes narrowed. "Why would he do that?"

"He might need your help."

"You see what happens when I try to help." He laughed mirthlessly. "My good intentions are the stuff of everyone's nightmares. I'm a Jonah, Nicky. Don't you know that yet?"

"What *would* you do?" she persisted.

"I would see that you were safe. I would *try* to see that you were safe, you and Robin."

"And then?" She wasn't sure what she wanted him to say. But the question hovered between them. She was asking whether there was . . . any chance of a future, one that included the two of them. She was revealing her heart, surrendering her pride, but she had to know.

She watched him swallow, and her heart sank. He didn't want her. He was honest enough not to claim otherwise. Her heart broke all over again.

Something of what she felt must have shone in her face. "Nicky," he said, almost desperately. "Davy's pardon doesn't include me."

"What do you mean?" she whispered.

"I go back to prison," he said shortly. "Davy doesn't go free unless I turn myself back in. I don't have a future."

Nicky stared at him, nonplussed. He was getting nothing out of this? He'd done it only for a friend. She'd believed he had traded Sanctuary at least in part for himself. She tried to breathe through the growing lump in her throat. But if he went back to prison . . . he had been sentenced to death. Surely, at least, that would be commuted. Kane's face was saying otherwise. His features could have been carved from granite, but his eyes were filled with despair.

"I don't understand," she finally said.

"That was the arrangement," he said. "One life. Davy or myself."

"Why? *Why* is this man so important?"

Nicky watched as Kane tried to move again, pain flitting briefly across his face. She knew how uncomfortable he must be, but she couldn't do anything about it. She didn't have the keys to his irons. Or a gun. Nor could she ever bluff Mitch.

"Why?" she asked again.

He smiled. It was such a sweet, sad smile she thought her heart would break.

"I didn't have a family, Nicky, not even what you and Robin had," he said. "My mother died when I was born, and my father hated me from that day. Kane, he named me, and he meant it with every fiber of his Bible-loving fanaticism. He tried to beat the devil out of me every chance he had. Davy lived on the next ranch. He used to bring me food, helped me hide. One day, my father discovered him doing that, and he started beating me. Davy wasn't much older than me, but he went after my father. He nearly died for that gallantry, and his father finally threatened mine if he ever touched Davy or me again. I honestly wonder whether I would have lived if Davy hadn't . . ." His voice trailed off.

Nicky felt shudders rock her body. She put a hand on Kane's leg, resting it there with the old trust.

After a moment, he started again, his voice halting. "My father killed himself a few months later. Davy's family took me in and raised me as Davy's brother. Davy married, had a son—my godson—and his folks died the year before the war started. He stayed on to manage the ranch while I enlisted in the Confederate Army. I was looking for some place to belong, I suppose. Davy had married, had a wife and son, and I needed something of my own. I thought maybe the army would provide it."

"It didn't?" she said.

"Don't let anyone tell you war is adventure," he said dryly. "It's blood and fear and pain and more fear. You never stop being afraid. Death is so damn capricious. It doesn't make sense why the man next to you dies and you don't. You stop making friends. You stop wanting to belong, because that belonging hurts too damn much."

Her hand had settled in his lap. She wished she could hold his hand, tighten her fingers around this. "You become more and more alone, because you can't stand the loss any longer." He swallowed. "And then it was over, and I came home, believing, thinking I would never kill again."

She waited, her body tense. She knew he was saying these things for her, not for himself. He thought he was a dead man. He was trying to make her understand, so she wouldn't feel so betrayed, and he was giving up the last thing he had—his pride—to do it.

"Some government agents came to Davy's house, shortly after I arrived. They'd raised the taxes impossibly high and were going to evict him. Alex, my godson, was twelve. I'd just been telling him some glorious war stories, and . . . he took it in mind to raise a rifle against a deputy sheriff.

"A deputy shot him . . . a kid, damn it, and he was going to shoot again. I killed the bastard first. Davy was blamed as much as I. Damn it, Nicky, it was my fault, my doing. If I hadn't filled Alex's head with war stories, maybe he never would have reached for the rifle."

"Alex?" she asked softly.

"He survived. The bullet went in the shoulder. But Davy and I had to go on the run. We were both pretty

angry, not only at what happened to us but to others."
Kane shrugged his shoulders. "So we did what we could
to balance the scales . . . and survive."

"When I was taken, Davy tried to rescue me. That's
how he was captured. That deputy had died, and we were
both sentenced to hang. Two days before we were to hang,
a marshal showed up at the prison and offered Davy's life
in exchange for Sanctuary. I had the reputation; Davy
didn't. And then I met you and Robin, and . . . I wanted
to take your uncle's offer. I thought that was the answer.
That's why I went back to Masters—the marshal—to bargain for more time. I thought if they waited, then I could
just hand over Sanctuary peacefully. Your uncle told me
he was dying. A few months in exchange for a number
of lives they would lose in trying to take it." He stopped.
"I wouldn't have let you or Robin be hurt, Nicky. If you
don't believe anything else, believe that."

"Did the marshal give you the time you asked for?"
she asked.

"No."

"Then your friend will die?"

He replied through clenched teeth. "Not if they find
my body. That was part of the bargain. If I died in the
attempt, then they would have to honor their end."

"So that was why you wanted to come back? You knew
my uncle would kill you." She gazed at him in amazement. "But how did you imagine the authorities would
find you in time?"

A very long moment passed during which he refused
to meet her gaze. Then he spoke in clipped tones. "I asked
your uncle to leave my body where Masters would find
it. I suggested an example might be appropriate. And—"

"You asked me," she finished.

"Long odds against either," he said, "but they were all
I had."

She shook her head slowly. Then, leaning over, she
touched her lips to his. "You're a fool, Kane O'Brien. That
posse doesn't have any idea where Sanctuary is, does it?"

"Oh, I'm sure they have an idea," he said. "They'll get
here eventually. I had to give Masters something. He'll be

searching this whole territory, if I know anything about men."

Nicky was silent for a moment, the last of her anger draining away. "My uncle's thinking about turning himself in," she said cautiously. "He might need your help to do it."

"With my vast experience of failure?" Kane said drily. "He needs me like a boil on his backside."

She found herself smiling. Even giggling. But it was a nervous giggle. "I don't think I'll tell him that."

He eyed her suspiciously, as if she were capable of pulling wings off a trapped fly. "He has no reason to trust me."

"But he does," she said gently. "For some reason he still does. Or else he thinks he doesn't have any other choice. I told you Hildebrand planned to take over Sanctuary. Others are just waiting for a chance. They don't know how sick Uncle Nat is, but they know something's wrong. He can't stay here. He has no place to go. And no time. I tried to talk him out of it. I don't want to see him in prison, but he's determined. He just wanted to make sure I . . . agreed that he could trust you."

Kane was silent. Nicky didn't know what he was thinking. But she had heard the anguish in his voice, the stark honesty of his words. Any lingering doubt she might have about him was outweighed by her need to believe him.

"Kane?"

He swallowed hard. She could see the movements of his throat. "Can you?" he said after a moment. "Can you trust me again?"

She hesitated, then announced evasively, "Whether I trust you or not, I can't . . . stop caring."

He moved again awkwardly. "You must," he said. "You're smart and brave . . . and beautiful. You'll find a good, solid husband."

"I don't want a good, solid husband," she said, her voice plaintive.

He smiled, a sad, wistful twist of his lips. "You just haven't had much of a choice."

But Nicky knew he was wrong. She remembered her

uncle's words. *Your mother was like that. Once she fell in love with John, nothing else mattered.*

She looked at his face, remembered the agony she'd felt when she had to choose between him and the uncle who had raised her, knew he'd felt the same agony when faced with a choice between his lifelong friend and her. He'd done his best, as she had, to choose the path that would bring the least harm to those he loved. And how could she fault him for that?

She couldn't.

Suddenly, all her doubts—and questions—faded away. Maybe she would always hurt a little because he hadn't chosen her above all else, that he had gambled with her trust, but she could live with that. What she couldn't live without was him. They had to get out of this mess—all of them—somehow.

Nicky brought the canteen to Kane's lips again, watched as he took some more water. She didn't want to promise him anything, because she still wasn't sure what her uncle planned. She knew, though, that one way or another Kane O'Brien was going to live. No matter what she had to do.

"I have to go," she finally said.

His eyes searched her face intently, as if he were memorizing it, and then he gave her that devilish smile she'd seen his first day in Sanctuary. She thought then it was both devilish and devil-may-care, but now she knew better. She knew how much he cared about a great many things.

"You were a sight for sore eyes, Miss Thompson," he said. "Thank you for that. And for the water."

It was an attempt to make light of his situation. A gallant attempt, and Nicky thought her heart would break all over again. She didn't want to leave him like this. Not trussed up like an animal headed for market. She hesitated. She wanted to reassure him, but she guessed now he wouldn't accept, or believe, reassurances. And why would he? Whichever way he looked was death.

She leaned over and kissed him lightly, pressing her cheek next to his, then she rose.

And ran.

Chapter Twenty-four

Despite Kane's discomfort, both mental and physical, he slept on and off. He was totally exhausted, and he was used to discomfort.

But he kept waking. Every time he moved, he hurt. His wrists were raw behind him, his arms nearly numb from their pinned position. He tried his best not to feel, not to think about things he couldn't change. When he was in the Yank prison and his stomach was so empty it ached and his body so cold he could barely move, he'd tried to think of cloudless days and bright sun. Now he couldn't envision those kind of days without thinking of Nicky, the way her brown hair caught the sun and her eyes sparked with mischief. Those memories hurt more than hunger or cold ever had.

He willed blankness even as he wondered what was taking Thompson so long to decide what to do with him. Despite Nicky's questions and kindness, he harbored few illusions about Thompson. Regardless of what the man had told Nicky, there was no doubt in Kane's mind that Thompson would kill him. It was only a matter of where and when.

The real question was whether his own manipulations had worked to achieve his two goals: that Thompson believed a posse was imminent and would finally send Nicky and Robin away, and that Masters learn of his death in time to save his friend.

Now, at least, he had a better than even odds chance. Nicky would try to contact Masters. He felt sure of that in his heart. She had forgiven at least part of his deception; he didn't think he ever would, though.

He wished he had some more water. His mouth was so damn dry. He closed his eyes again, thinking of Nicky's touch, the sound of her voice as she said she couldn't stop caring, the feel of her cheek against his before she fled.

He tried once more to sleep. It seemed only seconds after he closed his eyes that he heard the door open. Light again blinded him.

Rough hands pulled at him, and then his hands were free. Agony streaked up and down his arms as they moved. Then before he could comprehend what was happening, his ankles were also free. He expected to be tied again, expected Comanches to hustle him off to a horse. He tried to stand, made it to one knee but no farther. His legs were as cramped as his arms.

"Take your time," a rough voice said. "Just not too much."

He tried again as his eyes slowly adjusted to the light. He could finally see forms. Thompson. Evers.

A hand took his arm and helped him to his feet. He stood there for a moment, swaying. Every bone in his body complained, but he managed to stand.

After a moment, he felt steadier. The light moved away from his face, and he saw Thompson. The outlaw leader looked as tired as Kane felt, and a hundred years old. "I want to go to that marshal," Thompson said. "I need your help."

Kane absorbed the words slowly. So Thompson's words to Nicky hadn't been a ruse. He looked at the man standing in front of him, and admiration surged through him. He had guts, this man who had fought the law all his life and was now prepared to surrender for the sake of his family. Even if Thompson was dying, Kane suspected jail was not the way he wished to end his life. Kane looked at Evers, who stood silently at Thompson's side.

"Does he agree?"

"No," Evers said for himself. "But it's what Nat wants. I won't fight him."

"Once we're away from Sanctuary, Mitch will go on his own way," Nat Thompson said.

"Andy?"

"Andy and his wife—a few others—left earlier. It's near dawn. Can you travel?"

"Considering what I thought I would be doing this morning, yes," Kane said with irreverent self-mockery.

Thompson ignored it. "I'm giving you the same chance that marshal gave you," he said. "You do this right, and you might live to save your friend. But if you make one wrong move . . . I'll make sure no one ever finds any part of you."

Kane nodded. "Nicky?"

"She and Robin are outside. So is your horse. It's not quite dawn. There's a way out that not even the guards at the entrance know. We'll take that."

Kane rubbed his wrists. They were chaffed raw, but that was a minor inconvenience. He stretched, feeling the pain in his ribs from Evers's blows. The man was eyeing him as if he'd like to deliver a few more. Dislike—and distrust—flashed between them.

He looked again at Thompson. The older man's movements were slow, almost trancelike, and Kane wondered if he'd taken something to help him tolerate the journey ahead. Kane didn't waste any more time. He followed the others through the door, aware he didn't have a gun, and mounted a horse already saddled for him. Robin was mounted, holding a basket; Kane surmised the hawk might be in it. Nicky sat stiffly on her mare.

The five riders moved slowly away from the office. Thompson deliberately kept them at a walk down the still-dark street. Once they were outside town, though, Thompson spurred his horse into a gallop, and they headed toward the cliff where Kane had found the young hawk a lifetime ago.

• • •

HILDEBRAND swore. It seemed he had been riding forever. The worst part of the journey had been on an old nag he'd stolen from an Indian farmer more than a day after Diablo and the woman left him and Calico hogtied. He and Calico had finally managed to untie themselves and start walking. They'd both known they couldn't return to Sanctuary. The damn girl had evidently overheard something, and now Thompson would want their heads. They had ended up blaming each other, and Calico had swung at him, the fight escalating into a deadly contest between them. Hildebrand's hand had found a rock and brought it down on Calico's head. Again and again.

Five hours later, he'd wandered upon the lone homestead of an old Indian and his wife. Both were visible in the fields. He stole a pair of trousers and shirt, and a swayback old horse, barely avoiding shotgun blasts from the injun as he came running.

Two days later he reached Gooden. He heard about Yancy and went looking for him, hoping he had found a new partner. He found him wounded and aching for revenge, the same kind Hildebrand had in mind. Hildebrand had the advantage of the two. He now knew the location of Sanctuary. Calico hadn't blindfolded him as he had Diablo.

Neither Hildebrand nor Yancy had money after their respective experiences. They had used up what cash they had at Sanctuary. Hildebrand had the worn-out old nag, and Yancy's horse was in Gooden, where he dared not show his face. Lack of resources, though, had never stopped Hildebrand. He rode into town, waited till nightfall, robbed a drunk and took his gun, then held up a general store. After clubbing the owner with the butt of his gun and taking what firearms he needed, he stole two horses, leaving his own nag behind.

When he met back up with Yancy, they had all they needed to return to Sanctuary. They even had a plan. An embittered and hurting Yancy had discovered that a lawman was in cahoots with one of Thompson's people. That news should gain them entrance into Sanctuary, where they would enlist the guards and other guests. It should be easy enough to convince them that Thompson's judgment could no longer be trusted.

Money and revenge both awaited them in Sanctuary. They had a score to even with Thompson, with the high and mighty Nicky Thompson, and with Diablo. With any kind of luck, they could settle all those debts with one blow. With that pleasurable thought, Yancy and Hildebrand rode hell-bent for Indian Territory.

KANE marveled at the ingenuity of the hidden exit. The grays of dawn were lightening the sky when they reached a rocky cliff that Kane had previously explored. Mitch Evers dismounted and walked over to a series of boulders that Kane now saw shadowed a large crack in the wall. Kane remembered searching this area, but he'd never suspected an exit. Bushes that had shielded it were gone now, and he recalled Thompson saying that Andy and others had left earlier. The blacksmith must have used this same exit.

Kane waited, glancing at Nicky. She was silent. She appeared to be watching Mitch, every movement he made. Once, she looked back toward the town of Sanctuary. He wondered if she did so with regret. But she'd said nothing to him since he had mounted. Robin too had been uncommonly silent, and Kane wondered whether he had been warned to say nothing until they left the valley.

Nat Thompson was sitting on his horse, his back ramrod straight. It was the kind of straight that came from effort, not naturalness. From the tenseness of his shoulders, it was clear that he was suffering a great deal of pain. Kane's admiration for him spiraled. Admiration and gratitude. Thompson was swallowing his pride and his righteous anger against Kane in one last selfless act for his wards. Whatever else he had done in his life, Nat Thompson was dying nobly.

Evers pushed aside another rock, then signaled to the others to dismount. Kane slipped from his horse, still feeling the bruises Evers had inflicted. He stood alone as

Robin and Nicky dismounted easily. Robin gave him an uncertain glance; Nicky didn't look at him at all.

Thompson led his horse over to Kane. "I'll lead. Robin, you follow me, then Nicky, and O'Brien. Mitch will stay behind and push the rocks back into place, then trail us."

Kane felt naked and vulnerable without a gun, especially since Thompson and Evers were clearly anticipating trouble. The fact he didn't have one plainly indicated that he wasn't entirely trusted.

They walked into the cave. Thompson leaned down and picked up a lantern, lighting it from a match he struck on the cave wall. The cave was narrow, and in some places the ceiling was low enough that Kane, the tallest of them, had to bend his head. The cave became stifling after a while, and Kane wondered how long it was. They stopped periodically, and once Kane saw Thompson lean against the wall for a moment.

They were all quiet, and the sound of the horses' hooves and the riders' spurs echoed through the passage in an oddly melodic way. Yet Kane felt very much alone. The others were a family, even Evers. He was the interloper, the outsider no one quite trusted. Only once had Nicky looked back, and then it had been a quick glance that was solemn and sad—or had it just seemed that way in the dim light? But then why shouldn't she be sad? She was leaving everything she knew, all that had been safe for her and her brother. An uncertain future awaited her. She would soon lose the person who had raised her, her home, her security. Everything.

Though he was not responsible for her uncle's illness, he was certainly responsible for the rest of it. No matter how sweet that kiss hours ago, how tender her hands, she'd had time to think. They couldn't be good thoughts.

The passage seemed to take hours. Time, though, was impossible to judge in the dark cave. Kane wondered how Thompson managed it. By exerting the same will, apparently, that had kept a town full of killers in line. He was fighting a different battle now.

They stopped for a few moments. Robin's hawk whistled inside the basket, and Kane heard the boy's mumbled reassurances. A canteen passed its way down. Mitch had caught up with them, and he took it silently from Kane before passing it back. Then Nicky's hand accepted it and, in doing so, got her fingers entangled with his. For a moment, they touched before she drew the canteen, and her hand, away; they started moving again.

The interior of the cave grew lighter, and Kane realized they were nearing the exit. The cave broadened and walking became easier. He saw some carvings in the wall, primitive etchings of animals. Some tribe had once used these caves, and the valley beyond, probably for safety, just as Thompson had.

As Kane walked into the sunlight, he saw plains before him. They were on a small plateau, jagged rock towering above them. From this position, they could see for several miles. Everything was quiet, empty. Thompson had seated himself, awaiting the others. His face was white, wet with sweat despite the coolness of the day. Nicky was kneeling next to him, holding a small bottle. Thompson lifted it to his lips, seemed to shudder. His shoulders had slumped.

Nicky rose and turned her attention to Kane and Evers, who were standing next to him. "He can't go farther now. He has to rest."

Evers nodded. "O'Brien, help me with these bushes."

Kane looked back at the exit. A pile of underbrush had been shoved to one side, apparently by Andy, who had left the exit unobstructed for Nat Thompson. He and Mitch stacked the brush up over the entrance.

"Get some rest yourself," Evers said. "I don't suppose you've gotten much lately." There was a small note of satisfaction in the observation.

Kane ignored it, and the throbbing in his chest. "You going to keep guard?"

"Yeah," Evers said. "But I'll also be keeping an eye on you. Nat might trust you, but I don't."

Kane couldn't fault him for that. Were he Evers, he wouldn't have trusted himself either. Only now that his and Thompson's interests coincided could he put his full energies into seeing the Thompsons safely away from Sanctuary.

Kane went over to Nicky, who was sitting next to Thompson, her face puckered in worry. Thompson had obviously spent his last reserves on the long trek through the cave.

Kane wasn't sure he could make it to Gooden. Or anyplace else.

Thompson moved slightly, took a sip from the bottle of laudanum, then looked steadily at Kane. "Nicky," he said, "see how your brother is doing."

Nicky glanced from her uncle to Kane, then back again. She was obviously reluctant to leave his side. "Please," Nat said. "I want to talk to O'Brien."

Her reluctance grew. It showed in the face Kane now knew so well. "If it's about . . ."

Nat tried to smile, but it was more a grimace. "It's not about you," he said.

She looked at him suspiciously, but then got to her feet and went over to her brother, who was trying to calm his hawk.

Thompson was leaning against a rock. His face changed as pain obviously struck him again. Kane felt his own gut tighten in reaction. He wished like hell he could do something to help.

"I don't know if I can make it," Nat said. "Swear you'll take care of Nicky and Robin."

"I'll get them someplace safe," Kane promised. It was all he could promise. He still had an appointment with the hangman. "I know some people who will look after them. I've already given Nicky the name."

"I have some money in my saddlebags. Not much, but enough to give them a start. I just don't want them alone."

"I'll see they get it, that they're taken care of," Kane promised. "You've no need to worry about that."

"Mitch . . . he's a good friend. But he's been outside the law so long, he wouldn't know how . . . to settle down. I don't want Robin to go that way."

Kane nodded, his throat tightening. "Get some rest," he said.

"We can't stay here long. This is a blind spot for

the guards. I made sure of that, but when they find us missing . . . "

"You can't travel now."

"Go on without me," Thompson said. He reached inside his shirt and pulled out a map. "This is what you need. Trade it for Nicky's and Robin's safety."

"You can do it yourself," Kane said. "We all need a little rest." He knew it was foolish. Thompson had little to look forward to, whether he died here or in prison. But Kane knew he wouldn't leave the man. Not to die alone.

Thompson's eyes searched his. "We would have made a good team."

Kane grinned. "We still can. Just get some rest."

Thompson nodded, took another sip of the laudanum, and closed his eyes.

Kane continued to sit there for several minutes, oddly pleased that the man found some kind of comfort in his presence. He wondered how long he had before Masters could no longer stop Davy's hanging. He should have taken Thompson's offer to take Robin and Nicky and go on without him, but he couldn't. How do you value one life above another's? He couldn't do it any longer, even though Thompson's life was short. He could no longer weigh loyalties and lives against each other.

Thompson's breathing seemed to ease, and Kane knew he had finally fallen asleep. Kane stood painfully and went over to Robin and Nicky.

Robin had taken some meat from his saddlebags and was feeding the hawk. "How's Uncle Nat?"

"Sleeping," Kane said. "Why don't you two get some rest, too. Evers is keeping watch."

Nicky searched his face, frowning at what she saw, but she didn't say anything in front of Robin. Instead, she turned to her brother. "Robin . . . try to get sleep. We have a long ride ahead."

"But I'm not tired." His eyes were wide-awake with the adventure, and Kane remembered how long it had been since he'd been outside Sanctuary's walls.

"You will be," Kane promised with a slight smile. "And you don't want to slow us down, do you?"

Robin shook his head. Kane wondered how much he had been told about his own role in all this, whether Robin knew that he had intended to betray his family, but nothing of that showed in his eyes. Kane looked at Nicky, and she seemed to understand. She shook her head.

He touched the boy's shoulder. "You've done amazing things with the hawk," he said, as he watched the bird eat from the boy's fingers. Some hawks would never do that.

"He caught a bird the other day . . . while you were gone," Robin said.

"Then he's probably ready to let go," Kane observed.

Robin's face fell.

"Letting go is sometimes the greatest love of all," Kane said.

He wasn't just talking about the hawk now, and somehow Robin seemed to know. He looked toward his uncle, then back to Kane, his face troubled.

"Is that what Uncle Nat is doing?"

Kane nodded. "We all have to help him do it. That means you getting some rest."

A wetness glimmered in Robin's eyes, and Kane wondered if he knew more than anyone thought he did.

"All right," he said and turned away, his hand touching the hawk's sleek head.

Kane looked down at Nicky, standing beside him. Somehow, her hand had slipped into his. She was shivering, although the sun was up now, warming the air. He took a few steps to where the ground curved up against rocks and sat, pulling her down beside him. He held her in his arms, trying to quiet the tremors.

He wondered whether she had gotten any sleep the past night before they left. He doubted it. He scooted down, taking her with him until they were both lying on the ground, and he held her, his lips touching her hair, his arms sliding up and down her arms in a soothing motion. Finally she quieted and lay still next to him. His own eyes closed as his arms wrapped tightly around her, holding her body close to his.

•   •   •

A CRY from the hawk awoke Kane. Nicky was still lying in his arms, and he tried not to wake her as he looked around. Robin was talking quietly to the hawk. Mitch Evers had reappeared, and the sun had climbed several hours higher in the sky.

He shifted, moved Nicky. She didn't wake, which was, he thought, indicative of her level of exhaustion. Kane stood and went over to Evers. "Thompson still asleep?"

Evers nodded, his grizzled face wary.

Kane met his gaze directly. "I know you don't trust me," he said. "You don't have any reason to. But I want you to know I'll do my damndest for them."

"You hurt them in any way, and I'll hunt you to hell and back."

Kane nodded, thinking that Evers would have to stand in line for that particular honor. "You think your 'guests' will come looking?"

"Not without a leader. Now that Hildebrand's gone . . ."

Kane had a bad feeling about Hildebrand. When Evers and the Comanches had found Nicky and him, he'd said they had found Calico dead but no sign of Hildebrand. Calico was deadly, and if Hildebrand had gotten the best of him . . .

Where had he disappeared to?

"What about the Comanches who were with you?" Kane said.

"They left last night after taking what they wanted— and after they discovered they couldn't have you." Evers gave Kane an unpleasant smile. "They were looking forward to some entertainment."

"Can't say I share their disappointment," Kane offered.

Evers ignored the comment. "They said they would keep a lookout, but we can't depend on them now that they have liquor and food. Nat was the only one who could ever handle them, and I don't think he can do that now."

Evers stalked quietly over to Nat Thompson, watching him for a moment, and Kane followed him.

The laudanum had evidently done its job. Some of the

pain lines had eased in Thompson's face, and he didn't look quite as pale. Evers's face was twisted with a pain of its own, and Kane realized their friendship was as deep as the one between him and Davy.

Nat Thompson groaned slightly and his eyes opened, trying to focus.

Kane knelt next to him, waiting several minutes as Thompson struggled to sit. Time was pressing down on him now, and Kane prayed softly that the outlaw leader could ride. He studied Thompson's face. "Can you go on?" he asked.

Thompson nodded his head. He looked over at Evers, his eyes glazing over for a moment. "Remember that time we held up a stage office in San Antonio? I was shot up all over the place and still rode two days straight. Give me your hand." Evers leaned down and grasped it, pulling Nat Thompson to his feet. The man swayed for several moments, then steadied.

Kane went over to Nicky, who was still sleeping. He leaned over and gently shook her. He knew she hadn't had much sleep for the past five or six days, but she woke almost immediately. "Your uncle's ready to go," he said.

Rubbing a hand across her face, she asked, "How is he?"

"Probably better than you at the moment," Kane said, seeing the dark pouches of exhaustion under her eyes.

She sat up and Kane offered her his bandanna and canteen. Nicky quickly rinsed her face with the lukewarm water, then rose to her knees. Her hair was tangled, her face smudged from the trip through the cave, and her clothes ill-fitting, but Kane thought he had never seen anyone quite as appealing as she was at that moment. Her gaze, as it met his, was steady. She reached out her hand, and he took it, his fingers tightening on hers as he drew her up.

He didn't want to let go.

But the others were all waiting, all mounted except for him and Nicky, and he released his grip on her. He followed her to the mare, then cupped his hands into a lift.

She looked down and gave him a grin, and instantly some of the weight lifted from his shoulders.

They set out at a slow pace, with Evers, who knew the area best, leading, followed by Nat Thompson, then Nicky and Robin riding side by side and Kane taking up the rear. They were a motley bunch, Kane thought. And God help them if they ran into trouble.

BEN Masters stopped his horse, pausing to wipe the sweat from his brow. Fifteen men rode behind him. Fifteen deputy marshals.

He had several maps, one plainly showing Wichita Mountains. He wished to God he'd gotten more information from O'Brien. Instead, he had to bank everything on two words from a dying woman's lips. But what she said had concurred with what O'Brien had said.

Prior to leaving, Ben had wired the governor, asking for more time for Carson. He'd lied, saying he received the location of Sanctuary from the man called Diablo. He still had hopes for O'Brien. He didn't know what had spooked the man in the hotel room, but his gut instinct told him he hadn't been wrong. Somehow, somewhere, O'Brien was going to do something right.

Ben had to believe it. Everything else had gone wrong, God help him. And now he had to finish this business and keep his promise to Mary May. What in the hell was he going to do with a little girl?

First things first. He and his posse had been out three days now, and the only sign of O'Brien was his gray horse, which they'd found the second day. The damn horse had been wandering in circles, and Ben's tracker had lost the original trail. The land itself seemed completely empty. No sign of the Indians he understood claimed this as their land. Hell, no sign of life at all. No tracks. No O'Brien.

Were they a day away from Sanctuary? Were they even going in the right direction? He hated this feeling of uncertainty, of wandering in the godforsaken prairie. He was tired of feeling alone, even when he was with other lawmen. Ben wiped his face again and led his small troop of lawmen deeper into Indian Territory.

Chapter Twenty-five

Hildebrand and Yancy made good time. The moon was nearly full, enabling them to travel by night. The incentives were right: revenge and money. Sanctuary should be a few miles away.

Hildebrand couldn't forget there was a marshal involved, probably a posse, which was why they moved so fast. He and Yancy didn't talk much. They'd never particularly been friends; they'd run with their own gangs. But their interests coincided, if not particularly their trust.

They stopped at a water hole. Yancy didn't want to, but their horses were nearly gone. Hildebrand didn't want to lose another one. Damn Diablo to hell. His only regret was that Diablo wouldn't be at Sanctuary. Thompson and the girl would be, though. That was some compensation.

Both he and Yancy were watching for Comanches. Hildebrand thought he could bluff them, too. He had a couple of bottles of whiskey with him just in case.

They reached the entrance to Sanctuary. Hildebrand saw a guard up in the rocks encircling Sanctuary. Only one, which was unusual. He waved. A shot splattered the ground nearby, and his horse shied. Then another man appeared and the two in the rocks seemed to confer. One started down the rocky incline, his rifle in his hands. When he reached the bottom, he lifted his rifle into shooting position, while the guard overhead kept a rifle on them.

Hildebrand recognized the man who had climbed down. He was one of the guards with whom Hildebrand often played poker. His name was Moses, a nigh-unto unforgettable name.

"Hildebrand," the man said. "What in the hell are you doing here? I thought Thompson—"

"Kicked me out? He did. But I heard in Gooden that some lawmen might be on their way. I have friends here. They need to know Sanctuary's no longer safe."

Moses' eyes narrowed. "Posse?"

"Could be. Marshal named Masters was snooping around in Gooden. He was getting real close to a woman who worked for Thompson. Diablo was going there, too, and I always thought there was something wrong with him."

Moses studied him a moment. "Heard Calico was killed. Wasn't he with you?"

"Diablo took us both when we were asleep. I managed to get away, but it sort of made me wonder about him. Where's Thompson?"

"No one's seen him today," Moses replied with a frown. "Or the woman or kid. And the blacksmith's shop is closed. A few others are missing, too."

"Evers?"

"No one can find him, either."

Hildebrand saw his revenge melt away. And money. If Thompson was gone, so would be his cache.

"How long ago was he last seen?"

"Last night. Diablo was with them."

"Diablo?" Hildebrand's mouth pulled down on one side.

"He came in with Mitch Evers and the girl," one of the guards said. "But no one's seen them today. They sure as hell didn't go through here, though."

Hildebrand cursed. "He must have made a deal with the law. Is there another way out?"

"Not that I know of, although there's been whispers

from time to time. But I don't think Thompson would make any deal. He hates lawmen."

"Then why are they all gone? Even Evers. Sneaking out in the middle of the night?"

"Thompson wouldn't do that," the guard protested.

"Maybe Diablo took Thompson by force," Hildebrand said. "You know Thompson hasn't looked too well lately."

"But Mitch . . ."

Hildebrand shrugged. "He could be dead. I think we should warn the others. See if anyone knows about another entrance."

Moses hesitated.

"You want to fight off a posse?"

"We can hold this place."

"Not if there's another entrance you don't know about."

Moses hesitated. "Okay. Go on in. Look." He waved to the guard above, and Hildebrand and Yancy rode through the narrow trail into Sanctuary.

An hour later, they had gone through every inch of Thompson's house and office. No money anywhere, including the safe. At Hildebrand's urging, fifteen guests and six armed guards held a conference. Thompson had obviously deserted them and taken his money with him. One man allowed he had seen Thompson doubled over yesterday, and others suddenly voiced thoughts they had kept to themselves: Thompson was ill.

Which meant he couldn't travel fast, Hildebrand said. And Thompson must have money with him, and lots of it. *Their* money. He was a low-down double-crossing son-of-a-bitch.

They didn't have time to search for a secret exit. Hildebrand suggested they split up into two separate groups and search the area for tracks, one going to the left, one to the right. If one party found tracks, they would fire three rifle shots.

The "guests" at Sanctuary sacked the general store, looking for their guns; they found none there, but they did find a box of Winchesters and ammunition in Nat Thompson's basement, hidden behind several casks of wine. They emptied the general store, taking what they could and setting fire to the rest.

No man voiced a doubt now that Thompson had taken his family and fled, which meant the law must be on the way. In their collective anger, they also set fire to the hotel, Thompson's house, and the stable, though they took out the horses first and claimed them. Nat Thompson always kept a good supply for those who might need them.

The rest of Sanctuary would burn. Flames were already whipping from one structure to another.

The men mounted, money and revenge on all their minds.

KANE saw the glow behind them, the slight darkening of a clear blue sky. He spurred his horse forward until he reached Evers and gestured for the man to look behind.

Evers turned in the saddle, his lips frowning. "They've discovered we're gone," he said.

Kane nodded.

Evers hesitated, then reached into his saddlebags and pulled out Kane's holster and pistol, handing it to him. "They might scatter or they might come after us," he said, then added in a low, warning voice, "I'll still be watching you."

Kane took the gunbelt and buckled it on. "What about a rifle?"

"Nat has an extra one on his saddle if you have need of one," Evers said shortly, then added angrily, "This is all your doing."

"Thompson's dying," Kane said. "You know that. Your 'guests' would have made a move sooner or later. They were just waiting for an opportunity."

Evers glared at him, turned and trotted up to Thompson. The whole party had stopped, and they were looking back at the faint, fiery glow and the drifting smoke. Regret mixed with pain on Thompson's face. Robin's gaze was riveted on the smoke. Nicky looked at Kane, then away quickly. He wondered what she didn't want him to see in her face.

The loss of Sanctuary *was* at least partly his fault. It was bound to happen anyway, given Thompson's sickness, but he had hastened the event. He had accomplished his goal. Sanctuary was finished as a hideout. He had something to show to Masters. He should be pleased. Satisfied. Instead, he felt empty. Tired.

And it might be too late for Davy. He might also be responsible for leading Thompson and his family to their deaths. But he had no time to dwell on that. They were all running for their lives.

An hour later, they heard three shots, a space between each one. A signal. All of them drew up, listening.

Nat Thompson was barely hanging on. "They found the trail," he said.

"Where are your damn Comanches?" Evers asked.

Nat shrugged. "You know they've always been more threat than actual use."

Kane hesitated. "That shot was faint. They're a fair distance behind."

All eyes went to Thompson. There was no way he could ride hard enough or long enough to keep in front of healthy men who were bent on catching them.

"Is there a good place to ambush them?" Kane asked. It was time, he knew, to take over. Up until now, there had been no reason to challenge Thompson or Evers. They were going where he wanted to go.

"About an hour ahead," Evers said. "There's a hill, more like a pile of rock."

"When we get there, you take Thompson and his family and go on," Kane said. "I'll stay and delay them."

"Hell, you will," Evers said. "I don't trust you any farther than I can throw you."

"Then you can stay with me," Kane challenged.

Nat Thompson looked at his nephew, then niece. "I'll stay behind with Mitch. O'Brien will go with Robin and Nicky."

There was a long silence. "I won't go without Uncle Nat," Nicky said.

"Neither will I," chimed in Robin.

The three men looked at each other helplessly.

Kane broke the deadlock. "Let's get to those rocks. Then we can argue it out."

Nat Thompson nodded, somehow bringing an image of strength to the gesture. He set the pace again, a strong pace, the others deferring to what he could do. Kane didn't even want to think what it cost him. He swore silently.

He caught up to Nicky and rode alongside her. Mitch fell to the rear. Robin grinned at him. The boy seemed almost oblivious to the danger they faced; this journey was an adventure to him, and Kane understood. Robin didn't realize yet how ill his uncle was, or exactly how much was at stake. For Robin, leaving Sanctuary for the first time since infancy, it must seem as if a whole new world was opening before him.

Kane said a rare, brief prayer for him. He wanted that world to broaden for Robin—and for Nicky.

If only they survived the next few days.

THE sun had started its downward descent when Kane and his companions reached the rocky formation that jutted from the ground. As large as a substantial hill, it appeared entirely composed of rocks and boulders.

Nat Thompson could barely sit his horse. He was swaying back and forth, obviously badly in need of the laudanum. "I can't go any further," he said.

Evers dismounted, then helped his friend down. Thompson seemed to crumble for a moment, then stood and looked at the others. "I want to talk to Nicky and Robin alone," he said. Kane's gaze met Evers's, and they both dismounted, walking their horses out of hearing distance, both of them judging the rock formation for places to hide. They were only too aware of the minutes ticking by, but neither said anything. Kane had never liked Mitch Evers, but he'd come to respect his loyalty to Thompson. Mitch could have ridden off, saved himself. He must know he would be prosecuted along with Thompson, or killed by the men they'd left behind. His options had become as slim as Kane's and Thompson's.

Evers had never said much, particularly to Kane, and he certainly wasn't going to start now. Instead, he climbed up into the rocks, obviously searching for good roosting places. If the men from Sanctuary followed their tracks, they would pass right below here. With rifles, a good shot could take down two or three before the others would have time to draw and aim. And then the sun would favor those in the rocks.

A second man could throw the pursuers into chaos. Kane intended to be that second man, no matter what anyone said. He followed Evers up into the rocks, and his gaze went toward the space Evers was studying. There was just enough room for a man between two boulders, both of which would serve as good protection. Unless someone climbed up from the other side.

Kane started searching himself. He found another good spot, one from which a shooter would have a clear view, rock barriers to duck behind and a good view to protect the other man. He saw Thompson below, huddled with Nicky and Robin. Kane suspected what he was telling them: that he was going to die soon in any case, that they must go on without him. Nat Thompson intended to stay here alone, and Mitch wasn't going to let him.

Neither was Kane, even though the thought of shooting someone again was sickening. He kept thinking that part of his life was over. He wondered whether it would ever be over. Probably not until he was dead.

One thing he knew for sure—he couldn't run away from this fight. He had set everything into motion. He was damn well going to see it through.

Kane looked down again. Robin appeared to reel from whatever Thompson was saying. Nicky put her arm around the boy and held him tight. Nat Thompson held out his hand to Robin in a gesture that touched Kane even though he couldn't hear the words. Thompson wasn't a sentimental man. Nicky stood straighter, and Kane wished he were there next to her, holding her.

Thompson signaled for Kane and Evers to join him, and they looked at each other. Understanding flickered between them, and Evers smiled briefly. They climbed down and joined Nat Thompson.

"I want you two to leave," Thompson said. "Mitch, you get the hell out of here, maybe go to Mexico. Diablo can take care of my niece and nephew. I can't go farther, but I sure as hell can still shoot."

"No," Evers said. "We've been together twenty-five years. I'm not going it alone now. There's no way you can make me."

A muscle throbbed in Thompson's cheek. He turned to Kane. "Take Nicky and Robin and get out of here."

"Three of us have a better chance of stopping them," Kane said. "Robin and Nicky will be safer if I stay here. They can take a note from me. Someone will hear shots— your Comanches, or . . ."

"Your posse?" Nat finished dryly.

The time for lying was over. "I'm not sure there is one," he said, wishing to hell he'd given Masters more information.

Thompson blinked, then smiled slowly. "You're a devious son of a bitch," he said. "But it doesn't matter now. I want you with them."

Kane didn't like sending Nicky and Robin on alone any better than Thompson did. Their chances were better, though, if three men were to ambush the pursuers. "We can hold them up for days," he argued. "They wouldn't know we aren't all still together, especially if we scattered our three horses after Nicky and Robin leave."

There was a silence as the other two men considered his plan. After a moment, he asked, "How many do you suspect are behind us?"

"If the guards joined up with our paying guests, as many as twenty," Thompson said.

"And they would," Evers said, "once they realized you'd left. There's always been rumors about how much money you had stashed at Sanctuary. You had control only as long as they were afraid to cross you."

"And now they feel I crossed them," Thompson said.

Mitch shrugged his shoulders. "We all know they were

just looking for a chance to take over Sanctuary. You didn't owe them a damn thing."

"They may not view it that way," Thompson said. He looked again at Kane. "I don't think Nicky will go alone."

"She will," Kane said slowly, "if she thinks your life depends on it."

Thompson glanced up sharply at him.

"We tell them none of us will survive without help," Kane said. "But we might be able to hold out if they can reach Gooden."

Evers stared at him. "You really are a sneaky son of a bitch."

If Kane's heart hadn't been so heavy, he might have appreciated the observation, coming as it did from a man who had helped create Sanctuary.

Nat looked at him. "It might work, but what about your friend?"

Kane met his gaze. "Hell, they'll have Sanctuary *and* a body. Nicky will tell them where they can find us."

There was a silence. Then Evers spoke up. "Both Nicky and Robin can handle rifles," he said. "I think Diablo's right. The longer we can hold them off, the safer they'll be. They would know if there were just one or two of us. Some might check ahead. But if we move around these rocks, they'll think we're all here."

Thompson straightened his shoulders. "All right." He turned to Kane. "You explain this to Nicky. I'm going to switch saddlebags with her. Mine has the money; hers has most of the ammunition. Mitch, you unsaddle the three horses and take the gear up into the rocks."

Thompson leaned against the rocks for a moment, waving off Kane as he took a step forward. "What are you waiting for? We don't have time."

Kane nodded. He headed toward Nicky and Robin, who were standing uncertainly near their horses. Nicky lifted her eyes to him, large beseeching eyes asking him to do the impossible. Robin had tears in his eyes, though he was trying his best to hold them back.

Kane reached out and put a hand on the boy's right shoulder. The hawk was perched on Robin's left shoulder.

"You and that hawk have a lot in common," he said. "Lots of courage. And now I'm going to ask you to do something very hard."

"We're not leaving," Nicky said flatly, obviously prepared for a fight.

Kane turned to face her. "The three of us can hold off an army for a few days," he said, "but we don't have enough water or ammunition to last indefinitely. If you two stay here, we don't have a chance. The only one we do have, any of us, is if you ride for help."

Nicky studied his face for deception. He held her gaze. It *was* the only chance.

"I can't go," she whispered. "Everyone I love is here."

"What about your brother?" Kane asked. "You have to give him a chance. All of us a chance." He didn't elaborate. He didn't say that neither he nor Evers nor Thompson had a chance even if they were rescued. All three of them were gallows bait.

She swallowed hard, indecision in her eyes.

"Find a man named Ben Masters," Kane said before she could object again. "Or he might be using the name of Ben Smith. Tell him your father and I were coming in to give ourselves up. Tell him you're the reason I left Gooden. Tell him I did what he wanted. He'll help you."

"What about you?"

"I'm a survivor, love," he said lightly. "I survived a war. I survived a Yank prison camp, and I survived two years on the run. I'll survive again. But I need your help. Yours and Robin's."

A wetness glimmered in her eyes. "You don't have to stay." He knew then that she realized more than he was saying. She always did have a certain innocent wisdom.

"Yes, I do," he said gently. "I started this. I'm damned if I'm going to run now."

"I love you," she whispered.

He leaned down and brushed his lips against hers lightly. "You're a lovely lady, Miss Thompson. I wish I could have courted you properly."

She put her arms around his neck and stood on tiptoes, her lips reaching for his. "It looks like I'll have to wait a while," she murmured, and then their lips were locked together. His arms went around her, crushing her to him. He recognized their mutual desperation, the shared knowledge that any chance they might have had for a life together was all but gone. She was his sun and moon, the one good bright and shining star that justified his life.

He felt her tears on his cheek, and he thought how remarkable it was that she could cry for him, that she could love him after all she knew. It was a gift, one of the few he'd ever received, and by far the greatest.

He finally released her lips. "Always remember," he said, "I loved you. I never wanted to hurt you. I'd rather put a gun to my own head." He leaned down, touched his lips to her forehead. "You and Robin had better go."

He turned and faced Robin. He held out his hand and Robin took it, his lips quivering. "Don't forget to let Diablo go," he said. He meant both Diablos, and a quick look of comprehension in Robin's eyes told him the boy understood.

Kane turned to help Nicky mount.

She gave him one last look and ran over to where Evers was unsaddling his own horse. She gave him a hug, and he wrapped his big arms around her. "Get along with you now," he said. "We're depending on you."

Then both Robin and Nicky were in their saddles, Nicky looking slight on the mare. Kane slapped the horse's flank, and Molly bolted into a run. Robin followed.

All three men watched them go, then turned their attention to getting their guns, ammunition, blankets, canteens, and saddles up into the rocks. Kane hesitated before scaring off the three remaining horses, but none of them wanted to see the animals caught in a crossfire, and they couldn't hide them up in the rocks.

KANE heard the riders first. He and the other two men had barely settled down in the rocks, each selecting the location best suited to protecting the others as well as affording a clear line of fire. Kane had a box of ammunition lying next to him and a rifle in his hands. He took his six-gun from the holster and placed it on a rock next to him for easy access. He and the others were about two hundred feet from each other.

Their first goal was to convince the attacking outlaws that five shooters were lying in ambush so they would have no reason to ride on ahead. Time. They had to give Nicky and Robin time.

The pounding of horses' hooves grew louder. A lot of hooves. Kane stretched out, then positioned his rifle between two rocks. He'd rubbed the barrel and its sight with dirt to keep the sun from glinting on it.

The riders came into view, and he started to count. Fifteen, seventeen. Nineteen. Then he couldn't count any longer. They were directly beneath him. He fired a shot, aiming his rifle at a shoulder. The man went down, taking the horse with him as it stumbled. The next man ran into the first downed outlaw, then the air was full of rifle fire, yells and the sound of milling, confused horses.

Kane aimed again and through the sight saw Hildebrand. He pulled the trigger but missed. The man had sensed the bullet, though, and looked up, aiming toward the rocks where Kane sat. He ducked between the boulders, heard the ping of a bullet against rock.

He looked up again, and twisted his body, snaking through the crevices to a second location. Then he looked again. The riders were seeking shelter now: a nearby gully, several of the nearest rocks, behind one dead horse.

He fired, aiming to confuse rather than kill. His companions obviously had more deadly intent. Kane saw one man after another go down. He marveled once more at Thompson's endurance, his will. Kane saw one man starting to climb the rocks; he couldn't be seen by either Thompson or Evers. He aimed for the chest; this time he couldn't indulge himself. He saw the man fall and then tumble down.

He moved again, taking his canteen with him. A sudden silence had fallen below, and men were huddling outside rifle range, obviously trying to decide how to proceed. Kane sat back in the rocks, took several sips of water and reloaded his rifle. It was going to be a long afternoon.

• • •

NICKY and Robin heard distant gunfire. They both drew to a stop.

Robin looked at Nicky. "I want to go back. We can help."

Nicky wanted to, too, with all her heart. She wished she had never left.

But Kane had made sense. She was doing the right thing, as hard as it was to do, for Robin, for her uncle, for Kane.

Always remember I loved you, he'd said to her. *I never wanted to hurt you. I would rather put a gun to my own head.*

And his admonition to Robin. *Don't forget to let Diablo go.*

He'd been saying good-bye. And he *was* putting his gun to his head. He'd known it, and she'd known it.

"Nicky?" Robin was peering at her through apprehensive eyes. "Maybe we should go back."

She shook her head slowly. It was too late now. If they went back, they could be taken, and used to lure her uncle, Mitch, and Kane into the open. Their best chance was to do as Kane had asked: find help.

"We can't," she said, swallowing the lump in her throat. What sounded reasonable an hour ago didn't sound that way now.

"But . . ."

Choices. Always choices. Life-and-death choices. Loyalty choices. Robin or her uncle and the others? Which ones to make? Had Kane's hurt as much as the ones she'd had to make? Would the second-guessing, the pain, ever go away?

"We have to go on," she finally said. "We have to get help." But help meant the law, and another kind of finish for the three men sacrificing themselves so that she and Robin could live.

Dear God in heaven. She'd never prayed before; that had never been part of her lessons. But she started praying then. For her uncle, for Mitch. For the man called Diablo.

She dug her heels into her mare. She had to find the marshal named Masters.

BEN Masters had been riding alongside the stream shown on the map. They had been traveling nearly three days, slowed by an imperfect map, and he was more frustrated than he'd ever been in his life. Something inside told him time was essential. Instinct, perhaps. Maybe just worry. They had stopped to water their horses, when the ears of one of the horses pricked up.

Ben raised his hand, quieting the talk between the men, and they fell silent, all of them listening intently.

"Gunshots," one lawman said.

"Hell of a long way off," said another.

They all looked at each other, then without any additional words, vaulted into their saddles and headed north toward the faint sounds of gunfire.

Ben stopped them periodically to listen again, to make sure they were headed in the right direction. It was difficult to tell on the open prairie, but the firing did sound closer. And then the third time they stopped, there was nothing.

Silence. Dead silence. Even the wind had stopped blowing.

He listened intently. Still nothing. It might have been hunters, but then again maybe not. It had sounded more like a pitched battle. He signaled the riders to go forward again at a slower pace. He had to think of the horses, though urgency was driving him.

They had gone another thirty minutes or so when he spied two riders in the distance. He divided his troop, sending one group straight and the other to the left. He would have them in a vise.

Minutes later, he realized he didn't need a vise. The riders headed directly toward his group, which was the nearest. As they approached, both riders appeared to be young boys. He signaled by hand for the deputy marshals to put away the guns they had drawn.

One rider came directly to him, while the other held

back, a hand on a rifle in its scabbard. As the first inched his horse closer, Ben saw dark brown eyes study him intently, the gaze resting on the marshal's badge. It was then that he realized the rider wasn't a boy at all, but a woman.

"Ben Masters?"

He nodded. "Who are you?"

"That doesn't matter," she said. She hesitated for a moment, then reluctantly continued. "Kane O'Brien told me to find you. He . . . and two others are pinned down maybe five, six miles from here."

"By how many?"

"I don't know. The attackers came from . . . Sanctuary," she said, leaving a lot unsaid.

His eyes flickered, but he didn't waste time with questions. He looked at her horse and that of her companion. They were obviously tired. "Can you lead us?"

She nodded, but didn't move. "Kane said we could trust you." It wasn't a question exactly, but she obviously wanted a confirmation.

"I owe O'Brien," Ben said. "You can trust me." She hadn't asked in what way or to what degree she could trust him, and he hadn't promised anything specific. But implicit in the words was a sincere offer of help.

She studied him another minute, then nodded.

The boy behind her merely looked rebellious. His hand remained on the rifle.

Ben watched the woman nod to the kid, say something, then both turned back toward the direction they'd come. He signaled to the other group, which had stretched out to the left, and they turned, galloping at an angle so they would all meet ahead.

Ben eyed the woman riding in front of him. She was older than she'd first appeared and a superb horsewoman.

Several questions ran through his mind.

What in the hell had O'Brien done?

Would they be in time?

Or was this a trap?

Chapter Twenty-six

Kane saw the men below him huddle, then separate, some disappearing out of sight, and he knew they would be trying to climb the rock formation from the other side. Others found closer cover.

He had recognized Yancy and wondered briefly how he and Hildebrand had hooked up. They were a dangerous pair. But so were the others now that they had a leader. He kept his attention on Hildebrand, but the outlaw kept himself out of range while urging others into it.

Dirt exploded not far from Hildebrand, and Kane was reminded again that Evers and Thompson were damn fine marksmen. Had the rifle had a few more feet of range, Hildebrand would be dead. As it was, he scurried backward several more yards.

Shooting started again. Kane aimed at a man running from a gully toward a corner of the rock formation and pulled the trigger, hitting the earth just in front of the moving figure. The man darted back toward the gully, going in head first.

Then the air was full of shots. Someone had seen the flash of his rifle, and several bullets pinged near him. He crawled back to his alternate space, and aimed again.

He heard a grunt of pain to his left. Either Evers or Thompson had been hit. Kane aimed again, and this time he shot to kill. Other lives depended on him. He shot twice more, both times hitting his targets. Then his place was marked again, and the rock around him was peppered with bullets. He ducked, hoping either Evers or Thompson could draw fire while he changed position again.

He reloaded. He had one more box of ammunition for the rifle and only six bullets for his handgun. He looked at the sky as bullets continued to strike the rocks around him, and then one ricocheted and pieces of metal slammed into his arm. It would hurt like hell in a few moments but was manageable. He tore off the sleeve of his shirt and tied it around the wounds.

Kane heard shooting to the left. Either Thompson or Evers was still alive.

One yelled over to him. "Diablo?" It was Thompson's voice.

"Yo," he replied, letting them know he was all right. He didn't ask how *they* were. He couldn't afford to let the opposition know one of their number was wounded.

Kane snaked back to the other position and looked back at the sky. The sun was disappearing behind him. Late afternoon. Night would be the dangerous time. Hildebrand's men could crawl unseen into the rocks, then strike at daybreak from above or the side.

But Nicky and Robin should be safe now, far enough away that Hildebrand and the others could never catch them. And if they led a posse back, well then . . . Davy would be safe, too. He really couldn't ask for more.

He wanted to live, though. He really wanted to live. It hadn't been all that important until he'd met Nicky. He had a natural instinct to survive, and he hadn't wanted to die by hanging. But he'd given up hope of ever knowing love—of having a home and family—long ago. Then he'd met Nicky, and he knew exactly how good it felt to hold a woman he loved, how it changed the color of the sky, and the brightness of the moon, and the fresh scent of the wind.

Taking another gulp of water, he peered down the sight of his rifle again. It was more difficult to see the outlaws now, either because they'd taken better cover or the afternoon shadows curtained them. The pain in his arm was beginning to bother him, too, and he felt blood trickling down his skin. The wounds weren't bad enough, though, to hurt his aim.

Sensing a movement to his right, he shot at it. There was a scream and thrashing sound, and he felt sick. He heard the sound of a rifle coming from where Evers or Thompson had settled, and knew that one of them, at least, was still alive. He shot again, just to let them know he was still alive and in relatively one piece.

The shot was returned, just missing his head, and he ducked down. He wiped away the sweat beading on his forehead and dripping into his eyes, then reloaded with his rifle. Kane thought he should move back to the other spot, but he was tired. So damned tired. How long since he'd had a full night's sleep? Not since he'd left Sanctuary that first time. A week ago? It seemed a year.

"Nicky," he whispered. He hoped with all his heart she was safe. He hoped she would find a good man to love. Have ten children. He smiled at the thought of small replicas of her. He wished he could be the father.

There was a scraping sound to the side of him, and he swung his rifle around just as a man came in view. He fired and the man went tumbling down, yelling as he rolled over and over and landed in a heap at the bottom. Kane peered around, and, as he did, a bullet whizzed by him, then another from the opposite direction. They were bracketing him. This was a hell of a way to die, but preferable to a noose. He wondered how his companions were doing, who had been hit, and how Thompson was holding up. Hell, he wondered if either was still alive.

There was movement below again, another strategy session apparently, then Hildebrand's voice. "We just want the money, Thompson, and you can go."

There was no answer, and Kane knew a loneliness even deeper than the one he'd experienced those nights before his scheduled hanging.

"Go to hell," he yelled, not wanting them to think they were all dead.

Then there was another voice. "That's a damn good

suggestion." It was Thompson's. Kane hoped only he heard the weakness of it.

"You can't hold out forever," Hildebrand said, but then he seemed to stiffen.

Another one of the attacking outlaws stood up from behind a boulder as if listening to something. Then a third bolted for his horse standing not far away. Kane heard a scrambling in the rocks beneath him and saw several men race for their mounts. Suddenly, the outlaws were all scrambling for the horses as riders approached. Kane saw a small black mare at the front, a slight form atop her back, then he recognized Masters. He swore softly at Nicky's recklessness just before he collapsed down among the rocks, too tired now to do anything but wait. Hell, let Masters do some work for a change.

But then he heard a rifle shot come from his right, and he glanced over to see Nat Thompson. He was standing, firing steadily down at the last straggling outlaws. Kane wanted to yell to him to sit, to duck back behind the rocks, but then he realized what Thompson was doing. He was going to end his life his own way.

Almost fatalistically, Kane watched, motionless for a moment, as Yancy paused before mounting his horse and then swung his rifle toward Thompson. Kane came to life, aimed his own rifle, fired, and watched Yancy go down, but he was too late. Yancy's bullet had caught Thompson. Sanctuary's founder swayed on his feet for what seemed eternity, then slowly sank to the ground.

Kane watched as the newcomers fired at the outlaws who weren't able to mount, either because they were too far from their horses or because the horses had bolted. Another group of riders took off after Hildebrand and those few outlaws who had been able to mount and follow him.

Kane stood and scrambled his way over to where Nat Thompson lay, his body covering Evers's. Kane checked the pulses in their necks. Both were dead. He stood there for a moment, wishing he had a hat to take off, but that was up somewhere in the rocks. No matter what the two men had been or done, they both had died protecting Nicky and her brother.

For a moment, he thought about standing up, as Nat had, with his gun drawn, inviting the posse to shoot. It would be easier in some ways than facing his sentence. But he couldn't do that to Nicky. She'd lost enough for one day. So instead, he tossed the rifle aside, raised his hands and started the torturous climb down.

When he reached the bottom, Nicky was there, waiting, her heart in her eyes. Masters was beside her, and Kane looked at him for permission to lower his hands. He didn't want to be shot now by some trigger-happy deputy. Masters nodded, and Kane lowered his arms. The minute he did, Nicky flew into his embrace. He held her tight for a moment as her hands seemed to grasp at every part of him, as if she didn't believe he was whole. After a moment she looked up. "Uncle Nat?"

Kane met her gaze, was aware that Robin was now standing next to them. "He's . . . dead," Kane said slowly. "He and Evers." He hesitated a moment. "You know he was dying. He went the way he wanted to."

Tears glistened in her eyes, and he pulled her closer to him again, while his gaze went to Robin. The boy was valiantly trying to keep his face straight, his eyes dry.

"Where is he?" Robin finally asked.

Kane thought about telling him not to go look, but it was Robin's decision. He was becoming a man. He would have to be a strong one in the next few months, the next few years. There would only be him and his sister. Kane's hands tightened around her, not ever wanting to let her go. "Straight up," he said to Robin. "Behind those two large boulders about halfway to the peak."

It was only then that Nicky moved slightly, her eyes searching his face and then moving to his arm. "You're hurt," she said.

"A scratch."

That didn't satisfy her. She untied the cloth he'd wrapped around his arm, wincing when she saw the raw gashes. "More than a scratch."

"I've survived a lot worse," he said dryly. Then he hesitated. "I'm sorry about your uncle. But I think he died the way he wanted to. He wasn't the kind of man who could tolerate wasting away."

"I know," she said. "I knew that when I left. I knew he wouldn't be alive when I got back. I think Robin did, too. And Mitch wouldn't have known what to do without Uncle Nat." There was a sad fatalism in her words.

His hand touched her face. So much wisdom. So much compassion. She had known, and she had left. And he also knew, now, that she had done it only because he'd asked her to.

He closed his eyes for a moment as he memorized the feel of her. In some ways, her slender body seemed fragile next to his, but he knew she was made of a special kind of steel.

"O'Brien?" Masters's voice jerked him back to reality.

He looked up. Six or seven "guests" and guards from Sanctuary had been rounded up and were being hand-cuffed. He saw another eight bodies lying on the ground. Some of the outlaws had escaped, but Kane had seen a number of deputies making chase. A few might get through, but not many. He hoped like hell Hildebrand would be taken.

Kane finally acknowledged Masters, who was standing several feet away. "This what you wanted?" he asked bitterly as one arm held on to Nicky, the other swept the death-littered landscape.

Masters merely looked at him, his eyes sliding from him to Nicky and back again.

"Davy?" Kane asked.

"He's alive," Masters said.

"Sanctuary's about thirty miles north. What's left of it. The man who operated it is up in those rocks. Dead."

Masters looked around. His eyes lingered for a moment on Yancy, and Kane saw strong emotion replace his usual imperturbable expression. "I recognize a lot of faces."

"A bonus," Kane said. "I want something in return."

Masters's eyes turned wary. "What?"

"Safety for Miss Thompson and her brother."

"Still looking out for everyone but yourself?" Kane was startled to see the slightest twinkle in his eyes.

"I want your word," he insisted.

"Who is Miss Thompson?" the marshal asked.

Nicky straightened and shook loose of Kane's arm, although her hand dropped to his and clutched it tightly. "Nat Thompson was my uncle. Sanctuary was his."

"But she didn't have anything to do with it," Kane said.

Masters was looking her over carefully, taking notice of the trousers and shirt. "She's why you left Gooden in such a hurry, isn't she?" he asked.

Kane hesitated before answering. "She saved my life on the way to Gooden. I never would have made it if it hadn't been for her. And then she heard part of our conversation . . ."

"And you saw her leave?" Masters said.

Kane felt Masters's eyes bore through him, then fall to where his and Nicky's hands were locked together. "I want your promise to look after them," Kane reiterated.

"No," Nicky exploded. "I don't need anyone looking after me. I don't need anyone. Neither Robin or I, except . . ." She looked at him, pleading, hope still alive in her gaze.

Kane's heart trembled. After everything he'd done, she still wanted him, loved him. It seemed a miracle. But it was too late. He had promised to go back.

"Promise, damn you," he demanded of Masters, even knowing he had no leverage.

Masters grinned suddenly. "I think you should do it yourself."

Kane went stiff with astonishment, even anger. He didn't like being toyed with. He wanted to hit Masters. He wanted it very badly. If Nicky hadn't been holding on to his arm . . .

"Hell," Masters said, "from everything I knew, I expected to lose half my men going into Sanctuary. Not only did I not lose one, I suspect we've just taken some of the most wanted hombres in the country. You're right, O'Brien. It does deserves a bonus. I don't think I'll have any trouble convincing the Texas governor that you've become a valuable citizen."

Kane was too astonished—and cynical—to believe what Masters was suggesting. He knew the reputation of the governor, and how badly he'd been wanted. The doubt must have shone in his eyes.

"The governor's under a lot of pressure to stop some of the lawlessness," Masters said. "He can't afford to fight me, not and risk being associated with those land grabbers. The federal authorities wanted Sanctuary closed down a damn sight more than they wanted to make a martyr out of you. They decided that weeks ago. I was going to tell you in Gooden, but—"

Kane listened. Absorbed. Then comprehended. With calculated intent, he took his hand from Nicky's and, totally disregarding the pain in his arm, hit Masters in the chin as hard as he could. Immediately four men were swarming around him, pinning his arms behind him, but Kane didn't take his eyes from Masters, who had fallen to the ground.

The marshal shook himself, looked at Kane ruefully, then rubbed his chin and looked at the blood on his fingers from the cut lip.

"You let me believe there was no chance," Kane said.

Masters got up slowly. "I didn't think you would do what I needed you to do if you thought it was *your* life on the line. You obviously don't value it enough," he said. He turned to the men holding him. "Let him go. I had that one coming."

Kane took another step toward him.

"*That* one," Masters said, warningly.

"You're a bastard."

Masters didn't reply to that statement, only shrugged, then turned away and started to oversee the roundup of prisoners.

Nicky looked up at Kane. "Does that mean . . . ?"

"I don't know what it means," he said, unable yet to accept Masters's statement. Nicky was looking up at him so hopefully, he was afraid to believe.

He and Nicky watched as Robin started back down.

The boy hit a soft spot and started tumbling. Kane caught him just before he hit the ground, and held his shoulders for a moment.

"I'm sorry, Robin," he said. "So damn sorry."

Robin looked up at him. "You told me I had to learn when to let go."

Kane nodded.

"But it hurts."

"It always hurts, Robin, when you lose someone."

"Then I won't care about anybody," he said defiantly as he angrily wiped a tear from his eye.

Kane had to smile. He could tell Robin it wasn't that easy. He'd tried during the war. He'd tried during the past few months. Life didn't work that way.

"It's far better to care and lose," he said softly, "than never to care and never lose. I know. I tried both."

Robin looked dubious.

"Would you rather not have had your Uncle Nat at all?" Kane asked.

Another tear came out of Robin's eye and this time the boy ignored it. "No."

Kane knew how he felt. He hadn't known Nat Thompson well, but he'd felt grief that moment Thompson fell. Since his early childhood—and all the failures to please his father—he'd tried not to care too much about anything, but now he knew those attempts had been as useless as trying to hold back an ocean.

Nicky reached a hand up and touched his face. Her fingers ran over the scar. "The marshal was right, you know," she said.

He hesitated, unsure of what she meant.

"You're looking out for everyone but yourself," she explained. "Do you always do that?"

Kane was nonplussed for a moment.

"Yes," Ben Masters said, having returned to hear the end of the question. "He saved my life during the war. A Reb saving a Yank, and he ended up in prison for doing it."

"I told you it was a mistake," Kane growled.

"I know what you told me," Masters said. He looked

at Nicky. "The only way I could recruit him was to offer his friend's life. He wouldn't do it for his own." Masters smiled sympathetically at Nicky. "He's a stubborn man."

Kane's suspicious mind started working again. "What do you want now?"

"Well, I was hoping to pay back a debt, but now I think I owe you again. No other lawman's ever gotten a bag full of desperadoes this easily. Good way to end my career."

Despite the rather flippant words, something dark suddenly flitted over his face, and Kane wondered about it. "You said I had to go back."

"In the meantime, I fixed it so you wouldn't," Masters said. "You and I need to take a trip to the capital for an official pardon, but that's it."

"Davy?"

"He gets one, too."

Kane didn't trust himself to speak, felt a little like he'd stepped into a dream.

Masters hesitated a moment, his somber gaze resting on both Nicky and Kane as they stood together, then his lips cracked into a faint smile. "I think the reward money due on this lot of thieves and murderers will give you both a good start."

"I don't want blood money," Kane said, still thinking about Thompson up in the rocks.

Masters shook his head. "Someone's gonna get it. I don't think you want me to be the one."

Kane looked at Nicky and Robin. Both shook their heads.

Masters suddenly looked impatient. "You claim the government took your friend's land . . . and some other folks', too. I don't disagree with that. This gives you a chance to take honestly from the government what you were taking dishonestly. Hell, give it to your neighbors if you want."

Kane hesitated. Maybe he *could* right some wrongs. There was certain poetic justice in it. "We won't take any for the two men up in those rocks," he said.

Masters nodded.

"No one gets money for them," Kane insisted.

Masters nodded again.

Kane turned to Nicky. "Is that all right with you and Robin?"

Nicky nodded and squeezed his hand tightly, her eyes glinting with tears. "I think Uncle Nat would approve." She looked up into his eyes. "Can we bury them here? I don't think they would want to go back to Sanctuary."

Kane looked at Masters, who shrugged his consent. "I'll get some men to help."

"No," Robin said. "Kane and I will do it." There was a new quality to his voice, a sureness that hadn't been there before.

"The three of us," Nicky added, leaning into Kane's arms.

Kane felt his throat choking up. *The three of us.* It sounded fine.

Masters moved back, as if respecting their grief. "I'll round up the others on the other side of the hill. I'm sure someone has a shovel. I'll send the prisoners ahead with most of the deputies. I want to see Sanctuary. Then we'll go to Austin, get your pardon arranged." He walked away without waiting for an answer.

Kane looked at both Nicky and Robin, still uncertain as to whether they could, would, forgive his part in this.

Robin returned his glance with sudden understanding. "You have to let go," he said. "I know why Uncle Nat brought you along. He knew you would look after me and Nicky." He held out his hand. "Looks like you're stuck with us."

With one arm around Nicky, Kane closed his long fingers around Robin's hand. He couldn't say anything. He couldn't believe what was happening. He couldn't believe he was going to live—he *and* Davy—and that he finally was going to have a family of his own.

He couldn't believe any of it.

But then Nicky reached up, and her lips touched his, and he knew it was real.

"I love you, Kane O'Brien," she said.

"But not Diablo?" he asked softly.

"My devil?" she said. "I think he was always a bit of a fraud."

He tensed slightly.

"I mean, what devil always looks after everyone but himself?" she asked with a wickedly teasing smile. "I think you should put him away for good before you ruin his reputation, or," she added wryly, "you get yourself killed." She looked at him with such tenderness that for the first time in his life, he felt truly wanted, truly worthy of love.

You have to let go. His very name had always symbolized unworthiness to him. So had the one he'd taken: Diablo. But because Nicky loved him, he could let go of his past, of the pain of his father's hate and his lifelong feeling of being an outcast.

His heart seemed to burst with the realization. With hope he'd never known, with love he'd feared even to dream existed.

The feeling gave him the courage to turn her to him. "Will you marry me?" he asked. "I know that it's too soon . . . and that I don't have much to offer, or . . ." He kept rushing his words, afraid to stop, to hear the answer that would shatter the illusion.

She put her fingers to his lips. "Of course I will," she said with a glorious smile.

He turned to Robin, one eyebrow raised in query.

Robin grinned. "I approve."

By unspoken but what seemed common consent they all turned and looked up at the rocks, where Nat Thompson lay. The sun had dipped below the horizon, and the sky was a brilliant gold. The rocks were tinged with it.

"I think he's smiling," Nicky said, her voice a little unsteady.

Kane hoped that was true. "I think so, too, love," he said, and as he said that last word, he knew wherever he went now, he had a home. He belonged.

The most unlikely people had given this miracle to him: a marshal and an outlaw.

He held Nicky next to him, sharing her feelings—a bittersweet mixture of grief and hope, of love lost and love found, of betrayal felt and forgiven—and looked toward the setting sun. But it wasn't setting at all, not for him. In the golden haze of evening, Kane saw, instead, a glorious dawn, and a succession of dawns.

He felt Nicky's hand grip his harder; Robin had left and gone to the basket on his horse. They watched together as the boy took the hawk out, then raised his arm. The hawk hesitated a moment, then spread its wings and flew into the sky, circling several times. There was a cry, and the three of them saw another hawk rise from the craggy pile of rocks.

Diablo circled once more and then headed toward the other hawk.

Robin moved closer to Kane and his sister, and Kane put his hand on the boy's shoulder as they watched the two birds circle warily, then head to the other side of rock formation. They disappeared for several moments, then one of the hawks reappeared and flew back down to Robin's arm, screeching plaintively.

"Go," Robin said, and Kane heard the gentle harshness in it. "It's time to go to your own home."

The hawk screeched again and lifted off, circling one last time before disappearing.

Kane looked down at Nicky and Robin and saw their smiles, Nicky's tear-tinged, Robin's proud.

A time for good-byes.

A time for beginnings.

Epilogue

Nicky and Kane exchanged their vows before the same federal judge who handed Kane his pardon.

They had five witnesses: Davy Carson and his wife and son, Ben Masters, and Robin. Robin gave away the bride, and Davy was Kane's best man.

Davy had been in Austin with his wife when Kane, Nicky, and Robin arrived with Ben Masters. He had been released as soon as the governor had received the telegram about the destruction of Sanctuary.

Nicky could hardly believe the past week, the hard riding, the return to a burned-out Sanctuary. She'd thought she would feel some sadness, seeing her home in ruins, but she hadn't. She had looked at the rubble and felt nothing. Her grief was for the two men buried in the shadow of rocks some fifty miles away.

The subsequent ride to Austin had been exhausting. There had only been six of them: the marshal and two deputies, Kane, Robin and herself. Ben Masters had driven them relentlessly. He had business back in north Texas, he said. A debt to pay.

"Another one?" Kane had asked, wondering aloud what hell Masters was going to put that person through. It was obvious to Nicky he hadn't forgiven the man who had sent him to Sanctuary. But Ben, as he insisted Nicky call him, had just clamped his lips together and ignored the question.

Nicky had come to like the taciturn lawman during the long ride and thus had asked Ben to the wedding when Kane had not. It was obvious Kane had felt used and manipulated, and, though he'd won his freedom, he hadn't liked the way it had been done one bit. No amount of persuasion on her part had dented his resentment.

In Austin, Nicky had watched as Kane greeted the man for whom he'd been ready to sacrifice everything. She had stood back shyly while the two men clasped each other's shoulders and exchanged wry smiles, as she'd discovered men do when they feel deep emotion and don't know how to express it.

Davy had been the first to speak. "Thank you," he'd said, and Kane had grinned and shrugged off the gratitude before turning to the woman who stood next to him. "Still as pretty as ever," he'd said, and Nicky felt a moment of jealousy. Then he had turned to her, and she'd seen the love that he still had difficulty in expressing.

Martha Carson had helped her select a dress for the wedding. Nicky hadn't wanted white. She was used to being careful with money and wanted something she could wear again. So they found a simple but lovely green dress that complemented her coloring, and Martha helped curl her hair and thread flowers through it.

"You're lovely," Martha said.

"Am I?" Nicky said doubtfully as she looked at her short hair.

"Your husband-to-be certainly thinks so. He can't take his eyes off you." Martha chuckled. "I've never seen Kane O'Brien befuddled before, but you sure have him tied in knots."

Nicky smiled and in the mirror she saw a new Nicole Thompson stare back at her. There was a glow about her face, and she *did* look pretty. She turned around and hugged Martha. "Thank you."

"Thank you," Martha said softly. "Thank you for making Kane happy. I was afraid he never would be. He always joked a lot, but he was so lonely. We tried hard to make him feel part of the family, but we knew he never did. He always held back. . . ."

"He told me a little about his father," Nicky said.

"Probably only a little of it," Martha said. "That man almost destroyed Kane. I'll never understand how he survived and became the man he is. He always considered himself worthless, no-account, despite the fact he was the best friend anyone could have, the most loyal . . ."

Nicky's happiness dimmed as she considered Kane's background and the terrible decisions he'd had to make during the past few months. Her heart swelled with pride, and she was determined that he would know that same pride in himself.

And then they were in front of the judge, and she watched Kane intently as the vows were exchanged. His eyes were a bit uncertain, and she felt his nervousness, realizing it came from that feeling deep inside that he was unworthy of her, unworthy of anyone. Her hand reached out and clasped his, threading her fingers through his in complete trust.

His stern expression melted into a smile.

"Do you take this woman, Nicole Thompson, as your lawful wife?" The judge's words barely penetrated the communion suddenly flowing between them.

His response was soft but sure, and then his lips were on hers and there was no hesitancy at all as his eyes smiled down on her.

There was a dinner after the ceremony. Ben Masters was quiet, preoccupied, reserved. He had, in fact, refused the invitation, and only Nicky's cajoling changed his mind. He was obviously uncomfortable, though, and Kane all but ignored him. But Nicky felt she owned Ben. So did Kane, if only he would admit it.

They were midway through their wedding dinner when Nicky put her fork down and looked over at Ben. The man's slate blue eyes were fixed on his plate. "Thank you," she said suddenly. "Thank you for everything you've done for Kane."

Ben looked over at Kane's face, which had suddenly gone still. "It was my job," he said.

"It was more than that," she said. "And I'll always be grateful."

A muscle in Kane's cheek twitched. His lips flattened slightly, and she could almost tell what he was thinking. He hadn't really forgiven himself for the manner of Nat Thompson's death, which was why he hadn't been able to forgive Ben. But it was time, she knew. It was time to put all the bitterness to rest, and no better day than today.

Nicky refused to drop her gaze, willing him to forgive both himself and Ben. Suddenly, Kane's face seemed to relax and the last of the haunted look left his eyes.

"Maybe it's just as well I made that mistake four years ago," he conceded.

Nicky wasn't sure what he meant, but Ben Masters apparently did. He grinned, held out his hand, and Kane took it.

"What are you going to do now?" Kane asked. "More . . . outlaws?"

Ben shook his head. "There's a little girl waiting on me. I'm a lawyer by training. I think it's time to return to a different kind of law."

Kane hesitated. "I never did say thanks."

"Neither did I," Ben said. Nicky still didn't entirely understand the exchange, but she knew something important was going on. A friendship was being forged, and Kane was learning to let go of hurts. Slowly, but surely.

Hours later, Ben left, heading for the livery stable, and Davy and his family started back toward San Antonio. With Kane's reward money, Davy was going to try to get his ranch back, his and the others. Kane would follow in another week, with Robin and Nicky, to look for a ranch of their own.

But now the time was theirs—hers and Kane's. Robin had gone to his own room in the hotel, and Nicky intended a very private celebration.

Once inside their room, Kane turned to her. "Thank you," he whispered.

She grinned happily. All the shadows were gone from his eyes, all the ghosts. Maybe they would return on nocturnal visits occasionally, but they were no longer constant companions.

"I love you," she said. "I love you so much I want to burst with it."

He chuckled. "I think that's what *I'm* supposed to do."

She tickled the back of his neck, and he immediately made progress toward being ready to burst.

He had to do something else first, though. He had to hold her. Just hold her. And tell her how much he loved her. He'd only done that once before, and that was when he thought he would die.

Now he wanted to say it with hope. With dreams. With promises he thought he could keep.

His mouth moved to hers and his hands savored her face, and he said *I love you* in every way he knew. Finally, he took his lips away and held her face in his hands. "I love you," he said in a voice crackling with feelings he'd always been afraid to recognize.

She smiled, her lips trembling, her eyes bright with mist, and Kane O'Brien, Diablo, knew he'd ascended to heaven.

About the Author

Patricia Potter has become one of the most highly praised writers of historical romance since her impressive debut in 1988, when she won the Maggie Award and a Reviewer's Choice Award from *Romantic Times* for her first novel. She received the *Romantic Times* Career Achievement Award for Storyteller of the Year for 1992 and most recently was nominated for another Career Achievement Award, this time for Best Western Historical Romance of 1995. She has worked as a newspaper reporter in Atlanta and was president of the Georgia Romance Writers Association.

Award-winning author Patricia Potter sweeps us to misty Scotland for her next historical romance, where passionate intrigue swirls in an ancestral mansion, weaving a seductive trap for ...

THE MARSHAL AND THE HEIRESS

Available in August 1996 from Bantam Books

U.S. Marshal Ben Masters stared down outlaws and desperadoes every day, but when he became the guardian of newly orphaned Sarah Ann, he faced trouble of a different kind. Word came that the four-year-old was the lost heir to a Scottish estate, so he took her across the ocean, never expecting a household divided by ambitions ... or his head and body warring over Sarah Ann's remarkable aunt. Lisbeth Hamilton possessed a swift intelligence Ben's sharp mind appreciated, a tempting figure his fingers ached to caress—and a future jeopardized by her niece's claim. When Sarah Ann's life became threatened, Ben's lawman instincts pointed to Lisbeth despite the protests of his newly awakened heart.

How do you tell a four-year-old girl that her mother is dead?

U. S. Marshal Ben Masters worried over the question as he stood on the porch of Mrs. Henrietta Culworthy's small house. Then, squaring his shoulders, he knocked. He wished he really believed he was doing the right thing. What in God's name did a man like him, a man who'd lived with guns and violence for the past eight years, have to offer an orphaned child?

Mary May believed in you. The thought raked through his heart. He felt partially responsible for her death. He had stirred a pot without considering the consequences. In bringing an end to an infamous outlaw hide-out, he had been oblivious to those caught in the cross-fire. The fact that Mary May had been involved with the outlaws didn't assuage his conscience.

"*Sarah. Promise you'll take care of Sarah.*" He would never forget Mary May's last faltering words.

Ben rapped again on the door of the house. Mrs. Culworthy should be expecting him. She had been looking after Sarah Ann for the past three years, but now she had to return east to care for a brother. She had already postponed her trip once, agreeing to wait until Ben had wiped out the last remnants of an outlaw band and fulfilled a promise to a former renegade named Diablo.

The door opened. Mrs. Culworthy's wrinkled face appeared, sagging slightly with relief. Had she worried that he would not return? He sure as hell had thought about it. He'd thought about a lot of things, like where he might find another home for Sarah Ann. But then he would never be sure she was being raised properly. By God, he owed Mary May.

"Sarah Ann?" he asked Mrs. Culworthy.

"In her room." The woman eyed him hopefully. "You *are* going to take her."

He nodded.

"What about your job?"

"I'm resigning. I used to be a lawyer. Thought I would hang up my shingle in Denver."

A smile spread across Mrs. Culworthy's face. "Thank heaven for you. I love that little girl. I would take her if I could, but—"

"I know you would," he said gently. "But she'll be safe with me." He hoped that was true. He hesitated. "She doesn't know yet, does she? About her mother?"

Mrs. Culworthy shook her head.

Just then, a small head adorned with reddish curls

and green eyes peered around the door. Excitement lit the gamin face. "Mama's here!"

Pain thrust through Ben. Of course, Sarah Ann would think her mother had arrived. Mary May had been here with him just a few weeks ago.

"Uncle Ben," the child said, "where's Mama?"

He wished Mrs. Culworthy had already told her. He was sick of being the bearer of bad news, and never more so than now.

He dropped to one knee and held out a hand to the little girl. "She's gone to heaven," Ben said.

She approached slowly, her face wrinkling in puzzlement; then she looked questioningly at Mrs. Culworthy. The woman dissolved into tears. Ben didn't know whether Sarah Ann understood what was being said, but she obviously sensed that something was very wrong. The smile disappeared and her underlip started to quiver.

Ben's heart quaked. He had guarded that battered part of him these past years, but there were no defenses high enough, or thick enough, to withstand a child's tears.

He held out his arms, not sure Sarah Ann knew him well enough to accept his comfort. But she walked into his embrace, and he hugged her, stiffly at first. Unsure. But then her need overtook his uncertainty, and his grip tightened.

"You asked me once if I were your papa," he said. "Would you like me to be?"

Sarah Ann looked up at him. "Isn't Mama coming back?"

He shook his head. "She can't, but she loved you so

much she asked me to take care of you. If that's all right with you?"

Sarah Ann turned to Mrs. Culworthy. "I want to stay with you, Cully."

"You can't, Pumpkin," Mrs. Culworthy said tenderly. "I have to go east, but Mr. Masters will take good care of you. Your mother thought so, too."

"Where is heaven? Can't I go, too?"

"Someday," Ben said slowly. "And she'll be waiting for you, but right now I need you. I need someone to take care of me, too, and your mama thought we could take care of each other."

It was true, he suddenly realized. He did need someone to love. His life had been empty for so long.

Sarah Ann probably had much to offer him.

But what did he have to offer her?

Sarah Ann put her hand to his cheek. The tiny fingers were incredibly soft—softer than anything he'd ever felt—and gentle. She had lost everything, yet she was comforting him.

He hugged her close for a moment, and then he stood. Sarah Ann's hand crept into his. Trustingly. And Ben knew he would die before ever letting anything bad happen to her again.

Aboard the Lady Mary on the Atlantic Ocean
1868

"Annabelle!"

Ben tried to keep the irritation from his voice as he stuck his head under the lifeboat. The shirt he had grabbed and thrown on without buttoning flapped in the wind.

Damn, but it was cold. He'd known cold before, but not like this; the icy ocean wind seeped through his bones. It didn't help his bad leg, either, which had stiffened during the voyage.

"Annabelle, come on, now. Come out of there." He cooed in the soothing voice he'd used many times before to try to lure his prey from hiding. Unfortunately, the present outlaw wasn't responding one bit better than those in the past.

"Mr. Masters?"

He pulled his head out and squinted up at Mrs. Franklin T. Faulkner. The dowager, who had sat at the captain's table with him the night before, had her mouth pursed in disapproval.

If only his fellow marshals could see him now. They would laugh themselves silly.

"I'm looking for my daughter's cat," he explained curtly, then turned back to his mission, digging deeper under the lifeboat. Sarah Ann would be inconsolable if she lost the half-grown calico cat they'd rescued off the streets of Boston. The cat, though, had been ungrateful. Once adopted and feeling safe, she delighted in scampering out the cabin door to antagonize the ship's rat-catching cats. Apprehending her tested every one of Ben's hunting skills.

"A cat?" Mrs. Faulkner said.

"A cat," Ben confirmed, his hand stretching toward the ragged bundle of fur.

"Annabelle?" she added in a disbelieving tone.

Ben didn't answer. He wished the woman would scurry away as quickly as Annabelle had escaped his cabin minutes ago. The thought amused him. The hefty Mrs. Faulkner couldn't scurry if her life depended on it.

"Mr. Masters!" The voice was indignant.

He cursed audibly and heard a shocked gasp in response. He clenched his teeth. He was used to being on his own or with men as rough as himself. He would have to temper his speech as well as his actions for next few months. But for the moment, politeness be damned.

He almost snatched Annabelle, but she reached out and raked his arm with her claws. He grabbed one of her paws and started dragging her out. "Gotcha," he said with as much satisfaction as if he'd bagged a killer after months of hunting.

Annabelle suddenly feigned docility, though he didn't trust it, not one bit. She snuggled against him, purring contentedly. Ben swore vengeance silently, though he would never take it. Except on occasion, Annabelle wound him around her little claws almost as securely as Sarah Ann had twisted him around her small fingers. Something about babies did that to him, he was discovering.

Prior to meeting Sarah Ann, he'd never experienced wet baby kisses or rough kitten-tongue swipes across his cheek. There was something rather endearing about both, though he wouldn't have admitted it out loud. So he just simply glowered at Mrs. Faulkner as he slowly, awkwardly, emerged from under the lifeboat with his trophy clutched tightly against his chest.

Mrs. Faulkner's gaze went to his bare chest, then drifted upward to his half-shaven face. He knew soap still clung to parts of it. He hastily buttoned his shirt with one hand.

"My apologies for the state of undress," he said stiffly.

Six months ago, he wouldn't have cared how anyone saw him; after weeks, sometimes months on the trail of an outlaw, his clothes and beard would be in a sorry state, and it wouldn't have mattered. But Sarah Ann's future, her acceptance as a peeress, may well depend on him and his actions. He still couldn't quite believe the events of the past month, the news that was now sending him to Scotland.

Mrs. Faulkner looked at him oddly. "Your child's a dear little soul, but she doesn't favor you at all."

Ben loathed the woman's curiosity, even as he felt strangely satisfied by her words. Sarah Ann was lovely with her red curls and green eyes, a tiny replica of her mother. The fact brought a pang to his heart.

"You don't think so?" he said, forcing disappointment into his voice. He wanted to be rid of Mrs. Franklin T. Faulkner and her thinly veiled questions. He suspected she had ulterior motives in mind, principally her unmarried daughter. If she'd known some of the things he'd done, she wouldn't be so eager to see him as son-in-law material.

He had been sparse in sharing with other passengers information about Sarah Ann or himself, saying only that he was an attorney traveling with his daughter. He was, by nature, a cautious man. A lawman had to be.

Besides, there were still too many unanswered questions for him to reveal more. If Sarah Ann found a new home in Scotland—a family who would care for her—he would return to America. It would . . . crack his heart, but a family of her own would be far better for her than a man who knew more about hunting outlaws than drying tears. And if all didn't work out to his satisfaction, well, then, the two of them would come back together and he would return to his original plan.

He had taken precautions, though. He officially adopted the child. A great deal of money apparently was part of Sarah Ann's potential inheritance, and it was his experience that money corrupted. The greater the amount at stake, the greater the corruption.

"Poor motherless child." Mrs. Faulkner obviously wasn't going to give up. "You should marry again." Her eyes were avaricious on behalf of her daughter.

"Sarah Ann's mother died just a few months ago," he said abruptly, trying to end the conversation.

"Still, she needs a mother's hands."

"She needs Annabelle right now," he said. "Please excuse me."

A loud "humph" followed him as he headed for the stairs, then "What a doting father."

Ben grinned. He decided he and Sarah Ann would take their meal in their cabin tonight rather than risk sitting at the captain's table again with Mrs. Faulkner and her marriageable daughter.

In the cabin, he found Sarah Ann standing in the middle of the small room, her wide green eyes anxious, her underlip trembling.

"You found her," she exclaimed happily, and Ben felt ten feet tall. A hell of a lot taller than when he'd brought in a man to hang.

As she took the kitten from him, she saw his bleeding hand and scolded Annabelle.

"Bad cat," she said, but there was no bite to her words. The cat licked her cheek with apparent satisfaction rather than remorse. Sarah Ann put Annabelle in her basket and shut the top, then touched Ben's bloody scratch.

"Doth it hurt?" she lisped with concern.

Ever since he had said he needed her, she'd taken the role of caretaker very seriously. Sometimes she even seemed like a mother, very grown-up in some ways, yet very much a child when she sought comfort.

He smiled. A cat scratch was nothing compared to the wounds he'd suffered. "No, sugarplum," he said. "It doesn't hurt at all, but we'll have to be more careful to keep Annabelle inside the room."

Sarah Ann looked remorseful but pleaded to be allowed to "fix" his hand. She carefully washed it as he had done with her small cuts.

"Tell me 'bout my new fambly," she demanded.

He'd already told her repeatedly, but she never tired of hearing it, which was just as well because he wasn't very good at fairy tales.

"Well," he said, drawing it out, "there are two Ladies Calholm. There's Lisbeth Hamilton and there's Barbara Hamilton. They were married to your uncles, Hamish and Jamie."

"My Papa's brothers," Sarah Ann coached him. She had never known her papa. He'd died at a poker table before her birth, leaving her mother the pregnant widow of a known crooked gambler. Alone with a baby daughter to support, Mary May had turned saloon girl and confidant to outlaws, not the best of heritages.

But now there was another heritage, a brighter one,

Ben hoped. For it seemed that her scapegrace father had been the third son of a Scottish marquess, and with all three sons dead and no other grandchildren, Sarah Ann was heiress to a title and a vast estate. The notion had seemed fanciful to Ben, more fairy tale than real, but Silas Martin, the eastern attorney acting on behalf of the Hamiltons' Scottish solicitor, had convinced him that it was all true. Despite his own personal feelings and plans—and even a temptation to ignore the summons to Scotland—he couldn't deny Sarah Ann the knowledge of her heritage and the chance to know her real family. So, having been her guardian for only a few months, he'd closed his newly opened law practice in Denver, packed a few belongings, and here they were—on a ship bound for Scotland. "That's right," he said. "They are your aunts."

"Who else is there?" Sarah Ann asked eagerly.

"There's your cousin, Hugh," Ben continued. He tried to hide his anger. Silas Martin had said that Hugh Hamilton, who stood to inherit the title behind Sarah Ann, had tried to bribe him not to search too aggressively for Sarah Ann's father. Ben wondered just how far the would-be heir's ambition would drive him.

Already, an unusual number of deaths had occurred in the family, and Ben had never trusted coincidence. The Hamiltons seemed prone to tragedy, which looked like a recipe for disaster to Ben. He didn't believe in curses, but if he did, surely one had been visited upon the Hamilton family.

It was up to him to see that the curse—or whatever it was—didn't extend to Sarah Ann. And God help anyone who tried to interfere.

He let nothing of his concern show in his face, though, as he spun a tale of magic castles and Scottish lakes. And princesses.

"Am I a princess?"

"No, but I think you'll be a lady."

That always made her giggle. He had tried to explain about titles—about lords and ladies and marquesses. His own knowledge was incomplete, possibly wrong, but she loved hearing about them.

"And I get to curtsy?"

"Yes indeed," he said, "just as Cully taught you. She must have secretly known you were a real lady." He had been enchanted the first time Mary May had taken him to meet her daughter, and Sarah Ann has performed a perfect curtsy for him. She had won his heart then and there.

"Will they like me?" she asked with anxiety.

"Of course." He hoped to God it was true. But how could anyone not adore her, with those wide eyes and wistful smile and tumbling red curls? And her eagerness to like and be liked.

"And will they like Annabelle and Zusanna?" Zusanna was her doll, her inseparable companion. She clung to it as she did to the scarf she presently wore around her neck—the last presents her mother had given her. She wore the scarf even in her sleep, claiming it kept away the "bears," her name for nightmares. But it didn't always work. Too often, he woke to her whimperings and knew the night demons remained with her.

In answer to her question, he nodded and she threw

her arms around his neck. "I love you, Papa," she said. "So does Annabelle."

His heart clutched at the overwhelming tenderness he felt. Tenderness that almost squeezed out the foreboding that chilled his bones.